DEV...

THE I...

J. KENT HOLLOWAY

SEVEN REALMS PUBLISHING

The ENIGMA Directive, Book 3: Devil's Child

Copyright © 2012 J. Kent Holloway

ISBN: 978-0-9854325-7-7

Cover art © 2012 by Christian Guldager
Cover design by J. Kent Holloway

Published by Seven Realms Publishing, LLC

4420 Carter Road #6
Saint Augustine, Florida 32086
www.sevenrealmspublishing.com

Printed in the United States of America

BOOKS BY J. KENT HOLLOWAY

THE ENIGMA DIRECTIVE SERIES
Primal Thirst

Sirens' Song

THE DARK HOLLOWS MYSTERIES
The Curse of One-Eyed Jack

The Dirge of Briarsnare Marsh (Coming Spring 2013)

The Night of the Willow Hag (Coming early 2014)

STAND ALONE NOVELS
The Djinn

To Lee, Sara, Robyn and your significant others...my "Kentucky Cousins" who have been so wonderfully supportive of me these last few years.

ACKNOWLEDGMENTS

It's always so difficult to write this acknowledgments. It's not that there's no one to thank…quite the contrary. The reason it's always so difficult is that there are simply too many people to thank. Too many people that I owe so much too. Too many people that have stood by me through thick and through thin since I gave into this insane calling that is called professional writing.

But for the moment…for this book in particular…there are a few that have stood out during the ordeal of crafting this story. First of all, I want to thank Brett and Robyn Denney, as well as Trip Gray. It's hard being a writer some times. We're our own worst critics. And you guys have been instrumental in the last year or so for encouraging me in ways you'll never know. So thank you for that.

Also, I absolutely must thank my editors, Gabrielle Harbowy and Fanny Darling. Wow. You just wouldn't believe the amazing job these two awesome ladies did. A guy couldn't get any luckier than to have these two having his editorial back. If you find any typos or mistakes in this manuscript, then it's because I did something stupid after they finished their meticulous edits. It's my fault, not theirs.

And finally, I really must go back to where it all started once again and thank my friends…the Destination Truth team…that inspired it all. Josh, Rex, Ryder, Gabe…you guys have grown to be dear friends of mine and have encouraged me in so many ways. It's such an honor to have you guys as my inspiration for Jack and the team.

~ J. Kent Holloway
December 20, 2012

ONE

No matter how many times a mallet-sized fist flies toward your face, you always have the same reaction—close your eyes, scrunch your neck down a bit, and hope for the best. Sometimes you get lucky and they miss. Unfortunately, as I stared down the aborigine smuggler's long muscular arm hurtling at light speed in my direction, I knew my luck was about as dried up as my canteen had been for the last two days.

The giant's fist slammed against my jaw, twisting my head in an unnatural left-leaning spasm. Blood spewed from where a tooth bit down deep into my lower lip. It hurt like a mother, but at that point, I just felt lucky to have teeth at all.

"Please, Dr. Jackson," said a calming, subtle voice from somewhere behind me. It was tinged with a thick Australian accent. "Be reasonable. The longer you keep your silence, the longer Charlie M'nenga here will continue to...um...try to pry your mouth open. After all, you have so little to lose at this point."

I glared at the massive brute hulking above me while trying to wrestle free of the nylon ropes securing me fast to the wicker chair. I was in a rather sparse hut, nothing more than an old moth-eaten rug covering the dirt floor. Two netted hammocks hung unoccupied to my right, suspended by posts supporting the straw ceiling above.

The man speaking so eloquently behind me was Arthur Blaisemore—I've called him Artie for as long as I've known him. Just for spite, because I know how much he hates it. He's a competitor. Sort of. While I was a cryptozoological researcher, trying to hunt down strange creatures from all over the world in order to understand them better—and hopefully, protect them—Blaisemore was really nothing more than a poacher. A scumbag mercenary who hunted cryptids for profit and prestige.

The little weasel strode around to look me in the face, his arms stretched behind his back. He was just as scrawny and weak-jawed as I remembered. The man had a pale, ferret-like face with a wisp of sandy blond hair combed over one side of his balding head. He also sported a single gold cap on one of his incisors that seemed to glisten no matter how low the light was in a given room. A new addition to his appearance—or rather, a subtraction, I should say—was that he was now missing the index finger on his left hand.

He motioned for his aboriginal subordinate to step aside and moved into the bigger man's place, bending over to look me square in the eyes.

"Tsk, tsk, Jackie Boy," he said, an icy grin stretching the corners of his mouth. "Why are you so bloody stubborn? All we want to know is where you hid the baby bunyip."

The bunyip…the silliest looking Australian animal to be seen by man since the platypus popped out of whatever hole had coughed it up and the reason I was in the pickle I now found myself in. The super-secret government agency I work for, *ENtity Identification and Global Management Agency*, or ENIGMA for short, had heard that a large ring of poachers and river pirates were carting off cryptids in the Outback like they were going out of style. Despite orders from my superiors to the contrary, my team and I had come out to put a stop to it. And like most of my plans, it hadn't worked out exactly the way it was supposed to.

We'd bribed the right people and leaned on a few more for good measure, and we finally found the camp where the poachers had set up shop in the uppermost tip of Queensland. Under the direction of our team's field agent, and Captain America wannabe, Scott Landers, we had made a daring nighttime ninja raid of the camp. In no time at all, we'd found the bunyip cub. And yes, I was relieved it was just a cub. Full grown bunyips are known to grow as large as six feet in length and weigh over five hundred pounds. The little critter we'd found was only about fifty pounds, so we grabbed it from its cage, and hauled butt out of there as fast as we could.

The plan would have worked like a charm, if we'd given the little bugger a sedative like I'd suggested to begin with. But no, my team hadn't seen a need. So when it was jostled awake by our scurrying footsteps toward the riverbed and our awaiting boat, it started shrieking to beat the band. Its cries alerted the patrolling guards and woke up the rest of the camp. Then things had *really* gotten messy. All par the course for yours truly. Unfortunately.

So, ushering Landers and my best friend Randy into the boat, I'd handed them the whining sack of wrinkles and fur and headed toward the smuggler's own fleet of river boats to try to disable them. That's when I got caught…just as I was puncturing the gas tank of the last vessel with a KA-BAR knife.

In hindsight, I guess we should have taken our chances on the open water, but then, no one's ever accused me of being a Ph.D.…which is sad because I honestly am one.

"And I'm telling you, Artie, I have no idea where it is," I said, spitting a congealed clump of blood from my mouth. The taste of copper coated my teeth, but I smiled up at the lead poacher anyway. "It must have taken a whiff of your awful dime-store cologne and high-tailed it out here."

The cold smile melted from his face as he stretched to his full height and nodded at Charlie. The big lug lumbered over to me and balled up his fist yet again. I wasn't sure how much more of a beating I could take. The pirate's knuckles had already bruised at least two ribs. I was having trouble breathing from the pain to my sides. One eye was starting to swell shut and the other's vision seemed off by multiples of three.

"Wait," I said, looking at Artie.

He moved over to me, shoving the larger man aside like a gnat. Bending down once more, he looked me in the good eye and tilted his head. "Yes?"

I swallowed, or at least tried to against the sandpaper rough dryness of my throat. I wasn't joking when I said I hadn't had any water for two days. We'd been rationing before we even found the camp. And I'd been holed up in a cramped cell dug into the muddy soil for the last twenty-four hours, while the pirates awaited the return of Blaisemore to meet out whatever justice he felt necessary to the foreign interloper who'd stolen their prize out from under them.

"Could I have something to drink first?" I asked, coughing to clear my throat.

He eyed me before turning his filth-eating grin up a notch and stalking past me. I tried to turn my head to see where he was going, but unless I transformed into Linda Blair at her worst, that just wasn't going to happen. After several seconds, I heard the sound of metal plates clinking together and the flow of liquid into a glass.

"Jack," Artie crooned from behind me, "you really must forgive me. We tend to become so uncivilized out here in the bush."

He suddenly appeared again with a metal mug and a covered dish. The smell from the plate was intoxicating, sapping the feeble remainder of saliva from my lips.

"Water," he said, hiking up the mug before hefting the plate. "And my favorite delicacy in the world. Sautéed koala. They are yours as soon as you tell us where your friends have taken the bunyip."

I blinked. My eyes never wavered from the plate.

"Koala?" I asked.

He nodded, a proud gleam flickering across his eyes.

"Koala?" I thought maybe he'd misunderstood my original question or something. Felt it bore repeating.

His head tilted slightly, as if questioning my concerns over the species of the food set before me. "It really is quite delicious."

"Are you kidding me? I'm not going to eat a freakin' koala!" My brain kept screaming at me to shut up, but my mouth would have none of it. "They'd taste all...eucalyptusey."

Arthur's face screwed up in a vengeful grimace as he hurled the plate across the room and jabbed a finger against my chest.

"You think you're funny, don't you, mate?" He glanced over to his monstrous goon and nodded once more. "He's not going to tell us anything. Feed him to the crocs."

A malicious grin crawled up Charlie's face and he lurched toward me.

"Crocs?" The parched lump in my throat grew three sizes larger than it had been just two seconds earlier. "Where'd you get your degree in villainy from? The University of Clichés?"

"Shut up, Jack. I'm sick of that mouth of yours. It's been an obnoxious pain for as long as I've known you and I'm rather pleased to finally be able to shut it up." He moved to the side, allowing the muscle-bound enforcer access to my bonds. "I'm sure I'm not the only one who'll be happy either. Maggie, I believe, might even pay me handsomely when I tell her I've taken care of you."

Maggie...is she here? Is she part of this?

A shudder rippled down my spine at the thought. I didn't even want to think about what she'd do to me if she'd been there at that moment. Sure, we'd sort of made up since the triton ordeal last year...but then, not a month later, I'd run into her new boyfriend—an eco-terrorist goon named Deiter—and ended up putting the bruiser in the hospital for six weeks. Needless to say, all bets were off from that moment on. Last time I'd seen her, she'd not only renewed her vow to put a bullet in my kneecaps if she ever laid sight of me again, she'd upped the ante. Apparently, she now had plans for the parts of my anatomy slightly higher than my kneecaps. She always was a temperamental and complicated woman. No, Artie was right. If Maggie was involved in this little smuggling ring, she'd probably give up her share of the loot just to see what my captors had in mind for me.

"Wait just a minute," I said, as the big black man snatched me to my feet and refastened my hands behind my back. "Maybe we can work out some kind of deal. I can help you catch another one or something."

Arthur slithered around to face me; his gold-toothed grin shining brightly at me.

"I know you're smarter than that, mate. By their very nature, cryptids are near impossible to find, much less catch." For good measure, as if he could contain his fury no longer, his bony hand flashed out across my skull in a girlish slap. "We spent months tracking that cub down. Its parents are already long dead. For all we know, that cub was the last of its kind." He shook his head as he moved toward the door of the tiny hovel. "No, the whole situation is going to make my employers extremely unhappy. The discovery of that bunyip would have sliced away years of painstaking research and you threw that all away in a single night."

The aborigine shoved me forward. I would have fallen flat on my face if he hadn't grabbed my arms in time.

"Let me talk to them," I said, as I was forced to the open door. Arthur stood to the side, smiling coldly at me. "Maybe we can make some kind of arrangement."

"They know you too well, Jack. You've been a thorn in their side since before you joined up with ENIGMA. They'll be happy to see you go as well." He stepped out into the balmy night and directed a handful of guards to take me to the edge of the water for chow time. The excitement rustling through the obviously bored-out-their-mind poachers was palpable at the command.

Without another word, Artie stalked off to another hut on the south end of the complex, while I was quickly shoved away from camp to the water's murky edge. Though it was dark, the full moon shined down on us, offering a silvery halo that gleamed off the water's surface. I could make out the forms of massive, log-like objects floating lazily in the current.

Crocodiles.

Charlie's hand pushed against my back, forcing me to take a single step into the river.

"Hold on now," I shouted, trying to turn to face my captor. "I'm telling you, we can figure something out."

When I finally managed to wheel around, I was greeted by the barrels of six rather nasty looking guns pointed directly at my head. Unlike preparing to get hit in the face with a fist, no amount of eye-clinching or neck-scrunching was going to stop a bullet at such close range. Charlie nudged the barrel of his gun toward the water. His message clear.

Either walk in or take a bullet to the face.

Neither option was particularly appealing at the moment.

I looked back at the waiting crocs and then to the armed smugglers bearing down on me.

Ah, crap.

I took another step into the water. The lounging crocodiles remained still, the ethereal gleam of their eyes shining blankly in the darkness, as if they hadn't noticed the tasty little morsel traipsing right onto their buffet line. I only hoped their disinterest would last.

Okay, God. You closed the mouths of lions for that Daniel guy. How good are you with oversized lizards?

I'd only recently started talking to God and wasn't quite sure I was doing it right. Up until my trip to Malaysia the year before, I'd pretty much discounted any notion of some divine being that watched benevolently over us. Events during that little excursion had changed all that. But I was still a newbie. Wasn't quite sure if my prayer would only work if I spoke it in King James English or not. So I repeated it—only this time, to make Sir Lawrence Olivier proud.

O' Lord, as thy shut the mouths of the lions for thy servant Daniel, I beseech you to do the same for...crap! What's the King James word for "me"?

Apparently, it didn't really matter because a low growl reverberated from the waterline to my left a second later. I turned to catch the fleeting image of a serpentine tail descending from the shoreline into the murky river. The water rippled as the other crocs quickly followed their brother.

"Keep moving," the big man said from behind me, and I heard the tell-tale sound of the hammer being pulled back on his .357.

I scanned the surface for any signs of the waiting crocodiles and came up empty. They had all disappeared. Tensing, I took another step out, moving deeper into the water.

"You know, if I get a parasite from this water, I'm really going to be ticked," I grumbled, as the river rose up to my waistline. "I heard they crawl through your urethra. Not a pleasant image for anyone."

"Oh for the love of…" I heard Charlie growl just before the crack of a gun echoed all around us.

I froze, then started patting myself down. There didn't seem to be any holes in me, so I spun around to look at the massive smuggler. A perfectly round mark appeared in the center of his forehead, just before a stream of crimson oozed down into his stunned eyes. Then, he fell silently, face first, into the water.

I looked at the other guards, bewilderment plastered across their own faces, as they stared at their fallen comrade. Then, five more shots rang out, leaving five dead guards immediately in their wake.

Landers, I thought, scouring the terrain for signs of my friends. A flash of light flared up over a hundred yards away in the center of the broad river. Then, I heard the sound of an outboard motor whine to life and a small speed boat coasted quickly toward me.

The crocs lurking in the water jittered off at the approaching watercraft. But I couldn't say the same for the thirteen pirates bearing assault rifles who were now heading my way from camp. Artie's scrawny form led the way, as he pointed and shouted curses in my direction.

I looked at my approaching friends, turned back to the smugglers still sixty yards away, and threw them a wave before diving into the water. A few seconds later, one of my oldest and best friends, Randall Cunningham, was hauling me into the boat, a huge grin plastered across his face.

"I sure am glad to see you guys," I said, as Landers maneuvered the vessel around.

"Yeah, we weren't exactly sure how we were going to get you out of there," Randy said, handing me a cigar. "Lucky they have no imagination when it comes to killing people."

"I said the exact same thing." I clutched the cigar in my teeth with a grin as he lit it with a covered match. It was a ritual. Every time I narrowly escaped death, I had to have a cigar. The philosophy was simple, if illogical…if I was going to die from something, I'd rather it be from smoking. I'd given the things up for a time, back when I'd been dating a missionary named Nikki Jenkins. But our on-again, off-again relationship was currently back to the more common "off" status, so I allowed myself to enjoy the smoke without guilt.

I turned to the grim visage of the Marine-turned-ENIGMA-agent manning the wheel. "Uh, Scott? We still have a little problem. Those guys have faster boats than us."

"No," he said, throwing me a slight smile and holding up a black, rectangular box in his hand. "Their boats aren't gonna be much of a problem at all."

He pushed a red button on the box, and the night sky behind us exploded in four balls of fiery awesome. The smuggler's vessels were smashed to splinters by the concussive force of the C-4 charges Landers had obviously planted before their daring rescue.

"Nice." I couldn't contain my own smile as I took a long pull from the stogey. I jerked slightly as something rubbed up against my leg. I glanced down to see the soft, cuddly features of the bunyip nudging me with its broad snout. Tiny nubs that would one day became tusks protruded from its mouth. "Okay," I said to it, "Now to get you to your new home."

I picked the little guy up and placed him in my lap, as we sped through the dark waters of the Queensland River. Next stop, home, and a long vacation. I couldn't wait.

TWO

I limped my way through the halls of ENIGMA headquarters, nestled in a series of non-descript buildings in a business district of Arlington, VA. My little Jack Russell terrier, Arnold, limped right alongside me. Oh, he wasn't injured. Just having sympathy pains…if dogs can have those anyway. But he wasn't exactly an ordinary dog either, though I'd never told a single soul where he came from. Needless to say, having him limp in sympathy with my own aches is not as crazy as it might sound.

And why shouldn't he feel bad for me? After all, I had enough body aches to keep most people incapacitated for at least a week. I'm not bragging—I'd just as soon be one of those people, wrapped up in my blankets at home watching Oprah while the black eyes and bruised ribs mended. But Director Anton Polk, I guess you can say he's sort of my boss, demanded a debriefing of our trip to Australia. Which basically translated to a major chewing out for disobeying his orders not to go in the first place.

So, I pulled myself from my much needed R&R, hopped the first plane from my modest two-story townhouse in Florida, and made my way to the one place on earth I wanted to be the farthest away from.

I came to a set of elevators and mashed the button. The lobby was barren, like the desert wasteland of the Mad Max movies. Only the single security guard, Maurice, nodded me in when I'd entered the building. It wasn't surprising. It was Saturday. The few office personnel who actually worked in the building had a zillion better things to do with their time than to come here and listen to Dr. Obadiah Jackson get reamed by the Director.

The elevator door pinged open and I stepped through. Arnold bounded inside as well, his tongue lolling to one side as his tail wagged furiously.

"Heh. Yeah, I know you're excited," I said to him, crouching down to give him a good pat. "Polk is definitely not going to like seeing you, is he?"

Director Polk had forbade all non-cryptid animals access to any part of the ENIGMA complex. He despised animals. Hated them was a better word. I think it probably has to do with the nearly head-exploding bouts of sneezing that occurs when he gets within five feet of anything walking on four legs. Which, of course, is precisely the reason I always insist on having Arnold tag along whenever I make an appearance. Plus, Arnold loves the crotchety little desk-jockey. I couldn't help the chuckle that escaped my lips as I stood up and waited for the elevator to reach its destination…thirty-three levels straight down into the Virginia soil.

That might sound unusual to the uninitiated. It's not. The fact is, as I've mentioned before, ENIGMA is super-secret. Totally black-ops. Not too many people outside the President and a handful of congressmen even knew we existed. Established in the late 60s by President Nixon when an outbreak of cryptid sightings terrorized several communities throughout the world, ENIGMA was developed to investigate such sightings. On paper, it was created to track down these cryptids and study them. Sometimes, we're expected to contain them.

But like most institutions, it eventually lost sight of its goals. It began developing strategies and scenarios in which the strange creatures we studied might be used for more, um, unsavory things. Military. Living weapons. Really nasty stuff.

I know firsthand how nasty. It was one of ENIGMA's own experiments that killed someone very dear to me two years before. I shuddered at the thought, just as the elevator slowed to a halt and the doors opened up before me. I could hear my windbag of a boss shouting the moment I stepped from the elevator. I heard Landers' name. The Director didn't actually use my name in his profanity-laced tirade. But I was quick enough to put the pieces together from a few catchy expletives.

The grin broadened on my face. I can't explain why I take such a perverse pleasure in making the man so miserable. I suppose it's just one of those simple joys in life.

Arnold and I hobbled through the long corridor until we came to the doors leading to the reception area of Polk's office. I tapped on the door and popped my head in. Arlene, his secretary, looked up from her desk and threw me a wide smile. I swear you could melt the entire Arctic region with those pearly whites of hers. Arlene was a looker. An ex-runway model in her younger years. Now that she was just south of fifty, she looked even more amazing in my opinion.

"Hey, gorgeous." I winked and nodded to Polk's interior office doors. "How's he doing?"

"Oh, you've really outdone yourself this time, Jack," she said. "I've never seen him this upset before—" Her speech cut off when she saw the bruises all over my face. I could imagine I didn't look in the best shape. Cuts. Scrapes. And though the swelling had gone down enough for me to see through it, my eye was still six shades of blue. "Wow, Jack. We need to get you some Kung Fu lessons or something."

"Well, you should see the other guys."

"Landers was there, right?"

I moved over to Polk's door and rested my hand on the knob. "Yeah, but what's that got to do with it?"

"Because with Scott, it means all the other guys have bullet holes in their heads. It doesn't count. You still need lessons." She gave me a compassionate smile again and nodded toward the office. "You better get in there. And I'm not so sure you should take Arn—"

Before she finished the sentence, I turned the handle and stepped into the Category Five hurricane that was Anton Polk's fury.

"Jackson." He was standing, or rather pacing the floor before he turned and spotted me. His eyes burned as he pointed his spindly index finger at a chair on the other side of the long conference table. "Sit."

My dog plodded victoriously into the room, his head held high, as if he was the guest of honor. The Director's eyes widened simultaneously with the reddening of his face. I half expected steam to shoot out of his ears like Elmer Fudd in a Looney Tunes cartoon.

"And he stays outside." His heat-seeking finger targeted on Arnold. "You know better than to bring him…"

"Anton, calm down," came the gruff voice of Senator John Chesterton Stromwell, or J.C. if he liked you well enough. I hadn't even noticed his presence as I'd entered the office—which is saying something, considering the immensity of the man. He was seated at the far end of the table. His bushy Theodore Roosevelt mustache barely contained the obvious amusement at seeing the Director so upset. Or maybe it was from seeing Arnold, who trotted over to the larger-than-life politician and pounced into his lap. The senator cooed in his ear as he scratched the terrier's underbelly. "We're not going to get anywhere with you acting like a bad imitation of Old Faithful. You need to settle down."

At the senator's words, Polk drew in a breath. His face lightened a little, as if he'd been oxygen deprived and had finally taken in enough air to ventilate his brain. He stared at Stromwell for several seconds before leaning forward and resting his hands on the table. His head dropped as he continued his breathing exercises, something he'd been instructed to do by his cardiologist whenever his blood pressure rose to volcanic proportions.

Landers sat quietly in a chair next to him. His back rigid against the seat. His head held high, almost stiff, at perfect military attention. The freakin' boy scout. I guess the years since leaving the Marines would never quite remove the spic-n-span gleam to his razor sharp discipline. He'd been getting a royal chewing-out before I stepped into the room, yet his demeanor was as calm and placid as if he'd been having afternoon tea with my elderly neighbor, Gladys. He shot me a knowing look and then let his eyes fix on the chair next to me. A silent plea for me to take a seat.

I took the cue and sat down.

"I'm just tired of him, John," Polk wheezed, still pointing furiously at me. "I'm tired of his insubordination. I'm tired of his constant lack of respect for me and this office. I'm tired—"

"We're all tired, Anton," Stromwell said, leaning back in his seat. Arnold repositioned himself to lie squarely on the man's oversized belly. Perfectly content. "Including Jack. He was put into this position for a very special reason. To keep an eye out for anything that smacks of unethical behavior toward cryptids—whether within the organization or out. When you prohibited him from going to Queensland to look into the bunyip poachers, you were effectively telling him not to do his job."

"That's exactly what I told him two weeks ago," I said, raising my hands in the air.

"Shut up, Jack," the big man glared at me as he stroked the top of Arnold's head. "We'll get to you in a minute." He turned his attention back to Polk. "I'm not sure where this animosity you have for the boy comes from, but you're going to have to—"

My phone chimed, alerting me to a text message. Stromwell glared at me for the interruption. Apologetically, I pulled the phone from its clip and flipped it open.

"We're in the middle of something here, Jack." The senator's voice left no room for misinterpretation. He wanted my full attention.

The problem was, I'd already seen who the message was from. And since I hadn't heard from him in about five years, I couldn't very well just put him aside. If John Stephens was trying to contact me—especially by text—then it was probably important.

"I know, Senator," I said, glancing down at the digital display on my phone and scrolling down to the meat of the message. The breath was almost knocked from my lungs as I read it. *Hospital?* "But this is important."

"Whatever it is, it can wait," Polk spat. "See, this is exactly the rotten attitude I've been telling you about. He just won't listen."

I stood up and cradled the phone back in its clip.

"Sorry, Senator, but I've got to go." I patted my thigh and Arnold leapt down from Stromwell's lap and moved over to me, his tail wagging happily.

"We're not done yet, boy," Stromwell all but growled the sentence. Though he liked me, especially since I'd saved his daughter, Nikki, from an ENIGMA experiment gone horribly wrong, he had been none too happy with my people skills while working for his pet agency. "This meeting will determine whether you should be scheduled for a disciplinary hearing. It's not something to be taken lightly."

I walked over to the doors and opened them before turning back to the room. "And I can't take a friend lying in a hospital bed right now lightly either. You want to put me before the disciplinary board? Go ahead. Right now, I'm going to see my friend."

"Jack, wait..." I heard Scott say as I slammed the doors behind me.

I waved a curt goodbye to Arlene and made my way out of the building. I had a plane to catch.

Johnny, my friend, I thought to myself as I hailed a cab. *This had better be good.*

Oddly enough, considering I'd been to every continent on the planet and darn near every country, it was my very first honest-to-goodness visit to New York City. Something that, as a Southerner, I secretly prided myself on. Oh, sure, I'd been here before...for airport layovers before catching my next flight to Lord only knew where. But I'd never really stepped foot onto the bustling sidewalks of Manhattan.

And what an experience I'd been missing! The buildings towered on all sides of me, like a thousand giants looming in the sky. It was almost suffocating, if not intoxicating. But I had no time for sightseeing, as I strode up the majestic steps of the New York Presbyterian Hospital in Northern Manhattan. The automatic doors slid open for me. I stepped toward them and made my way to the front desk to inquire about Johnny's room.

After following the directions I was given, I hesitated outside of room 514. It had been so long since I'd last seen my childhood friend. We'd grown up together in the foothills of the Appalachians in Eastern Kentucky. From opposite worlds, Johnny was from a poor black family. The middle child, in a household of seven kids, he'd always had a hard time fitting in…even within his own family. Maybe that's why I'd taken an instant liking to him. He had been as much at odds with his own parents, as I had with mine. But where I had come from two middle-class scientists, who were also devout Bible-believing Christians, his was an uneducated farming-class family. He aspired for greater things. I just wanted to stay home from church every once in a while.

In the end, we both ended up where our parents had wanted us. Though Johnny had never taken up the family farming business, he remained a man of the earth. Living off the land as if he'd been sculpted from the very soil his bare feet had so often tread. Last I heard, he made a decent living as a professional hunter and tracker. Winning numerous competitions and becoming somewhat of a celebrity back home.

What he was doing in New York City, I had no idea. And how he'd landed himself in a hospital suite was an even bigger mystery. Standing an easy six and a half feet tall and build like the Colossus of Rhodes, he'd make even the meanest street punk think twice before attempting something stupid against him. But in this city, that was the only thing I could think might have happened.

His text message had been cryptic, to say the least: IN NYC-PRESB HOSPITAL. NEED YOUR HELP. That's all it said. Leaving my overactive imagination to concoct a whole diorama of possible scenarios. Seeing as how NYC-Presbyterian was a teaching hospital, housing one of the finest trauma units in the country, I had quickly dismissed any notion that he was here for a more mundane reason.

I grasped the door handle and prepared for the worst. Turning it, I took a breath, and stepped into the room.

Though it was semi-private, only one bed was occupied. It contained the battered form of my childhood friend. He'd definitely seen better days. The lumps, bruises, and lacerations covering most of his body made my recent injuries look like a playground brawl.

His right arm was slung up in a harness hovering above his bed, encased in a stiff fiberglass cast. Enough bandages to enshroud an Egyptian mummy adorned his head, left arm, and both legs. His left hand clutched the TV remote control as he cycled through channels like he'd forgotten to pay his cable bill and was waiting for them to shut it off.

When he noticed me standing in the room, he stopped his channel surfing and grinned brightly at me.

"Boomer!" he said, using his old nickname for me—don't ask where it came from. But the point is, anyone who knew me long enough quickly learned that using my given name was anathema to me. My parents had thought they were being very clever in naming me after Obadiah, one of their favorite of Old Testament prophets. To a boy growing up in the wilds of Kentucky, the name quickly became a sore subject. Most people just shortened my last name and called me Jack. Johnny had never been *most people*. "It's good to see you, man." He tried to sit up and looked over my shoulder expectantly. "What? Randy's not attached to your hip this time?" He chuckled.

"Nah. Left him back home, working on a project." I smiled. Back in the day, the three of us had been a force to be reckoned with. Though, truth be known, neither Johnny or Randy would have hung out with each other, if not for me. They just didn't have enough in common. Got on each other's nerves too much. "And it's good to see you too, pal," I said, moving to his bedside and sitting in a chair. "You've seen better days though."

He eyed his cast before turning to me, his smile broadening. "Nah, it ain't any big deal, really. Just me being stupid. Looks like you've gone three rounds recently, yourself." He nodded at my face.

His avoidance of the matter at hand was telling. He wasn't comfortable yet explaining what had happened, nor why he'd messaged me. Appalachian pride. It was both admirable and infuriating. But I knew he'd get around to telling me everything when it felt right. We spent the next twenty minutes in idle chit-chat. Catching up on old times. It felt good. It would have felt even better if he didn't wince every time he laughed. This brick wall of a black man was in unbearable pain. He never once pressed the button on his morphine drip. A testimony to his pain threshold—or maybe, once again, that infernal pride.

"John," I said, when I couldn't take any more beating around the bush. I'd never been good with subtle small talk. "Let's cut the bull. What's going on? What happened?"

His eyes darted away from mine, gazing past the open window to the imposing glass skyscrapers surrounding the hospital. It looked as though you could just reach out and touch the one directly across from us. I imagined, involuntarily, just how easy it might be for Spidey to actually websling around town.

I shook the image from my head and leaned forward. "Come on, man. You called me here for a reason. Someone did this to you. I need to know who."

He looked back at me, drawing in a breath before shaking his head. "Not *who*, Boomer. *What*." I watched as an involuntary shudder rippled down his traumatized body. "Something big. Scary as all get-out."

For Johnny to admit something was scary was saying a lot. Back in our early teens, I'd seen him stand stock-still as an enraged black bear charged him from fifty yards away. He'd casually put a bullet between its eyes before it was able to pounce on us.

"What was it? Maybe I can help."

His eyes flickered down to his chest. His good hand scratched at the back of his head. He was shaking. "You're not going to believe me."

"Try me."

He took another breath and looked up at me.

"Okay," he said. "How 'bout...the devil."

THREE

I STEPPED OUT OF THE HOSPITAL INTO THE WHIRLWIND ACTIVITY OF THE city. Though it was only about three in the afternoon, the sun had already drifted behind the range of skyscrapers littering the landscape, producing a sort of twilight feel.

It was symbolic of my mood. Grim.

Johnny had told me what happened, but I was still trying to make sense of it. Being well known as one of the nation's best trackers, he'd been contracted by the mayor's office to locate and kill a strange, flying animal that had been terrorizing the city's population for the better part of a month. Witness accounts were conflicting. Some said it looked like some type of dragon or pterosaur. Others claimed it was merely an oversized carrion bird. And there were even a few who believed gargoyles had actually broken away from their stone prisons and were harbingers of the imminent Apocalypse.

Only in New York.

Just before he'd arrived, however, things had escalated. The creature changed from just another drunken apparition on a Saturday night tourist binge to a killer. At least two native New Yorkers had been found slain—a homeless man in Central Park and an escort trying to make her subway train at an ungodly hour. Witnesses to both maulings described the culprit as a vicious devil-like creature made of mist and shadows.

But my old friend had never been superstitious. He was a pragmatist to the core. He knew whatever was haunting the rooftops, killing the city's citizens was flesh and blood. An animal. As far as I know, there'd never been a biological species on earth that John X. Stephens couldn't hunt.

And hunt he did. For three nights, he waited patiently. Perching behind a blind on the roof of a tall tenement building on 34th Avenue, he'd watched the night sky for any signs of the mysterious creature. On the fourth night, his perseverance paid off.

A series of strange shrieks and rhythmic clicks had echoed across the horizon, followed immediately by a black silhouette flying just below the skyline. Johnny estimated the wingspan to be at least twelve feet across…maybe more. The sight had chilled my friend to the bone, but failed to paralyze him. He was, after all, a hardened hunter. A professional. Readying himself, he'd taken aim at the beast and fired. And had royally ticked it off for his efforts.

The creature had been hit. No question about that. If Johnny said he hit it, he definitely did. But apparently, getting struck in the chest by a 7.62x54 mm copper-jacketed slug didn't really mean much to it. With a screech, it had diverted course and bee-lined straight for my friend.

Johnny had shuddered uncontrollably when he'd recounted what the beast looked like. A dull sheen clouded his sunken, haunted eyes as he'd remembered with the crystal clarity what only he could.

"I'm tellin' you, Boomer," he'd said. "It was the devil. A living, breathing demon straight from the pits of Hell."

He'd gone on to explain how the beast's leathery wings were tipped with lethal-looking spikes at the ridges that could easily be used for tearing its prey apart. It stood on two sinewy, fur-covered legs attached to formidable talons, curved inward, giving the appearance of cloven hooves. The bone structure and posture had brought to mind some creature from *Jurassic Park*, like a Velociraptor or something similar—only covered head to long serpentine tale in fur. Its torso was immensely broad, sporting large, powerful simian arms that reminded John of a silverback gorilla. But it had been the head, my friend said, that sent slivers of dread down his back. Shaped like the skull of some great horse, with two twelve-inch horns cresting the brow, its mouth protruded in a sinister equine grin.

Then, the creature had pounced. After that, John only remembered waking up in the ICU.

Of course, the description had not been lost on me. I'd heard it, albeit not in so detailed terms, a number of times before. The common description of the Jersey Devil—either the wild imaginings of a large number of madmen since the Revolutionary War or the modern equivalent of the chimera of legend—was always of some strange hybrid of horse, goat, and bat.

But my friend's description also presented me with another conundrum. The Jersey Devil, to my knowledge, had never wandered this far north before…preferring to reside in its lush, primal habitat of the Pine Barrens in Southern New Jersey. By all accounts, if it truly existed, it had never been migratory.

I rubbed my neck, pondering these inconsistencies, as I meandered to the curb and hailed a taxi. I had a few places I needed check out before it got too dark and I couldn't think of a better place to start than the scene of the first crime. Um, so to speak.

After climbing into the cab, I told the English-challenged cabbie to drive me to Central Park, and leaned back in my seat. As the driver slipped into traffic and lead-footed the gas pedal like I'd just asked him to "follow that car," I pulled out my cell phone and scrolled down my contacts. I was going to need data before I could really proceed with my investigation and there was no better person to get that from than Wiley Garrett, ENIGMA's very own boy genius.

If my life was an Anton Strout novel, Wiley would be called a "technomancer"—someone with the ability to manipulate any technology with only a thought and a whisper. As it stands, he's just your average, everyday mega-geek techno wiz who still has vintage *Star Wars* sheets on his bed. Rumor has it, he has an impressive collection of them. He graduated from MIT at

the ripe old age of 15, went to work for the NSA soon after that, and got
bored with the whole affair after cracking one of the most complex algo-
rithms ever designed in a whopping 14.6 minutes. He'd come to work for us
soon after around his twentieth birthday.

The phone rang twice before he picked up.

"Jack! Hey, man." Wiley's voice cracked. I heard the distinct sounds of
electronic gunfire and I recognized the screams of blood-soaked aliens in
the background. He was apparently busy playing *Halo*. "You know, Polk's
been looking for you, dude. Has me monitoring your cell phone and email
accounts—"

"Wiley, just chill for a sec, okay?"

My body lurched into the passenger side door as the cabbie hooked a
sharp right turn.

"Watch where you're going, buddy!" I yelled at the driver and then
turned my attention back to the pimple-faced geek on the other end of the
line. "I need some info, Wiles."

I gave him my grocery list of necessary information, then asked him to
contact Randy and Scott. I had a feeling I would be needing their help with
this one. Landers wouldn't want to come…he'd always been Mr. Do-As-
I'm-Told. But Randy would convince him in the end. Randy, however,
would follow me to the pits of Hell if I asked and he'd drag any poor sap he
could find right along with us.

"Oh, and Wiley?"

"Yeah, Jack?"

"Make sure Nikki doesn't catch wind of this. She hears about it and
she'll want to tag along. And that's something I don't need right now.
Understood?"

"Absolutely," the pudgy little nerd squeaked. "But what about the director? What should I tell him?"

"Tell him the truth. I'm off to find a mug more gruesome than his."

Before Wiley could stutter a customary monosyllabic response to my insults of the boss, I ended the call and tried to enjoy the rest of the ride to one of the nation's most breathtaking parks.

꙰

Central Park in the early days of April is an amazing thing to see. The air is still crisp and fresh, budding with flowers that brighten the walking trails like a stream of lights on a Christmas tree…even in the dim light of dusk. The smell of spring wafted on a light breeze as I strolled the paved walkway through the blossoming Spruce and Oak trees lining both sides of the clearing.

Knowing a blind search of the sprawling 843 acres of pristine wilderness for clues to the creature I was hunting would be like searching for a contact lens in Yankee Stadium. I'd have to use my brains for a change. Narrow the search a bit.

I'd taken a few minutes to talk to local food vendors and homeless denizens of the park, trying to gather any information available. Most refused to talk about the sightings. The few that did had very different accounts of what they'd seen and I quickly surmised I would get nothing of any value from any of them.

It wasn't until I spoke to a couple of mounted NYPD officers patrolling the park, that I'd been able to ascertain the location where the homeless man had been killed. I'd been warned that the park wasn't safe at night—especially to tourists—and I should leave the area as soon as possible. But in the end, the officers had given up what little information they knew when they realized it wasn't so easy to get rid of me.

Using the GPS app on my iPhone to navigate the unfamiliar territory, I found myself wandering the emptying trails, making my way slowly to a tiny, perfectly manicured glade in which the first supposed victim of the "Devil" had been torn to shreds. I passed by the famous, stylized bronze statue of

Balto and suddenly found myself wishing I'd brought Arnold along for the trip. Not only would he have loved the city, his sniffer would have been an invaluable asset in my search.

I arrived at the spot which the officers had marked on my map and scanned the grass. It was just starting to turn green with the passing of winter. I looked, hoping to find anything that law enforcement and the forensic specialists might have missed. The sun was now almost completely behind the tree line and I was forced to pull out my Mini Maglite for a better look around.

I scanned the ground, walking as lightly as I could over the fresh cut lawn. I honestly wasn't expecting to find anything, but I had to start somewhere and going to the crime scene had always seemed to work for Monk. When my hunch proved correct and I came up empty, I tried a different tact. Pocketing the miniature light, I reached into my cargo pants and pulled out another small object that appeared suspiciously like the Maglite.

But this one was different. Equipped with a special UV-emitting bulb, it was designed to illumine any biological specimens within its range. I grabbed the small bottle of Luminol from another pocket and sprayed the strange smelling chemical along the ground near my feet. Alternate Light Sources, or ALS to crime scene technicians, were fantastic at making hairs, fibers, and other objects visible to the naked eye. But you needed a special chemical to illume any trace amounts of fluids such as blood, fecal matter, and even urine. Hence the Luminol.

I looked at the sky. It appeared dark enough.

I flipped on the ALS and cast its strange amber light back and forth over the darkened ground. I stepped methodically forward in short choppy steps. This sort of work took painstaking patience. If you rushed it, you risked contaminating any evidence that could potentially be found.

After ten minutes of scouring the Luminol-soaked ground, I let out a heavy sigh of defeat. I was just about to reach down and turn the light off when my eyes caught something silvery-blue to my left. I turned to look, fearful the illuminated object would disappear from sight like a wisp of fog. But it didn't. Five or six drops of something sprinkled a square-foot patch of St. Augustine grass.

I crouched down to get a closer look. The silver hue intensified as the light's beam drew closer to it.

Yeah. That's definitely biological, I thought, rummaging in my messenger bag for two evidence tubes. Gloving up first, I carefully removed samples of both biologically contaminated and untouched grass. I was just sealing the tubes shut when the area to my right erupted in a loud, blood-curdling cry.

I jerked to full height and spun around, seeking the source of the disruption. Whatever had screamed sounded human. And terrified. Very, *very* terrified.

I stuffed the evidence into my pack and bolted through a thicket of maple trees to the south, where the shout had originated. I was surprised by how few brambles raked my face as I ran haphazardly through the darkened woods, but soon remembered that the entire park was landscaped, despite its *au naturale* appearance.

I ran nearly a hundred yards before another series of shouts broke out about fifty yards to my right. The original voice I'd heard was screaming, followed by yelling from numerous other individuals.

Instinctively, I reached to pull my Glock, only to remember I hadn't brought it. A gun in New York City is basically like posting a neon sign on your forehead saying, "Hey cops! Arrest me now!"

I hesitated. I was up against unknown odds, with no weapons, and in a strange environment. The city had done a lot to clean up the park of crime in the past decade, but there were still about a hundred random acts of violence a week taking place within the forested acres of land. I was in no mood to be added to those statistics. But still...someone was in trouble.

Crap. I'd never hear the end of it from Nikki, I thought. I took off running again, having no idea what I would do when I actually caught up to the voices.

Fortunately, I didn't have long to dwell on it. A minute later, I broke free from the tree line and entered into a clearing. My breath caught in my throat.

Thirteen black-robed and hooded figures loomed over a panic-stricken, immaculately tailored blond man. He was sprawled on the ground, cringing in fear. Of all the things I might have expected to see on my first outing to Central Park, this was definitely not anywhere on the list.

FOUR

THE ROBED FIGURES LOOKED AT ME AS I BARRELED INTO THE CLEARING, their faces hidden beneath dark hoods. From their tensed posture, they were just as surprised to see me as I was them.

At least for a millisecond.

Recovering their bearings, they swung their arms up, bringing twelve rather long, curved, and pointy-looking daggers to view. I recognized the blades as kukri knives…commonly used by the Gurkhas of Nepal.

"Ah, crap," I said, backpedaling two steps. "Hey, look…sorry to interrupt your *Rocky Horror Picture Show* rehearsal here. I'm just a tourist. Got a little turned around is all."

Three of them stepped around the still-cringing man on the ground and moved toward me with the grace and speed of a litter of jungle cats. Swinging their blades with synchronous precision, they lunged at me. Instinctively, I darted to the left, tucked in my legs, and rolled from their attack.

"Now come on!" I shouted, coming to my feet. "Can't we talk about this?"

Their shadow-shrouded faces remained neutral, their silence deafening, and they leapt in my direction again. A little more prepared, I sidestepped the first and, in the same fluid motion, threw my steel-toed hiking boot into the groin of the second. The third sideswiped me from behind, knocking me to the ground.

As Arlene, Polk's secretary, had pointed out, I've never been much of a brawler. But what she didn't know was that I had been enduring Landers' ridiculous sparring matches for the last year. He was a firm believer in always being prepared. He'd hoped that in spite of my abysmal shooting skills, surely I'd be good with something simpler, like hand-to-hand combat. He'd been wrong about that, too. But I manage. In a pinch.

Besides, I fight dirty.

Before my assailant could bring his blade down into my back, I grabbed a handful of dirt and flung it behind me into his eyes. With the creep temporarily blinded, I rolled underneath his weight and sent him flying off me. The dagger clattered to the ground and I dove to grab it before he recovered. I was just barely fast enough, because the moment I stood up, the blade clutched tight in my hand, all three of the hoods had surrounded me. I glanced over my shoulder and saw their ten compatriots watching the fray like a circle of couch potato Nazgul from *The Lord of the Rings*.

"Wait a minute," I said, shaking my head in a nervous chuckle. "This is a hazing, isn't it? You guys are in some kind of over-the-top fraternity and this is an initiation, right?"

The three creepy attackers stepped silently forward. Two of them sheathed their stainless steel weapons. The third's hands clenched into a tight—feminine—fist.

A woman?

Through the slit of my still-swollen right eye, I peered deeper into her cowl to see a shock of long silver hair protruding from the side. When I say silver, I'm not talking the cottony whiteness of a geriatric head of hair. I'm talking about the precious metal. The sheen was almost blinding, even in the dim light of the streetlamp beside us.

They gave me no more time to examine her face, as they once again pounced in unison. The one to my right dove at my legs, while the left-hand goon grabbed at my shoulders. I crashed to the ground with a thud and found the silver-haired vixen resting comfortably on my lap. Looking at one of her partners, she held out her hand. His kukri quickly found its way into her palm and she brought the blade to my throat.

"What business do you have here?" her silky voice seethed from under the hood. She sounded young. Really young. But her voice held such clarity and strength that I knew she was the group's leader. I didn't have time to ponder that, though, as I felt the edge of the knife biting into my neck. "What do you have to do with this man?"

She pointed to the prone form of the young thirty-something-year old man I'd seen upon stumbling into the glade. Branches and strands of grass tangled within his thick, James Dean-esque brown hair. His slightly dainty, but handsome features were contorted in a rictus of fear as he stared up at the remaining Robed Wonders standing over him.

"Him?" I nodded over at the man. "Never seen him in my life." Her dagger pressed deeper against my skin. "I'm telling you the truth. I was just looking around. Heard that guy screaming like a little schoolgirl and came running. I thought he was being mugged."

How was I supposed to know his muggers had just come from an Addams Family *reunion?* I thought, biting my tongue to keep from actually speaking the words. This was one example of a time where my mouth could literally be the death of me.

"That's unfortunate for you," she said. I could just make out the outline of dark burgundy lipstick, spread evenly across a tight pair of lips. The skin of her exposed neck could only be described as alabaster, like some sparkly vampire-wannabe. A nose stud adorned one nostril. The girl was like some goth chick from hell. "Because you will meet the same fate as he."

"Um, please tell me you're going to send him on an all-expense-paid trip to the Virgin Islands," I said, throwing her my best rakish grin. "That'd be very original as far as shared fates go."

Her knife eased a bit, a faint trace of a smile spread across her shadowed face.

Darn it. I knew Randy and I should have kept working on that stand-up routine.

"I'm sorry," she said, her grip tightening on the dagger's handle as she prepared to slide it across my throat. "We can't take any chances. Our mission is too important to leave witnesses." She leaned forward and whispered in my ear. "You're cute. Just not *that* cute."

I felt her body tense against me. She was about to make her move. I struggled to throw her off, but her partners-in-crime had my arms and legs well secured. For the third time in less than a week, I found myself in the precarious position of clenching my eyes shut and hoping for the best...

Oh well...at least it's not Artie, I thought as I prepared for the blade to slice into my neck.

Blam!

My good eye popped open at the crack of gunfire, its source a good distance away. The creep holding my arms fell over, clutching his shoulder, and moaning in pain.

Blam!

A cloud of dirt billowed from the turf not two feet from my hands—close enough to send the goon holding my feet scurrying back to his friends. The silver-haired goth bent down, kissed me on the forehead, and then whipped out a weird-looking spray bottle. With a quick double tap, a cold mist shot from the nozzle onto my face and clothes.

"Looks like you get to live," she said, and slithered off my prone form. "At least for now."

She turned and ran to the others and I watched as they melted deep into the shadows of a stand of maple trees to the south. Like ghosts.

Or bloody satanic ninjas!

"For the love of..." I heard myself mutter as I picked myself up from the ground and looked around. I felt the soft trickle of blood streaming down my neck. I pulled out a handkerchief and applied it to the superficial wound.

I glanced around the park for signs of my benefactor. Whoever had taken the shots was really good. It was too soon for Landers to have arrived, so I had no idea who had come to my rescue. Not seeing any immediate signs of the gunman, I walked over to the traumatized victim and reached out a hand to pull him up.

"Th-thank you," he said. His hands were shaking and he self-consciously stuck them in the pockets of his very expensive dress slacks. "I d-don't know what w-would have happened if…if you…"

I waved him off. "I get that a lot. Don't mention it."

The sound of footsteps to my right drew my attention. The shadowy outline of a well-built man of about six feet entered the clearing and for the second time in thirty minutes once again, found myself completely speechless.

The older man's grizzled face cracked into a wicked grin as he tilted his head toward me. "Obadiah," he said. His vintage 1873 Winchester lever-action rifle hung casually across his back in a sling. He was sporting the same flannel shirt he always wore when he went hunting…despite the warmer temperature.

"D-dad?"

"I don't know what I'm gonna do with you, boy." He shook his head as he stalked over to us and looked the would-be victim up and down with a disapproving look. "Just blundered right into a hornets' nest to save the *princess* here, when you should have taken some time to spy out the terrain. If I've told you once, I've told you—"

"Dad, what are you doing here?"

"Princess?" the stranger asked in a huff of disgust.

I glared at him before turning my attention to Dr. Oliver Jackson—my estranged father. Or rather, I guess, not-so-estranged now that I had finally come around and joined him in his belief in Christ. You see, he and my mom had always been a bit of an embarrassment to me. Top researchers in their respective fields, they'd skyrocketed to great prestige in the scientific community…that is, until they professed their faith in an "unscientific superstition" like God. Of course, I *could* have tolerated that if, in their religious zeal, they just hadn't named me Obadiah.

Still, in the two years since professing my own faith, I had to admit that our relationship had grown somewhat. Even so, it still didn't explain why my burly family patriarch was stalking through Central Park at the exact same time as me. Or why he was packing his hunting rifle like a modern day Grizzly Adams.

"I'll repeat. What are you doing here, Dad?"

"John called me," he said with a wink and slapped me on the shoulder. "Told me what happened and I came to help out."

"That's funny. He didn't mention that."

"Told him not to. Knew you wouldn't like it."

"You were right."

I couldn't believe this. Dad was a paleontologist…a dinosaur doctor, as I liked to rib him. The creatures he hunted were long dead. Mostly dirt and dust. They'd hardly try to have him for dinner if he made the wrong move. I'd intentionally kept him out of my business for that very reason.

Oh, sure. There was probably no better outdoorsman in the world. He'd give Landers a run for his money. And he'd pretty much taught John Stephens everything he knew about tracking, shooting, and hunting animals of all shapes and sizes since yours truly had never been all that interested. But come on! It's my dad. I couldn't have him join me on my hunt for the tourist version of the Jersey Devil.

"I think we can discuss this later," my dad said, looking over his shoulder. "Those shots are sure to bring in the cavalry and I'd just as soon be long gone before they get here. This pea-shooter of mine ain't exactly legal."

I nodded. "Good point." I looked at the rescued *princess*. "I think you should come with us. I've got some serious questions you're going to need to answer."

തക

The three of us sat in a cramped booth in a nearby diner and I scarfed down a chili and cheese slathered hotdog in three bites. Fighting the forces of darkness has a way of making a guy hungry. Facing an overbearing and demanding father can downright starve a man.

Dad sat next to me on one side of the booth. Our stranger was nearly hugging himself into a nervous ball on the other side. After downing a keg-sized Coke, I looked up from my dinner plate. "Okay," I said to the man we'd rescued. "How about telling us your name, first of all."

His hand, still shaking from his ordeal, popped a ketchup-heavy fry into his mouth and nodded.

"Um, my name's Davenport. Alex Davenport. I'm a reporter. I was working on a story when I was accosted by those...those..." A fit of nervous shakes prevented him from finishing the sentence.

"Yeah, we get it. Question is, what kind of story were you working on that drew out such unsavory characters?"

"I think I can answer that one, Obadiah—"

"Jack, Dad. Please. Call me Jack."

"That's the most ridiculous thing I ever heard of, boy. I'll call you by your God-given name and you'll respect it when in my presence. It's a good name. Godly name. You should be proud of it."

Davenport glanced between us, confusion painted on his face.

"But..." I tried to protest.

"No buts," Dad said, pointing a thick, calloused finger at the reporter. "Now, as I was sayin', our boy here's on the same trail as us. Hunting himself one *devil* of a story, I'd say."

I looked at Davenport. "Is this true?"

"Of course, it's true." Dad threw up his hands in irritation. "You never believe a word I say. I've never once told you a single untrue statement and—"

"Dad?" I held up a hand to silence him. "You're not helping here."

"I, uh, I don't know w-what he's talking about," the reporter said, his eyes darting from me to Dad in a nervous twitch. "I was just investigating the murder that occurred there in the park a few nights ago. Just checking out the crime scene and they attacked me."

"Now who's a liar?" Dad leaned forward, slamming his palm against the table. "I saw you, son. Saw what happened. I'd been watching you from the moment you set foot into that clearing."

I looked at my dad. "What happened then?"

"He saw it. Or rather, he heard it at first...wings flapping in the darkness above the tree tops." Dad took in a mouthful of his salad. Just another irritating thing about him...he'd always been such a healthy eater. "Davenport here followed the creature. Watched it perch itself up on a nearby tree branch. Then got himself a bright idea."

Yes, Oliver Jackson really talks like that. The man holds three Ph.D.'s, speaks four languages fluently, and he still talks like Jed Clampett from the *Beverly Hillbillies*.

"And what was that?" I turned my attention to the unnerved reporter, watching his reaction during Dad's narrative.

"Turned on his camera and took a snapshot. Heh. I imagine it would have made one heckuva postcard."

"Why did you lie to us, Davenport? Why not just tell us?"

"I don't have a clue who you are!" He practically spat out the words. "For all I know you could be one of...one of *them*. Or worse, another reporter. This is the story of the century. The thing I caught on that camera...well, it would have been phenomenal. Proof of a Jersey Devil-like creature roaming the treetops of Central Park. I'd make a fortune."

A cold chill washed down my spine; a single question crept into my head.

"Um, what newspaper did you say you worked for again?" I asked.

"I didn't say..."

"What paper?" My voice elevated an octave. I was getting irritated.

"The... *The Fortean Inquisitor.*" His face simultaneously turned ten shades of red as he mouthed the words.

"Oh for the love of..." I threw my hands in the air. A tabloid reporter. Chasing after another UFO-abducted-alien-baby-who-eats-alligators-in-the-sewer story. "That's just swell."

I turned to my dad. "What happened to the camera?" There was no point in asking Davenport. He wasn't going to tell me the truth any longer. As an ENIGMA employee, I couldn't let the photograph of the creature get into the hands of the public. Yeah, I know. Keeping the public in the dark makes my skin crawl too. But it's part of my job.

"Those bozos took it from him. Still had it when they skinned out of the park."

"Well, then," I said, shaking my head in annoyance. "We're just going to have to get it back, now aren't we?"

FIVE

We left Davenport, still shaking, in the rundown diner. After locking my dad's Winchester in the extended cab of his old Ford F-250 pickup, we made our way back to the clearing where I'd been attacked. I hadn't been able to finish looking for the clues I'd been searching for before running into the Darth Sidious Look-alike Brigade and I still had plenty of time to kill before Landers and Randy's flight arrived.

"So, what exactly are you lookin' for, son?" Dad asked, watching me scramble up the tree where the reporter had seen what I'd decided to simply call the JD, to keep the name short and sweet.

"Not. Sure," I grunted, pulling my legs over the nearest branch and perching on top. "Physical evidence. Anything that might be used to identify the creature."

I pulled my UV light from my messenger bag and clicked it on. The amber-hued light drifted back and forth along the branch, illuminating a few scuff marks biting into the bark, but little else. Frustrated, I plopped down on the branch and let my feet dangle in the air. My eyes drifted to the dirt below while my brain sorted the options for our next move.

"Well, what are you doing now?" Dad asked, his hands folded across his burly chest. "Ain't no time for a break."

"I'm thinking!" The words were a little sharper than I'd intended. His presence in this whole affair was starting to put me on edge. And if he thought he was going to tell me how to conduct a cryptozoological investigation, he had another thing coming.

"Your little light gizmo didn't show you what you needed?" The man smiled at me behind his bushy salt-and-pepper Hemingway beard.

"No. It didn't."

"Well, why not use the good sense God gave you, boy. Look with your eyes, not with your gadgets. Use what I taught you when you were a kid."

I knew what he was getting at. When I was a kid, my dad had tried to teach me how to hunt on more than one occasion. There were two reasons I'd refused to let him: First, the thought of killing Bambi's mom had definitely not been my idea of a good time. Honestly, just imagining killing a defenseless woodland creature sent waves of nausea and revulsion through my gut. The distaste for it has followed me my entire life…despite the number of cryptids I'd killed in self-defense over the years. The second reason I'd declined every invitation to join Oliver Jackson on his regular weekly hunts was far less noble. The crazy old man had always gone at the most sacrosanct of times…Saturday morning! I'm sorry; I wasn't going to miss *Thundarr the Barbarian* for any kind of father/son bonding. But even though I'd never gone hunting with the old man, he'd insisted—at times other than during Saturday morning cartoons—on showing me the finer points of tracking game. The knowledge had come in handy on more than one monster hunt when I was starting out. More recently, I'd started relying more heavily on newfangled high tech forensic equipment than my own senses.

I pocketed the Alternate Light Source, then pulled my Mini Maglite from my pack, and shined it once more over the tree bark. Still didn't see anything. This wasn't making any sense. The creature, if it was as described by countless witnesses should have left some trace of its presence, if it had perched in this tree.

I focused my thoughts on what I knew of the creature…from Johnny's description, as well as the popular mythos behind the Jersey Devil. All eyewitness accounts reported the JD to be half-horse, half-goat, with bat-like wings. Bat-like.

Bat-like?

I looked at the large tree on which I was currently perched. The bark was extremely light brown, almost silvery in patches. Its leaves, which were only just beginning to sprout seemed asymmetrical and rough to the touch.

"Dad? Any idea what kind of tree this is?"

He smiled knowingly at me and nodded. "Now you're thinkin' like a hunter, boy," he said, showing me his bright teeth in the moonlight. "If I ain't mistaken, that is a…" He paused for a second, as if in thought. "A *celtis occidentalis.*"

I sneer at him and shrug. "Seriously? You're giving me the Latin nomenclature?"

He sighed. "A hackberry tree, son."

I had thought that it was. So the question an experienced tracker needed to ask himself now was: Why would the winged creature we were hunting be hanging out in a hackberry tree? Why not a maple or an elm, which were wider and taller with much stronger branches?

I looked down at my dad, who was eyeing me appreciatively. He knew where my thoughts were taking me. The paleontologist in him had already figured it out.

"We're talking about a possible food source, aren't we?" I asked, clutching the limb directly above me and pulling myself up to the next level.

"Now you're usin' your brains, kid. And what sort of physical evidence would you expect to fi—"

I found it before he had a chance to finish the sentence. On the drive back to Central Park, I'd used my time to Google some information on the flora and fauna common in the Pine Barrens of New Jersey where the JD is known to dwell. I then cross referenced similarities with the Park. One common denominator was the hackberry tree, which produced its fruit in autumn. But the berries were hearty and often survived the harsh northern winters well into spring. So when I saw the two different piles of berries carefully laid out on the branch near the tree's trunk, I wasn't surprised. The first pile of berries appeared to have been chewed on…only the husks and the seeds still remained. The other group of berries looked to be the creature's "to-be-eaten" pile since they revealed no bite marks at all. The JD had probably been interrupted by Davenport while in the middle of a meal and had taken off. Strange, though—I wouldn't have thought a creature like Johnny described to be an herbivore. It just seemed too bloodthirsty. Too violent. Then again, maybe it was simply an opportunistic omnivore. Still, the berries were a great piece of evidence. The half-eaten ones could contain saliva that we could use to identify its DNA. Carefully, I pulled a plastic baggie from my pack and proceeded to take a sample of the putrid berries with a pair of tweezers.

"Got it!"

"Now see," came a rasping male voice I didn't recognize from somewhere below me. "That makes me curious. What exactly have you *got?*"

I glanced down to see a short, thrumpy-looking man. He wore a wrinkled button down shirt and slacks that looked about a size too short on him. The man's round face was stern and even though he was looking up at me, his thick, square chin bulged above a stump of a neck. He wasn't so much overweight as he was a brick wall.

"Well? You going to explain why you're up in that tree?" The man brushed absently at his neatly cropped mustache.

"Um, and you are?" I asked, lowering myself from the tree. I dropped and turned to face the stout man. That's when I saw the shiny piece of metal clipped to his belt. "Oh, you're a detective." I nodded to the police badge.

"Detective Sergeant Michael Grigsby," he said, pitching an unfiltered cigarette in his mouth and lighting it. "We got a report of some gunfire in this very area earlier tonight. Just came out to look around and found you monkeying around in that tree. Gotta ask myself, what would make a grown man do that at three in the morning?"

Casually, I palmed the bag of berries in my hand and slipped them in my pocket. It was horrible forensics. No telling what state they'd be in when I removed them later, but I couldn't very well explain to the policeman that I was foraging for the food source of a winged cryptid responsible for two maulings in his city, now could I?

I eyed my dad, who simply smiled and nodded his head toward Grigsby. His message was clear: *Yes, son. Go ahead and tell the nice police officer.* He was definitely amused, which annoyed the crap out of me.

"Er, well—"

The detective wouldn't let me finish. "You see, it's like this. I'm investigating a very nasty murder that occurred in this very area not more than a week ago. Strangest thing I've ever seen. Limbs torn right off the man's body. Head snapped off like a chocolate bunny at Easter." He gave my dad the onceover before stepping up closer to me and letting out a plume of smoke. "So when I hear reports of gunfire in the same clearing as my homicide…well, you can see why I might be a little suspicious."

"Yeah, I can understa—"

"So, I show up and you're saying something about finding something. And don't tell me you were lookin' for a contact lens. If I had a nickel for every time I heard that one…" Grigsby placed his hands on his hips, resting his right palm on the grip of his .38 service revolver.

This guy's still using a revolver? When was his gun issued? 1978?

"Okay, I'm going to be honest with you." The words slipped from my mouth before I even had time to think. Normally, I'd be lying through my teeth when approached by an official law enforcement representative, but I could tell this guy was too bright to believe one of the government's "weather balloon" stories. Besides, I'd never been the best liar in the world—though I'd definitely given it a lot of practice. Just ask my ex-girlfriend Nikki. "I'm a member of a government scientific think-tank. We're kind of looking into the death of your victim, as we think it might be related to some of the research we're doing."

All right, so maybe I wasn't ready to tell the detective everything. But I wasn't lying per se. More like a series of omissions really. But despite my elective honesty, the detective's eyes belied the fact that he just wasn't buying it. His brow furrowed as he moved over to the tree I'd just climbed down from and placed a meaty hand against its bark.

"Think-tank, eh?" He shook his head in mock amusement. "And my victim just so happens to be part of some experiment gone wrong? Son, do you have any idea how ridiculous that sounds?"

His words made me shudder. If he'd known just a portion of the events in Malaysia two years before...what happened to Vera...or even the crazy ordeal with the mermaids in Greece, he wouldn't think it ridiculous at all. But he'd obviously misunderstood my point.

"It's not like that." I looked over at my dad for support, but his eyes were fixed on the treetops, silently whistling his own innocence of the entire affair. *Thanks a lot, Dad.* "Look, your victim might be connected to other unsolved deaths that occurred in Manhattan in the last month. We think the culprit—"

"Suspect."

"Okay, the...um, suspect...is more than likely an unclassified species of animal. We're trying to track it and then transplant it back to a safer environment."

The detective grinned at my dad. "Is he serious?"

"As a heart attack," Dad said, returning the smile before scowling at me. "Unfortunately. Apparently, it's what he does for a living."

The stocky man threw his cigarette butt to the grass and smashed it with his foot. "Look. It's late. I'm tired. I need to get your information so we can wrap this up and I can climb back into my cozy little bed."

He pulled out a notepad and a tiny eraser-free pencil—like the kind you get playing miniature golf—and nodded to me first. We proceeded to give him our information, however, I managed to avoided revealing ENIGMA's name during the exchange.

Grigsby folded the notepad and stuffed it back into his shirt pocket. Then he stuck the blunt end of the pencil into his mouth and bit down.

"Now here's how I see things," he said, nodding to the both of us. "You two haven't done anything wrong…well, except for maybe climbing a park tree, but I'm fuzzy on the tree-climbing laws around here. But here's a word of wisdom for you: Leave this homicide investigation alone. I catch either of you within spitting distance of a crime scene again, I'm going to take you to the nearest precinct and have you booked for any number of nasty infractions I can come up with. Understood?"

"Loud and clear," I said.

"Good. Now I'm going back to bed. But remember, I see your faces where they don't belong again…"

He let his words trail off as he stalked off into the shadows of Central Park.

⁂

I dropped my dad off at his hotel and decided to get a room myself. It was around four-thirty in the morning and we still had about another four hours to go before Randy's plane arrived. It'd give me at least a handful of hours sleep before we had to get back on the case. Once in my own room, I carefully extracted the baggie of berries—they'd remained surprisingly intact—from my pockets, sealed them in a protective FedEx pouch, and addressed it to Wiley back in Arlington. He'd be able to get the necessary tests done on them and hopefully we'd have some answers soon. Then I text-messaged the computer nerd, telling him where the team could find me once they landed in NYC. After his lengthy reply, I slipped into the skin-tight sheets of my bed and crashed into a dreamless slumber.

I awoke a few hours later, semi-refreshed, to a knock at my door. I groggily pulled myself out of the ultra-soft bed, pulled on the hotel's complementary bathrobe, and opened the door. My dog Arnold bounded into the room, leapt onto the bed, and let out a single bark. His tail wagged furiously against the rumpled comforter.

"So they brought you, huh?" I asked him before I turned back to the door and saw Randy, a dumb grin sprawled across his face.

Randall Cunningham was my most trusted ally on all the earth. We met in high school, when his first attempt at petty theft landed him in some potentially major hot water. I'd stepped in at the last minute, saved his skin, and we've been friends ever since. He's also the tech manager of my team and could be a royal pain in my neck. But I wouldn't have survived half the things I had if it wasn't for him. He was my Watson, my Boswell. And I wouldn't go on a monster hunt without him.

"I couldn't get anyone to watch him," he said, absently stroking the narrow tuft of hair sprouting just below his lower lip. That's right. The dweeb actually had a soul patch and a thick mop of sandy brown hair that stuck out in every direction. "Besides, you know how he gets when you leave him home for too long. He'd have been completely unbearable for weeks after you got home."

Randy moved into the room, threw the overstuffed duffle bag onto the floor and plopped down on one of the chairs around a small round table. I looked at him, but he wouldn't return my gaze. A bead of sweat glistened on his brow. He was nervous about something, but I couldn't quite discern what.

I was about to ask him what he was hiding when a grunt beside me brought my attention back to the door. Agent Scott Landers practically filled the doorway with his Superman-like awesome. Kind of made me sick. Standing a full six-foot-two, with a lean, muscular build, the former marine was about as near perfect as a guy could get. Square jaw. Tanned skin. Spiky-gelled hair that was the exact opposite of Randy's—meaning, it was meticulously controlled.

To be honest, for the first year and half that I'd known him, I'd never much liked the guy. From the moment I first met him in an Amazonian jungle, I had thought he was a stiff. Then, he'd betrayed us. He'd been assigned by higher-ups within ENIGMA to work with a whacked-out, honest-to-goodness mad scientist named Sashe Krenkin, who was resurrecting experiments from an old Soviet project, hoping to create the perfect biological killing machine. The jenglot. A pack of homicidal mutants with a voracious appetite for blood that had nearly killed me and my team. In a way, I guess they did kill one of them—my friend Vera Pietrova.

And Landers had been part of the whole thing all along. Sure, in the end, he'd come around to help us. Saved my butt big time, too. But it had taken me a very long time to learn to trust the guy. In fact, it hadn't been until well after our ordeal in Greece last year that I had begun to develop anything remotely resembling camaraderie. I'd never admit this to him, but he was slowly becoming…well, a friend. It didn't mean that I would ever ease up on the G.I. Joe jokes, though.

Landers moved into the room, carefully placed his own bag on the floor, and took a seat next to Randy without a word. But I couldn't help notice the fleeting glance he gave my friend as I moved to shut the door.

"Okay, the gang's all h—"

Before the door could swing shut, a very feminine, very shapely leg blocked the jamb. My eyes tracked the leg up gentle curves, all the way to the soft, smooth pout of Nikki Jenkins' upturned lips.

"Now, we're all here," she said, pushing the door open again, walking to the bed, and sitting down to rub Arnold's belly. His legs kicked hard at the affectionate attention.

Having not seen Nikki for about six months, I couldn't take my eyes off of her. She looked amazing. Dressed to the hilt in a very expensive-looking suit with a hem just above her knees. Her golden hair was completely loose, and seemed to flow over her shoulders like a cascading waterfall. The professional look suited her…nicely. When I'd first met her in Malaysia, she'd been a missionary, working in a small, secluded village in a dense rainforest. She hadn't worn any makeup then and was more comfortable in a baseball cap and cargo shorts than anything she might buy at Macy's.

I kept staring at her, my mouth slack with nothing to say. It was probably for the best. Her emerald green eyes burned with a subdued anger as I looked her up and down. And let me tell you, for such a small package—Nikki only stood at five-foot-three—those eyes could make even the toughest men cringe. She was readying herself for a fight. She knew I hadn't wanted her to come along on this.

Well, duh. In addition to the fact that our rocky relationship would foster some seriously distracting issues, she was a freaking missionary for crying out loud. She was no cryptozoologist. No field researcher. And definitely not a soldier like Landers.

I looked at Randy with a scowl. "What's she doing here?"

"Why don't you ask me?" Nikki said, her voice smooth but with an edge of irritation. "I'm getting real tired of you ditching me every time you get a potentially dangerous investigation."

Arnold growled in agreement with her. I took in the pair, Nikki's fingers doing a number across the dog's chin.

"Oh, you're in on this too, mutt?" I turned back to Randy. "You want to explain?"

My friend blew out a sigh before looking up at me, a sheepish grin across his face.

"She somehow caught wind that Scott and I were gearing up." He scratched nervously at his soul patch before continuing. "I mean, come on. You know how she is. She's like a bloodhound. She forced me to tell her where we were going. I didn't have a choice."

Ordinarily, I would argue with him, but given the look on Nikki's face, I knew he was right. She could be a nasty little tyrant when stirred up and at the moment she was more stirred up than a vat of my Uncle Hershel's famous chili.

Can we say, awkward? I thought, rolling my eyes with a sigh. This was going to be a disaster. This was exactly the reason for our current split. Six months ago, I'd kept her in the dark about an investigation I had been working in Guam. A complete waste of time. The cryptid that had been sighted turned out to be a hoax. But when Nikki found out about it, she'd been furious. I'd flat out lied to her, which had been the last straw.

Long story short, Nikki and I had kind of a weird relationship. Actually, although we were on the outs at the moment, she was still very special to me. She'd introduced me to Christ…helped me to finally accept the reality of His presence in my life. She'd done a great deal to help me grow in my relationship to Him.

Whether she wanted to admit it right now or not, we were also very attracted to one another. We both cared for each other deeply. On the other hand, I often wanted to throttle the girl where she stood and I knew the feeling was very mutual. Especially when she got all "hard-headed" like she was at that moment.

Great. First Dad. Now this. This hunt is definitely starting out on the wrong foot.

"Fine. You can stay," I said, throwing my hands up in submission before moving to the bathroom sink to brush my teeth. "Now, I'm starving. I'll fill you in while we get something to eat."

SIX

"How in the world did you manage to get us on the roof of Trump Tower?" Nikki asked while I strapped the restraining harness securely around her. Tiptoeing, she looked over the ledge of the building at the jagged cityscape cut against the nighttime sky. Millions of pinpoint pricks of light shone through pane glass windows of hundreds of high-rises littered throughout Manhattan.

"Uh, you know...I've got a few friends here and there. Some broad I know named Ivana," I said with a roguish grin, stretching out several thin cords attached to a large nylon canopy before following her gaze off the fifty-eight story skyscraper. A sudden bout of vertigo hit me square in the gut, forcing me to inch back to the safety of the roof. *Geeze, I hate this.* "Now are you sure you know how to fly one of these things? This is your last chance."

"No, I'm good." She could hardly contain her grin. The smile looked good on her. It had been far too long since she'd graced me with one and though I still had my reservations about Nikki being here, it was starting to feel like old times. "You're the one who hates heights, remember?"

"Yeah," I said, pulling on my own harness and stringing out the paraglider's lines. "Don't remind me."

The plan had been simple. After I debriefed them about the creature, we'd laid the groundwork for our first, full-on search for the creature stalking the concrete jungle of New York. We'd decided to wait until it was dark. Then, Randy, Landers, and my dad would take their positions at a temporary base camp we'd stage in the heart of Central Park. They'd monitor six IR— infrared—cameras we'd positioned in key locations on city rooftops, as well as those mounted on Nikki's and my helmets. Randy set up a miniature radar station on the top of Trump Tower and headed back to camp in Central Park where the others were waiting. If anything of significant size flew within range of the array, he'd pick it up. Add to that the two FLIR thermal imagers that Nikki and I both had attached to our shoulder harnesses and we were good to go.

Of course, that left the second stage of the plan—the part I wasn't particularly keen on: paragliding off the top of Trump Tower and soaring through the canyon of buildings all around us. Never mind the fact that I wasn't particularly fond of heights. The big problem would be the legal ramifications if we got caught. Since 9/11, the New York City authorities weren't exactly jumping for joy at the thought of would-be daredevils flying unchecked in the region. If we were detected, we'd have some major explaining to do. And I didn't exactly have official government sanction to pursue this particular little act of insanity.

Plus, though I'd used paragliders a few times before, I'd never really mastered them. It was a delicate operation. The controls were extremely sensitive. Too much wind, we'd shoot right over the rooftops. Too little, we'd slam smack dab into the side of a building. Neither were particularly encouraging possibilities.

"So, we going to do this, or what?" Nikki was beaming from ear to ear. She scooted closer to the edge of the building and climbed up onto the ledge. The skirt of the canopy wafted slightly off the graveled roof and settled gently back down. Then, she looked at me mischievously.

I gave her a scowl, climbing up to stand next to her. "You think this is really funny, don't you?"

"Immensely."

"Well, don't enjoy it too much. You'll be right next to me if I plummet to my death."

My eyes locked onto hers, unwilling to pull away from her gaze.

I'd never met a girl as volatile, or as courageous. Yet, she was also loving and compassionate. She'd willingly risk life and limb to protect the most wretched of the world. Yet at the same time, she was no stranger to violence and could shoot the wings off a fly at thirty yards with a .38. She was a dichotomy. A missionary by profession. An adventurer by association. And in all the time I'd known her, I'd never quite pieced together what exactly she was to me.

There was no doubt in my mind that I loved her. With all my heart. But was that enough? Could our feelings for one another overcome our fundamental differences? I had no idea. Our characteristics and personalities seemed to constantly put us at odds. In the end, all I knew was someone extraordinarily special that had been put into my life and I wanted her to remain part of it.

"Well, if you fall," she said, shining her white smile in my direction, "you're on your own 'cause I'm not about to try to catch you."

And with a maniacal laugh, she pulled the lines of her paraglider taut, catching the air within the sails, and leapt from the building. In a rush of wind, she was yanked up into the air, flying through the concrete canyon as if she'd been born with wings.

"Ah, crap," I said and leapt from the building two seconds later. Immediately, I felt the thirty foot wings expand and was yanked up with a jerk of rushing air. Settling into the harness chair, I grabbed the brakes of the glider in a dead man's grip. "I am *so* going to die."

"You're not going to die, Jack," Nikki's voice echoed through the tiny speaker inside my helmet. I'd forgotten about the radio transmitters.

"Don't count on it, Nik," Randy cut in. "He's really bad at flying those things."

"Nobody asked you, Randy." I shifted my weight to the left and angled toward my high-flying companion. "She's right. I'll be perfectly fine."

"Now, I didn't exactly say that," she laughed into the mic as a gust of wind pulled her up higher. "Just that you wouldn't die."

Sheesh, everyone's a comedian around here, I thought, winging my way around the corner of the tower and onto Fifth Avenue while trying to avoid looking down at the bustling streets nearly sixty-five stories down.

"How we doing, Scott?" I asked.

"Looking good, Jack." The ENIGMA agent's voice was stoic as usual. Stern. Humorless to the core. At that point, it was something I could appreciate. "You and Nikki maintain your positions for nine blocks, then hang a left on 65th Street. It should put you right over the park."

Maneuvering the airfoils with gentle pulls on the brakes, I gained on my partner and we quickly found ourselves flying in tandem. I looked over at her, gleefully watching the city below. I could only shake my head at her enthusiasm. The girl truly had no fear of anything. I watched her closely. Her ponytail, sticking out of her helmet, flapped against the current of air keeping us aloft. She laughed wildly from the exhilaration of flight. Her eyes were large and bright, the color of the ocean just after a hard rain. Her smile was infectious, beaming nearly from ear to ear.

She is just so beautiful. Geeze, why do I keep screwing things up with her?

I was mesmerized by the avian grace in which she handled the flying contraption and I soon realized my mouth hung wide open in admiration. Unfortunately, she noticed it too.

"What?" she mouthed with a half-smile, avoiding radio chatter. She didn't need to ask. She knew exactly what I was thinking. She was so intuitive that way. It was both maddening and alluring at the same time.

I merely nodded the question away and pointed ahead. We were approaching our turn. Scanning the horizon, I let my mind drift back to our objective. Losing focus on an expedition could get someone killed.

"Jack, do you copy?" Randy spat into my ear, reinforcing my need to concentrate.

"Roger that." *And don't say it*, I thought, but knew he would anyway. My friend was so predictable that way.

"My name's not Roger," he said for the millionth time since I'd known him. "But we've got a bogey popping up on the radar. It's coming your way at nine o'clock. It's big and it's moving fast."

My head whipped left; my eyes peering into the halogen haze of the street lamps far below. It played havoc with my eyes.

"I can't see anything. How far away is it?"

"Dude, it's right there. You should—Hey!"

"Boy, it's on top of you," my dad growled into the microphone. "It's on top of you!"

I looked up to see a hideous black shape zoom down from overhead. Its nearly fifteen-foot wing span arched back in a diving tackle toward my paraglider's canopy.

"Holy smokes!"

Instinctively, I jerked the brakes to the left, sending me spiraling around to my right and narrowly missing the dive-bombing cryptid by inches. Now below me, I could clearly make out the creature's strange chimeric features in dizzying detail.

Its body was huge, reminding me of images of the mythological mino-taur. Powerful ape-like arms bent at the elbows as it pulled itself out the fast dive. Its squat, irregular legs seemed to bend backwards like the hindquar-ters of goat and tapered off into two hoof-like claws. The single six-inch talon near the heel of the foot reminded me of a Velociraptor's. As it veered skyward again, I could just discern the long, curved shape of two horns protruding from the monster's horse-like face…its menacing mouth curled in a vicious snarl as it made a beeline straight for…

"Oh crap!" I shouted into the headset. Glancing around frantically, I caught sight of my partner, now moving quickly away from the on-coming beast. "Nikki, it's heading for you! Get out of here now. I'll lead it away."

The JD barreled up, directing its ire toward her. With a kick, she swung the contraption around to the right and avoided its impact in a maneuver similar to the one I'd just had to make.

Letting go of the right brake lead, I reached down to my hip, pulled the .40 caliber Glock Landers had secured for me, and aimed at the creature.

"Jack, don't shoot!" Landers voice crackled over the earpiece. I'd forgotten that with the IR camera attached to my helmet, they could see everything I saw, as if looking through my own eyes. "If you miss, that bullet will descend to the park. It might hit someone. Or worse, you might hit Nikki."

"Well, what the heck am I supposed to do, genius? That thing's going to make short work of her if I don't do something fast."

The beast had already corrected its angle and was once again tailing my former girlfriend. A quick look over her shoulder and Nikki abruptly turned right then left, in a tight zigzag pattern.

Dang. She's good.

The creature flew past her once more, its massive arms extending out toward her. Though it missed her body, its claws raked against two of her lines, severing them and sending her whirling out of control in a downward spiral.

"Nikki!" I shouted as I dove toward her. I wasn't sure what I could do if she wasn't able to stabilize the sails, but I couldn't just watch her plummet to her death. Before I could reach her, however, she managed to regain tentative control, adjust her weight to the remaining cords and descend slowly toward the ground. Leaving me completely alone with the airborne beast that now had its glowing red eyes fixed on me.

"Jack, we've got problems," Landers voice echoed inside my helmet.

"You think?" I jerked my glider to the left, arcing my path around in an attempt to outrun the creature.

"I'm not talking about the Devil," the agent said. "I'm picking up some chatter on the police band. You've been spotted. They're scrambling a chopper even as we speak. They'll be here in minutes."

"Well, tell them to take a number!" I leaned forward to pick up speed. By the time they got here, I'd more than likely be a smear on the sidewalk below.

A hideous screech bellowed from behind, forcing me to turn to see the creature swooping toward me with an unearthly speed. At this rate, it would be on top of me in seconds. I had limited options. None of them were particularly good…especially with my current skill level at aviation.

So, I chose the craziest idea of the bunch.

Taking my cue straight out of a James Bond script, I yanked down on the reigns of the brakes, expanding the nylon canvas to its full capacity. The increased air pressure yanked me straight into the air, letting the angry cryptid fly past and underneath me. Then, holding onto the air brakes with one hand and taking steady aim with the other, I fired three shots. Two missed, luckily plowing into the concrete structure of a nearby building. A single bullet smacked the creature's right wing, sending it barreling out of control with a howl of pain.

Before the monster hit the green lawn of the park below, it pulled up at the last second and streaked across the sky, out of range of more gunfire.

Yes. I did it. I could hardly contain the grin spreading across my face. *I am definitely going to need a smoke after this one.*

"Randy, is Nikki…"

"She's fine, Jack. Landed safely. Scott is already en route to extract her. Now get out of there before that police chop—"

Before he could finish his sentence, a blinding light burned against my face and the *thump-thump-thump* of chopper blades belted out their rhythm in front of me.

"Unauthorized pilot," a voice—a very angry sounding voice—bellowed from loudspeakers attached to the helicopter. "This is the NYPD. Land immediately or we will open fire."

Oh swell, I thought as I maneuvered the glider toward the nearest clearing in Central Park. Already a swarm of blue and red lights were converging on the park lawn where I was about to land. I only hoped Nikki and Landers had managed to slip away unnoticed. *How in the world am I going to explain this to Stromwell?*

SEVEN

A HANDFUL OF TV NEWS REPORTERS HURLED ACCUSATORY QUESTIONS AT me as the boys in blue shoved me into the back of the patrol car. Apparently, a crazy man flying in the heart of New York City was considered exciting news. I wondered if I'd have been better for ratings if my paraglider had crashed into the trees instead of safely bringing me to terra firma.

If it bleeds, it leads, I thought, desperately craving a cigar to chomp between my grinding teeth. A high-flying, near-death experience…plus an impending arrest definitely warranted a Cuban. But the cops had confiscated my smokes, along with just about everything else I had on me.

All in all, not one of my better moments, I thought as one of the police officers climbed into the front of the unit and drove me to the nearest precinct. My brain was already scrambling for a cover story before I was even taken to the inevitable interrogation room. Besides the fact that ENIGMA was supposed to be super-duper top secret and would not acknowledge its existence to the local LEOs, telling the truth with Detective Grigsby yesterday hadn't exactly worked according to plan either. *So, genius…what are you going to tell them?*

I didn't have much time to think of a good explanation. A few blocks north and we were pulling up to the precinct-building smack dab in the middle of Central Park.

Huh. Who knew they had one of those inside the park?

After parking the patrol car, I was yanked out of the backseat, the cuffs digging deep into my wrists, and ushered through the green double doors of the station. I was escorted through a series of non-descript hallways and shoved into a small, windowless room containing just a table and two metal chairs—bolted to the floor. I leaned back in the uncomfortable seat and closed my eyes. I knew the game all too well. They'd let me sweat. They'd keep me in the room for hours before anyone so much as poked their head in to "check" on me. The name of the game was fear. The more intimidated I was, the more likely I would be straight up with the cops when the inter-rogation began. Or the more mistakes I would make.

I opened my eyes and began mentally tracing the crisscross patterns of the ceiling tile above me while replaying the events of the day with crystal precision. After flying wing-to-wing with something like the Jersey Devil, the psychological games of the NYPD just left something to be desired.

The Devil.

The thing had been even more impressive than I would have ever dreamed. Just as Johnny had said, the thing had been roughly the size and shape of a silver back gorilla, the cryptid was an imposing figure. Add to that the leathery, webbed wings and you had yourself the makings of a regular nightmare.

I shuddered at the thought of those wings fluttering past me on currents of wind; dive-bombing me with single-minded determination. But one question kept flitting through my thoughts like a hyper-kinetic Super Ball zig-zagging inside a racquetball court...why hadn't it killed me? The creature was certainly fast enough. Its maneuverability had been surprising for a wingspan that long. It could have knocked me from the sky with ease.

But it hadn't. I replayed the scene over and over in my mind's eye. *No. Though it got awfully close, the more I think about it, the more I believe it had merely been checking us out. There hadn't seemed to be any animosity in the creature's move-ments.* I grimaced at a sudden thought. *Um, until you shot at it, you knucklehead.*

I chided myself. I simply hadn't learned. Last year, a rival of mine, Clar-ence Templeton of an eco-terrorist organization called ARK, had pointed out my propensity to kill more cryptids than I actually studied. At the time, I was knee-deep in flesh-eating mermaids and a crazy Russian femme fatale who had a vendetta against me. I hadn't really had the time to worry about such issues when swimming for my life from a school of amphibious monsters. But upon my return home, the dwarf's words had haunted me. I'd resolved myself to be much more careful about it in the future.

"And you failed miserably," I said out loud, remembering at least four other times within the past twelve months that I'd taken pot-shots at creatures I was supposed to be investigating.

"Failed miserably at what, I wonder?" came a vaguely familiar voice from behind me.

I turned to see Detective Sergeant Mike Grigsby straightening his tie as he strolled into the room, being sure to close the door behind him. He sported a rather casual smile as he moved around to the other side of the table and sat down in the opposite chair. He tried to shift it to draw himself closer to the table, but the bolts held it fast to the floor. His face shifted to a reddened pallor for an instant before he played the whole thing off by leaning back, placing his hands behind his head, and crossing his legs.

"Go on," he continued. "You failed miserably at what?"

I eyed the large detective before leaning forward across the table.

"I failed miserably…" I glanced around the room in a mock display of a paranoia and whispered conspiratorially, "…in the last fantasy football league at the office. This kid named Wiley, a real computer geek, tore us all up that season. It was embarrassing."

Grigsby belted out a laugh, a genuine smile stretching across his face.

"Somehow I knew you were going to try to give me the run-around," he said, pulling a stick of gum from a front shirt pocket, unwrapping it from the foil, and popping it in his mouth. Still leaning back in his chair, he closed his eyes. He chewed the gum in slow, deliberate bites for several seconds before opening his eyes to look at me with a wink. "Look, here's the deal. I know you're not a terrorist. You know you're not a terrorist. I also don't think you're a suspect in my Central Park homicide either." He paused, letting his spiel sink in while he chewed on his gum some more. Then he sat up in his chair and leaned in toward me with the same mock conspiratorial demeanor I'd used just minutes before. "But you *are* up to something. In *my* city. And whatever you're up to, it's liable to put some of the people I'm sworn to protect in danger. That makes me real curious. Understand?" His grin dissolved, replaced immediately with a stern look of determination.

I liked the cop in spite of myself. He was a good man, I could tell. Not at all the typical New York pompous windbag you see in the movies. Genuine. Dedicated.

And totally unprepared to handle a ten-foot tall, winged monkey buzzing around in his city.

It was time to play it straight with Grigsby. But only to a point. He hadn't exactly believed me the last time I'd tried to be honest. Of course, Landers would have a cow. He's all about the whole "need to know" thing all government spooks recite like a freakin' mantra. It had caused our fair share of arguments in the past, I can tell you that.

"Detective, I've already told you why I'm here," I said, willing the most sincere and honest face I could muster. Which is funny because whenever you actually try to do that, you always come across looking guilty as sin. "I work for a government agency—"

He held up his hands and shook his hands.

"Stop. Stop." Grigsby's eyes narrowed as he glared at me. "Whether that's a bunch of bull or not, I don't even wanna know. 'Smatter of fact, I've been instructed to not even try. Of course, I couldn't resist prying just a tad. But you start talking about government agencies and experiments and whatnot…well, I figure I best shut you up now."

I stared at him. Blank-faced.

"Whoever you work for, they're apparently some pretty powerful people," he answered my unspoken question. Sort of.

"Um, come again?" I asked with a tilt of my head.

"You're free to go, Jackson. I can't hold you. Order came down from the Commissioner himself. You're to be released."

I wasn't sure whether I should smile at that or beg for them to keep me incarcerated for a while longer. Wasn't sure what would be worse—a few nights getting cozy with a felon named Shifty or having to face the larger-than-life senator from Texas, whom I knew pulled some major strings to get me out of this mess. I decided to muster my most rakish grin.

"Well, Detective…it's been really nice chatting with you and all, but I…"

"Don't even play that game with me, bub. You're trouble. You and I both know it. The sooner you get out of my city, the easier I'm going to breathe."

"Well, as soon as I'm finished here, I'll definitely—"

Once more he interrupted me. "Oh no, Jackson. You've been instructed to be on the next flight back to whatever hole you came from. Whoever pulled the strings to get you out of this, is pulling *your* strings as well."

He reached into his breast pocket and pulled out a crinkled sheet of paper, folded several times into a tiny square. With a certain air of satisfaction, the brick wall of a detective unfolded it and handed it to me.

I unfolded it and read: *Jackson. Time's up. Thin ice, boy. Return immediately. JCS*

Stromwell's terse note left no room for doubt. Though I doubted the big guy would have a problem with what I was doing, my position with ENIGMA had been on, as the senator put it, thin ice since Polk had been appointed chief director of the agency. For whatever reason, he'd had it in for me since day one. The note was a warning.

I sat there, staring at the paper in my hands. This was crazy. It was my job to investigate cryptids after all…and there was one major player currently taking a literal bite out of the Big Apple.

Grigsby cleared his throat. "Just so we're clear, bub," he said, standing and walking around the table to me. He bent down, unlocked my cuffs, and loomed his bulky frame over me. "In case that little love note ain't enough, I'm going to give you my own friendly advice. I so much as catch a whiff of that cheap cologne you're wearing anywhere near one of my homicide scenes again, I'm going to personally see to it that you regret it."

I glanced up at him, before tilting my head down and sniffing at my shirt. *Cologne? But I don't wear any cologne.* Sure enough though, a strong musky odor—somewhat earthy—wafted up from the fabric of my shirt. The smell wasn't that bad, but I certainly didn't recognize it as a store-bought scent for men, either. *Strange.*

I turned my attention back to Grigsby. I wasn't quite sure what to tell him. There was no way I was going to leave New York until I had gotten to the bottom of the Devil attacks, no matter what Stromwell demanded. But at the same time, there was something about this flatfoot cop that I couldn't help but like. The guy had brains. And he wasn't afraid to use them either…which was always a plus.

I decided avoidance was much better than lying.

"So, can I go now?" I asked, standing up from chair while rubbing at my reddened wrists. The Boys in Blue had gotten a little gung-ho with me during my arrest—you know, suspected terrorist and all—so now I could add abrasion burns to my wrists and bruised ribs to the injuries I'd already sustained during my excursion to Australia.

He nodded, opening the door and gesturing for me to leave. "But I'm tellin' ya, Jackson. Leave town. Tonight. And only come back when you want to take in a Broadway show or somethin'."

"You got it!" I said, quickly stepping from the room and walking down the hall toward the property retrieval desk. "You take care now, y'hear?"

∂∾∽

Twenty minutes later, and some major finagling to get my Glock back— the cops in this town definitely did not like the idea of a paragliding daredevil wielding a firearm for some reason—and I stepped back out into the lush green backdrop of Central Park. The sun was just poking up over the canopy of trees that painted the landscape and the cool, brisk air of early morning caressed my sleep-deprived face like the longing touch of an old girlfriend that had been out of your life for far too long.

Thankfully, the rush of news crews and reporters had dwindled away, so I wasn't bombarded by a hoard of flashbulbs and microphones fighting for their exclusive interview with the nutjob who'd parachuted from Trump Tower. I took a deep breath, enjoying the early morning air.

I glanced around, looking for the Chevy Suburban Landers had rented at the airport, but it wasn't anywhere in sight. A twinge of worry shot down my spine as I thought about Nikki. What if she'd been hurt when she'd crash landed in the park? What if they weren't here to pick me up because they were now at the hospital with her? A putrid sick feeling settled in the pit of my stomach at the thought.

"Dr. Jackson?" came an oddly familiar voice from behind me, making me jump.

I spun around to see the handsome face of the tabloid newspaper reporter I'd rescued from the park from two nights before. His chiseled features stretched into a smile as he approached, holding out his hand.

"Alex Davenport," he said, his hand still outstretched. I didn't take it. I just wasn't in the mood. "You know, from the—"

"Yeah, I know...*The Fortean Inquisitor*," I growled, turning back around and walking out of the circular grounds of the NYPD Central Park Precinct. *Maybe they had to park off 85th Street or something*, I thought, ignoring the fact that the reporter was following me.

"Dr. Jackson, I just have a few questions for you, if I may," Davenport said, catching up to me with long, steady strides. "About the creature. About your part in all this."

I just kept walking, my eyes still scanning for signs of my friends.

"Well, if you won't tell me about that, what can you tell me about..." He flipped through a few pages in his notebook and looked up. "The ENtity Identification and Global Management Agency?"

I stopped in my tracks, but didn't turn to look at him. My brain raced. How had he known about ENIGMA?

"That's right," he said. I could hear the smile in his voice without having to see it. "I know all about the little shadowy government outfit you work for. After all, a renowned cryptozoologist dropping off the academic radar two years ago isn't something that goes unnoticed. It leaves a curious person to ask where you've been all this time."

I finally looked at him, but kept my mouth shut tight. The less I said, the better, I figured. So, I decided to let him do all the talking.

And he was certainly willing to talk. "So, after our meeting the night before last, I did some digging. And the funny thing is...since your extended 'sabbatical' you've told people you are taking, you've been popping up all over the map. Malaysia. Peru. Guam. Scotland. A little incident in the Cyclades, ring any bells?"

He paused for effect before continuing. "Weird thing is there always seem to be two common things that show up wherever you are. Lots of chaos and a single whispered word: ENIGMA."

I started meandering toward the sidewalk on 85th Street once more, avoiding his gaze. *Where the heck is Randy? Landers? Heck, at this point, I'd settle for Arnold.* I was starting to sweat just thinking about what the kid was telling me. I was already in enough hot water with Polk as it was. The last thing I needed was for this brash, young reporter to start printing stories about the agency...even if it was in a grocery store rag.

"So I've been researching ENIGMA for the past few hours and discovered the word, at least in the context of cryptids and monsters, appeared back in the late sixties during the Nixon administration. Oh, trust me, the information was scarce, but I started to put the pieces together. A top secret, black ops agency that hunts down strange creatures around the world. Very cool stuff. My readers will love it!"

I spun around on him, a finger poking at his chest and a scowl across my face. "Look, Slick, I have no idea what the heck you're talking about," I growled. "But your voice is really starting to grate on my nerves. So, go ahead and write whatever you want—"

He ignored my outburst, reached into his inside jacket pocket and pulled out a folded piece of paper.

"And my research must have caught someone's attention, because I received this email just an hour ago," he said, holding out the paper to me. "Totally anonymous. I couldn't even begin tracking the IP address. But I thought you might want to see it."

I opened it and glanced down. My breath caught in my chest at the grainy black and white digital image I was looking at. It was a picture of a blood-soaked crime scene and though there was no indication on the photo itself, I knew it had been taken in Madagascar about a year before. My eyes scanned the page, resting on the bloodied corpse of my old friend, Anthony Kowskowitz—better known to those who knew him simply as Witz. A mercenary who had pulled my butt out of the fire when we'd taken down Sashe Krenkin's secret complex in the Siberian wilderness two years before.

My eyes moved slightly to the right of Witz's body and landed on an oval shaped object resting intentionally on the floor next to him. I bit my lip as I stared. The object was a severed head. The grotesque and mutated head of Vera Pietrova, my team's former medic.

You see, last year, someone had murdered Witz. Put a bullet clean through the center of his skull. They'd then placed Vera's head next to the body as a message to me—though I sure as heck had never figured out what that message had been. Shortly after that, a hit squad had started hunting me. I had assumed it had to do with the case I had been working on at the time, but discovered shortly after that my assumption had been wrong. The bad guy in that investigation had no idea who put a hit out on me...and trust me, if it had been her, she would have told me. She was just that twisted.

I pulled away from the photo and looked up at Davenport. "I…I don't know what this has to do with me," I lied, hoping my voice sounded more convincing than I thought it did. I handed the sheet of paper back to him.

He glanced down at it once before folding it back up and slipping it back into his coat pocket. "Now see," he said, his face stern and sullen. "That's where I know you're lying to me. There was more to that email, Dr. Jackson. Much more."

I stiffened at his words.

"You see, the sender of that email claims to be responsible. For it all. For the death of your mercenary friend. For placing that weird head thing next to the body. Everything. And whoever sent it wanted me to give you a message…" His voice trailed off as if in thought, but he didn't continue speaking.

He had my attention now and he knew it. I twirled my finger around in gesture for him to continue. "And?"

He looked up at me and smiled. "And, I'll tell you what that message is if you let me tag along on your mission here and let me have the exclusive story on the monster." His face grew serious again. "Plus, I will keep what I know about ENIGMA from any article I write."

I shook my head. "Uh-uh. No way."

"Freakshow."

The word he uttered froze the very blood in my veins. To the casual listener, the word Freakshow would carry with it images of strange circus sideshows with bearded ladies, monstrously overweight men, dwarves, sword and fire eaters, and a few lizard-scaled humans. To me, however, it was not merely a word. It was a name. The name of a homicidal, insane killer I had faced a few years back before joining ENIGMA.

"Freakshow," I mumbled out loud, oblivious to Davenport grinning widely next to me. My initial encounter with him, he'd kidnapped me and dumped me on a desert island in the middle of the Pacific Ocean and unleashed a few monstrosities on me in a webcast version of *Survivor* meets tooth and fang. The rules had been simple. Survive until dawn. Wagers had been placed on how long I would survive. I hoped I had disappointed every single viewer of the masochistic reality show. I had never been able to find a single trace of the man since, despite my vow to the contrary.

I glanced back up the reporter. He had me over the barrel. There was no way he would give up the information without a deal. I knew that much from observing the near ravenous hunger in his eyes.

A beat up old F-250 pulled up to the curb of 85th Street, distracting me for a second from the conversation. My dad sat stoically in the driver's seat, both hands firmly on the wheel. I winced at the old rust bucket he was driving. He hadn't bothered to buy a new car since the year I graduated high school and you could tell. The few pieces of metal that hadn't been eaten out by the ravages of time still showed up in that blood red color he'd insisted on when he bought it. All except for the driver's side front quarter panel that was just a slightly darker burgundy.

I glanced back to Davenport with a smile, opened the door to the pickup and motioned toward the open cab.

"Okay," I said quietly. "Get in. Let's make a deal."

EIGHT

"WHO'S THIS?" LANDERS ASKED, POINTING TO DAVENPORT AS THE THREE of us strode into the hotel room.

The drive from Central Park to my East 48th Street hotel had taken longer than expected. Morning rush hour traffic had been a beast and I'd considered getting out and jogging the remainder of the way on more than one occasion. During the gridlock, Dad had explained that the reason they hadn't been at the station to pick me up upon my release was that they had been busy getting their tails chewed out by Chief Director Polk via Skype conference call. Once they'd received notice that I'd been released, Nikki, who was none the worse for wear after her harrowing encounter with the Devil earlier, had asked my dad if he'd be willing to go and pick me up.

"Trouble," I said in answer to the ENIGMA agent's question. I pointed to an unused chair over to the corner and looked at the reporter. "Sit."

"But—"

"I told you on the way here. You do what I say…no questions asked."

He looked at me, then did a three-sixty and took in the rest of the team. Shrugging his shoulders, he moved over to the chair to the kitchenette, plopped down with an exasperated huff, and crossed his legs casually.

Arnold trotted over to him, gave him a brief once over, and then curled into a ball at his feet. I couldn't tell if the mutt was standing guard to protect him or keep him in line. In the end, I figured it was pretty much a little of both.

"All right, Jackson," Davenport said, ignoring my dog completely. "But remember…I'm the one holding all the cards here. However, I'm a good sport. I'll play along for now."

"What's he talking about?" Landers asked. "You never did answer my first question either, by the way?"

I ignored the question for a second time, moved over to the door, and opened it.

"Time for a Powwow. I need some coffee in the worst way and we can fill each other in down in the café." I nodded to my father. "Can you stay and babysit?"

"Now wait just a minute—" Davenport began to protest, but I stopped him with an upraised hand.

"Hush!" I chided. "This is a sensitive issue. I need to brief my team. Alone. I promise we won't do anything without you."

When the disgustingly handsome reporter clenched his teeth, but nodded in submission, I looked once more to my dad. "Okay?"

"Why the heck not? It's not like I have anything better to do with my time." Though his gruff voice conveyed his disgust at the assignment, the gleam in his eyes told me he was being highly entertained by the entire affair.

Great. He's going to want to come on all my expeditions. There'll be no living with him now.

Ten minutes later, Landers, Randy, Nikki, and I were huddled in a single booth in a small breakfast diner four blocks away from the hotel. I pulled in a steaming gulp of my vanilla flavored coffee and closed my eyes in bliss. Too bad my spiky-haired team member had to screw it all up with his incessant nagging.

"What's going on Jack?" Landers said. "Who is that man in your hotel room? And why aren't we all packing our gear and heading back to D.C.?"

I took another sip of my coffee before looking up at them again. Randy merely shook his head, knowing exactly what I was going to say. Well, sort of. There was no way he could be prepared for what I was about to tell them about Davenport.

"I'll answer your third question first," I finally said, feeling quite confident the spook was good and miffed at me for the moment. "The reason we're not packing our gear is because we ain't leaving. Not yet anyway—"

"What do you mean, *we're not leaving*? Jack, we have direct orders from Polk himself. We have no choice—"

"Now see? That's exactly where you're wrong. We have all sorts of choices. I chose to have a vanilla coffee. I chose not to have a half dozen donuts. I chose to even have this discussion with you in the first place." I gave him a shrug. "So, I guess I can choose not to listen to that pompous little pinhead too. I'm not going."

"But Jack, Scott's right," Nikki had decided to put her two cents in. Her argument wasn't at all unexpected. She was the most level-headed of the bunch—unless you really ticked her off. Like I seemed particularly gifted at doing. I shuddered at the very thought. "This isn't just coming from Anton. It's coming from my dad as well. They want us back. There are too many risks here…of exposing ENIGMA. Our mission. We're in New York City for crying out loud. How do you expect to keep this thing quiet here? It's just too dangerous."

I could almost hear the senator's words—his own syntax—coming straight from his daughter's lips. No matter what that man said or did, she would always side with him. Which, for the most part, wasn't a bad thing. Stromwell meant well most of the time. But he was dead wrong about our current mission.

I glanced at Randy. "What about you?" I asked him. "What do you think?"

He took the last swig from his own coffee, laced with just a hint of whiskey to sooth his nerves no doubt, and smiled at me. "Heck, you know me, bud. I go where you go. You may be a crazy S.O.B., but you're way is always a whole lot more fun than Polk's."

I smiled at that before addressing them all again.

"Look, you guys don't need to get in any more trouble because of me. Go on home," I said, forcing a humorless smile. "But I've got a great friend that's laid up in a hospital bed because of this thing. People are dead because of it. There's a good chance the creature will keep on killing whether we leave or not...which will eventually expose its species to the world anyway. And I can't just sit back and do nothing because I'm afraid the world will find out about us. Heck, this is exactly the reason we were created to begin with. To investigate these kind of cases and to put a stop to it if we can. And I aim to do just that...with or without you."

They stared at me for several seconds without saying a word. Finally, Landers let out a breath and leaned back in the booth.

"You know Polk will have your hide for this," he said. It wasn't a question.

I nodded.

"This is exactly what he's been wanting—you blatantly disregarding his orders in front of the senator, as well as the board of directors," Landers continued. "It's his ticket to having you removed from the agency."

I growled at that. "Do you think I give a flip about that, Scott? Do you? That place has brought nothing but grief and misery to me ever since I joined it. Do you honestly think I—"

"Hey bud?" Randy spoke up. "On this, I kind of have to agree with Scotty. Without you there, the bad guys are pretty much free to turn ENIGMA into one big mad science lab. They'd go back to taking the cryptids that you discover as a private researcher and turning them into weapons. So, yeah, I think you *do* care. You care a lot."

"But for the moment, he cares more for his friend," Nikki said with a nod. "And those people that are in danger from whatever we ran into last night. No, Jack. I get it. I understand." She glanced over at Landers before saying, "All right. I'm staying too."

"So am I," Landers said, his face stern. "On one condition."

"Okay. What's that?"

"That you tell me who that guy in your room is and what he has to do with any of this."

I smiled and told them.

❧❧

After breakfast, we made our way back to the room and discussed a plan of action—constantly aware that a stranger, a reporter no less, was in our midst. But all the best laid plans typically fall apart the second you step out the door. And that's exactly what happened to us a few hours after dark as we made our way to our cars, prepared for the evening's search.

Davenport's phone chirped and with practiced ease, he palmed it from his coat pocket, accepted the call, and brought it to his ear in one swift motion. I couldn't help notice the brief wink he threw at Nikki as he spoke into the receiver.

"Yeah," he said with an arrogant confidence that seemed out of place for the career path he'd chosen. If I'd decided to become a sleazy tabloid reporter, I'd say I would probably wear a bag over my head most of the time. Forget trying to act like a modern version of Cary Grant. "No way. Really?"

A pause from the other end. I could just make out the murmuring of a gravelly female voice on the other end.

"Where?" he continued, holding up a finger at Landers who was climbing into the Suburban's driver seat. "Okay. I'm on it. Thanks."

He closed the phone and looked up at me, his eyes wide with excitement.

"There's been another attack. This one just off Broadway."

I looked down at my watch. Not even half past seven. The creature had no particular time schedule that I could discern.

"Did you get a specific address?" I asked, powering up my own phone in order to use its GPS system. Upon booting up, my screen flashed brightly for a second, then chimed eight times in quick succession. A tiny digital number blazed across the LCD display. I had nearly twenty messages. Most likely all from Polk. Ignoring them, I pulled up the GPS app and punched in the address Davenport recited. "Okay." I looked at my team, a grave expression painted on my face. "Looks like there's a change of plans. We're going to the crime scene."

Davenport cleared his throat behind me. I spun to face him. "What?"

"Um, it's just that I don't know how you guys think you're going to get within a hundred yards of that place," he said.

"We've snuck in tighter places than that in my time, kid," I growled, half turning back to face Landers in order to hash out a whole new plan.

"Not this time," he said. "The victim supposedly is a big time player in town. Way high profile. Every piece of brass in the city will be there. Press. There's no way you're going to sneak in under the radar on a case like this."

A lump grew in my throat. *High profile.* From what I'd gathered, the two previous victims had hardly made headlines. Davenport's grocery store rag seemed to be the only media outlet that had even the remotest interest. But throw in a celebrity or someone affluent and the crime scene was likely to be a circus. Lots of cameras. And lots of cops keeping their eye out for nosey busybodies trying to sneak into the scene for an exclusive. *The kid's right,* I thought, squatting down to give Arnold a scratch behind the ears as I pondered our next move. *It's not going to be easy.*

I turned to Landers. "We really need to get into that scene," I said. "Any ideas?"

Of all of us, Scott was the most experienced in *sneakery*. Years of service in the marines and then in covert ops had taught him quite a few tricks of the trade. It was almost second nature to him. But he shook his head. "Not off the top of my head. But the more people we have, the less likely we'll be able to pull it off, I can tell you that."

"Agreed." My mind raced through the possibilities. Our options were bleak to say the least.

"Um, if I may, I might have a solution," the reporter said with a sly grin. "How good are you with dead bodies?"

NINE

THE VAN THAT RANDY, DAVENPORT, AND I OCCUPIED PULLED UP ON THE scene—its red and white strobes blazing a swath of light through the crowd as we approached the yellow crime scene tape at Broadway and East 29th Street. The reporter's friend, a body removal technician for the Medical Examiner's Office, clutched the steering wheel in a white-knuckled gripped.

"I can't believe you talked me into this again, Alex," the man said. "Last time we did this, we both almost got busted."

"Don't worry about it, Louie," Davenport said with his trademark white smile. "We'll be more careful this time. Besides, with what I'm paying you, you should be able to take care of some of those gambling debts you owe Gambone. So relax."

The reporter's plan, as much as I was loath to admit it, made sense. The only way we would be able to get into the crime scene was to appear like we belonged there. But impersonating a police officer or a Medical Examiner investigator was just too risky. Too high profile. What we needed was a disguise that wouldn't stand out. That no one would give a second glance to. If this had been some shindig at an uppity, high class party, then waiters would have been appropriate. At a murder scene, the most innocuous people amid the chaos would be the M.E.'s transport crew.

I mean, let's face it…no one likes a dead body. No matter how long you've been a cop or how many bodies you've seen sprawled out on the curb of some street corner, there's always a hint of your own mortality staring back at you in those dead eyes. The last thing you want to pay attention to after you've done your preliminary examination of the corpse is to watch it be hauled off by the Medical Examiner's hired help.

At least, that was our hope.

A uniformed patrolman lifted the tape up for the transport van to drive through and waved us in. A few minutes later, we were standing outside a three story building displaying a dark blue sign that read TOMATO. Apparently, it was some sort of party, wedding, and anything else you can imagine supply store. What that had to do with a tomato, I couldn't fathom, but hey, it was New York.

Louie, Davenport, and Randy strode around to the back of the van, opened the double doors, and pulled out a rickety old stretcher that was probably about as old as I was. I shuddered to think about how well it would hold up if the victim was heavy set, but pushed the thought away as we moved toward a huddle of detectives and officers blocking the view of the alley in which the body presumably was found.

"Any word on who the victim is?" I whispered to the reporter who'd been on the phone with his office for most our nerve-racking drive over here.

He nodded, keeping his eyes fixed on the small army of officers littering the streets. "A United States senatorial candidate," he said. "Max Schildiner. The guy was pretty well-liked. Had a good shot at winning the election in November from all accounts."

I rolled my eyes at this news as we drew nearer to the alley. *Great. Just great. This thing just got political. Stromwell is definitely going to be ticked when he hears about this. Then again, it might just be the nudge he needs to make this investigation official.*

Forcing my whirlwind barrage of thoughts to focus on our current task, I took in the scene around us. Hoards of onlookers crowded around the street, gawking at the scene unfolding before them with slack-jawed enthusiasm. They were kept at bay simply by several sawhorse barriers and a handful of uniformed officers. Three portable florescent boom lamps were erected around the scene, brightening the dimly lit street as if it was high noon instead of pushing midnight. The illumination would be a problem if I needed to break away and look for any evidence, but I figured I'd cross that bridge when I came to it.

A uniform nodded to us as we approached and smiled at Louie. "Four of ya? Think that's a little overkill, bub?"

The body removal guy just shrugged. "Union's playing havoc with us lately," he said, popping a cigarette in his mouth and lighting it. "Too many back injuries. They're experimenting with requiring at least four per stiff, but I don't think it's gonna fly."

The cop laughed at that. "Yeah, I doubt the city's gonna want to pay all the overtime it would take to handle that kind of manpower," he said, motioning us through the throng of detectives, crime scene techs, and at least a handful of guys with FBI stenciled on their windbreakers.

Great, I thought. *Just absolutely perfect.*

I assumed that most of what needed to be done to the body, evidence-wise, had already been taken care of. I'd heard that in New York, it sometimes took body transport teams up to twenty-four hours to make removals and the cops around there were apparently pretty used to it. I was banking on the fact that they would be more than pleased we had made it there in record time and would let us do our jobs without much interference. But the presence of FBI agents could potentially complicate things. Though I suspected they would be involved in any murder of a senatorial candidate, the devious side of my personality couldn't help wondering if Polk had sent them to keep an eye out for us.

I looked around uncomfortably as we were ushered into the blood-spattered alley to the east of Tomato's. The confined space looked like the interior of some horrible slaughterhouse. There was very little of Max Schildiner left intact. The torso appeared to have been eviscerated from the sternum down to the mid-section exposing the entrails that now hung limply to his left side. The man's fleshy throat hung open in a stringy mess—the hyoid bone exposed completely. There was no head that I could see, just a mass of flesh and hair in a clump on the concrete where he lay. The creature had apparently crushed the victim's head to powder, leaving only the ragged flesh of the face, teeth, and a few bone fragments behind. His arms and legs had been flung individually down the alley—well, three of the limbs had anyway. One arm rested precariously above us on a nearby fire escape railing. It's hand opened and outstretched as if waving down at us.

"Oh, geeze—" Randy said, his nose curling up in disgust. "This is so freakin' gross."

I could sympathize. We'd both seen some pretty gruesome things in our time, but the man we were now looking at would have given Humpty Dumpty a run for his money.

"Come on," Louie the Transporter whispered. "We can't fool around. They'll get suspicious." The overweight, balding man pulled out several sets of latex gloves and passed them around. "Let's get to work."

Without further complaint, we folded down the stretcher near the bulk of the victim's remains and stretched a sheet of clear plastic over it. Careful-ly, I moved around the body so that my back was to the on-looking cops behind me, flicked on my UV light, and gave a cursory inspection of the body. The florescent lighting that been set up made spotting anything useful nearly impossible. It was just too bright for the small flashlight to do any good. Thankfully, the victim would be coming with us when we left, so I'd be able to spend some quality time picking through the evidence while we made our way back to the morgue.

"Okay," I said, reaching down to the torso and grabbing hold of its belt. "I need to get a better look at the overall scene. The body's not going to show me anything. At least not here anyway."

Randy and Louie grasped other areas of the man's tattered suit and we hefted him up onto the stretcher in a single swing.

"And how do you suppose you're going to do that?" Randy asked with a queasy voice. I couldn't blame him. The stench coming from Schildiner's bowels was overwhelming. I had fought back the urge to puke at least three times already—

That's it! The thought screamed inside my skull. *Jack, my boy, sometimes you are pure genius.*

I took in a huge gulp of air, inhaling the pungent aroma wafting up from the bloodied corpse. My eyes locked onto the mass of bone and flesh before my eyes, devouring every disgusting detail and I found the onslaught of nausea overtaking every one of my senses in a full assault. I retched uncontrollably.

"Ah, gol!" I said, spinning away from the body and dashing over to the nearest wall. Then, I let my dinner come up in all its disgusting glory. I heard the chuckles from a few of the police officers huddled at the ally entrance as I heaved against the brick wall my shoulder now rested on. The chunky fluid burned at my esophagus as it expelled out of my mouth.

I crashed to the ground, taking in deep breaths in hopes of stopping what I had so willingly allowed to happen. Cradled on my hands and knees, I slipped out the small UV flashlight and scanned the pavement for anything that would catch my interest. Catching onto the plan, Randy walked over to me, placed his hand on my shoulder and effectively blocked the view of the cops staring at the "rookie" body transport tech now crouched down on the ground. They didn't even bother to lower their voices as they laughed at me. The jerks.

"See anything?" Randy whispered, bending down toward my ear.

"Not yet. I'm not sure—" My words caught in my throat. The amber-hued light had picked up the trace of something silver just to my left. "Wait a minute." I brought the light back around until I found the spot again. Sure enough, a circular pool of some sort of organic liquid coated the pavement near my knees.

"Ah-ha!" I whispered, reaching my hand back toward my friend. "Got a tube handy?"

He palmed an evidence tube to me and I carefully scooped up a sample before corking it and dropping it in my jumpsuit's front pocket.

"Any idea what it is?" Randy asked.

I shook my head, still trying to get my intentional bout of nausea under control. I wasn't finished with my search, but knew I wouldn't be very effective if I kept retching every time I caught a whiff of Schildiner's bloody entrails.

"What's going on here?" I heard a gut-wrenchingly familiar voice echo from the entrance of the alley behind me. "Why isn't that body gone? We've got the media so close they oughtta at least take me to a movie first."

Grigsby. Crap. Definitely not *who I needed to run into tonight.*

"Sorry Chief," Louie said in his nasally voice. "Got a newbie here. He just needs to get acclimated to everything. He'll be okay though."

There was a nerve-wracking pause for several seconds as if the detective was considering something. Then, "Well, tell 'im to hurry it up. We can't hold this street closed much longer."

I relaxed when I heard Grigsby start talking to another police officer and walk away from the scene. I let out the breath I'd been holding and stood up, being sure to keep my back to the street, and dusted my pant legs off.

"Hey, yous guys," Louie said, presumably to Randy and me. "We need to wrap this up. One of you need to get that arm off the fire escape. The other, grab that leg on the other end of alley. Then, we're out of here."

I looked up at the fire escape, the arm still hung precariously from its perch. *Ugh. I really,* really *hate heights.* But I also figured a bird's eye view of the scene might reveal some clue I might otherwise have missed by staying on the ground. I looked over at Randy.

"Give me a boost to the ladder," I said to him.

"You sure?"

I gave another glance skyward, then nodded. "Yeah. It might do me some good to take a look from a better angle."

Without another word, my friend bent down to one knee and locked the fingers of both hands to form a makeshift step. I placed the heel of my foot into his upraised palms, leapt to the dangling fire escape above, and pulled myself up. I was halfway up when a thought struck me like a baseball bat to the side of my head.

"Where the heck is Davenport?" I asked, scanning the alley.

Randy spun around, taking a quick three sixty, and then shrugged.

"Oh, he left shortly after we spread the plastic on the stretcher," Louie said with a hoarse laugh. "The little weasel's probably gonna stiff me on what he owes me too."

What the heck? A chill ran down my spine, but I couldn't quite put my finger on why. It had been the reporter's idea, after all, to come along to the scene. *So why skin out without saying anything? Where'd he go?*

Pushing the questions from my mind, I climbed the remainder of the ladder until I reached the first platform of the fire escape and the mangled arm of the senatorial candidate. Taking a quick peek over the railing to see if any of the officers were paying attention, I pulled my UV light out once more and shined it on the dismembered appendage. I was now higher than the florescent lights below and the amber glow shone brightly against the carnage.

And I was instantly greeted by a huge silver blotch that covered the arm's tattered shirt sleeve. It looked like the same substance I had discovered on the pavement. Taking a tube from the inside of my jumpsuit, I scooped another sample into it, sealed it with the stopper, and pocketed it once more.

I then leaned over the fire escape railing, careful not to rub up against the blood smeared wall, and peered down at the scene. But if I had expected to see anything new, I was sorely disappointed. It just looked like one big bloody mess to me. Sighing in resignation, I grabbed the arm, stuffed it into a red biohazard bag, slung it over my shoulder like some macabre Santa Claus, and began making my way back down to the alley.

I was halfway down, when I spotted something strange out of my peripheral vision. I turned to look out toward the street, past the crime scene tape, and into the crowd. Something out there had grabbed my attention, but I didn't know quite what it was. *Something familiar. Something—*

I scanned the crowd, focusing my attention on each wide-eyed, slack jawed gawker milling around. After passing about six on-lookers, my eyes landed on her. She was wearing a hoodie, pulled up over her head—which is exactly what had piqued my interest to begin with. A mane of silvery hair flowed from the corners of her hood. She was dressed a little more casual than the last time I'd seen her, but there was no mistaking that sterling silver hair of hers.

It was the girl from Central Park who had attacked Davenport. Suddenly, Davenport's disappearing act made a lot more sense. Chances were, he'd seen the hooded woman and decided that retreat was the better form of valor.

And left us high and dry. Swell.

I scrambled down the ladder and casually tossed the bagged arm on the stretcher before turning to Randy who was just putting the remaining limb on top of the pile.

"We've got a situation," I whispered to him as we pulled one side of the plastic pouch around and sealed it with evidence tape. "Across the street. In the crowd. The crazy girl who attacked me in Central Park two nights ago."

"Where?" Randy's head popped up around shoulder as he gawked into the mass of people milling around the scene.

"Don't look!" I hissed. "Trust me. She's out there."

Louie, ignoring our conversation, went around to the foot of the stretcher and directed us to move to the head. In unison, we lifted the stretcher off the ground, but the wheels refused to unfold so that we could set it down on the pavement.

"Pull the lever," Louie chided. "No, not that. The long bar just underneath the—heck, you, Jack, is it? Come over here and hold this end."

I did as I was told while the expert transporter moved Randy out of the way and pulled the correct lever. The wheels came down in one swift motion and locked into place.

"I'm going to need you to make a distraction," I continued talking to Randy as Louie worked at strapping the cadaver down. "Nothing too obvious, but enough to let me slip around without being spotted. I have a feeling once the body is inside the van, she'll be long gone."

After several seconds of futilely trying to fit the straps into their locking mechanisms, Louie threw up his hands in exasperated disgust. "Screw it!" he growled, moving back to the head of the stretcher. "They have got to buy us some decent gurneys soon. These ones are falling apart." It was as if he didn't even notice we were there.

Once in his position, we started wheeling the gurney toward the cluster of police officers that were busy making a human wall to prevent the crowd from seeing too much of the scene. Randy was the one who came back to our discussion.

"What kind of distraction?" he hissed as we drew closer to the cops.

"Be creative. Just be subtle about—"

Before I could finish the sentence, my friend pulled the wheel release lever, sending the gurney and its contents sprawling on the pavement and at the feet of fifteen mortified police officers. Blood and body parts flew everywhere in a tidal wave of gore and all chaos broke loose. Cries of dismay erupted from the onlookers across the street and the cops scrambled out of the way of human debris.

Great, Randy. Way to be subtle about it, I thought, but took full advantage of the turmoil he'd created. As the officers scrambled to contain the mess, I moved toward the van. "I'll be right back," I shouted over my shoulder. "I'll get something to clean this mess up."

With everyone's backs to me, I stalked over to the transport vehicle, climbed into the back, and slipped out the sliding side door away from any straying eyes of law enforcement. Then, as casually as a person dressed in a body transport jumpsuit could, I crouched under the crowd control barrier and slipped through the crowd until I had a clear path toward my target.

Glancing up ahead, I could just barely make out the hooded figure tucked protectively in the midst of the onlookers. Since she was still there and not bee-lining into the shadows, I could assume she hadn't seen me come this way. Or she hadn't recognized me from the park. Either way, things seemed to be going my way for a change.

Still trying to maintain a casual demeanor, I stuck my hands in my pockets and walked lackadaisically toward the mystery woman. I was within five feet of her when a rough, calloused hand seized the back of my shoulder and wheeled me around.

"Well, if it isn't Dr. Jackson," Detective Sergeant Mike Grigsby said with a grin that would make the Cheshire Cat green with envy.

Ah, crap.

TEN

"I THOUGHT THAT WAS YOU MAKING A MESS OF MY CRIME SCENE," Grigsby said, shaking his head as he folded his arms across a thick, barreled chest. "*But no*, I thought to myself. *He wouldn't be that stupid, now would he?* Apparently, I was wrong."

I smiled defensively at the detective, casting a quick glance back at my prey. For now, she seemed oblivious to my current predicament, but I wasn't sure how long that would last. I couldn't risk losing her because of this puffed-up Dudley Do-Right.

"Detective Grigsby!" I beamed, spreading my arms in greeting while turning up the charm-o-meter to nuclear radiant. "It's not what you think…"

"Really?" he said, tilting his head to one side. "And what is it that I *think*, exactly?"

I could only blink at the question. I hadn't expected it. I was used to dealing with dirty cops from every corrupt department the Third World had to offer. When it came to detectives with brains, not to mention integrity, I was completely lost.

"I, um…well, I figure that…"

Some movement out of the corner of my eye grabbed my attention. The hooded female had turned away and started picking her way through the throng of people at a slow, but steady gait. I wasn't sure if she'd caught onto me or if she'd decided she'd seen enough, but it really didn't matter. I was running out of time, as well as options.

"Here, let me help you," Grigsby said, sticking an unfiltered cigarette into his mouth and lighting it with a cheap Bic lighter. "What I *think* is that you disobeyed your superiors and didn't return home like you were told. I *think* you decided to stick around and play detective. I *think* you impersonated a Medical Examiner employee in order to gain entry into a restricted crime scene. I also think, for the record, that you think I'm a complete moron!"

The last sentence came out as more of a snarl than any form of English I'd ever heard. But his meaning was just as clear to me. I was in deep trouble and he was effectively letting me know it. But I just couldn't worry about it right now. I turned to locate my quarry, who had finally made her way through the crowd and was heading east on 29th at quicker pace. Something had spooked her and she was wasting no time making good her escape.

"Excuse me. I'm sorry," Grigsby said, snapping his finger at my face as he exhaled a plume of smoke from his nostrils. "Am I keeping you from something?"

"Well, now that you mention it—"

"Detective Grigsby?" came a voice from behind. We both turned to find Alex Davenport stepping up to us, stark determination on his face and digital voice recorder in his hand. I had no idea where he'd been the last twenty minutes or so, but he was definitely a sight for sore eyes at that moment. "I'm a reporter with *The Fortean Inquisitor* and I—"

"I know who you are, kid," he said, holding up his hands to keep the reporter from approaching any further. "You're going to have to move back to the, um, designated *press* area." I think the detective might have blown a blood vessel in his attempt to keep from chortling at the word "press" in dealing with Davenport. "We'll have a news conference just as soon as we can."

Grigsby turned back to face me, but the young reporter darted between the two of us, pressing the red button on his recorder.

"I'm not finished, Detective. I'd like to ask you—"

Before Davenport could finish his sentence, I took off, running as fast as my legs would carry me in the direction I'd last seen the hooded figure. I'd lost sight of her momentarily, but I believed I'd be able to pick up the trail as long I wasn't encumbered by any well-meaning local LEOs along the way. And from the sound of things behind me, it was going to be a very tight race. I could hear Grigsby shouting furiously at me before barking orders into his radio as he took off in pursuit. I had only a few seconds lead and I was determined to make them count for everything they were worth.

The sidewalk along West 29th was entangled with scaffolding where workers had labored through the day, renovating the tenement building along that section of the street. If I wasn't careful, I'd likely strike my head on one of the metal bars and find myself splayed out across the pavement like a Christmas present just waiting for Grigsby to open. At the same time, I knew the same skeletal metalwork would create just as much havoc for the cops who were now chasing me down the street.

Five breath-heaving minutes later, I jerked to a stop at Fifth Avenue and spun around, searching for any signs of my target. Another minute later, I spotted her head bobbing casually among the dwindling crowd of late night revelers. She was heading south on Fifth and I quickly took a right and bolted after her once more. As if sensing me, she turned and stared me down, then bolted across the still-heavily congested street to the other side and fled down a darkened alley. I jumped out into the street, nearly running right in front of a Yellow Cab, and pulled to a stop in the same alley.

It was narrow, cluttered with large plastic garbage cans, empty liquor bottles and a variety of things I personally had little interest in identifying. The stench of urine and vomit wafted up to my nose and for the second time that night, I suppressed the urgent need to hurl. But despite all that, I could just make out the shadowy form of my target near the other end, sprinting away from me as if she was being chased by a pack of angry yetis.

Though my left side was cramping up, I sucked in a deep breath and ran after her. Fortunately for me, close-quarters combat hadn't been the only thing Landers had put me through this last year. He'd also concocted a strict training regimen and forced me to follow it. Though I wasn't in the best shape of my life, my endurance was much stronger and I found distance running a lot easier than I would have a year ago. Looking up ahead at her, I could tell that she was running out of steam. If I could just keep it up a little while longer, I'd be able to catch up to her and hopefully get to the bottom of how she was involved in all this.

I watched as she rounded a corner, now only twenty yards away from me. I crossed the distance, preparing myself for the sharp right turn just as I made it to the end of the alley, but was suddenly hit by a sledgehammer jolt of white-hot electricity shooting down my limbs. I felt the world spinning chaotically around me as I slammed into the ground, rolling to my side just enough to avoid smacking my face directly into the pavement.

I could feel my legs and arms spasming uncontrollably as I looked up just in time to see the hooded figure step out from the shadows, a stun gun gripped tightly in her hand. I heaved for breath, trying to sit up as she slinked over to me, pressed the soles of her vintage Converse sneakers down on my chest, and pursed her lips. A wisp of her silvery hair glistened in the moonlight, but even that was dull compared to her near pure white teeth as she smiled down at me.

From my vantage point, I was able to get a better look at her than the first time we'd met. She was fairly young—probably eighteen or nineteen years old, with a strong chin and soft, pale skin. Her lips were rather thin, but colored with dark, burgundy-tinged—almost black—lipstick. Her large eyes were a similar color to her hair and I had to wonder if she was wearing special contact lenses. They were...unnatural to say the least. Her physique was well put together...short, probably around five feet and some change. And though she was wearing a frumpy looking hoodie that draped like a tent over her torso, I could tell that she was well-toned and reasonably fit.

"Though I can't say I'm disappointed to see you again, Dr. Jackson," she cooed, flicking a strand of hair from her face, "I find myself in a very tenuous predicament."

She knows my name, I thought. My mind raced with all the implications that fact presented. *How the heck do the psycho-vixens always know who I am? What? Do I have a freakin' neon sign plastered to my forehead? Sheesh, maybe there's a "Women Who Hate Obadiah Jackson" website I don't know about.* Well, I'm pretty sure that's what I was thinking—I'm not really sure because I couldn't stop my body from convulsing from the jolt her stun gun had given me.

Her smile broadened as she read the expression on my face. Still pinning me down with her foot, she pocketed the stun gun and reached around her back, withdrawing the familiar curved blade of the Kukri knife and once more crouched down to straddle me. The knife found its place once more against my throat, though with slightly less pressure than on our first encounter.

"That's right, Dr. Jackson. I know exactly who you are and what you're doing here." Her voice was almost a purr. I was very much aware of her weight bearing down on me as she leaned in to sensually whisper her next words in my ear. "Oh, when we first met, I didn't know you from Adam. But all a girl needs to find things like that out, is to know the right people. But I'm getting ahead of myself. We're not quite ready for you yet, Jack. There's more that you need to discover on your own before we talk."

She pulled back, reached her free hand into the pocket of her hoodie, and pulled out a tattered piece of cloth with a tartan pattern weaved into it. The sound of footsteps pounding against the asphalt echoed down the alley we'd just come from. She gave a brief glance over her shoulder before turning back to me and smiling.

"That's my cue," she said. She placed the fabric on my chest, leaned in once more, and kissed me on the cheek. Then, she pulled away and stood up, brandishing the knife in warning.

"Who are you?" My brain was finally beginning to recover from the shock of her attack and was only now able to put enough thoughts together to form a coherent sentence.

She winked at me. "You'll find out soon enough," she said, before sheathing the blade behind her back and dashing down another alley and out of sight.

Ten seconds later, I was surrounded by seven very angry looking cops—each with their service weapons pointed directly at my face.

❧⸱❧

I was sitting impatiently in the back of a squad car when Detective Grigsby climbed into the front seat and turned to face me. The grin that stretched across his face was by no means congenial.

"Dr. Jackson," he said, popping a cigarette in his mouth. He didn't light it this time. "What am I going to do with you? I've tried being reasonable. Tried being understanding." He closed his eyes and took a deep breath. "I honestly don't think you're a bad guy. You mean well. But you're interfering with several on-going homicide investigations and I just can't let that fly."

He opened his eyes once more and held up the tartan cloth for me to see.

"So, I'm curious...what's this?" he asked bluntly.

I glanced at it and then turned my eyes back to Grigsby. "I have no idea. Looks like something from a kilt to me."

His smiled widened. "Ha! Yeah. Some poor Scotsman is probably walking around with half his skirt on right now, eh?"

I laughed at the suggestion. "Could be."

The detective's face dropped all semblance of cordiality. "Dr. Jackson, stop. You can do a lot around me that I'll allow, but do not think I'm an idiot. I think you know exactly what this thing is. After all, you risked an evading charge to catch up to the broad who gave it to you. Must be something really important, don't you think?"

So he knows about Silver. Great. Honestly, I'd hoped that he would have just assumed that I'd been trying to escape getting caught at the crime scene. I hadn't wanted him to know about the girl. At least not until I knew more about her.

"So, who is she?" he asked, not giving me a chance to answer his last question.

"Met her on Match.com. She stood me up and I wanted to find out why." It was an attempt at humor, but at this point, even I was in little mood for my lame jokes. "Honestly, I have no idea who she was. She just looked suspicious and I wanted to ask her a few questions."

He nodded knowingly at this comment. "Suspicious, eh? How so?"

I shifted in my seat, trying to ease the pressure on my arms still hand-cuffed behind my back. "Uh, I don't know. Shifty eyes. Fidgety feet. She just looked like she was up to something and I wanted to find out why. I was making my way over to her when you caught up with me. She took off and that's why I did too. Wasn't trying to *evade*, as you put it. Just wanted to find out if she knew anything."

He eyed me for several seconds, then tossed the tartan fabric in my lap. "And you have no idea about that? Or why she gave it to you?"

I glanced down at it and really examined it for the first time. I was taken aback when I noticed some type of family crest stitched into the cloth. A large red and yellow shield, colors separated by a diagonal line cutting it in two. Two crisscrossed swords rested in front, blades long and tipped in red. But it was the object on the top of the shield that really drew my attention. In the place where similar crests would feature a stylized lion, an eagle, or even a gryphon...this one sported a large and menacing black bat.

"Well?" Grigsby said, interrupting my reflection. "What about it? Any idea why she would have given that to you?"

I couldn't pull my eyes away from the bat crowning the family crest. Apart from the heraldic symbol's wings, there was nothing to suggest the image was connected whatsoever to the Jersey Devil. The bat looked more reminiscent of the logo on a bottle of Bacardi than the medieval representation of the cryptid I was now hunting. After a few seconds of contemplation, I shook my head at his question. "Honestly have no idea." I looked up finally, making sure my eyes locked on his. "Seriously. No clue."

He nodded at that and without a word, opened the patrol car's passenger door and got out. He hadn't been gone a quarter of a second before my thoughts wandered back to the cloth and the mysterious woman that had given it to me.

'We're not quite ready for you yet,' she had told me. *What the heck is that supposed to mean?*

I wasn't sure how much time had passed from the moment the detective had left me until he returned. Somewhere in my analysis of the evening's events, I had dozed off. Or flat out passed out from exhaustion. I can't be sure either way. But I jumped in my seat when my car door opened with a screech, and Grigsby grinned when he saw it.

"Get out," he said. "You're coming with me."

"Where are we going?" I asked, scooting out of the patrol car's backseat.

The cop pulled out a set of keys, turned me around, and unlocked my cuffs. He then walked past me and pointed to a late model black Impala parked three cars away. "I'm going to take you to what you wanted to see," he said without looking at me. He opened his car door, got in, and started the engine before I'd even made it to the passenger side. Once I was in, he waited for me to buckle my seatbelt, and then continued. "You wanted to see tonight's victim up close and personal. Well, I'm going to let you do just that."

ELEVEN

THE TWENTY-MINUTE DRIVE TO THE NEW YORK CITY MORGUE WAS ONE of almost complete silence. With both hands firmly gripping the steering wheel and his eyes fixed straight ahead, Grigsby drove the slick, halogen-lit streets with a cigarette clenched between his teeth and a scowl on his face. I wasn't quite sure what his game plan was. Wasn't sure why he'd be taking me to see Max Schildiner's mangled remains. But for the moment, I wasn't going to look a gift horse in the proverbial mouth. The fact was, aside from the terrible lighting conditions and the scrutinizing gaze of an army of law enforcement officials, I had become too distracted by Silver at the crime scene to properly inspect the body in the alley. Besides the strange liquid I'd found on the pavement, as well as on the severed arm, I'd come up empty. And I had a very distinct feeling a closer examination of the corpse would prove most fruitful.

"Um, so..." I said, my eyes roaming at the rolling cityscape speeding past us. "The tartan cloth. Do *you* have any idea what it is? What it means?"

He didn't answer for several seconds as he moved onto an off ramp and coasted into a dark, dingy portion of the city. Of course, the dinginess might have been caused more by the light drizzling rain that had recently started to fall and the blossoming purple-orange of the dawn sun as it edged its way up from the overcast horizon. Everything around us seemed to be carved from marble and tinted in various shades of gray. Once we were moving along 1st Avenue at a brisk pace, the detective cleared his throat.

"Every New Yorker with a television knows what it means." He rolled down his window and exhaled a stream of smoke from his lips. The crisp air surging into the cracked window slapped me across my groggy face, giving me a much-needed jolt to my worn-out system. "I can't believe you don't."

He turned to look at me briefly before bringing his eyes back to the road. "You sure you don't know anything?"

"I'm not exactly from New York, now am I?" I said, turning my attention to the large blue and white building that we pulled up next to. The letters THE MILTON HELPERN INSTITUTE OF FORENSIC MEDICINE were stenciled on the side. The building was affixed to a much larger complex, a hospital from what I could tell, though not the same one that Johnny was holed-up in.

Grigsby drove up to a gated entrance to a parking garage, rolled down his window some more, and spoke to the guard at the security station. After identifying himself to the overweight woman inside the guardhouse, the gate swung open and the detective drove into the dimly-lit garage, snaking his way through the concrete labyrinth until he found a good spot. Once he parked the car, I turned to face him and asked the question that had been on my mind since his reply about New Yorkers with TVs. "So what does it mean, Sergeant? What's the big deal about that crest?"

He studied me for several seconds before shrugging. "It's the family crest, and political logo, for Senator Thomas Leeds. He's running for his third term this year and the TV's been overrun with commercials. They always end with that crest and the catchphrase: LEEDS LEADS." He cocked his head at me and threw his cigarette out the still open car window. "Really? You haven't seen it?"

"I haven't really had much of a chance to catch the latest American Idol, Detective. I'm kind of hunting a mons—uh, I mean, I'm conducting my investigation."

But even as I spoke the words, my mind was racing with about a million thoughts. *Leeds. Leeds. Why does that name sound so familiar to me?*

We got out of the car and moved across the pavement to an elevator. Grigsby pushed the down button and we waited for the elevator's car to crawl its way up to us.

Of course, there's Marc Leeds, but I don't think that scrawny little weasel is connected here. I scowled involuntarily at the thought of the man I had once called friend. A man who had betrayed me. Who had been working for a nameless enemy organization the entire time he'd been on my team. On top of it all, I suspect he's the one responsible for breaking into my house last year and stealing both the only specimen of uncorrupted jenglot DNA known to man and my former mentor's extremely coded journal I'd recovered in Greece. A journal that could very well have given me the answers to many of the odd events that had been plaguing me the last few years. *Forget about Marc, Jack. Just a coincidence. So what does this Leeds have to do with Silver? Or the Jersey Devil?*

The elevator dinged, the doors opened and we stepped inside. I was so caught up in my whirring thoughts that I didn't even notice which button the detective pressed. All I knew was we were moving down. A few minutes later, we reached our floor and stepped out into an institutionally white corridor with checkerboard tiled floors and harsh florescent lights installed in the ceiling every few feet. The smells of Formalin and antiseptic assaulted my nose.

Grigsby stalked down the hallway with a purpose and I could do nothing but follow his lead. "Um, this isn't some sort of trick is it?" I asked with a nervous grin. "You're not taking me to some kind of looney bin are you?"

He chuckled at this and kept walking. "That'll be our next stop, but first, I'm going to be true to my word."

We rounded a corner and moved up to a security station. A balding, middle-aged man with a paunch stretching the buttons of his security uniform shirt looked up from his magazine in a bored, non-committal way.

"Who ya here for?" was all the man said. He nervously flicked his comb-over out of his eyes, which seemed to strain against the temptation to look back at the magazine—which I could now see was the latest *Sport Illustrated Swimsuit Edition*. The detective flashed his badge, as well as his picture ID. "Detective Sergeant Grigsby. Here to see a decedent that was just brought in. A Max Schildiner."

The security guard stuffed the magazine in a drawer with a huff and rifled through a stack of papers affixed to a clipboard. After a few seconds, he looked up at us and said, "Examination Room 12. Dr. Steiner will be the pathologist, but he's not in yet." The guard glanced at the clock on the wall behind us. "It's a bit early and Steiner's day shift. Probably won't be here for another hour or so."

"Not a problem," Grigsby said with a broad smile. "We're not here for the post. We just need to look at the, um, body for a few minutes."

The man's brow pinched into a tight knot. "Now, Detective, you know that ain't allowed. No one sees the Morts 'til a doc is present."

"Uh, excuse me," I said. "Morts?"

The guard glared at me and shrugged. "It's what I call da stiffs. Ya know…rigor *mort*is an' all dat. Nobody but me calls dem dat, but I'm sure it'll catch on sooner or later."

"Ah," was my witty reply.

Grigsby smiled at me, shaking his head before turning back to the security officer. He made a show of reading the man's nametag and went dead serious.

"Gerald, is it?" the detective asked.

The man nodded.

"Well, see…we have a problem." The detective reached into his shirt pocket and pulled out a notepad and pen. He jotted something down and closed the pad before looking back up at Gerald. "We really need to see those remains. It's vitally important that we do. And you desperately need to keep your job. So, you're going to let us into Examination Room 12 and walk away for a few minutes."

The guard's nicotine stained teeth shown in the harsh light as he laughed out loud. "Really? And how do ya suppose I'm gonna lose my job if I don't do dis for ya?"

Grigsby leaned in closer to the man conspiratorially. "Because if you don't, I'll report that half empty bottle of vodka you keep in your desk drawer." The detective's smile returned. "You know, the drawer you just shoved that swimsuit magazine into."

Gerald involuntarily looked toward the drawer, then back at Grigsby. He opened his mouth to protest, but was immediately interrupted by the detective.

"Aah! Don't try to deny it. I saw it clear as day."

The man closed his gaping maw, stood up, and grabbed a set of keys hanging from a hook in the wall to his left.

"Come on," he said with a sigh and started walking down the corridor. As we followed him, I looked over at Grigsby.

"Why are you doing this?" I asked.

Our footsteps echoed down the hallway. Though the Medical Examiner's Office was open 24/7, we passed only a handful of droopy-eyed employees as we made our way to the examination room.

He looked over at me with a genuine smile. "Call it a hunch." He pulled out a stick of Wrigley's gum and stuck it in his mouth. An attempt to curb a nicotine craving, I guessed. "I'm not entirely sure what you and your little 'think tank' is all about. But something tells me you know more about my homicides than I do. I figure it's my job to use whatever resources I can to find out the truth." We walked a few more feet in silence before he added, "But don't think for a minute that you're off the hook with me. If this doesn't pan out, your butt's going to jail."

"Peachy," I said, shoving my hands into my pockets as we came up to the door of Exam Room 12.

The guard stopped at the door and looked at the two of us. "This is as far as I go. Yous guys are on yer own now."

Grigsby nodded, allowing Gerald to slip past us before opening the swinging door. He gestured for me to enter first and I complied.

The last time I had been in an autopsy room had been in college. My post-graduate work. We'd been required to dissect several human cadavers and I'd never quite acquired a taste for it. I figured that was probably a pretty good thing, actually.

Without saying a word, my companion moved to the southern wall to a series of large metal drawers. He scanned the labels inked with various names until he eyed the one he was looking for. He pulled on a pair of latex gloves and opened the vacuum-sealed door, then pulled out the tray containing the various pieces of what had once been a promising senatorial candidate.

"We only have a few minutes," he said, stepping away from the remains. "Do what you need to do and let's get out of here."

I stared at the mass of bone and tissue, still enveloped by the shroud of clear plastic. Through the years, I'd seen a lot of maulings, dismemberments, and carnage brought on by all kinds of teeth-filled nasties that clung to the shadows of our world. Most of the time, discovering such tableaus in a natural environment, was somehow more manageable. Easier to deal with. The circle of life. Seeing such destruction in the antiseptic confines of the stark white autopsy room seemed almost...obscene.

My gloved hand hovered over the plastic as I paused to take a deep breath.

"Well?" Grigsby said, a single eyebrow arching.

"Geeze, dude. Give a guy a sec to gather his nerves."

He smiled, but there was no humor in it. "I'd love to, Jackson. But the truth is we don't have time for you to *gather your nerves*. Dr. Steiner and his tech will be here soon and we can't be anywhere nearby when they get here, *capice?*"

Without responding, I reached across the tray and took hold of the plastic, peeling it back to reveal the macabre contents. Taking another deep breath, I let my eyes pour over Schildiner's body with as much detachment as I could muster. Which, to be perfectly honest, wasn't very much at all. Something was just weird about examining the corpse this way…under the scrutinizing eyes of the NYPD detective. I felt nervous. Agitated.

Suddenly, I spun around on Grigsby. "What?" My voice elevated an octave as I spat the word.

"Pardon?"

"What do you want from me?" I asked. "Why'd you bring me here? What do you expect me to accomplish?"

The detective eyed me, his face unreadable, but he remained silent.

"Seriously," I continued. "This is just creepy. One minute, I'm your least favorite person. You've been trying to run me out of town since *day one*. Now all of a sudden, we're chums. Buddies. Someone you decide to break into a morgue with. Call me paranoid, but something just doesn't jive."

Grigsby maintained his silence a few seconds more before giving a quick nod of resolution. "Okay," he said, taking a quick breath as if steeling his resolve. "All right. It's *that!*" He pointed at the remains. "I've been working homicide now for over ten years. I've seen everything. Or at least, I thought had. Until these killings started. Until these…these mutilations."

He tenuously sorted through the carnage until he picked up one of the pieces—a femur, if I wasn't mistaken, with skin and muscle tissue hanging on in shreds. He then pointed to a couple of deep grooves carved into the bone. "I brought you here because of this. Those marks aren't caused by any knife I've ever seen and I want to know what made them. I want to know what's going on and, quite frankly, you seem to be the only one around here that has a clue."

I leaned in for a closer look at the deep linear indentions he was indicating and gave him a sympathetic look. "You know what caused them," I said. "You just don't want to admit it yet."

"Humor me."

I nodded and took in a breath. "All right. They're tooth marks."

"You're right. I already had figured that out, genius. But I've had three wildlife experts look at the similar marks on my other victims. They couldn't match them to any known species of animal."

I shrugged. "That's because they weren't created by any catalogued species."

He let out an indignant laugh. "And I suppose you're going to tell me that some giant gargoyle thing caused them, right? That is, after all, what the witnesses are claiming."

A gleam of sweat beaded down the detective's face. He was nervous. Possibly even scared. And it was completely understandable. Everything he ever believed about the world was suddenly being turned upside down. He was a man of reason. Logic. Deduction. He was used to hunting bad guys. Murderers. Monsters in their own right, but not the kind of monster I was asking him to believe in.

It's like this. When it comes down to it, people are going to believe what they want to believe. It doesn't matter what the facts are…people are wonderful at manipulating facts to fit their preconceived ideas about the world around them. For most people, cryptids are something that just doesn't fit into their idea of a rational world. To come face to face with evidence that throws all that rationale out the window…well, that was enough to make even the strongest man sweat.

"Not exactly a gargoyle," I said softly.

"Then what? What is it? What is out there killing these people?"

I shrugged. "Have you ever heard of the Jersey Devil?"

Grigsby stared at me as if I'd just grown three horns on my head and a tail. "You're saying a freakin' fairy tale monster is my suspect?" He threw his hands in the air with a laugh. "I don't know who's crazier—you or me for even entertaining the idea that you might be able to help."

To emphasize his point, he draped the plastic over the body and began to slide tray back into the cooler door. A glint off the carcass caught my eye and I reached out to stop him. "Wait," I said, opening the bag once more.

Pulling out a pair of tweezers, I carefully extracted the item that had caught my attention and held it up to him. "See this?"

He looked at the thin strand of hair I held within the tweezers and shook his head. "It's a hair. So what?"

I smiled. "This, Detective Grigsby, is everything." I held it out to him one more time, letting him take it into his hand to examine more closely. "I can already tell this hair doesn't belong to our victim. Even without a head, it's easy to see he was fair haired. This one is dark. Second, it's thicker, more course than human hair. Ergo, it comes from an animal. But not from a domesticated one like a pet—it's too thick for that. This comes from something with a very heavy coat of fur. Something wild. Something that quite possibly settles in for the winter. Hibernates maybe."

"So, now you're saying a bear is my suspect?"

"I'm saying that once I have this strand of hair analyzed for DNA, we'll be a lot closer to figuring out exactly what it is." I delicately took the hair from his hand and placed it in a plastic baggie I'd pulled from my pocket. "But I think we can safely assume you don't have a bear problem in Manhattan."

"Why do you say that?"

My face turned serious as I handed him back the hair safely protected in a plastic sheath now. He seemed so fascinated with the specimen, I wanted to allow him a chance to really study it. "I've seen the thing. It's why I was paragliding through town the other night. The creature nearly killed me." I intentionally left out any mention of Nikki. I didn't want to implicate her in any way if this new-found partnership with the NYPD turned sour. "Your *suspect*, as you put it, can fly. It has wings. At least fifteen feet across. And yes, it eerily matches the descriptions of Jersey Devil sightings through the centuries."

His wide eyes stared at the clear baggie in the palm of his hand as I pushed the tray back into its drawer. There was nothing left to see that I hadn't already seen before. The same blood and guts from the senatorial candidate. The same severed limbs. The same sense of revulsion when I considered the potential for future victims if this thing wasn't stopped soon.

"Look, I know it's a lot to take in all at once—"

"No," he said, shaking his head. "No, I get it. I believe it. I'll deal with it..." His eyes couldn't seem to pull themselves away from the hair in his hand.

"But?"

"Hmm?"

"You can deal with it, but I sense there's a 'but' coming," I explained.

After a few seconds, he absently handed the hair standard back to me and held out his hand. "Let me see that crest again," he said. I pulled out the crest and handed it to him. He scrutinized the cloth for several seconds before looking up at me, his eyes dark. "The 'but' that you sense coming is this: If all this is true, then we have a major problem."

"You mean besides a big scary gargoyle-like monster that likes to tear its hapless victims into jerky?"

Obviously not amused, he held up the crest for me to see. "Senator Leeds. It's his crest. I don't think that's a bat we're looking at. I think it looks more like *a big scary gargoyle*."

The implications hit me in the face like an aluminum baseball bat. "Oh."

"Exactly," Grigsby said. "Somehow—I'm not sure how just yet—the senator is mixed up in this thing in all kinds of ways."

TWELVE

WE FINISHED UP AT THE MORGUE WITHOUT RUNNING INTO THE MEDICAL Examiner or anyone else who might raise an eyebrow at our unauthorized examination and Grigsby drove me back to my hotel. The detective was uncharacteristically quiet as he maneuvered his unmarked Impala expertly through the grid of New York City streets. His silence was understandable. He'd gone quickly from a relatively rational world where the biggest monsters out there were of the gun-toting human kind. I was asking him to believe in a whole different breed—of the "hide under your bed until all the lights are off" variety. It was a lot for the average person to take in. A lot he'd have to sort through. So, I didn't press.

Of course, as exhausted as I was, I had no problems with getting the silent treatment from him either. It had been more than forty-eight hours since the last time I'd slept and I was starting to feel it. The only thing on my mind at that moment was melting into the hotel room sheets, stretched too tight over my bed, and sinking into the sleep of the dead.

Grigsby didn't stick around once he'd dropped me off—once again, perfectly okay with me because I had a date with a mattress. I smiled as the elevator ascended to my floor; searching for the keycard I'd stuck in the mess I called a wallet. Of course, I needn't have bothered. The moment my friends—who were apparently camping out in my room—heard me approaching, Randy opened the door and ushered me inside. That's when the maelstrom of questions started.

"Jack, what happened?" Randy said. "I saw that goon Grigsby putting you in cuffs and driving off with you. I figured you'd be bound up like Hannibal Lecter and on your way to Polk with a fully-armed police escort by now."

"Meh," I said before moving over to the sink and washing my face. I had hoped my non-committal answer and the mundane task of preparing for bed would dissuade them from asking more questions.

"Yeah, Jack," Nikki said, reclining on the sofa and rubbing Arnold's belly. "We were worried about you. What happened?"

I pulled out my toothbrush from my shaving kit and dabbed a bit of toothpaste on it. "I'm fine," I said, looking at my friends in the mirror. Randy and Landers were parked at the table near the door, sipping on coffee. Nikki remained on the sofa. Apparently, my dad had the good sense to not be there at the moment. Conspicuously missing too, was the tabloid reporter, Davenport. "Grigsby and I had a little powwow. That's all. He's decided he'd actually like our help on this, so he's agreed to let us continue doing what we're here for."

"Well, what happened," Randy asked taking a sip of coffee and as was his habit, stroking at the little patch of fuzz growing just under his lower lip. "What did you find out?"

"Look," I spun around to face them, my toothbrush hung precariously from my lips. "Can we do the debriefing later? I'm exhausted. I just need a little shut-eye and then we can talk about this all you want. Promise."

I turned around, spat the toothpaste into the sink, and rinsed my mouth. Then I stumbled over to the nearest bed and leaving the Medical Examiner transport clothes on, plopped down on it, taking one of the zillion pillows and pulling it against me in a tight cuddle.

"Jack, I'm sorry," Landers finally piped in. "But we're on a schedule. Polk has been breathing down our necks. He wants us back ASAP. If you want us to risk our careers for this, we're going to have to wrap it up quickly. We need to debrief now."

Sure. Easy for the Boy Scout to say. They'd at least been able to get a bit of sleep. I'd been up for the past two nights. And considering I was already pretty banged up from my excursion to Australia, I was just plum worn out. I had to face facts. I wasn't as spry as I used to be and my team would just have to be patient with me.

"It won't take long, Jack," Randy urged. "I already filled them in on what we found at the crime scene. About the strange liquid we discovered near the corpse and about how you chased the crazy woman who attacked you in the park. We just need you to fill in the blanks."

With my face firmly planted on the mattress and my eyes rebelliously closed tight, I dug into my pocket and pulled out the strange tartan cloth Silver had given me, as well as the baggie containing the hair sample. I held them up behind my back and growled, "Here."

"What's this?" Randy asked as I felt the bag and tartan fabric pull free from my hands.

"Hair sample. Found on victim," I mumbled into the pillow. "Send to Wiley and have him run DNA."

"And the family crest?" Nikki said. "Where'd you get it? What does it have to do with the case?"

With a sigh, I rolled over in bed and told them everything. I told them about chasing the girl down until she tased me in the alley. I told them about the strange warnings she'd given me—about her comments about "not being ready for me yet"—and about her handing me the crest. And then I explained who the crest belonged to.

"Thomas Leeds?" Nikki said. "What's he got to do with any of this?"

"Are you kidding me?" Randy said, his eyes widening in disbelief. "You're telling me there's a 'Leeds' attached to a Jersey Devil case? For real?"

"Yeah, apparently, he's running for office again," I said. "Detective Grigsby seems to think that more than one of the Devil's victims have some sort of connection with the senator. He's going to check some things out and get back to me later tonight."

Randy shook his head. "You're not understanding me," Randy explained. "*Leeds*. That name doesn't ring any bells for you?"

"Are you talking about Marc?" Nikki asked. "Surely, there's no connection. Just a coincidence."

"I'm not talking about Marc." He looked back over at me. A lopsided grin stretched across his face. "Do you really not remember?"

My brain felt like it was stuck in a vat of molasses. My mental gears churned away, trying to connect the invisible dots that were apparently so obvious to my friend. But whether from exhaustion or something else, I just couldn't put my finger on it. I shrugged as I rolled back over onto my pillow. "Does it *really* matter, Randy? I just want to go to sleep..."

"The name *Mother Leeds* isn't ringing any bells for you?"

My eyes shot open at the name. Slowly, I turned back over and looked at him. *Mother Leeds*. "No way," I said, still staring at him as he continued grinning wildly.

"I know, right?" He said, nearly giddy with enthusiasm. "Can you imagine?"

"Care to fill us in?" Landers, who'd been sitting quietly by the door scribbling notes, demanded.

My heart pounded in my chest as I thought about the implications. Though I was still exhausted, the mention of the infamous Mother Leeds was like placing an IV drip of espresso directly into my veins. I looked over at the spook with a twinkle in my eyes.

"Mother Leeds," I said, "is said to have been the mother of the Jersey Devil. Depending on what account you listen to, anyway." I sat up in the bed, running my fingers through my greasy, exhausted hair. "Some say she was a witch. She got pregnant and cursed the baby."

"More than that," Randy said, between a gulp of coffee. "She basically told her family that she hoped the baby would be the devil."

"Right," I agreed. "The story goes that once the baby was born, it was a normal human child. But as it matured, it changed. Started turning into a strange, demonic-looking creature. At a certain age, the child is said to have gone berserk and murdered its entire family. Then, it fled out into the wilderness where it has survived to this day."

"And you think there's a connection with this senator and the Leeds of legend?" Nikki asked.

"You have to admit. It would be a huge coincidence if there wasn't."

"But aren't there a number of different stories regarding the Jersey Devil's origins?" Landers asked, leaning forward in his seat. "I mean, that's just one legend among many, from what I understand."

I nodded. "Absolutely, but all the legends have one thing in common..."

"The name Leeds," Nikki said, finally getting what had excited Randy and me so much. "And the hooded woman giving you the family crest of a highly respected United States senator—whose name just happens to be 'Leeds'—was like..."

No one had to complete her thought. It was like putting up a great big neon sign that pointed to the senator as our number one suspect. As the implications oozed their way into my exhausted brain, I let out a sigh and climbed once more out of bed.

"Okay," I said. "Here's the plan. I really do need a quick nap. But as soon as I wake up, Nikki and I will go visit Leeds' election headquarters and try to snoop around." I glanced over at Landers and Randy. "In the meantime, take my dad and scout out some good locations for tonight's hunt. We need to get a hold of this thing before anyone else is hurt and that's not going to happen if we don't have a few traps set up throughout the city."

"Why take your dad?" Randy asked. "I didn't think you wanted him involved in this."

I shrugged. "I don't. But he ain't leaving and if I'm honest with myself, there's no one better at hunting a wild animal than him. He did, after all, teach Johnny most of what he knows."

I laid my head down in the pillow once more, waiting for them to walk out the door. But after their exodus, I could tell by a disgruntled sigh behind me that Nikki was still there and not a little annoyed.

"Yes?" I growled into my pillow.

"Watch your tone, Jack," she snapped. "I'm just wondering what I'm supposed to do while you get your precious beauty sleep."

Honestly, I hadn't given it much thought. I'd never wanted Nikki to be part of this to begin with. In the last couple of years, every time she became involved in an ENIGMA investigation, she'd been unnecessarily put in harm's way. Sure, the Malaysian ordeal didn't count. She was already there. But during last year's excursion to Greece, she'd been taken prisoner by a psychopathic hussy with a grudge against me. And in the two days she'd been in New York, she'd already been attacked by a flying monkey with a major attitude and nearly plummeted to her death in the process. Truth be told, I kind of wanted her to get the hint and go home.

"I don't know," I mumbled. "You're near Fifth Avenue. Why not do what most women would love to do if they came to the Big Apple? Go shopping." It was a pretty mean thing to say, but that was the point. I wasn't a big fan of being held emotionally captive and that's exactly what she'd been doing to me since our current break-up. When she didn't respond, I figured the jab had been a little too sharp and added: "Honestly, I don't really know what you could be doing. Do you have any ideas?"

The uncomfortable pause continued for several more seconds. I could feel her eyes boring laser-precise holes into the back of my head.

"Well, I suppose I could do some research on the Leeds family," she said, then waited a breath before continuing. "Davenport and I could do some digging into—"

I spun around to face her at this. "Oh no! That little jerk left us high and dry last night," I said. "I don't trust him and I don't want you within twenty feet of him."

"I thought you said he showed up just in time to distract Grigsby so you could chase down your mystery woman?"

"That's beside the point. The creep is bad news. The answer is no."

The moment the words were out of my mouth, my brain screamed to pull them back in. But it was too late. Nikki's eyes widened with rage; her chin arched upward in utter defiance.

"Oh," she said, spinning around to grab the key to her rental car off the table. "Really."

She strode over to the door and reached for the knob.

"Nikki," I said, my voice pleading. "Wait."

She turned and glared at me.

"Is that an order?" she asked. "A high and mighty command from the Great Obadiah Jackson?"

"I didn't mean it like that..."

"Yes, you did, Jack," she hissed. "That's the problem. You *did* mean it. You want everything your way. You want me to behave the way you think I should. You want me to do all the sacrificing, but not sacrifice anything yourself. You want to run the show. You. You. You. That's the problem. With you. With us. Everything. And I'm sick of it."

"But..."

"I'll be back by noon," she said, her voice a bit more calm. She opened the door. "We'll go see Leeds then. But we're going to need to talk more about this."

She stepped into the hallway and shut the door behind her.

Swell. All I wanted was a little sleep. Didn't want it to turn into World War III.

A low whine sounded from the floor beside the bed, then Arnold jumped onto the mattress, curled up beside me, and sighed. He eyed me with curious disdain.

"Yeah, I know, buddy," I said while scratching behind his ear. "I really am an idiot. But I'll fix it. I'll fix..."

And I drifted off to sleep.

∂∽✑

The shrill *threep* of the hotel phone jolted me awake. My heart pounding, I reached over, picked up the receiver, and mumbled, "Nikki, I just fell asleep. It can't possibly be noon yet."

No one replied. I could barely make out the sound of breathing on the other end, but that was it.

"Hello?" I said.

More breathing, then I heard the click of the phone hanging up and a dial tone.

I held the receiver against my ear for several seconds, my eyes closing almost as soon as the person on the other end hung up. Forcing myself awake, I replaced the receiver and snuggled back into my pillow.

THRRREEEEEP! THRRREEEEEP!

My hand shot out and grabbed the phone before the third ring.

"Hello?" My voice was a little more biting this time. I glanced over at the clock beside the phone. Nikki hadn't even been gone fifteen minutes.

"Jaaaack," cooed the slightly accented, male voice on the other end. "It's been far too long, no?"

I bolted up from the bed, wide awake. Even though it had been at least five years since I last heard it, I knew the voice as well as I would an old friend's.

"Freakshow." It was the only word that could squeeze past the lump now lodged in my throat.

I wasn't exactly sure why I was so surprised he'd be calling. He had, after all, already been in touch with Davenport. Told him about me and worse still, ENIGMA. Ever since the reporter had told me about the clandestine emails from the sociopathic game show host from Hell, I knew the creep was up to something. Still, after all this time—I mean, I'd spent the better part of a year after my abduction trying to track the nutjob down—I hadn't even come close. Having never seen the man in person (he'd communicated with me on the island through a system of loudspeakers), I had nothing but a nom de plume to go by. Even the webcast's IP address had offered no leads since it was randomly changed at irregular intervals. The new website information would be sent out by invitation only to the crème de la crème of high society whenever a new contest was being announced. Needless to say, I never received an invitation.

After a while, I had to move on with my life. My research. I gave up the search and eventually, he'd just sort of been forgotten. Oh sure, he'd reserved a very special place in the back of my subconscious, but for all intents and purposes, he'd just become unimportant to me. Now, after all this time, I was on the phone with the man with the Hispanic sounding accent and affinity for Latin American cryptids.

"Ah, Jack," he said. "You remember me. I'm touched."

"Don't be," I said. "I haven't lost much sleep since our last encounter. You're nothing but a mere footnote in my memoires. A short story at best."

The man on the other end of the phone laughed. That high pitched, psychotic laugh I remembered all too well. "That, my friend, is about to change."

His statement chilled me to the bone. Nervously, I pulled the receiver tighter to my ear and spoke.

"What is *that* supposed to mean?"

A soft chuckle. "Simple. It means I'm tired of sitting on the sidelines. Tired of watching you from afar. Tired of seeing everyone else have all the fun." He breathed heavily into the microphone as if puffing on a cigarette. "You cost me dearly during your performance on my show, Jack. Not only could I not replace the cryptids you dispatched during that encounter, I lost my shirt as well. I had high stakes against you and you cheated me out of a large sum of cash.

"So, ever since then, I've been watching you. Biding my time. Occasionally, throwing a ringer into your expeditions." He paused and I could almost hear the smile spread across his face. "How did you like the surprise I sent you in Greece last year? At the airfield?"

I gripped the phone tighter as my heart pounded inside my chest.

"The assassins," I hissed. "They were yours?"

"Well, of course they were mine," he laughed. "You didn't think that Ekaterina would be so bold do you? She has other plans for you. We don't exactly see eye to eye on your role in the overall scheme of things."

That little tidbit set my Spidey-sense on overdrive.

"Wait," I said. "See eye to eye...are you telling me that you two are working together?"

"Oh no...nothing quite so mundane as that. However, we do have a common benefactor. An individual with great interest in you, Jack, and your work with ENIGMA."

"And this benefactor...he was behind Krenkin? The jenglot? And the tritons?"

Silence on the other end. Then, Freakshow cleared his throat.

"Speaking of the jenglot...such an absolute shame about poor Vera, isn't it," he said, his voice now almost a glass-shattering shrill. His excitement was almost palpable. He was nearly orgasmic in his delight. "Such a beautiful girl. Well, I suppose, not there at the end. But at one time—"

That's when I remembered what Davenport had told me. Freakshow had claimed responsibility for killing my pal Witz and desiccating Vera's jenglot body—beheading her and placing it at the murder scene. I felt bile rise in my throat. My temples pounded. And I swear, I literally growled into the phone.

"You're going to pay for Madagascar," I whispered. "For Witz. For Vera—"

"Tsk. Tsk, Jack. Don't be so cliché. It's unbecoming."

"What do you want?"

"Why, I thought it would be obvious." His tone became instantly serious. "I plan to renew our game."

"Look, weirdo, you can forget it," I said. "No more games. As a matter of fact, I'm hanging up."

I moved the receiver toward the cradle when I heard the madman shout, "Wait. You might want to listen to this..."

My hand froze, hovering inches over the phone. Taking a breath, I lifted it once more to my ear, but said nothing.

"Jaaack?" he cooed. "You still there?"

I continued saying nothing. He knew I was still there. I wasn't going to give him any more satisfaction from this conversation than he was already acquiring.

"I can hear you breathing, Jack," he said. "So you must still be there, right?" A soft, icy chuckle echoed on the other end of the line. "I'm going to play it with you straight. No tricks. No lies. I want you to know exactly what's coming, but I also want you to know there's not a bloody thing you can do to stop it. So when it happens, don't beat yourself up too hard, okay?"

"Spit it out!" I was losing my temper with this guy, which ticked me off even more. It meant I was playing right into his hands. He was baiting me and I was falling for it, hook, line, and sinker.

"Wow, Jack," Freakshow said, sucking in a breath in mock umbrage. "A tone like that might make a fella think you're not happy to hear from him."

I sighed into the phone. "Just tell me what you've got to say so I can get back to sleep."

"Oh yeah! The big investigation. Almost forgot all about that. Giant gargoyle skimming the rooftops of the Big Apple. Now, that's got to be one wild ride. No wonder you're being short with me. It's the stress, isn't it? You know, I know this psychiatrist...he worked wonders for—"

"Freakshow! Enough with the games. Tell me what you have to say." I paused for effect, then added, "Please."

"Oooh, the magic word. Sure. I'll let you get back to your beauty sleep, mi amigo," he said. "Okay, here's the deal. Before your little investigation is over, one of your teammates will be taken from you. As a matter of fact, they'll be well on their way to becoming my next big Internet star. You see, I've recently realized that the quickest way to get to a man's soul is through his friends. So if you have any unresolved issues with anyone on your team...you better patch them up now."

He let out another shrill laugh and then the line went dead, leaving me gripping the receiver tight in my shaking hand.

THIRTEEN

I'M NOT QUITE SURE HOW LONG I SAT ON THE EDGE OF MY BED, ABSENTLY cradling the phone receiver in my lap while staring off into space and trying to come to grips with what I'd just been told. Freakshow was most definitely up to something. And from the sound of it, he was eyeing someone on my team—someone he planned to kidnap, as he'd done me five years before, and use for his sick little crypto-gladiatorial webcast. From experience, I knew this was no idle threat. If the man wanted to take one of my friends, he could do it with little to no effort.

That is, unless I figured out who he planned on taking and cut him off at the proverbial pass. The problem was that from my brief encounters with the man, I was convinced that he truly was insane. In his world, up was down and down was an intelligent shade of the color blue. No matter how hard I tried to anticipate his next move, Freakshow would change it four random times just to throw me off the track. There could be no way to know exactly who he'd have his sights on.

A soft whine came from Arnold, who nuzzled up against my leg. He no doubt sensed my anxiety and wanted me to know all would be well. And where my dog was concerned, I knew he truly believed it. Heck, if the mutant K9 had any say in the matter, he'd tear Freakshow's arm clean off if he tried to take anyone in front of him. He'd certainly proved he could do it when I'd found him on that desert island anyway.

I gave a quick scratch to his upturned belly, hung the phone up, and pulled out my own cell phone. It was scrambled for security reasons and I figured it would be much more difficult for Freakshow to listen in if he had a mind to. Flipping through my contacts, I found the one I wanted and pressed the button. Three rings later, the line on the other end answered to a series of labored breaths.

"Jack!" came Wiley's wheezing voice. "How's the investigation going?" More heavy breathing.

"Wiley? What are you doing? Sounds like you're about to have a heart attack."

"Oh." More huffing. "Just working..." A grunt. "Out."

"Well, take a break for a minute before you have a stroke."

I heard movement on the other end, followed by more bouts of labored breathing. Then a deep sigh.

"Sorry about that, Jack," the pudgy computer whiz said into the phone. I heard him take a gulp of something to drink. "Figure I needed to start...ya know, start losing some weight and stuff, so I've been working out on my—"

"Wiley, I've got a problem," I said, cutting him off. For some reason, I had a really bad habit of doing that and I swore to myself that I'd make it up to the little nerd someday. "I need your help on something."

"Is it about the case? 'Cause Mr. Polk specifically told me I was not, under any circumstances, to help you with this 'inane inquiry' as he put it. I mean, I've already sent those berries you sent me to the lab...ya know, what the boss don't know won't hurt him, right? And don't worry...I'll do the same once I get that goop from the crime scene and hair sample Landers called me about a few minutes ago. But I gotta be careful. If I keep bending the rules, I'm going to get caught and then I'll be no help at all to you guys."

"No, it's not about the case. It's about something else. Something much more dangerous."

I could almost hear the muscle's in Wiley's hands tighten around the phone. I had said the magic word. Though the boy genius was destined to spend the majority of his life behind a computer terminal, he had eternal aspirations of one day joining us in the field. Even more, he wanted to experience firsthand the dangers we faced on a regular basis. Since that wasn't going to happen any time soon, he'd learned to live vicariously through me. My dangers became, in essence, his own. Only problem is that where Freakshow was concerned, any snooping on Wiley's part could put him in the wacko's crosshairs. He could quite literally be placed in danger himself. What I was about to do was not something I took lightly.

"Listen, this is serious, okay?"

"Absolutely," he replied, a little too eager.

"I'm not joking. You're going to have to be exceptionally careful on this one. If you get caught, you'll have more than your job on the line."

"All right, Jack. I understand." He took another drink. "Just tell me what you need."

I pulled the business card Davenport had given me when we first met and read off the email address listed to Wiley. "I need you to hack into that account. You should find some emails sent by a man calling himself—"

"Freakshow?"

I swallowed. "How...how did you know?"

"I'm already in."

"What? Already...how?"

"I'm a genius, Jack. What can I say? Set my weights and stuff up in my lab, so I was right here at my computer." I heard a few keys tapping. "Anyway, the owner of the account—Alex Davenport—flagged the emails as high priority, so I clicked on them first."

I grinned. "You never stop amazing me, kid," I said. "Now listen. Davenport hinted that Freakshow gave him a secret message or something...something explicitly for me. Do you see anything like that?"

I heard him hum some non-melodic tune for several seconds, before he responded. "Nope. Nothing like that," he said. "There's an attachment with a photo—oh." He let out a soft moan. He'd obviously found the scene photos of Witz's murder. Of course, Wiley had seen them before—around the same time I had, but no one would ever get used to the carnage those photos showed.

"Wiley, it's okay," I said. "Don't worry about it. I had a feeling that whatever private message Freakshow wanted me to know wouldn't be there anyway."

"Um, okay." His voice was unsteady. I had a feeling he was about to lose his lunch if I didn't distract him soon.

"Okay, kid, the next phase of the operation is right up your alley. I need you to do whatever you can to trace Freakshow's IP address. Also, he just called my hotel room. Maybe you could trace the call. See if the number is registered to a real name. Maybe even figure out where he was calling from…a location and anything else you can dig up on him to help me find him."

"Sure thing. Shouldn't be a problem." His tone was a bit more steady now. He was in territory he could handle. Which might be dangerous in its own right. The last thing I needed was for Wiley to get cocky.

"Don't count on it. Wiley, I'm serious. The man's as dangerous as they come. And the way he handles his webcasts, we already know he's tech savvy. If he catches wind that you're onto him—"

"He won't," Wiley said, a touch of pride in his voice. "I'll be careful. Promise."

"I know you will." I paused, trying to decide if I should confide a bit more to him—just to let him know how serious the situation was. But ultimately the less he knew, the better. "Let me know as soon as you find something, okay?"

He let out of muffled affirmative and I knew that he was already stuffing his face with Lil' Debbie snack cakes.

"Thanks, kid," I said, hanging up the phone.

Taking another breath, I stood up from the bed and made my way to the bathroom. There was no way I'd be getting back to sleep any time soon, no matter how exhausted I was. So, I figured I'd best get my butt in gear and get ready for the day's investigation.

A shower, a shave, and a phone called to a very brusque Nikki later, and I was walking from the hotel lobby to her car, idling in the circular drive. I couldn't help but look over my shoulder from the moment I left my room.

❧

We drove to the Thomas Leeds' campaign headquarters in complete silence. Nikki, for her part, was still miffed at my behavior from earlier that morning. I, on the other hand, was still brooding over my conversation with Freakshow. It made for one awkward thirty minute drive.

It took us forever to find a parking spot—no wonder New Yorkers typically didn't drive in their own city—and we ended up having to walk four blocks before we came to the corner of West 48th and 10th Avenue where Leeds' HQ was located. The two of us strode in silence as we approached the building and I realized that it was time for a little damage control before we started interviewing the senator about a giant winged creature terrorizing the city.

"Look, Nikki," I said, my voice cracking a little from an atrophied voice box.

"Jack, listen," she said at the exact same moment.

We stopped, turned to face each other, and smiled.

"Let me go first," I said, taking her hands and giving them a soft squeeze. "I know we've been having problems lately. And I'm afraid we don't have time right now to explore all of them, so let me just address the current elephant in the room. The way I acted earlier...the things I said. The way I treated you and tried to keep you away from this investigation. I'm sorry. I want to blame it all on just being exhausted, but that's not really an excuse. I'm just on edge. Johnny's laid up in the hospital. We're chasing a killer monster. And the last thing I wanted was for you to once again be placed in danger because of what I do for a living."

Not to mention being the possible target of a madman with a murderous game show and a vendetta against me, I thought. Of course, I hadn't known about Freakshow until the last hour or so.

"Hold on...before you say anything," I continued, throwing her my very best lopsided grin. "I know you can take care of yourself. Heck, you can take care of yourself better than I can take care of me. But I care about you, ya know? You're a missionary. You should be traveling the world helping people, not chasing after—"

"Jack, stop," she said, her face turning solemn again. "That's not what I wanted to talk to you about. I know all that. I'm not mad at you...well, at least, not horribly so. But I need to tell you something before we get any closer to Leeds' office."

The serious tone of her voice—the way she squeezed my hand tighter—told me I was probably not going to like what she was about to say. I tried to swallow, but found my throat parched.

"Um, okay? Tell me."

She looked up at me as she brushed a golden strand of hair over one ear and forced a weak smile. "Well, I thought we might could use some help with interviewing the Senator," she said, then squeezed my hand another time while scrunching her neck apologetically as if preparing for a blow.

Oh geeze, a three squeeze problem, I thought. *This cannot be good.*

"Jack, I asked Alex to join us."

"You did what?" I pulled my hand away and stiffened, my brows furrowing in a fit of irritation. And maybe a little fear.

"I just thought since this was his city—these were his people—he might have better insight into what's going on around the headquarters," she said calmly. So far, I hadn't reacted any differently than she'd expected. Which was a good thing. It meant she was prepared. "Plus, he's a professional interviewer. He might glean some information we can't."

"You. Did. What?" I repeated the question, this time a little softer.

"You heard me."

"Nikki! We don't even know if we can trust him," I spat. "I mean, the guy could be in cahoots with—"

I stopped myself before I said too much. Unfortunately, it wasn't soon enough.

"With who? Who might he be in *cahoots* with?"

"Um, I dunno. Kat, maybe? Or Templeton," I said, once more collecting my thoughts into some semblance of logic. "Don't you think it's just a little too convenient that we stumbled on this guy? Don't you think it's strange that this reporter just happened to be hunting the Devil when we came along?"

She rolled her eyes.

"Jack, he works for a tabloid specializing in the paranormal. I'd say it would be a lot more suspicious if he *hadn't* been investigating it."

"Besides, there's another good reason to let me tag along," came a voice from behind us. We both turned around to see Alex Davenport's handsome mug standing there. Apparently, we'd been so busy arguing, we'd not heard him walk up. "I have a press pass. Senator Leeds' staff would be wary of two strangers snooping around their office. But a reporter...well, that's just a day in the life of a senatorial campaign."

The tabloid reporter smiled at me, then turned to wink a Nikki. My fists clenched involuntarily at the prep school reject, but a quick glare from Nikki put me in my place. I knew better than to protest too much. Besides, as much as I hated to admit it, the press pass angle was actually a pretty good idea.

"Besides, Jack," he said, "we made a deal, remember?"

I cringed at the reminder. Whatever Freakshow had planned, he'd apparently shared some of it with the reporter. Since Wiley could find nothing more in Davenport's emails than the photos of Witz's murder scene, I had to assume the message had been given to him over the phone or by some other means. If I wanted to find out what that whackjob was up to, I'd have to play nice for a while longer.

"Fine," I said. "But I do the talking."

FOURTEEN

LEEDS' CAMPAIGN HEADQUARTERS WAS A BEEHIVE OF MANIC INSANITY. A maze of cubicles equipped with phone operators thanking callers for their generous donations and spewing the drivel that all politicians ooze cluttered the entire main floor of the office. Frantic volunteers rushed around in zigzag patterns, showering the floor with a trail of loose papers as they moved. The entire room seemed to buzz with a dull, subsonic roar that was almost deafening in its ordinariness.

"Welcome," said the beanpole of a man wearing a disheveled off-the-rack suit and a tasseled pair of penny loafers (complete with shiny pennies, no less). His thinning hair swayed over his bald spot as he strode over to us through the throng of tireless workers. "I'm Charles. Chuck. I mean, people call me Chuck. But I'm actually Charles Filmore. Senator Leeds' personal, um assistant."

He held out a hand for me to shake and it felt slimy with sweat to the touch. The squirrel-like man chittered away in a nervous string of sentences one could hardly call dialogue.

"How rude of me," he said, realizing how sweaty his palms were and wiping them on his pants legs before offering it to Nikki and then to Davenport. "I'm such a buffoon. But then, this really is the most pressing of times. The primary elections are just around the corner and Senator Leeds has so many engagements. I've got a million things running through my head at once. But then, that is the nature of the—"

"Mr. Filmore," I said, perhaps a bit more harshly than he deserved. Though they looked nothing alike, the senator's personal assistant reminded me a lot of Wiley—with his nervous energy and good-natured over-eagerness to help. But then, I wasn't very patient with our resident tech-head either. "I realize," I continued with a little more calm, "that this is a busy time for you. My colleagues and I were just hoping we might be able to speak with your boss about a...um, story we're working on."

"Story?" Chuck asked, before shaking his head emphatically. "No. No. No. I'm sorry. I'm so sorry. No stories at the moment. Reporters are more than welcome to attend the senator's press conference tomorrow afternoon. But he really cannot be disturbed at the moment. Too much to do. Too much. Perhaps there is something I may help you with. I'm not authorized to say too much, but if you're just looking for a few simple sound bites, I could provide some for you."

The scrawny chatterbox was starting to get on my nerves. Took him ten minutes to utter the word "No comment." I straightened up, about to let him have it when Davenport stepped around me and smiled at him.

"Chuck," he said, flashing that award winning grin of his. "Completely understand. Things must be insane right about now."

The assistant nodded, his own dumb smile spreading. "You have no idea," he said. "Just no idea."

Davenport nodded sympathetically at this, then looked around conspira-torially while loosening his tie. "Look, pal. I get it. I've worked the political beat before. I know the pressure you must be under. And working for a guy like Leeds...well, I bet he can be real demanding."

Filmore's eyes darted left and right, before giving a curt nod of affirma-tive. "You've no idea. Truth be told, he's almost a tyrant."

I glanced over at Nikki, trying to contain a grin. So, the hack of a re-porter might be useful after all. He was going to squeeze the information out of the assistant without him being the wiser. After all, a tyrant of a politician wouldn't hesitate to utilize any means at his disposal to gain a political foothold, right? He might even be inclined to unleash a dark, family secret to get it.

"Yes. Yes. A tyrant all right," Chuck was still going on. "A tyrant against the status quo, that is. A tyrant for the people. Yes. He might drive us all a little hard, but it's only because he cares so much. So much. He cares so much for the little guy. Winning this election means so much to him because he wasn't able to see all his objectives for his constituents completed this last term. So, he pushes us. But that's a good thing, right?"

The smile quickly fell from my face. Things had not exactly gone according to plan.

"Absolutely," Davenport said, nonplussed. "But I'm curious about free time. Your employer's, in particular. Surely, he's not all work and no play. What does he like to do when he's not busy with the campaign?"

"Thank you, Mr. Filmore," came a stern feminine voice to our left. We turned to see a shapely redhead in a very expensive pant suit walking over to us. To say the woman was a knockout would be like saying that waffles are tasty. The newcomer's green eyes seemed to sparkle and she hit me with a radiant smile designed for knocking the wind out of anyone who happened to be in the vicinity when it was unleashed. "I'll take over for now. Senator Leeds has been looking for you."

The nervous bureaucrat nodded his apologies to us and scampered away like an abused puppy.

"I'm Aislynn Sommers," she said, shaking each of our hands. As she shook mine, her eyes continued to linger on me as her seductive smile broadened. "Senator Leeds' campaign manager. How can I help you?"

"Actually, maybe you can," Nikki said, drawing the lovely campaign manager's attention away from me. "We're doing a story on Senator Leeds' background. His family. You know, his roots."

"Ah, intriguing idea," she said. "I'll be happy to help you. But not here. Let's go into my office."

Without waiting for a response, she turned and began walking toward the back of the main office space, where a row of doors opened into more private offices. As we followed, I nudged Nikki and nodded to Ms. Sommers.

"She's the one," I whispered. "She's the bad guy who's behind all this."

She couldn't suppress a snicker at the comment.

"I'm serious," I said, nearly bumping into a near-panicked volunteer apparently on a coffee run. "I don't know how she's involved...but I guarantee you, she's the mastermind behind all this."

"How do you figure?" Nikki hissed back at me.

"She's hot."

This time, both Nikki *and* Davenport broke out into shared restrained chuckles.

"Really?" Nikki asked, looking over at the woman leading us, no doubt, to our doom. "That's your big Sherlockian deduction, is it? *She's hot?*"

"Think about. In the time that you've known me, has not every single hot woman I've encountered been an insane vixen bent on either eating my face off or putting a bullet in my brain?"

"You know, you might just be right," she said with a sly smile. "When we first met, you thought I was hot and I've wanted to put a bullet in your brain on more than one occasion."

"Mark my words," I said, rolling my eyes as we walked into the office Ms. Sommers had ushered us into.

We each took a seat while our hostess closed the door behind us and moved around to the other side of the desk.

"Now, this way, we'll have a little peace and quiet," she said, sitting down and gracing us with another alluring smile. "So what would you like to know?"

❧◈❧

An hour later, the three us stood up from our chairs and shook the red-headed mastermind's hand with appreciative accolades. Though Aislynn Sommers had been relatively forthcoming in answering our questions, we'd learned nothing new about the mysterious senator or his familial background. At least, nothing that wasn't already available in any press packet.

Yes, Thomas Leeds hailed from a small town in rural New Jersey. His family lineage could be traced back all the way to the first settlers within the colonies. As a matter of fact, he'd even been linked to clan of witch hunters in England around the seventeenth century. But as far as Ms. Sommers was aware, there was no connection between her boss and the Leeds family who were associated with the Jersey Devil legend.

Yeah. We mentioned the Devil and she didn't even bat an eye. That's how crafty she was. The beautiful campaign manager might have had Nikki and Davenport fooled, but not me. She knew more than she was letting on and I was determined to find out what.

"I've enjoyed our talk," she said as she opened the door to her private office and shook our hands once more. She stopped in mid-shake with mine, leaned forward and whispered in my ear, "If you'd like to know more, give me a call some time." And she palmed a business card into my hand.

I stealthily pocketed the card and smiled back at her.

"I'll take you up on that offer soon," I said, before catching Nikki glaring at me. Seriously, I was a magnet for beautiful, power-hungry women whose elevators tended not to reach the top floor...the Jenglot Sister-Queen in Malaysia two years ago, Ekaterina Stolnakanova in Greece last year, and now Ms. Aislynn Sommers. I wasn't sure why my ex-girlfriend was so surprised...or irritated for that matter. She's the one who broke it off with me, after all.

As we walked out of Aislynn's office, we nearly ran headlong into the blonde, six-foot-four former linebacker who was known to the world-at-large as Senator Thomas Glen Leeds. Like everyone else in this political maelstrom, he beamed his million dollar smile at us and looked over at his manager.

"Aislynn, I've been looking for you," he said in a strong baritone voice.

"Sorry, Tommy," she said. "Just giving these reporters a little background information on you."

"Oh?" he said, scrutinizing us with a little more attention than before. "Reporters, eh? Who with?"

I smiled back at the politician and shrugged. "We're actually freelance," I said. "Name's Jack. Jack Jackson."

I offered him my hand, but the moment I mentioned my name, he let out an audible gasp and stepped back. His mouth fell open, then closed and I watched as beads of sweat began to form across his forehead.

"Tommy?" Aislynn said. "Are you all right?"

If I were a betting man, I'd swear the senator had heard my name before.

"Senator?" I asked, taking a single step forward. He countered by backing up even more.

"You need to leave," he said with wide, fearful eyes.

I glanced over at Nikki and Davenport and gave them a quick shrug. His behavior was unexpected to all of us, including his campaign manager.

"You know who I am?"

"Yes, I know exactly who you are," he said, reaching into his coat pocket and pulling out a cell phone. "You have ten seconds to leave here before I call the police."

"Tom, what on earth are you—" Aislynn Sommers began to protest, but was cut off.

"They're not who they say they are," he growled. "They'll ruin everything."

"Senator Leeds," Nikki said calmly, holding out her hands submissively. "I promise. We're only trying to discover the truth behind—"

"I know exactly why you're here," he said, tapping the screen of his phone and lifting it to his ear. "You're trying to sabotage my campaign and I won't stand for it...Hello, police? Yes, this is Senator Tom Leeds. I have three trespassers in my campaign headquarters causing trouble—"

"Now hold on a minute," I said, taking another step toward him.

"He's coming at me!" Leeds shouted into his phone. "He's attacking!"

I stopped mid-stride, looked over at my two companions, and nodded toward the front door. "We need to get out of here," I said, already moving swiftly in that direction. "Even Grigsby won't be able to pull our butts out of this one."

The senator's outburst had drawn the attention of everyone in the room. The entire throng of supporters clogged every possible route to the front exit. As the swarm of devotees moved in on all sides, I inexplicably felt something warm and wet trickle across the back of my neck. I spun around to find the source of the spray, but could see nothing. But I had no time to think about it. Leeds had finished reciting the address to the dispatcher, had stuck his phone back in his pocket, and was shouting for us to get out.

"Crap," I said. "We can't get out that way."

I could already hear the sirens of New York's finest blaring through the streets outside. They certainly weren't wasting any time coming to the aid of a major politician in their town. I spun around searching for another way out when my eyes caught the slightest glimpse of a hooded figure and a trace of silver dart behind an office door near the back of the room.

"Silver!" I shouted, suddenly running after my mystery woman with no further explanation.

"Jack?" Nikki cried, bringing up the rear. "What are you talking about?"

I threw open the door in which she'd fled and dashed inside, only to find a long hallway with about twenty other doors lining the wall. At the far end of the corridor, I spied a bright green EXIT sign. The exit door was just swinging closed. Sprinting once again, I shouted over my shoulder, "The girl from the park. The silver-haired cultist that almost did a number on Daven-port!"

I flew through the exit and into an alley between Leeds' offices and a CVS pharmacy. I whirled around, to see my mystery woman rounding the corner.

"Head back to the hotel if you can," I shouted, running after her. "I've got to follow her. Figure out what she was doing here."

"Jack!" Nikki yelled. "What about the police?"

But I ignored her. Ignored her panic. Her dilemma. There were more pressing issues to deal with at the moment. Besides, she was in no real legal danger anyway. It was me…my name…that had set the senator off. My name he'd given to the 911 operator. I'd scared him. There was honest to God fear in the man's eyes when he realized who I was. And I had a feeling that my silver-haired pixie might know why. I couldn't lose her. Not this time. Nikki would make me pay dearly later, but if I could get some answers, it would be totally worth it. At least I hoped so.

Digging my heels into the pavement, I poured on the speed, leaving Nikki and Davenport behind, and negotiated the corner she'd just run around. I immediately caught sight of her trying to blend into the noonday crowd.

No. Definitely not this time, I thought. *But let's play it smart for a change, Jack. Use the brains the good Lord gave you.*

I slowed my pace, turned up the collar of my jacket, and melted into the crowd myself. The cops were just pulling up to Leeds' office, but they never saw me. And neither did my target. I couldn't help smiling. Finally something was actually going right for me in this investigation.

The girl led me down 10th Avenue, through nine blocks of heavy foot traffic, weaving in and out of the bustling pedestrians. She'd slowed down considerably about two blocks before, most likely believing that she'd managed to give me the slip. But I'd been tracking monsters for so long now, it was almost second nature—at least when I didn't let my impulsive nature get the better of me. Sometimes, I truly could be my very worst enemy.

But not today, I thought with a grim smile. *Not today.*

She hung a right at 39th and we ambled our way west toward...I glanced over at a street sign and suddenly picked up my pace. *She's heading toward the Lincoln Tunnel,* I thought, beginning to panic. I wasn't quite sure how far she could get in the tunnel on foot, but I didn't want to take any chances. Once she made it inside, she could be lost forever and I wasn't going to let that happen. Not again.

As we approached the entrance to the tunnel, however, she hung a sharp left and meandered into an alley between two buildings that looked as if they should have been condemned a few centuries ago.

Where are you going?

Flattening myself against the corner of the building, I peered cautiously into the alley. Despite it being afternoon, the narrow space was dark, shaded by the old tenements that jutted into the sky like two giant fangs. But though the girl was no longer in sight, I could hear her footsteps from around other end of the building.

Moving into the alley, I jogged toward the opposite end and once again, peeked around the corner—only to let out an involuntary gasp.

She was gone. Disappeared.

But it made no sense. This section of the alley was a dead end. A row of large rusted-out garbage cans lined the wall to my right, their contents long gone. A broom and dustpan rested against the dirty brick wall of the building, right next to a large metal door that led into the building. The door itself had been boarded up some time ago, its planks firmly secured.

There was no place she could be hiding.

I looked up at the side of the building. There was no way she could have scaled the walls to make it to the roof. The few windows that peppered the building were still intact, none broken to allow her to scramble inside and the fire escape had oxidized into scrap metal eons ago.

That left only one alternative.

I glanced down at the wet, sticky asphalt of the alley until I found what I was looking for. A manhole cover. Just as I had expected, it had been moved and not set properly back in place. I glanced over my shoulder once nervously, but didn't see anyone lurking about in ambush. Turning back to the manhole, I grabbed the broom and used it to pry open the cover. The stench that wafted up from the hole pounded me in the face with its full necrotic force.

"Sheesh," I whispered, as I swung my legs around to find the ladder leading to the sewers below. "Why can't bad guys ever find some place beach-like and tropical to hide in?"

I lowered myself to solid ground. In the pitch black confines of the tunnel, my other senses erupted with high def precision. Every smell…every trickle of water…all heightened the rate of my thumping heart as I reached into my pockets and pulled out the Mini Maglite I keep for just such an occasion.

"Okay, Creepy Hooded Girl," I said, taking in my bearings in the crisp white light of the LED. "Come out, come out, wherever you are."

I smiled nervously as I stepped off the concrete dais and into the stream of liquid filth that made up the New York City sewer system, picked a direction, and began to walk.

FIFTEEN

I DON'T THINK IT'S ANY SECRET THAT I'M NOT A BIG FAN OF TIGHT SPACES. It's not something I'm proud of. Just a fact of life. But for some reason, in my job, I've found myself in some of the tightest squeezes on the freakin' planet—both literally and metaphorically. Case in point: getting myself wedged underneath a cramped shelf of rock inside an ancient pyramid while being chased by a pack of blood-drinking mutants. Or how about navigating a really tiny, two man mini-sub crammed with five passengers and a school of really ticked-off mermaids swimming up your wake? I won't even mention the time I got stuck in a coffin and buried in a haunted cemetery while investigating a banshee in Ireland. No, seriously...I won't mention it. Ever.

So imagine my utter disdain as I felt my way through the near pitch blackness of that New York sewer, unsure if I was even on my quarry's trail. The oval swath of brilliant illumination pouring from my flashlight cast strange, dark shadows all around me. The trickle of water kerplunked into the muck just past the range of visibility. And all the while, I felt the curved 20-foot ceiling above me closing in around me as I sloshed through the watery filth. And I won't even go into the strange sounds and phantom growls echoing in this smelly underworld.

Yeah, I'm man enough to admit, I was a little on edge during my subterranean trek. This might—I hope—explain why I jumped when my iPhone suddenly chirped from inside my pants pocket. Taking a deep breath to try to calm my nerves, I used my free hand to pull the phone out while the other cast the flashlight around the chamber for a quick 360 before I answered. I didn't bother looking at the display to see who was calling. I already knew.

"Look, I know what you're going to say," I whispered into the phone's receiver as I kept moving forward. "But, Nikki, I knew the cops were after *me*, not you. It was a calculated risk. I couldn't let the silver-haired girl get away again."

"Oooh, Dr. Jackson," cooed a soft, feminine voice that distinctly was not Nikki Jenkins. "If you're *that* into me, all you have to do is ask me to dinner."

I tried to reply, but found my vocabulary picked that exact moment to take five. I recognized the voice. It was most definitely my silver-haired Nazgul.

Sheesh, how are all these wackos getting my phone number? I should get a 900 number. I could make a fortune.

After a brief pause, I managed to catch my bearings and offered a retort. "Dinner could be arranged." I whirled around the sewer tunnel, hoping to catch some glimpse of my prey. "Why don't ya come out and we can make plans."

"I'm not sure your girlfriend would approve."

I couldn't help chuckle over that. "Well, in all fairness, after leaving her to face the police so I could chase after you, even if she had been my girlfriend, I'm pretty sure she wouldn't be now."

There was a pause on the other end. The sound of rustling and a click. Then more silence.

"Hello?" I asked. "Are you still…"

"I'm still here," she said. "Just thinking."

"About?"

I was hoping her interest in me was genuine. Not because I found the nutjob attractive, but simply because it might be the best way to actually learn something about her.

"About a lot of things really," she replied, uncharacteristically solemn. Every time I had spoken to her in the past, she'd seemed to be so impish, taking delight in our games of cat and mouse. Now, she seemed reflective. Mournful, even. "About whether your reputation is as deserved as I had originally been told. About whether you know what you're doing. And most importantly, wondering if you have any idea of the danger you're in at this very moment."

Yeah. Definitely unsettling.

"Well, I don't believe the old stories of alligators in the sewers, sweetheart," I quipped. "I have a friend at the FBI who already checked it out."

"Dr. Jackson, have you figured out exactly what you're hunting yet?" She'd completely ignored my attempt at humor.

"Um, large winged mammal? Looks like a demon on steroids? Something similar to a Jersey Devil, maybe?"

"Very good." Her tone was unnervingly neutral. "And what do you really know about the Jersey Devil, Jack? What are they capable of? What are their habits? Where did they come from?"

The use of my nickname was intentional. She was attempting to ingratiate herself into my life. Become more familiar with me. Which, at this point, was good. The more personal we were, the more information I might able to glean from her.

"Honestly?" I said. "Not much. I have some people working on digging up research on it now."

"Well, let me ask you this then—it might help you. Might even save your life. What do you know about a place known as the Gateway to Hell?"

"Gateway to...? What's this all about?" Was this nutjob suggesting that the cryptid called the Jersey Devil was an actual demon? That it was some supernatural force that had escaped into our world? "Look, I'm in no mood to play games. Just tell me what you're driving at."

"That would take all the fun out of it," she said coyly, her previous delight in the *Game*, once more evident in her voice. "But therein lies all your answers. The origin of it all, actually. However, because you truly are in very immediate danger, I will give you two hints."

I rolled my eyes at this and growled. "Look lady, I'm standing knee-deep in the waste product of about a million New Yorkers. I'm really in no mood—"

"First of all," she said, ignoring my protests. "The Gateway to Hell is a very real place in the Czech Republic. It is a deep hole in the ground on which an ancient castle was built. The creatures you seek come from that very place. It is where they feel most at home."

"Okay?"

"But when the creatures were, um, removed, they sought similar habitats wherever they settled. They choose such places to make their nests. The Pine Barrens in New Jersey have plenty of caverns and deep boroughs, which is why it has been the perfect habitat for them."

"I'm still not following," I said, turning around and walking back toward the manhole in which I'd first entered the sewers. The fact was, I was lying to her. I was starting to understand exactly what she was getting at. But I'd discovered a long time ago that playing dumb often gets a competent investigator the best information.

"My God. He said you could be dense, but I never imagined—" She caught herself, but it was too late. She'd already revealed something she wasn't supposed to. Apparently, she had an associate who knew me. Maybe even personally. "Dr. Jackson, you happen to be tromping through the Manhattan equivalent of a huge cavern system. So tell me...if you were one of these creatures, out of your element in strange new land, where would you be more likely to set up shop?"

Yeah. It was exactly what I'd expected her to say. I found my legs moving quite a bit faster toward the exit, though not yet at a full run.

"But you came down here too," I said, my breathing a little more labored from exertion. Full blown panic was now building up inside me. On further reflection, those phantom growls I'd heard earlier might not have been as "phantom" as I'd originally thought. "If I'm in such great danger, then so are you. Why aren't you worried?"

There was another pause before she answered. "That brings me to the second hint actually," she said. Once again, her voice was solemn. And if I didn't know better, I'd say there was a touch of worry in there somewhere too. "That is *some* aftershave you're wearing, Jack. Where'd you get it?"

Aftershave? I tried to smell myself, but the filth and stink surrounding me prevented me from identifying what she talking about. But then, I didn't need to smell it. I already had. So had Grigsby. He'd commented on it during my interrogation at the Central Park Precinct.

...the heck is going on?

"The scent," I said. "What is it? Where did it come from?"

"The first time, I gave it to you—in Central Park, when I tackled you," she said seriously. "I didn't know who you were at the time. I thought you a threat to our cause. Of course, I never intended real harm to you. Just wanted to scare you and that reporter off. But that little aerial acrobatics stunt over the city two nights ago almost cost you dearly, didn't it?"

The implications were finally becoming clear. *Where is that blasted manhole?* I thought, now jogging briskly. *Why can't I find it?*

Those growls had returned. And they were louder than before. More fierce. Primal. Angry.

"But I took a shower since then," I pleaded into the phone. "Whatever you used to scent me should be gone now."

"And you'd be right, except for one thing—"

A splash of water from behind me. Something was coming my way. Fast. The growls were shaping into high-pitched shrieks.

"Jack, they're getting closer," she said, worry tingeing her voice. "You've got to find a way out now!"

"I'm trying, I'm trying!" I shouted, now at a full sprint. It was difficult keeping the phone to my mouth to talk as I sloshed through the water, but I still needed answers. "What's the 'one thing'? What am I missing? How did I get the scent on me again?"

"You got it when you were in Leeds' campaign headquarters," she said. "Whoever's behind all this sprayed you with the stuff because they knew you were getting too close."

The memory of something wet spraying against my back rushed back to me. I'd been surrounded by Leeds' people. The cops were on their way. Then the wetness. I'd looked around, but hadn't seen who'd sprayed me. Then, I'd spotted Silver clear on the other side of the room and had simply forgotten about it.

A screech exploded from somewhere up ahead of me. That's when I realized something Silver had been saying all along. She'd been referring to the Jersey Devil in the plural. *They.* Plural. *Them.* Plural. *They're getting closer.* Plural again.

"Ah, crap," I said. "Look, it's been fun, but I gotta go." I hit the *END* button on the phone and stuffed it back in my pocket. "Why couldn't it have been alligators?"

⇜⇝

"Crap, crap, crap!" I hissed as my legs sloshed through the sewer water. I wasn't sure how many creatures were now stalking me, but there were at least three of them and they were closing in fast. I'd managed to skirt past the one in front of me by veering left along a narrow artery. More than likely, it would lead me farther away from the manhole I'd originally entered, but I had no choice. I heard the beast's huffing and strange clicking sounds mere yards ahead of me in the darkness. Providence had provided me with the artery, so I took it without question.

Why on earth did I leave my gun back at the hotel?

Of course, I knew why. Going to see a senatorial candidate while packing a Glock-17 wouldn't have been the brightest thing I'd ever done…and *that's* saying something. Besides, how on earth could I have possibly known I would have been stupid enough to get sprayed by some weird scent that attracted the Jersey Devil to me like Sylvester to Tweety?

The splashes, howls, and clicks were getting louder behind me. Growing closer, though even with my Maglite I was unable to see anything more than dark silhouettes moving against the black backdrop of the sewer tunnels. Oh, and glowing red eyes. That was one thing the legends hadn't lied about. Those eyes were enough to stop a freight train with their glare.

"I mean come on!" I shouted out loud. "Who sprays people with Devil juice?"

Apparently, I was fixated on the *who* and the *why* in order to avoid dealing with the "*What the heck am I going to do?*" Which was reasonable, because let's face it, unless I managed to find an outlet, I was pretty much screwed. I'd seen the body of the Jersey Devil's last victim...or rather, the pieces that were left. Things were not exactly looking peachy for me at the moment.

A snarl suddenly erupted behind me and I whirled around to see a dark mass scrambling along the curved ceiling of the sewer toward me. I kid you not...it was literally crawling upside down along the vaulted ceiling until it kicked off with its feet, spread its leathering wings, and glided toward me. Without thinking, I ducked into the water and submerged. I felt the monster impact the water just ahead of me; its arms, legs, and wings thrashing against the filthy liquid.

Weapon. I thought, turning the flashlight off and stuffing it into my pocket. Remaining submerged, my hands blindly felt their way along the sewer floor. *Gotta find a weapon.* My hands patted frantically along the slimy bottom, but if there was anything useful to be found, I honestly didn't want to think about it. Giving up the search and resigning myself to whatever awaited me, I burst from the water, eyes clenched tight, screaming with panicked rage. My arms swung wildly, batting at the air like a fourth grader in a playground brawl. Only, there was nothing there to strike.

Opening one eye, I peered into the gloom. I couldn't see anything, but then, that didn't surprise me since it was pitch black. My instincts screamed for me to turn on the flashlight once more, but having no clue as to the night vision capabilities of the JDs, I thought it best to remain cloaked in darkness for now. After all, if I couldn't see *them*, there was more than a good chance they couldn't see me.

Right?

I stood stock still, focusing my ears for the telltale sounds of the cryptids that had been stalking me. After five heartbeats of silence, I let out my breath and slowly began blindly feeling my way along the tunnel wall. Eventually, I'd have to come to a ladder or an emergency exit. City maintenance needed access to the sewers to do their job and that meant they needed multiple entry and exit points. All I had to do was avoid the creatures for a little while longer and I'd be home free.

I've no idea how long I edged along the curved surface of the wall, letting my hands feel their way along the algae-coated concrete for doors, ladder rungs, or anything else that might point the way to my escape. And still, I heard no more growls, hoots, or even more disturbing, those strange clicking sounds the creatures had been making. It was as if the monsters so keen on tearing me to shreds just moments before, had simply lost all interest in me.

But that makes no sense, I thought, nearly slipping on a particularly slimy stretch of concrete. The water was becoming shallower, now only as high as my shins. *Why would they just give up on me like that? The thing nearly had me. It landed in the water next to me. All it had to do was reach out and...*

I suddenly stopped. There, just two and a half feet ahead of me, stood a very large, hulking mass of shadow. Two searching red eyes blinked as it huffed the air with unseen nostrils.

Click. Click. Clickety-click.

I tensed, chiding myself for getting my hopes up too soon.

Okay. Maybe they haven't given up.

I held my breath. Actually, the crimson glow of the creature's eyes gave me a certain amount of hope, if you can believe it. I realize that most movies or comic books like using red eyes for fictional monsters. The color just tends to give it a more sinister feel. But biologically speaking, the reflection of red against an animal's eyes typically indicated something with extremely poor night vision. Green or amber-green, normally signified excellent nocturnal sight. If my theory held true, the Jersey Devil was just as blind in the pitch black as I was.

More clicks and snorts came from the beast as its red eyes looked from left to right.

Unless it has some other mode of sensory input, I thought, my mind turning again to the chitinous exoskeletons of the jenglot...capable of literally seeing the world around them from sensors on their hide. I shuddered at the memory. *Swell. Always the optimist, Jackson.*

The creature sniffed the air a few more times before it lumbered slowly in my direction. I tried to make out details, but against the darkness, there was very little to see. It was definitely large—about seven feet tall—as well as broad and muscular. True to Johnny's description, its torso was shaped something like a large ape's, with round, sloping shoulders. I could just barely make out a trace of its leathery wings folded behind its back and long, slanting horns rolling from the top of its head. But as for specific features, I was completely blind.

Then again, I didn't have a whole lot of time to rationally think about what I was seeing, because it soon loomed right in front of me. It's long muzzle snorting more air, before it turned to look down directly at me.

Ah crap. Instinctively, my hands balled into fists as I waited for the inevitable to come. This was it. The thing was about to attack and the only recourse I'd have would be to fight it hand to hand. *Yeah. I'm so boned.*

It leaned in closer, its snout nuzzling my face, inquisitively taking in shallow drafts of my scent.

Sniff. Sniff. Snort.

Up one side of my neck and face and down the other, the thing practically inhaled me. Beads of sweat dripped past my forehead, burning their way into my eyes. Suddenly, I became aware that I'd been holding my breath since first realizing it was there. I felt lightheaded. Black splotches flared into my vision. I couldn't help it. I had to breathe, even if it gave my location away.

Then again, it had to know I was there. Even blind, the Jersey Devil was sniffing me like a blood hound over an Oscar Meyer wiener. There was no way it didn't know I was standing in front of it. And yet, it wasn't tearing me to shreds…wasn't ripping my arms out of their sockets like a ticked off Wookie.

Slowly, I let my used-up air slip slowly past my lips. The creature reeled back from my sudden release, but didn't appear startled. Or, more importantly, aggressive. After a few seconds, it pulled in for a better "look," gave me another pass of sniffs, then abruptly turned and began plodding down the tunnel again, completely ignoring my presence.

What the…? Those things were all over me just a little while ago, ready to take my head off, I thought as I began padding in the opposite direction from the creature. *That one seemed as docile as my granny's twelve-year-old cat. So what changed?*

A little more confident than before, I withdrew my Maglite and flicked it on. There was no doubt that those creatures—however many were hiding down there in the sewers—could take me out any time they chose, so a little light to illuminate the way wasn't going to hurt.

Okay. What just happened? What changed? I asked silently as I continued moving along the winding tunnel system. *Was it them? Did something happen to them? No. Not them. Me.*

Then, I understood. I'd been sprayed by some concoction that seemed to drive those creatures insane with rage. When I plunged into the water, it must have either washed the scent away or masked it completely with the...um, well, with whatever other scents one could find in a sewer. So that would mean...

"...our victims were definitely not random," I whispered into the darkness. "They were targeted."

Of course, that begged the question of who—which really didn't seem to be a huge mystery to me at moment. The two most likely candidates were Silver herself, or a man who had harbored familial connections to the creatures for centuries. *Our good Senator Thomas Leeds.*

I was brainstorming a way to prove my insane theory when I spotted it. A ladder bolted along the wall and leading up into the streets above. I smiled grimly and began climbing, still plotting my devious plan to catch the killer as I pushed the manhole cover aside and pulled myself out into the beautiful light of day.

SIXTEEN

"TELL ME AGAIN WHY I'M NOT TAKING YOU TO THE PRECINCT FOR booking?" asked Detective Sergeant Michael Grigsby as he clutched the steering wheel of his Impala and crept slowly through the congested blob of New York City traffic. "Senator Leeds is a demanding you be placed under arrest for your little stunt and you not only talk me out of carrying out the warrant, but convinced me to take you back to his headquarters in the process? I must be freakin' out of my mind."

I grinned back at him and sunk into my seat with a sigh. After escaping the sewers, I'd made my way to the hotel where my team, dad, and a royally pissed off Nikki were nervously awaiting my return. Before I could tell them anything about my ordeal in the sewer, they'd demanded I take a shower. Turns out, I needed three of them to get the filth off me and even after that, my dad hadn't been satisfied. To add injury to insult, he dug into his toiletry bag and offered me a bottle of, in my opinion, the vilest substance on the planet, his Aqua Velva. Even worse, the glass bottle had to be at least twenty years old. I'd taken it, reluctantly, but refused to actually apply any of it on me. If they didn't like my smell after I'd scrubbed my body raw, they'd just have to get over it.

I'd done what I could to patch things up with Nikki for what I'd done, but sometimes there's just nothing you can say that can make up for leaving your ex to fend for herself when a hundred police cars show up to arrest you. And she was more than just my "ex." She was my teammate. And, only by grace above, she was still my friend. At that moment, I wasn't so sure that was still the case. Of course, I'd been right...they hadn't been after her. She and Davenport had made it back to the hotel unmolested. But the pain of my abandoning her to an unknown fate was far too fresh for her to forgive at the moment. I could only pray that with time, she would eventually understand.

After doing what I could to mend fences, I filled everyone in on what I'd discovered since chasing Silver from Leeds' office and laid out my plan of attack to catch the senator red-handed. However Tom Leeds was controlling the creatures, I figured it had to do with the scent that had been sprayed on me. Which meant that whatever the stuff was, chances were good it would be at his campaign HQ. The real problem was getting back into the office to find it.

Enter the good detective.

"Look, I know this is risky," I said. "And I appreciate you taking a chance on me like this. But I really do believe it's our best bet to get the answers to your murders."

He glanced sideways at me, lit a cigarette and drew in a lungful of smoke. "What I don't get is how exactly a United States senator ties into this monster...this Jersey Devil thing." He exhaled and I watched as the plume was sucked through a slit in the driver's side window. "I mean, the guy's a mega-player in Washington, for crying out loud. How does he even *know* about this creature?"

I shrugged. "If my hunch is right, the relationship with the Jersey Devil has been in his family since the legend first started being whispered. It's been part of his life a whole lot longer than politics. My question is: What is he up to?" I sat up in the seat and looked over at Grigsby. "Besides the last victim, Schildiner, you weren't able to show any connection between others and Leeds?"

The detective shook his head. "Even Schildiner's connection doesn't feel right. Sure, he was one of Leeds' competitors, but he was a small fish. From what I've uncovered in my investigation, he didn't stand a chance of winning the election. So there's really no apparent motive for Leeds to sic these things on him.

"As for the others? We're still working on their background, but so far, there's no connection with any of them."

I shook my head. "There's got to be. We just have to dig deeper. I'm telling you...these deaths weren't random."

The Impala pulled up to the curb just outside the campaign headquarters, effectively ending our conversation. As Grigsby put the car in park, I looked out the window and drew a breath. This was either going to go marvelously or I'd be spending the next ten to fifteen in a Federal prison for threatening a member of Congress.

Exhaling, I held out my arms and nodded. "Okay. Let's do this."

It was the detective's turn to grin. He snapped a pair of handcuffs around my wrists and tightened them until they bit into my skin. His smile broadened.

"Hey, you don't have to take so much pleasure in this," I said.

"No, I do. I really, really do," he chuckled as he stepped out of the car, walked around to the passenger side, and pulled me out. His face had already shape-shifted back to his typical Joe Friday impersonation by the time we reached the headquarter doors.

The moment we walked into the large, open office space, a piercing cry of dismay erupted from the other end of the room and I saw the senator's weasely personal assistant, Chuck Filmore, making his way frantically over to us.

"No, no, no!" he shouted, his arms waving wildly. "What's *he* doing here? He can't be here. Senator Leeds would have my hide if he knew I let you bring that...that...hooligan in here."

"Hooligan?" I said, looking over at Grigsby. "Hooligan? Who says hooligan anymore?"

"Shut up," the detective said before turning his attention to the assistant. "I'm here on official police business. As you can see, we have the suspect in custody and before I book him, I wanted the three of us—i.e. me, him, and your boss—to have a little powwow to find out exactly what happened this morning."

The skinny bureaucrat in the cheap suit and ludicrous comb-over vehemently shook his head before the reply even left his lips. "Impossible. Simply impossible. The senator wants this man brought up on assault charges immediately. Any questions required by my employer can be handled through his staff of attorneys. Anything more is simply quite imposs—"

"It's okay, Mr. Filmore," came the silky voice of Aislynn Sommers, Leeds' campaign manager. We turned to see the leggy redhead sauntering casually over to us from her private office. "As a matter of fact, I was hoping to speak with Dr. Jackson again." She looked at me and smiled. I was surprised when I realized the smile actually met her eyes. She was being sincere. She really did want to speak with me and I sensed her motives weren't of the maniacal vixen-wanting-to-sink-her-talons-into-me kind of way either. For the life of me, I couldn't fathom why. I'd figured that after her boss had flipped out, I would be the last person on earth she'd ever want to see, considering how much I could really throw a monkey-wrench into the senator's chances of getting re-elected.

Then again, I thought, *maybe that's my answer.*

"Ms. Sommers, I'm sorry, but I simply cannot allow this," Filmore said, his face twisted in a vicious scowl. "Senator Leeds gave me specific instructions to—"

"And the senator isn't here now, is he?" she said, folding her arms and looking down at the sniveling assistant. "Now get back to whatever it is you do around here and let the grown-ups talk."

The little geek's face reddened to about the same shade as the beautiful campaign manager's hair, but he said nothing as he scampered off to his desk on the far side of the room. I watched as he picked up the phone, punched in a few numbers, and started speaking quietly into the receiver.

"My apologies, Detective..."

"Grigsby. Detective Sergeant Mike Grigsby." He let out a nervous cough, then spoke once more. "But my friends call me Mike, Ms. Sommers."

I threw the detective a quick double-take at that. The big balooga was actually flirting with the broad. Even more mind-boggling to me...his flirting, apparently, was not completely unappreciated. Her smile broadened at his words. "And my friends call me Aislynn," she said, absently tucking a strand of ginger hair behind one ear. I watched as her unnatural green eyes sized the police officer up, then twinkled with delight when she beckoned for us to follow her back to the same office I'd entered earlier that day.

We took our proffered seats and watched in silent appreciation as our host walked around to the other side of her desk and sat down. After several seconds of silence, she nodded at me and spoke. "Are those cuffs really necessary, Mike? I doubt Dr. Jackson is going to attack anyone with you in the room. And he doesn't strike me as the sort who will try to run either."

Her self-confidence and always-in-control demeanor ushered back the old nagging feeling I'd had when I'd first encountered the red-headed *femme fatale*.

She's the one. She's got to be in cahoots with the senator on this, I thought. *She's just too smooth. Too sexy. Too...*

I let the thoughts drift away. Yeah, clearly, I do have some major trust issues with women. Then again, as I've already mentioned, I did have quite the history with quite a few of them either trying to have me for dinner—in the bad way—or wanting to put a bullet in my kneecaps. I decided at that moment that I was going to keep a very close eye on this one. If she tried to spray me with any Devil juice, she'd have another thing coming.

"If it's all the same to you," Grigsby said, looking over at me with a mischievous grin. "I'll keep the suspect on a short leash for the moment. I prefer him this way."

She laughed cheerfully at this, then nodded. "So, how can I help you, Mike? I'm sure you didn't come all this way with your, um, prisoner just to get a positive identification from my employer."

Grigsby laughed. "You caught me," he said. "No, I guess I was just curious about a few things here. Jackson here claims he didn't do anything. Claims the senator acted completely irrational the moment he met him. Now, criminal-types always say they're innocent, but from what I've been able to gather, my suspect here is some type of scientist. An academic. Not exactly the sort that goes around assaulting politicians. I'm just trying to piece together exactly what happened before I ruin a man's life by charging him for assaulting a United States senator."

She eyed the detective for several seconds, then glanced over at me. Her amused smile never leaving her face.

"And the fact that you two have been investigating those horrific gargoyle killings together have nothing to do with it, I suppose?" she finally said with a chuckle.

Grigsby and I glanced at each other with widened eyes. I felt my heart clawing its way to my throat as my mind played through all the possible scenarios involved in our blown cover story.

"Er, how did you know we were working together?" I asked after several awkward seconds of silence.

She laughed at this as she opened her desk drawer, pulled out a pack of Camels, and popped one in her mouth. Holding out the pack for either one of us, she put it back in the drawer when we both declined, and lit her cigarette. After a long pull of smoke, she eyed me with a mischievous smile.

"Wasn't too hard to put together, Dr. Jackson," she said as a stream of smoke snaked its way through her nostrils and into the air. I couldn't help but wonder if this was what Smaug the dragon might have looked like when it was about to gobble up poor Bilbo Baggins. "Your little reporter act was pretty easy to see through...especially when you started focusing on Tommy's, um, less than gleaming family history. I've been following the news myself. I've heard about the killings. Heard the rumors about a winged creature skimming the rooftops at night. And I heard about your little paragliding operation the other day. They had your picture on the news and everything."

Closing my eyes, I silently shook my head at this. *My photo. On TV. That definitely does not bode well for my future employment opportunities.*

Ignoring my obvious discomfort, she snubbed the cigarette out in her ashtray and returned them both to her desk drawer. "I've been trying to quit," she said, indicating the cigarette butt in her drawer. "But after a day like today...who can blame me."

"You still haven't explained how you knew we were working together," Grigsby prodded.

"Simple enough," she smiled. "After the little scene my boss made over your partner there, I did some digging. I looked into his recent arrest and learned the name of the detective that released him."

"And when we came into your office together, the coincidence was a little too much to believe," I said, feeling like a royal idiot for not considering the possibility the detective and I would be linked. "Just swell."

"It's okay," she said. "Seriously. I'm glad you came back. As I mentioned earlier, I was hoping you would."

I cocked my head. "Why? To play spin doctor for your psycho senator?"

"Jack!" Grigsby scolded before turning his attention to Aislynn. "I apologize for that. From what I can tell in the short time I've known him, his mouth is often bigger than his brains."

"It's quite all right. I can truly sympathize with him." She looked at me and nodded her understanding. "I'm not here to play 'spin doctor' as you put it...but I am here to tell you what I know. And maybe to help you understand why Tommy reacted the way he did when he saw you."

"Okay," I said. "I'm all ears."

"I'd say you're all mouth if you ask me," Grigsby grinned.

I rolled my eyes at him and nodded to Aislynn. "Don't mind him. Go ahead. Share."

She leaned back in her chair and pulled her hair into a tight ponytail, slipped on a scrunchy, then leaned forward and looked us both in the eyes. "All right. After you ran out and after the police took his statement, I pulled Tommy into my office to have a little chat about everything. He was truly freaked. Of you. He told me about his family's history...the legend of the Jersey Devil and how it was all true. His family really were involved in the legend, though he wouldn't share with me how."

"So, he was afraid I was going to ruin his chances of getting elected by outing him, so he concocted that false police report," I said, a satisfied grin spreading across my face.

But the campaign manager shook her head. "Actually, that wasn't it at all. He called you a thief. Or rather, the company you work for. Something about how evil the group was and how they wanted to turn anything unusual into 'freakin' weapons.'" She paused for moment before looking me dead in the eyes. "Does that make any sense to you?"

I didn't answer. The words couldn't get past the lump in my throat.

"Anyway, he went on to say that you were the one who stole 'it.' He wouldn't elaborate on what 'it' was exactly, but did say that it was probably your fault those people were dead."

I pondered her words, absorbing them into my psyche. Letting their meaning wash over me as I ran the myriad of possibilities through my mind. I knew for a fact that I had nothing to do with the devil attacks, but what about ENIGMA? Ever since the ordeal in Greece last year—after hearing the things that the leader of an eco-terrorist group called ARC had told me about the agency I worked for—I'd been suspicious of whether they'd truly changed. I'd been appointed to the agency by Senator Stromwell for the very purpose of reigning in ENIGMA's black-ops directive of catching cryptids and developing military applications for them. But ever since Anton

Polk had taken over the agency, things had been awfully squirrelly around the office.

The fact that I'd been refused travel to Australia to protect the bunyips, for instance. That just reeked of something shady within the agency. Could ENIGMA have been protecting Artie Blaisemore and his crew? And could Leeds be right in assuming we had something to do with the Jersey Devil attacks? As I thought about it, I found it even more suspicious that not only Polk, but Stromwell himself had tried to stop my personal investigation.

In a way, the senator's paranoid measures to remove me from his office made perfect sense. And Leeds could possibly be in a position on Capitol Hill to know a little something about those I work for.

My mind reeled at all the implications.

"Dr. Jackson?" I heard Aislynn say, interrupting my train of thought. "Are you all right?"

Suddenly, I found myself needing a smoke in the worst way. The situation I was now finding myself in might not be a matter of life or death, but it was life-changing nonetheless.

"Um, yeah..." I said absently, before pulling myself together, taking a deep breath, and turning my attention back to our host. "So, the question is, if he's familiar with my agency—which is classified Top Secret, by the way—and he thinks that I'm responsible for the Jersey Devil murders, why not try to keep me here while someone else secretly calls the police? Why try to scare me away?"

The campaign manager shrugged. "Probably because of how it would look. Let's face it...Tommy's a shoe-in to win this election. It's only a formality. But if people get wind of any connection he might have with a mythological creature buzzing the city rooftops and tearing innocent civilians to shreds...well, you can imagine what that might do to the election," she said. "And even if he's not responsible for the deaths—"

"So you say," I added.

"Even if he's not responsible," she repeated, completely unfazed by my accusation, "it just wouldn't look good for people to get a whiff of his family connection, you know? So, he felt it best to have you removed and let the cops deal with you away from his headquarters. Quite frankly, he did exactly what New Yorkers are famous for...he ignored you and hoped the cops would deal with you in their own way."

"Aislynn, since we're being so honest with each other, there's something I'm obligated to ask," Grigsby finally spoke up. "I hate to, but it's got to be done."

"That's fine," she responded. "Ask away."

The detective loosened his tie and sat forward on the chair. "What was Senator Leeds' relationship like with Max Schildiner?"

"The latest mauling? I can certainly see why you might need to ask. No need to apologize." She paused for several seconds, obviously contemplating her answer very carefully before responding. "Actually, besides him being one of Tommy's opponents in this election, their relationship was rather cordial. Ideologically, they had very similar views about policy. He'd never say it, but I always had the feeling that if Tommy had to lose to anyone, he'd secretly hope it was Max."

Grigsby scribbled a few notes on his tiny reporter's pad, then looked back up at her. "And you can recall no incidents recently...anything at all that might have strained their relationship?"

Aislynn Sommers bit her lower lip as she thought about the question. "No. Nothing that I can..." She paused.

"Yes? Did you think of something?"

"No, not really," she said, but her voice didn't sound as confident. "It's just that there was something weird that happened a few weeks ago...after a townhall meeting we had in the Village. I saw the two of them arguing about something in the parking lot, but by the time it was over, the two were laughing and even shared a drink together.

"As a matter of fact, Tommy felt so bad about it, he'd sent Mr. Filmore to Max's office with a fruit basket and four box seat tickets to the next Yankees game."

More jotting in the notebook, then, "Did he happen to tell you what they were arguing about?"

She smiled once again, her confidence obviously returning. "As a matter of fact, he did. And it was silly. Max made a joke about stealing me for his own campaign. It was a sore spot for Tommy because we'd just had an argument earlier in the day about strategy and he knew I was unhappy with him. Thought there might be a chance he could actually hire me out from under him." She let out a little laugh at that. "As if Schildiner could actually afford me."

"And that's it?" Grigsby asked. "That was the entire argument?"

"Yes. Like I said, it was nothing. They went back to being very friendly later that night when we all hit a local tavern we frequent. Laughing. Cutting-up. No hard feelings at all."

Her story sounded pretty reasonable to me. If she was telling the truth, there really didn't seem to be any reason for Leeds to sic his own personal gargoyle on the would-be politician. From the look Detective Grigsby gave me, I could tell he agreed with me.

"Well, Aislynn, I won't take any more of your time," he said. "You understand from your own eyewitness testimony, I can't really charge Dr. Jackson with anything, right?"

"Oh, absolutely. I've already discussed it with Tommy, actually. He's agreed to drop the charges...which is another reason I knew you two were here for something other than what you claimed. If it was official, you would have known there were no more charges to file. It's why I told you that you could remove the handcuffs."

"Speaking of..." I said, holding out my arms and grinning at the burly detective.

With a mock scowl, he unlocked the handcuffs and pocketed them. We both stood from our chairs and made our way to the door. As my hand reached out to grab the handle, a sudden thought struck me and I turned to face our hostess once more.

"Ms. Sommers, I was wondering," I said. "Would it be possible to perform hand swabs on all your workers here?"

"Jackson!" Grigsby growled, his face flushing.

"It's okay, Mike," she said with a bright smile. "Like you said...more mouth than sense." She looked over at me. "And why would you need swabs of our volunteers, Dr. Jackson?"

I glanced at the detective, then at her while shoving my hands deep into my pockets. This was going to be tricky. How much could I share with her? On the one hand, if she really was behind the killings, then she'd already know everything I was going to say to begin with...so what could it really hurt? Then again, if by some microscopic chance, the red-headed hottie was innocent in the entire affair, she might just agree once she heard how important it was. I decided to play it straight.

"Look, it's about the mechanism for how the creatures are choosing their targets," I said.

"Creatures? As in, more than one?"

"Yeah, I've found evidence that there are more than one of them. What's more, I think they're being manipulated. Someone has concocted some sort of chemical that drives them batty—no pun intended." I smirked at the unintentional wordplay and continued. "The chemical emits an odor that sends them into a frenzy and they tear whoever's wearing the scent apart. I know. Someone sprayed the chemical on me earlier today when I was here. I was attacked."

Aislynn's eyes widened.

"But how?" she asked. "What kind of chemical? I was with you the entire time. I never saw anyone spray you with anything."

"It was during the chaos. While Senator Leeds was calling the police. We have a sample of the stuff and it's being analyzed right now. But whoever is behind this is obviously inside your headquarters and I'm guessing there might be traces on them. A swabbing might pick it up and then we'd be able to identify a viable suspect much easier. No muss. No fuss."

She leaned back in her chair once more and looked casually up at me as she tucked a strand of hair behind her ear again.

Could that be a nervous tic? A possible tell?

"That would be careless, wouldn't you say?" she said, her tone serious. "If the person who's doing this is smart enough to come up with this supposed solution that causes these creatures to attack, would they really be so careless to get any on themselves? What would be to stop the creatures from attacking him?"

"Or her," I added with a wry grin.

"Or her," she conceded with a nod. "But my answer has to be no. Not without a court order. I don't want to be uncooperative. If one of our staff *is* behind these killings, I want to know about it. But I can't risk the rumors that would start flying if we gathered everyone together for you to start collecting evidence off them. How would that look? Then, there's the whole privacy issue and probable cause. No, I'm sorry. I just can't allow it."

"But—"

"We understand perfectly, Aislynn," Grigsby interrupted. "No need getting your staff all worked up over a theory."

"But—"

"Jackson, she said no. Now that's the end of it."

I sighed, turned the knob, and opened the door. But before stepping out into the main office floor, I turned once more to Ms. Sommers.

"One more question, if I can?"

"Certainly," she said, genuinely amused.

"Have you ever seen a girl around here, a volunteer maybe, with silver-looking hair?"

She tilted her head to one side and nodded. "Mia has hair like that. The only person I've ever met with that hair color."

"Mia?"

"Yeah," she said. "She's in here all the time. She's Tommy's sister."

SEVENTEEN

"SHE'S HIS FREAKIN' SISTER?" RANDY ASKED, LEANING BACK IN HIS CHAIR.

Once Grigsby dropped me off, I'd collected the team—my dad and Davenport included—and had sequestered ourselves in the hotel's main conference room for a debriefing. I figured we were long overdue for what I call a "spitball session"; a ritual I liked to employ to get all the facts we'd gathered during an investigation into some semblance of order. After my meeting with Aislynn Sommers, I'd suddenly realized that things were swiftly slipping through my fingers and if I didn't get a handle on all we'd learned soon, I wasn't going to have the slightest clue which end of a Jersey Devil was up.

"That's what Aislynn said," I nodded, scribbling the name MIA on a whiteboard and then writing the words THOMAS LEEDS' SISTER? next to that. "Why would she lie about something like that?"

Randy shrugged. "Have no idea. Just doesn't seem likely given that your silver-haired goth chick is a creepy, knife-wielding witch."

"Randall Cunningham!" Nikki's stern voice echoed through the room. She was still not talking to me, so I found some comfort in the knowledge that her vocal cords were indeed still working. "Watch the stereotypes."

"Nik, come on!" My friend leaned forward and counted off his fingers in protest. "One. She dresses in a black hood and cloak. Two, she's got silver hair for crying out loud! *Silver* hair! And three, she's gotta be knee deep in some type of devil worship or something—otherwise, why go all sacrificial-altar on the reporter geek over there?" He nodded at Davenport, who looked as if he was about to swallow a horned-toad at the very memory of his ordeal in Central Park. "If she's not a witch, then what the heck is she?"

Nikki shook her head, got up from her chair, and walked over to the coffee maker. "I don't know," she said, pouring herself a steaming cup. "But neither do you. To call her a witch...it just seems so, I don't know...immature, even for you."

"Guys!" I said, tapping the board with the marker. "Let's focus. At this point, the only thing that matters is that we now know she's connected to both the cryptids *and* Senator Leeds. That's a major score in this investigation in my book."

"Obadiah." My dad sat across from me; his stern face staring at me like a granite statue. He'd never been one for silly games or triviality and I could tell by his cold expression he was about to lose his patience. "I think it's time we bring this little powwow to a more productive, and organized, line of inquiry."

"Such as?"

"Well, I'm looking at your little board there," he said, standing and moving to the whiteboard. He took the eraser resting in its cradle and wiped the board down. "Well, any time I need to wrap my head around a problem, I usually try to start at the beginning."

Without waiting for a response, he scribbled the word VICTIMS on the upper right-hand corner. Then,he handed me the marker and returned to his seat without another word.

"Yeah, that makes sense," Landers piped in, throwing me an amused grin. He no doubt loved seeing discomfort he was causing in my life. "It doesn't do much good looking at our suspects until we can figure out what connection our victims might have with them."

"Okay, let's talk about our victims then," I conceded, glaring at the ENIGMA agent before turning my attention to the tabloid reporter.

"Davenport, you were supposed to be doing some research in that arena. Find anything useful?"

He cleared his throat as he leaned forward in his chair, opened a manila folder, and scanned a few sheets of notebook paper. "Well, the first victim you already know about. You were investigating his murder scene in Central Park when we met."

"Humor me," I said. "At the time, the only thing I knew was what Johnny told me...and he'd been given the spin-doctored version of the facts from the mayor's office, I'm sure. Besides, it won't hurt to refresh my memory."

"All right. Well, like I said, our first victim was the one killed in Central Park. The guy's name was Ted Enders." The reporter waited as I scribbled the name, along with the location of his attack. "Basically, your every day average homeless dude. An Army veteran, serving in the first Gulf war; he fell on hard times in the early part of the decade. Got addicted to pain meds and eventually wound up on the streets. A few misdemeanor convictions for intoxication and public indecency. No known political connections. Nothing of real significance on this guy."

"Sounds like he was just in the wrong place at the wrong time or something," Randy said.

I shook my head. "But knowing what we know about how these things hunt, it makes no sense. When I was down in the tunnels with them...after that chemical was covered up by sewer water and Lord knows what else...they seemed relatively docile. The creature came right up to me, sniffed a few times out of curiosity and moved on. And from what I've been able to see of their faces, they have flat teeth, not fanged."

"So? What does the shape of their teeth have to do with anything?" Davenport asked.

"Plenty, Princess," my dad growled in response and it took all my strength not to laugh at the nickname he'd given to the reporter. "Flat teeth suggests the creatures are herbivores of some kind. Fangs are used for ripping flesh. Flattened choppers are better used for grinding vegetation. Kind of like a mortar and pestle."

"Which would explain the berries we found in Central Park," I added. "The creature was eating them when you started taking photos and scared it off."

"Okay, fine," Randy continued. "But if it wasn't just a 'wrong place-wrong time' killing, then how does he fit in?"

I shook my head again. "No idea. At least, not yet. But let's move on. Davenport, tell us about the next victim."

"Okay, now the second victim is a bit more interesting, given her connection with Thomas Leeds," he said, obviously impressed with what he'd been able to uncover. "Theresa McUllen. Killed walking to a subway terminal near Park Avenue. My sources aren't really sure where she was coming from, but they figured she was probably on *the job*."

"The job?" Nikki asked. "You say that as if it means more."

"It does. See, Ms. McUllen was a call girl. A very expensive one at that," he said. "But that's not the really interesting part. You see, it just so happens that she had also worked as a volunteer for one Senator Thomas Leeds."

That bit of news got everyone's attention.

"You've got to be kidding me!" Randy said. "That's a little coincidental, don't you think?"

"Is there any indication Leeds knew about her profession?" Nikki asked. "Could there have been some sort of black mail going on?"

Davenport shook his head. "From what a buddy of mine at the *Times* told me, he denies any knowledge of her vocation. Heck, he basically claims he'd hardly spoken two words to her the whole time she worked at his campaign headquarters."

"Yeah, right," Randy said. "A politician who isn't aware one of his staffers is an escort? Like we haven't heard that one a zillion times before."

"Yeah, I have to admit, it's a bit weak," Landers agreed. "And just a bit too convenient, as well, that our second victim would be a prostitute working for our number one suspect."

I shrugged. "What do you mean, convenient?"

"Just that Leeds doesn't seem to be an idiot. Granted, who else but us would even connect the Jersey Devils to him in order to make him a suspect...but it's still risky. From what you said, his campaign manager wasn't exactly keeping his family history a secret from you guys. Sure, in a perfect world, they would rather the family connection never be made at all. And Leeds tried to scare you off to distance himself from the whole thing...but when push came to shove, they didn't try to cover it up. So obviously, the senator didn't seem to think his connection to them was that big a deal. If he'd intentionally used them to kill the girl, I'd say he'd want to do everything he could to hide his relationship with the old legends."

I couldn't argue with the logic. From that point of view, our theory certainly had a few holes in it. Still, I wasn't quite ready to remove Leeds from our suspect pool just yet. The guy came across as someone cocky enough to pull something like that and say, "prove it" afterwards. No, the senator and his sister just seemed to be the best candidate for the killings.

"Well, let's move on to the final murder," I said, looking at Davenport once more. "Tell us about Max Schildiner." I wrote the name on the board and waited for him to review his notes.

"Okay, but we're all pretty much up to speed on him," the reporter said. "Basically one of two candidates competing against Leeds in the election. Insiders seem to confirm what Ms. Sommers told Jack. Schildiner and Leeds were pretty tight. No real problems at all and politically, they saw eye to eye on almost everything. I get the sense from some of my interviews that neither would mind if the other won. But they both were sweating what would happen if the third candidate, Lorn Jeffreys, won the race."

"Maybe we should take a closer look at Jeffreys," Landers said. "Maybe he stumbled onto Leed's family secret and somehow figured a way to use

the JDs to throw suspicion on one of his competitors while literally elimi-
nating the other?"

Davenport nodded at this. "Already looked into it. A few of my sources
are doing some background research on him just to be sure, but from what
I've already found out, I don't think it's possible that he's our man. Besides
being a family man and a deacon in his church, the guy has absolutely
nothing shady in his profile at the moment. But the kicker is, he's been in
Central America for the last month and a half helping out with the earth-
quake relief that's going on down there. There's no way he could be doing
this."

"Well, maybe he's hired someone," I said. "Someone with his obvious
clout wouldn't—" The sound of my cell phone playing the theme song to
the original *Star Trek* series interrupted my next statement. I reached into
my pocket and didn't even need to look at the caller ID to know who was
calling. It was Wiley's personal ringtone. "Tell me you've got something for
me, big guy," I said, as I punched the speaker button and set the phone
down on the conference table.

"Hey Jack!" Wiley said, breathing a little too heavily into his Bluetooth
headset. "Yes, I found out plenty. First of all, the lab results on those
samples you found in Central Park came back—the saliva from the berries,
as well as the hair standard—um, DNA analysis was inconclusive. Species
definitely unknown, but no doubt mammalian. Diana, down in the lab, says
the samples have distinctive characteristics with the mammalian suborder
Megachiroptera of the family *Pteropodidae*."

"Huh?" Randy asked.

"Our creatures have some common ancestry with what are known as
megabats," I said, tossing the idea around in my head a bit. It actually made
some sense. "Despite the name, not all megabats were *mega*, but they all
shared common characteristics that I've seen in our Jersey Devils." I started
ticking off a list on the board as I spoke. "One, well, bat wings—that's sort
of a given. Two, they have long snouts. Three, they're herbivores, specifical-

ly, they prefer fruits and nectar to anything else. Which, by the way, makes the megabat pretty docile when it comes to other animals. They typically don't attack except for self-preservation."

"What about echolocation?" Davenport asked. "Maybe that's how the killer is manipulating them. Messing around with their ability to navigate."

I shook my head. "Nah, actually, megabats don't have that ability. They use their eyes and acute sense of smell. They have excellent vision and olfactory senses. But hearing's pretty good too. No, I think Mia was telling the truth when she told me the chemical is the manipulative agent."

"Which were found on at least two of our victims," my dad added.

"Well, I have some good news about that too," Wiley's voice whined from the speakers of my iPhone. "Once I learned about the possibility of these things being some type of large, humanoid bat, I started doing research. Seems that certain species, like the flying fox for instance, exude a kind of protein from a gland in their neck. This protein comes out like sweat and the bat proceeds to lick the stuff all over their body. It acts as a primitive form of communication."

"Let me guess," Randy said. "It's some sort of warning system."

"That's one of its functions, yeah," Wiley agreed. "But that's not all. It's also used to attract mates, determine the alpha-bat—"

I glared at Randy. "Don't say it."

"Oh, come on!" he said. "I have about twelve good alpha-bat jokes to—"

"Go on, Wiley," I said, cutting my friend off mid-sentence.

"Well, the big use for this stuff...and the most significant to your investigation is that this protein can actually be used to identify others from within a bat's own colony. Or, more specifically determine if a visitor might be from a rival group."

I nodded. "That's actually excellent information, Wiley. I'm impressed."

I could almost hear the little geek blush from the other end of the phone. "Well, um, that's not all I've got for you Jack." I could hear him tapping away at his computer keyboard as he tried to collect his next bit of news. "I did some digging on that IP address and phone number you asked me to look into—"

I glanced around the room, my heart racing. More than one member of my team showed interest in what he was about to say, and I wasn't quite ready to spill the beans about my conversation with Freakshow. I grabbed the phone off the conference table and turned off the speaker before speaking.

"Now's not really a good time to discuss this," I whispered as I stood from the conference able and started walking to the other side of the room. "Kinda got an audience here."

"But Jack, you need to know this...that IP address for the email account? I couldn't get a line on it. It's routed and rerouted to ISPs all over the world. No way to trace it. Same with the phone number used to call your room. No name. No nothing. I'm thinking it's a burner phone or something."

"And that's important how?" I started counting backwards from ten to calm down. Sometimes, the kid could get on my last nerve. He meant well, but sometimes, his idea of important and mine were on opposite ends of the galaxy.

"It's not," he said. "But even though I couldn't get any info as to the identity of the caller, I was able to get a fix on approximately where the call was coming from."

That caught my interest.

"Jack, I can't tell you for sure...but there's a good chance that phone call came from somewhere in the hotel you're staying."

I felt the room begin to spin uncontrollably as he spoke the words. A tsunami of blood poured into my brain, as my heart pounded against my chest. Arnold, who'd been quietly playing with a ball in the conference room throughout the meeting, whined and cocked his head at me. He could sense my inner turmoil and I prayed to God that he was the only one who could. I didn't want to spook my team by telling them what was going on. At least, not yet.

But the shock of Freakshow being so close—never in a million years would I have been prepared for that bit of news. Ever since getting that phone call the day before, I'd never once even remotely speculated that the madman might have something to do with what had been going on. I just figured it was coincidence that he had called me now...after all these years.

Suddenly, Freakshow's words came back to me: *Okay, here's the deal. Before your little investigation is over, one of your teammates will be taken from you.* Involuntarily, I looked over my shoulder to my friends. Nikki. Randy. Landers. Even my dad. All potential targets. All possible ways for the creep to get at me.

Heck, my dad had even been threatened by an associate of Freakshow's. Ekaterina Stolnakanova had threatened to do some very horrible things to my dad in revenge for what I'd done to her grandfather. I'd tried to get him federal protection ever since the threat, only to be rejected by Polk. Freakshow had admitted to working with Kat, though he'd tried to show indifference toward her. But what if it was an act? What if my dad was the intended target?

Jack, you've got to tell them, I thought to myself. *They need to be warned.*

"Wiley?" I said quietly into the phone.

"Yeah, Jack?"

"Were you careful? Did you cover your tracks when you did your search?"

"You know me, Jack. I'm always careful."

"Well, double check, kid. Double check," I said, suddenly more worried than I'd been in a very long time. "And for the time being, do me a favor and hang around HQ. You've got everything you need there anyway. Until I say otherwise, hang tight there. Okay?"

There was some hesitation in his voice, but eventually he said, "Sure thing, Jack. If you think it's important."

"I do," I said grimly. "Cover up your search one more time and hang tight. I'll get with you soon."

And with that, I hung up and turned to face my team. My friends. My family. They all stared silently at me, worry painted across their faces. Only Davenport appeared indifferent. Which, in my mind, should be no surprise. I'd long ago given up believing in coincidences. If Freakshow had been in our hotel, then there was a good chance our little paperboy knew something about what was going on. And I figured it was about high time we found out just how much.

"Obadiah?" my dad said. "What is it, boy? What's wrong?"

I looked at them, anxiety pulling the muscles of my face tight.

"Trouble," I said quietly. "This investigation just got real."

EIGHTEEN

I LOOKED AT LANDERS, NODDED AT DAVENPORT AND SAID, "SCOTT, watch him. Don't let him leave."

"Wait. What?" the reporter asked, bolting to his feet. "What's going on?"

Despite Davenport's protests, the ENIGMA agent complied by standing up from the table, moving over to the door, and leaning back against it with his arms folded. Then, I proceeded to tell them everything. My ordeal five years before. The insane man who kidnaps his victims and forces them to play his own private little life or death reality show. I told them how he had contacted Davenport and leaked information about ENIGMA. About me. And finally, I told them about Freakshow's threat...to take one of my friends to be his next contestant.

Out of the entire group, only Randy knew the story. Landers, because of his security clearance, had known some of it—but I'd kept a number of things secret even from the government agency I currently worked for. But now, every one of them knew the whole story. I'd held nothing back—well, okay, I still hadn't told anyone about Arnold. But they were all now up-to-date on the most important stuff.

When I finished telling my tale, every eye turned suspiciously to Davenport.

"Whoa, whoa!" he said, waving his hands in the air submissively. "I've got nothing to do with this. The guy's only contacted me through emails. I've never met him and he's certainly never told me what he was planning to do. He just said I might be interested in following you guys around and wanted me to deliver a message to Jack when it was all over. That's it. That's all I know. I swear!"

"And what exactly is this message he wants you to deliver?" Landers asked, his eyes narrowing at the nervous writer.

"He wouldn't tell me. He said he'd let me know the message when the time was right. " Davenport looked from the agent, to me, and then finally to Nikki. His eyes pleading. Worried. "You've got to believe me."

"Actually, we don't have to believe you at all," Landers growled as he withdrew his sidearm from a shoulder holster and stepped toward him. Though he could be a pain in my rear and a real boy scout, Scott Landers took the security of ENIGMA very seriously. His reaction to this revelation honestly didn't surprise me, but I enjoyed it nonetheless.

"Scott, stop," Nikki said, standing up and walking over to stand between the agent and Davenport. "That's not fair. If what Jack says is true about this *Freakshow* person, then it stands to reason that he'd play Alex like he plays everything else. I believe him."

"Of course, you would," I said, rolling my eyes.

She spun around, fire burning in her eyes. "Just what is *that* supposed to mean?"

"Exactly like it sounds," I snapped, stubbornly meeting her glare. I wanted her to know I wasn't backing down on this. Whatever was going on with Nikki and me, I was just about fed up with it. Still, we didn't have time to fight at the moment and I knew I was going to have to swallow my pride. After all, she was right about the games Freakshow liked to play. The more I thought about it, the less likely it seemed that the madman would use a poser like Alex Davenport as a confidante. "She's right, guys. From what Wiley said, there was nothing in Davenport's emails to suggest the two of them were in cahoots.

"Wait! What?" Davenport croaked. "You hacked my email?"

"Shut up," Landers growled. "Let him finish."

I smiled at the agent, then continued. "Granted, Freakshow would know I'd have his email hacked, so I'm sure he'd be careful what he said, but—"

My phone buzzed, interrupting my train of thought. It was a simple, old-fashioned ring tone this time; the unlisted number not registering any specially pre-programmed tune to play. I punched the speaker button and said, "Hello?"

"Jackson, it's Grigsby," the gruff detective's voice crackled over the cell phone. He sounded as grim as I felt. "We've got another victim."

My heart paused briefly at the news. Another one. My brain whirled trying to wrap all the pieces of information we'd just been over into some sort of cohesive theory as to what was happening…anything to stop another human being from being murdered on the street. I tried to respond, but the words were catching in my throat.

"You there, Jackson?"

"Yeah," I finally said. My voice felt raw. "I'm here."

"Well, get your tail down here. You're gonna want to see this." Grigsby paused, then added, "But come alone. None of your crew need to see this, okay?"

I agreed, then wrote the address down on my notepad before hanging up. Sliding the phone back into my pocket, I looked at my friends and sighed. I was tired. So tired. I'd still not gotten a wink of sleep since coming to New York and exhaustion was mounting. Add to that the emotional stress of another victim and I was wound tight enough to pop. Still, this was important. I needed to see this new victim and assess whatever I could at the scene while it was still fresh. Sleep would have to wait.

"There's been another murder," I finally said. "I'm going down to check it out. In the meantime, you guys have work to do."

I explained that the next phase of the plan would be to explore the sewer tunnels I'd discovered earlier that morning. "I have a feeling those tunnels are where they're laying their nests. We find the nests, we'll find them."

Though neither Davenport nor Nikki liked it, the team agreed that the reporter would be confined somehow until we could discern just what role he played in Freakshow's little scheme. Despite Davenports claims we were "unlawfully detaining" him and charges we were hindering the rights of the press, Landers happily volunteered to handle the reporter's security, with Arnold's watchful eye as backup. While he was going to playing guard duty, I also asked Scott to check out any references to "The Gateway to Hell" and any correlation with places inside the Czech Republic. Wasn't sure Mia's clue would lead us anywhere, but it was worth a shot.

Randy and Dad were assigned the task of getting our gear ready for tomorrow's expedition and planned on setting up basecamp during the night so we'd be ready to go first thing in the morning. I warned the two of them to use extreme care and they assured me they wouldn't delve into the tunnels themselves until we arrived. Besides, Dad explained that he'd have his rifle nice and handy should any "black-winged nasty come a'callin'."

As for Nikki...well, I figured it was time I do whatever I could to end the little feud we were having. I explained as much to her before asking her to come with me and to my surprise, she agreed with just a *trace* of a smile.

Women. I'll just never understand them.

Grigsby had specifically ordered me to come alone, but he'd just have to deal with it. After seeing even the slightest of smiles on her face, I immediately committed myself to doing whatever it took to see it more often—whether the detective liked it or not.

As we walked out of the conference room and toward the lobby where we'd hail a cab, I thought of the other reason I'd wanted her to tag along. I just didn't want her out of my sight. Though I'd never admit it to her, I'd brave the fiercest of dragons and risk the sharpest of claws to keep her out of Freakshow's hands. If the creep had his sights set on her, he'd be in for the fight of his life.

❧

Given how late it was, the cab ride to the Upper Eastside murder scene seemed excruciatingly long. Though I could tell Nikki was appreciative of me inviting her along, she was still too perturbed by my past indiscretions to give any sort of opening for a worthwhile conversation. The only topics of conversation apparently allowed had to do with the current investigation…and my treatment of her new BFF, Alex Davenport.

She let me know just how much she disapproved of the way we'd treated him like some nefarious ne'er-do-well and hinted on more than one occasion that my irrational suspicion of him might be a transparent attempt at masking my own jealousy. I had to keep reminding myself of that slight, but very pleasant smile she'd given me just a few moments before. It was the only thing that gave me strength enough not to lash out as she began psycho-analyzing the decisions I frequently made in life.

"…I'm not quite sure what Oliver and Susan did to screw you up so bad as a kid, but it seems that every time you make a choice, it's based completely on…"

That was pretty much the gist of it. I can't be sure. I tuned most of it out. I couldn't have been more pleased when the cab pulled up to our destination on East 69th Street and we climbed out into a swath of red and blue lights flashing away the darkness around us.

The air was unusually chill for that time of year and I pulled my jacket around me and pulled up my collar. The ghostly vapors of my breath drifted in front of my face as I took in the scene. I could make out no less than twenty-three police vehicles, two crime scene vans, the Medical Examiner's transport van, and at least six different news crews. Either these Jersey Devil killings were starting to grab the attention of the media or we had ourselves another high profile death. I became even less at ease as my eyes searched for the body among the throng of law enforcement and gawkers congesting the upper Eastside street. Nikki seemed to sense my anxiety.

"What?" she asked. "Jack, what's wrong?"

So absorbed with my evaluation of the scene, I didn't answer for several seconds. Then, I glanced over at her and shrugged. "Where's the body?" I nodded to a string of uniformed officers hustling back and forth through the doors of a high rise apartment building to our left. "And why are they concentrating their investigation *inside* that building?"

"Jackson," came a gruff voice from behind us. "I thought I told you to come alone."

Nikki and I turned to see a red-faced Grigsby barreling over to us; a smoldering cigarette hanging from one side of his mouth.

"Sorry, Detective," I said. "But some things have come up. For the moment, she doesn't leave my sight."

Her eyes widened at this, suddenly understanding my ulterior motive for bringing her. I'd pay dearly for it later, but frankly, I didn't care. I had no doubt the Texan daughter of Senator Stromwell was more than capable of taking care of herself against most monsters we'd ever face. But Freakshow...Freakshow was no ordinary monster.

Grigsby let out a resigned sigh and smiled at her. "Good to see you again, Ms. Jenkins," he said with a strained, but sincere smile. "I'm sorry if I made you feel unwelcome. It's just that this one...um, well, it's going to be tough. For *all* of us."

I let his words sink in for a few seconds, turning the meaning over in my head a number of times before asking the obvious question. "What do you mean?"

He nodded over at the apartment building and said, "Better to show you. This one is a little strange. The attack actually happened inside the victim's apartment. Looks like something crashed through her plate glass window. Neighbors heard high-pitched shrieks—they swear it wasn't a human scream—as well as some type of struggle from within. They dialed 911, but by the time the first responders arrived, it was already too late. One of our officers saw the creature leap out of the window and fly off."

"You mean to tell me that the creature actually entered the victim's dwelling?" I asked. "Literally flew through her window and attacked her?"

He let the question go unanswered as he escorted us into the building and said nothing else for the entire thirty-seven story elevator ride to the victim's floor. Then, ushering us past a handful of crime scene techs that looked a little green under the gills as they hobbled onto the now vacated elevator, we made our way to the victim's apartment.

"Ms. Jenkins, I'm not really sure you'll want to see this—"

"Detective Grigsby," she interrupted, her voice near frigid. "I've served as a missionary in some of the most dangerous locales known to man. I've been involved in wars, nursed injured soldiers back to health, and dealt with villages where starvation, slave trafficking, and racial cleansing were every-day occurrences. I hardly doubt that there is anything on the planet that can be more disturbing than the things I've seen, so please," she paused, taking a deep breath to calm herself. "Please, don't try to coddle me. I'll be fine. I promise."

Grigsby smiled at her then motioned for us to step into the apartment. "Just watch where you step. They're still processing. Not everyone at One Police Plaza is ready to buy my theory that there are real-life gargoyles mauling New York citizens. And this one...Jack, this one is big."

He refused to say more as he led us through the foyer and into the ex-pansive living room of the luxury apartment. If I hadn't known better, I'd swear that a miniature tornado had whipped through the place, destroying almost everything in its path. The fifty-two inch LED television was the first item my eyes landed on, splayed as it was, across the couch after being knocked from its mooring on the wall. Shards of glass covered the hard-wood floors from where a glass coffee table had been hurled across the room. Crimson patterns of sprayed blood coated the walls, floor, and furniture of the entire room. As my mind processed each piece of destruc-tive fury, my heart grew tighter in my chest. The creature had reached a new pinnacle of rage on this murder. Something had sent it completely over the edge.

The shattered bay window in the front of the apartment gave full voice to my concerns. It just boggled the mind. It was a very rare thing for an animal to intentionally ignore the territorial boundaries of another. Instinct—the need for self-preservation—would normally prevent such things from happening. After all, another creature's territory meant home field advantage. In the case of territorial animals such as wolves, it would be an act of complete desperation to risk unnecessary confrontation with another pack. And though we now suspected that the Jersey Devils were some unknown species of a megabat, I had a hard time believing their behavioral patterns would be much different.

So what on earth had prompted the monster to disregard its own primal instincts, crash through a plate-glass window, and tear someone to pieces?

Grigsby cleared his throat, grabbing my attention from the devastation all around me. I looked over to see him standing over a body draped in a once-clean white sheet. Now, a moist stain of blood saturated the center of the material and I shuddered to imagine what lay underneath.

"I asked the M.E. boys to hold off on hauling her from the scene until you had a chance to look at her." His eyes were sad. Truly, hopelessly sad. I had no idea what could be so significant about our current victim that would mess with a hardened police veteran the way this one did, but the moment he pulled the sheet back, I had my answer.

Her face was a mangled mess of flesh, blood, and bone, and completely unrecognizable. But the hair...hair the color of a deep sunset was a dead giveaway. I instantly knew why Detective Grigsby was so upset. After all, he'd liked Aislynn Sommers from the moment he'd first laid eyes on her. Even flirted with her just a few hours before while we sat in her office interviewing her about her employer. And here he was, now standing over the mutilated remains of her body.

"Mike, I..."

"It's okay," he said. "Just part of the job. I'll deal with it. Heck, I only just met her. But no one should go out this way, Jackson. Nobody."

The Medical Examiner had already gathered the various body parts from around the room and had placed them in relative proximity to where they would normally be attached. There wasn't a lot in one piece. As a matter of fact, her remains made Schildiner's meat-grinded body looked almost whole.

I glanced over at Nikki, who stared numbly down at the body. Her jaw clinched tight as she took in every detail. After several seconds, she returned my look and I saw a tear streaking her cheeks.

"What's going on, Jack?" she asked quietly. "Why the escalation? Why were they so violent this time? And why on earth did they kill *her*, of all people?"

"I don't know." I hated the words the moment they slipped through my lips, but it was the truth. I was lost. Heck, I'd half-suspected Aislynn Sommers of being the culprit to begin with. Now, nothing was making much sense. "Any idea where Leeds was tonight?" I asked Grigsby while staring down at Aislynn's body.

"He's being interviewed now," he said. "But by all accounts, he was at a fundraiser. Lots of witnesses. Plus, I'm not sure he even had a motive for this."

And I wasn't sure whether whoever was responsible for such carnage even needed a motive. I was beginning to suspect whoever had unleashed these creatures had long since lost the ability for the rational thought required to actually have one. Some people, after all, just wanted to watch the world burn. My mind turned instantly back to Freakshow, but I pushed it aside.

No, this was too personal. From the little I knew about him, the creep would never kill for revenge or anything so mundane. He preferred his games for sheer pleasure's sake.

"Mia?" I asked, moving to my next suspect. "You said you were going to put out an APB on her earlier tonight. Any luck?"

The look on the detective's face answered the question for me.

"Okay, let's approach this from another angle," I said, taking another look at Aislynn's mangled body before taking the sheet from Grigsby's hand and covering her once more. "If it *was* Leeds or his sister, what would be the motive?"

"Well, with Mia, maybe it's jealousy," Nikki said, her voice a little more solid now that the body was covered again. "I mean, maybe *little sister* doesn't like her brother spending more time with another woman than her." She caught my dubious expression then smirked. "I know that sounds awfully Oedipal, but weirder things have happened." She paused as another idea materialized within her thought-stream. "Or maybe she's super protective. Maybe Aislynn represented some type of threat and Mia wanted to protect her brother from it."

I smiled. "Now that's more like it," I said. "Would definitely fit. It could also explain Schildiner and the prostitute too. Maybe the girl has some misplaced sense of loyalty. Sees dangers where there really isn't any and acts proactively."

"And Aislynn pretty much spilled the beans to the two of you today," Nikki continued. "Gave up the family secret like it was nothing more than grandma's casserole recipe. A major breach of trust, if you ask me."

I looked over at Grigsby, who continued to stare down the sheet-covered body, After a moment, he gave one shake of his head and looked up at us. "All of that is completely conjecture," he said. "No evidence to support any of it. And if you ask me, it just doesn't feel right. This…" He gestured at the carnage. "This is too personal. Sure, it was your monster you've been hunting, but you have to admit, it's beyond anything we've seen in the past. Whoever's controlling these things must have done something special to Ms. Sommers here. They wanted her to suffer." He paused a second, then added, "Besides, if you remember correctly, it was the silver-haired tart that pointed you in Leeds' direction to begin with."

Yeah, I had forgotten that. Mia had been the one to give me Leeds' family crest. She wanted me to find her brother. Wanted me to get involved. It wouldn't make sense for her to kill Aislynn to protect the family secret if she was doing the exact same thing. When I decided I wouldn't get anywhere with this particular line of thought, I changed gears. I decided it was time to try to figure out how the killer had escalated the attack…how he or she had gotten the creature to barge into their target's own home and do…all this.

My mind was spinning through all the possible ways, knowing what we knew of the protein secretions that seemed to corral the creatures, how the killer could have amped up the rage-factor of our winged beast and came up empty. The protein was just a protein. An organic chemical. Sure, I could see how it might attract the creatures to attack someone out on the street somewhere, but to pull them indoors? Into another species' territory? I just couldn't figure—

The blinding white illumination of a spotlight flashed through the open window as an NYPD chopper skimmed by the building, presumably searching for the fleeing creature. As it coasted past, the beam streaked across the sky and moved over to the building on the opposite side of us. Something shimmered against the light; a reflection of some kind. Then, a shadowy form bolted from its hiding place behind an air conditioning unit and dashed toward the rooftop stairwell.

"Mike, look!" I shouted, pointing over to the rooftop on the other side. He spotted the figure immediately, then pulled out his walkie-talkie and barked out a series of orders to his fellow officers.

The three of us inched up to the open window and peered over the edge, watching the chaos below as the radio crackled with up-to-the-second updates on the pursuit. Five minutes later, Grigsby's cell phone chirped. He answered, gave a handful of terse, indecipherable comments then hung up the phone with a grin.

"They got 'im," he said, as he started making his way to the front door.

"Him?" I asked, taking Nikki nervously by the hand and pulling her with me as I followed him. She jerked the hand away and glared at me defiantly. She wasn't about to have me play hero protector to her distressed damsel.

"Yeah," he said, leaving the apartment and moving toward the elevator. "*Him*. Seems the ID in his wallet says our suspicious person is one Charles D. Filmore. Senator Leeds' personal assistant. And we're heading downtown right now to interview him."

NINETEEN

THE FIRST THING I NOTICED UPON ENTERING THE 19TH PRECINCT'S interrogation room was the rancid stench of urine, bile, and vomit, as well as the disinfectant employed to try to mask them. The cleaning solution had failed miserably. My nose wrinkled involuntarily as I noticed the next thing in the room—the tears streaking Chuck Filmore's cheeks. The little guy was taking short, gasping breaths while his unsteady hands slowly pulled a Styrofoam cup of coffee to his trembling lips. He looked up at us as we entered, his puffy red eyes, silently pleading to us for mercy.

"I didn't do anything," he said, placing the cup down in front of him. He rested both shaking hands, palms down on the table, as if struggling to steady himself. "I swear. I didn't."

Grigsby didn't respond. Instead, with a non-committal grunt, he opened the manila folder he'd carried into the room and pretended to read through its contents. When Filmore realized he was getting nowhere with the detective, he turned his attention to me.

"Dr. Jackson, please," he said. "I've done nothing wrong. I was…I was…" The personal assistant broke down once more into a sobbing fit, bringing his hands up to cover his face as he cried.

I glanced over at the two-way mirror, knowing Nikki was watching the proceedings with both passionate interest and genuine concern over the NYPD's newest suspect. That's just the way she was wired…always thinking about the "little guy" in such ordeals. Always so compassionate for the downtrodden. It was one of many things that so attracted me to her…at least, when I didn't want to strangle her for it instead. Still, I couldn't help wondering what she was thinking at that very moment. Fortunately, I didn't have much time to dwell on it as Detective Grigsby suddenly found his voice.

"Mr. Filmore," he said dispassionately. "I'm going to keep this brief. What were you doing on the rooftop across the street from *my* crime scene? A crime scene in which a very close associate of yours had just recently been murdered, I might add."

Chuck sat back in the steel chair bolted to the concrete floor and loosened his tie. He was wearing the same Fifth Avenue knock-off suit we'd seen him in earlier that afternoon, though now it was stained with street crud where the cops had tackled him trying to make his escape. A ruddy abrasion marred his clean shaven chin and I couldn't help wondering how his head felt after being piled on by at least six large NYPD officers.

"I...I..." Filmore tried to answer, but was obviously having trouble formulating a coherent thought.

"Just relax, Mr. Filmore," Grigsby said. His voice suddenly softer, more calming than before. Slowly, he reached into a briefcase that he'd been carrying, pulled out a set of high-end night vision binoculars, and set them down on the table. "We haven't charged you with anything. This is just a friendly get together among friends...trying to piece things together in your co-worker's death. That's all. Right now, you're merely a 'person of interest' in this case. I just need to know why we caught you spying on us with these binoculars from across the street."

His face blushed as he eyed the expensive spy gear and struggled once more to come up with the right words. That's when it hit me.

"Oh, geeze!" I said, slapping my hand on the table and causing him to jump. "You were sweet on her, weren't you?"

His face reddened even more before he turned his eyes downward to stare at his shoes. I looked over at the detective.

"He wasn't spying on us and our investigation," I said. "He was stalking Aislynn. He's a peeping Tom!"

Grigsby turned to face Chuck. "Is this true?"

Filmore nodded, but said nothing.

"Please answer out loud," the detective said. "This interview is being recorded and we can't document nods and hand gestures. I'll repeat: Is this true?"

Filmore looked up at us sheepishly, nodded, and said, "Yes, it's true. I was watching her ever since she got home tonight. Like I do almost every night." He caught himself, then added, "Or at least, I did."

I wasn't sure, but I could almost detect an audible growl escape Grigsby's throat at the confession. He obviously didn't appreciate the little guy peeping on someone he'd taken a shine to.

"And tonight? Did you see the attack?"

Filmore nodded.

"Out loud, please."

"Yes. I saw the whole thing," he said with a quick sob. "The entire ghastly thing."

Grigsby asked him to describe the event as he'd seen it and the little guy, amid tears and nervous gasps told him everything. His account matched in every way what other witnesses had said.

"And the creature," I said. "Have you ever seen it before?"

Filmore looked down at his hands as he wrung them uncertainly. After a few seconds, he shook his head.

"No. Never," he said. "But I've heard about them. Know about the senator's connection to them." He paused, took a deep breath and continued. "And I know who's responsible. For Aislynn's death. For all of them."

Involuntarily, I leaned forward in my chair. He'd piqued my interest now and from the tightening of Grigsby's jaw, I could tell he was just as intrigued. But the wily detective knew better than to ask the easy question. Whoever really was behind the killings had no way of knowing we were onto the chemical method that was being employed to manipulate the creatures' actions.

"I thought you just said it was some kind of flying monster that killed Ms. Sommers," the detective said.

"I know, I know, I know," Chuck said, gesturing wildly. "But that's just it. It's the perfect murder, right? I mean, how could any court prosecute someone for a homicide when witnesses everywhere say it was some kind of creature. It's brilliant, really, if you think about it. Someone who knows how to control those things, who can train them, could basically just sic them on whoever they wanted. And no one would be the wiser, right?"

Grigsby pulled away from the table, stood up and started pacing the floor in mock contemplation. The big guy made quite the show, scratching the stubble of his chin as he voiced his thoughts for all to hear.

"So you're telling me that someone has the ability to actually point these gargoyle-things at a target and they would..."

"They would go after them," Filmore said, nodding. "Yes. Yes. That's exactly what I'm saying. And more importantly, I know who it is."

Unfortunately, I didn't have the patience of my NYPD counterpart. Slamming my fist down on the table, I shouted, "Oh for crying out loud, Sparky! Lay off the theatrics and just tell us! I don't have time for this."

Grigsby spun and glared at me as his meaty hands closed slowly into fists. There was no mistake this time...he most definitely growled.

Okay. So I overstepped my bounds a little. But come on! The weasely little drama queen was going to take all night before he gave it up. We didn't have time for interrogative games. Thankfully, I must not have damaged our chances for the truth too much because Filmore cleared his throat and leaned in conspiratorial toward us.

"Okay, but you have to promise me protection. If she finds out...if she learns that I've pointed you in her direction, she'll...she'll send those things after me too! I just know it."

I smiled victoriously, then nodded. "I can't speak for the NYPD, but I can promise federal protection if it becomes necessary. Sure." It wasn't exactly the truth. I wasn't exactly authorized to promise any kind of protection—federal or otherwise. After all, ENIGMA was an agency that didn't officially exist. Plus, I wasn't exactly on official business. Heck, the way things had been going, I might need protection myself. From Polk. Still, I would have told him we'd take him to see the *real* Santa Claus if I thought it would get him to stop rambling and tell me what I wanted to know.

Chuck nodded at this, took a sip of coffee, then nodded again. "All right," he said. His voice was a mere quivering whisper. "See, Mr. Leeds...he's actually been on the run for about fifteen years now. Running from his family. Their heritage. His past. He doesn't talk about them often, but one night while he was...um, a little inebriated and shaken up over a phone call he'd received that day, he sort of confided in me..."

It took every ounce of my being not to scream at the guy to just get on with it. But although I would never make a great detective, I'd done enough investigations in my time to know that some people just need to tell the story in their own way. And in my experience, the Nervous Nellie types were the absolute worst. I knew I'd just have to grin and bear it.

"...told me his family was some type of devil worshippers. Had been for centuries back in Europe, as a matter of fact. They'd apparently come to America fleeing religious persecution just like everyone else; only, they never found that freedom. They'd been hunted as witches since the day their ship first landed."

Filmore droned on about the Leeds' family history, then told the story we already knew about Mother Leeds and her alleged pact with the devil that had resulted in the birth of the creature that soon became known locally as the Leeds Devil, and later internationally as the Jersey Devil. He explained that from that moment on, the remainder of his family had lived in relative obscurity, sequestering themselves in the rugged terrain of the Pine Barrens and looking after their demonic "brother" and his offspring.

Enter Thomas Leeds, a young dreamer who wanted nothing more than to get a college education and break away from the evils his family had harbored for almost three centuries. His greatest desire had been to swear off the family traditions, go to law school, and enter politics. Needless to say, this wasn't exactly a welcome notion with his clan's matriarch—Filmore explained that every generation since the colonial times, the Leeds' clan choose a female in the family to rule over them—so the aspiring politician ran away. To Boston. Where he went on to earn his law degree and eventually take on a position in a very prestigious law firm in Manhattan. And from that point on, his destiny lay in the direction of Capitol Hill.

"And things were fine," Filmore continued. "No problems at all during his first term as a senator. But about a year ago, just before we started gearing up for his re-election campaign, the phone calls started happening."

"Phone calls?" Grigsby asked. "From who?"

"From the senator's younger sister, Mia," he said. "Apparently, the matriarch had died, leaving her in charge of the entire clan. And she wanted him to return to the family's homestead...wanted him to return to his obligations. She'd always despised the fact that the senator had left. Out of the entire clan, she'd felt the most betrayed by his leaving." Chuck took another nervous sip from the coffee. "Apparently, she'd only been around five or six at the time. She felt that he hadn't just abandoned the family...he'd left her as a young child, completely alone and unprotected. She'd never forgiven him for it."

"Wait a second," I said, shaking my head. "This isn't adding up. I saw her. I saw Mia at your campaign headquarters yesterday morning. She'd poked her head out of one of the offices and I chased her away. When I mentioned it to Aislynn, she casually told me who it was as if it had been no big deal. As if the girl stopped in to visit all the time."

Filmore smiled weakly as this. "She *would* act that way," he said. "She had no idea what was going on. Senator Leeds kept it secret from her. When Mia would come for one of her regular 'visits', he'd usher her in a private office before Aislynn or anyone else had a chance to ask too many questions. No, as far as I know, I'm the only one who knows what is really going on with the senator and his sister."

"So Charles, any idea where Ms. Leeds is currently staying?" Grigsby asked. "Any known associates? Forwarding addresses or phone numbers you might have happened upon in recent weeks?"

The assistant shrugged. "No clue where she's staying," he said. "Trust me. The senator's had me looking everywhere for her since the first killing. But I haven't been able to find a trace. Even hired a small army of P.I.'s to look for her, but they've turned up nothing. As for phone numbers or associates...sorry. Those were dead ends for me too."

I looked at my watch. It was now two in the morning and I knew we needed to wrap the interview up soon to get enough shuteye for the investigation in the morning. But I still had one question left.

"So any idea what her end game is?" I asked. "I mean, what happens if Senator Leeds refuses to come home?"

Filmore's face darkened; his eyes reclaimed their redness as a new batch of tears began to stream down his face.

"It's obvious, isn't it?" he said, dabbing his eyes with a handkerchief. "If she doesn't get what she wants, she's threatened to send those monsters after Tommy."

TWENTY

"JACK," LANDERS' VOICE CRACKLED IN MY EARPIECE. "YOUR DAD IS settled into home base and is monitoring our positions through the tunnels with our GPS trackers. On top of that, he'll be watching the motion sensors, IR cameras Randy setup for seven square blocks outside the sewer manholes, and keeping an eye on our own camera feeds as we explore. I've already mounted IR camera B-1 inside the first quadrant and we are about to begin our sweep." There was a brief pause. "How are *you* doing down there?"

I glanced at Nikki, who nodded back at me with a reserved and uncharacteristically cold smile. Our investigation the night before hadn't exactly smoothed things out between us the way I'd hoped and frankly, I was nowhere closer to discovering a way to truly patch things up with her than when she'd first broken up with me.

Arnold, who sat on the sewer's concrete walkway, simply panted happily and pretended to be just an ordinary dog completely oblivious to my current discomfort. Of course, I knew better. The mutt had been thoroughly amused over the cold shoulder I'd been getting from Nikki since the breakup. If I could speak mutant K9, I was almost positive his wide eyes and lolling tongue would be saying: *This is what you get for being a self-centered bonehead.* But since I didn't speak dog-ese, I can't be absolutely sure. My only consolation, as far as my traitorous dog was concerned, is that he thoroughly despised water of any kind. It's why he hadn't gone to Greece with us last year and why I knew beyond doubt that he would soon find himself immensely uncomfortable surrounded by the river of filth of the sewers.

Yeah. I can be that vindictive.

But to be fair, my own discomfort wasn't merely being teamed again with my ex or the unfaithful snarkiness of my pooch. No, it was much worse than that. It had been decided that our intrepid tabloid reporter could not be trusted alone in Landers' hotel room. Since the best place to keep a potential backstabber was right in front of us, the plan was to put him to work while we mounted a series of twenty-five infrared cameras throughout the tunnels. If I'd known that the team intended to place him with Nikki and me, I'd probably have cut him loose at the hotel and wished him on his merry way. As things now stood, I was going to have to put up with the creep making goo-goo eyes at Nikki for the better part of the day.

"Jack?" Landers said into my earpiece. "You there? I asked if you were okay?"

"I heard you the first time. And yes, we're all just peachy. Thanks for asking." I reached into my backpack and pulled out a long metal container. Opening it up, I eased the exquisitely rolled Cuban cigar into the palm of my hand, then brought it up to my nose, savoring its smell amid the putrid stench of wastewater.

I could feel Nikki's glare without even seeing it.

"What?" I asked, bringing the stogey to my lips and biting down on the end. "I ain't lighting it or anything. Just sort of anticipating everything horrible that could possibly go wrong down here."

Davenport smiled. "Oh, this is that *thing*," he said to Nikki. "That thing you mentioned, right? Where he smokes a cigar every time he escapes a near-death situation with his life?"

She giggled at this. I kid you not, the tough-as-nails, shoot-a-fly-off-the-wall-from-fifty-paces missionary actually giggled.

"Yeah," she said, still laughing. "He thinks it's rather charming, but it's really nothing more than an immature ploy to call attention to something amazing he's done."

I clenched the cigar tighter in my teeth and turned to look at the two of them standing next to the ladder leading up to the world above. The manhole cover was still open and the golden beams of the early morning sun shone through the circular opening.

With a grunt, I peeled off the foil on the self-adhesive back to the IR camera and mounted it on the wall about a foot above my head. "If you ladies would like to gossip," I said, flipping the camera on and turning to glare at them, "you're more than welcome to do it topside. Otherwise, we have work to do."

Arnold gave a little harrumph of agreement and I watched as he trotted a few feet ahead of us and stopped to make sure we were following. He let out a low growl of disapproval when he realized we weren't.

"Do you really think it's a good idea to bring that dog down here?" Davenport asked. "I mean, it could be dangerous. I'm not sure he'd be safe if those things attacked and—"

I spun around, irritation with the smooth-talking writer reaching its boiling point. Before I could stop myself, my index finger was jabbing at his chest.

"Look, buddy, maybe Nikki's right. Maybe I'm being too hard on you. Too suspicious about your connections with a homicidal maniac. Like it or not, I'm stuck with you for the time being and you're stuck with us. So there's something you should know about that 'dog' there." I removed my finger and pointed at Arnold, who now sat on his haunches looking up at us with a wagging tail. "There are very few dangers in this world that little fleabag can't handle. Because of that, he goes where I go. There's no one better to have covering your back." I paused, then grinned mischievously at him. "But don't take my word for it. Your friend Freakshow knows about him intimately. Why don't you ask him sometime."

I then turned to Nikki.

"And as for you," I said, my voice suddenly softening. One look at her and my fire had completely fizzled. "Look, I know this isn't the time or place, but I need to get it out in the open before we proceed. Nikki, you're supposed to be better than me. You always have been. It's in *you* that I set my own bar. Ever since I met you, all I've ever wanted to be is a man you could respect. Care for. Love. I swear I know I can be a self-centered cad at times and I know I need to learn to stop trying to protect you all the time. Stop lying to you. Heck, I just need to be more honest with you about everything. But I promise you...on everything I hold sacred, I promise you, I will do everything in my power to make it right." Self-consciously, I took the cigar from my mouth and tossed it in the water. "So can we just call a truce for a little while? At least until this JD mess is over?"

She stared at me, her mouth open in what can only be described as surprise. Maybe even shock. It was a good look on her. An even better look when I noticed the frost in her eyes slowly melting away and a genuine and warm smile spread across her face.

"Sure," she said. "Yes. I'm sorry, Jack. I've been so...well, my actions have been unforgiveable." She stopped for a second then pointed a finger at me. "However, understand this...even though I'm apologizing for my behavior, it doesn't excuse you from yours. I'm not letting you get off this easy, but for now, I'll concede that our fight is definitely a dangerous thing to have hovering over our heads. We need to focus on the investigation. We can worry about the other stuff later."

She held out her hand and I accepted, shaking it gently. Slowly. Savoring the warmth of its touch against my own skin. It had been far too long since we'd shared any physical contact and I suddenly realized how much I'd missed it. But she was right. I needed to get my head in the game or risk having it lopped off by the talons of the monstrous bat-like chimeras that haunted these very tunnels.

My headset crackled to life, breaking the spell and we both released our grips.

"Obadiah," my dad's voice said. "We've got ourselves movement about two blocks east of you. One of Randy's fancy cameras just picked up something big streaking by and dipping down into the sewers. I've marked its entry point on your GPS already."

"Got it, Dad. Thanks," I said, powering up my handheld global positioning device. "We're on our way."

"We'll start heading your way too, Jack. We'll meet in the middle," Lander's voice said in my earpiece. "Don't do anything stupid until we're close enough to back you up."

"Hey, you know me," I said with a grin. "I'm Mr. Cautious."

With that, we took off at a steady trot, moving toward the point Dad had marked while quickly setting up more cameras as we did.

∽∾

The tunnels we currently occupied were about six blocks west from where I'd found myself the day before. The water here was shallower, only about ankle deep, and the tunnel consisted of two parallel concrete catwalks with the stream of waste water in between. A tapestry of green algae and moss coated the walls on either side of us. The vaulted brick ceiling was palely illuminated by a series of wire-mesh framed sodium lights.

I found it curious that the lights hadn't been working the day before, but chalked it up to the ol' Jackson luck and pushed it out my head as we continued following my GPS to the entrance my dad had specified. We found it ten minutes later and came to a halt.

Taking my flashlight, I flashed the beam up toward the manhole cover now firmly set in place.

"If one of the JDs did come through here, they know how to cover their tracks," I said, reaching into my pouch and digging out the FLIR thermal imager. Flicking the switch, the thing hummed to life and I began scanning the cover, as well as the access ladder bolted firmly to the wall. The telltale red and orange glow of a fading heat signature radiated from the ladder rungs, as well as the heavy iron of the cover. "Strange."

"What?" Nikki asked.

I stared at the image on the tiny three and a half inch display and shook my head. "These heat signatures. They're obviously pressure points where something giving off heat has touched them, right?"

She nodded in reply, but waited for me to continue.

"Well, doesn't it seem odd to you that something like the Jersey Devil would bother with a ladder? Sure, it's too tight a squeeze for the creature to use his wings, but I find it hard to believe these things would need to use a ladder to move in and out. Heck, come to think of it, I have a hard time buying that they use manholes to begin with. There are plenty of other ways into the sewers. More cavern-like ways."

"Like subways," she said.

"Yeah. From what I know about the underground system around here, it's a labyrinth of David Bowie proportions," I said. "There are plenty of entrances that an animal could use. Our cryptids might be some kind of winged primate, but it seems highly unlikely they'd sneak in and out this way." I pressed the button of my com unit. "Dad, have you had a chance to replay the video of what you saw?"

There was nothing but static for several seconds, then my dad came back online. "Yeah, but it moved too fast. Just a flurry of black. Then it drops down into the tunnels, lickety-split. Frame-rate just isn't good enough to make a better ID."

"Thanks Dad," I said, before turning back to Nikki and Davenport. "Keep your guard up. I have a feeling we might have company...and I'm not talking about the cryptids either."

Davenport's eyes widened at the implications. He swallowed hard, then spoke. "Mia? You think it's her?"

I smiled mischievously back at him. "Don't worry, Princess," I said. "I'm sure she's got more in mind for us than finishing what she started in Central Park."

"Please stop calling me that."

Ignoring the request, I turned serious and added, "Just watch your back, guys. This could get hairy quicker than we first thought."

Understanding my concerns, Nikki slowly withdrew her air-compressed tranquilizer gun from its holster and held the muzzle parallel with her leg, but ready to use at a moment's notice. Of the entire group, only Landers could outshoot the blonde Texan. So when it was decided to come equipped with enough Ketamine to put down a rhino in hopes of possibly catching one of the creatures for study, she'd been chosen to carry the gun.

I smiled proudly at her then resumed scanning our immediate area with the FLIR, looking for evidence of where our mysterious visitor might have moved. I was a little disappointed to discover that the heat signatures were already fading from view. Fortunately, I had two advantages our silver-haired goth chick hadn't counted on: First, the piece of tartan cloth with the Leeds' family crest and second...

"Arnold," I whispered, patting my knee with my hands. "Come here boy."

When he complied, I held the tattered cloth down near his nose and scratched the little mutt behind the ears. "Can you find her?" I asked, looking him directly in his intelligent, disturbingly understanding eyes.

He returned my gaze, gave a brief huff of acknowledgment, then turned to his right and started trotting along the walkway away from us; moving in an eastward direction.

Grinning ear to ear, I looked at my team. "This might be easier than I thought."

Nikki rolled her eyes, shaking her head in complete disappointment. "You just *had* to say it, didn't you?" she said. "Just had to say something stupid like that."

My smile didn't falter as I started moving in Arnold's direction. "Hey, you're the one who taught me about faith," I said, watching the FLIR monitor as we walked. "You know, we don't always have to be the red shirts. Sometimes, we can actually be the Kirk or Spock instead of the security guy."

She returned my smile as she walked beside me and I have to admit, it felt good. But I couldn't allow myself to think about it at the moment. Despite trying to make light of our current situation, I believed we were actually in more danger than anyone realized. I hadn't wanted to say anything, but Arnold had picked up on Mia's trail pretty quick, indicating I'd been right about her being the black mass that had slunk down into the sewers on dad's monitor. And if Silver truly was lurking somewhere within the tunnels, it could only mean one thing…she was planning on stirring up the JDs with that homicidal concoction of hers.

No, Jackson. It's time to get your head in the game or you might not have a Nikki to patch things up with later.

Motioning my team for silence, we followed Arnold as he meandered his way through the disorienting maze that would have given Theseus a run for his money. I only hoped that the creatures on the other end would not be nearly as dangerous as the Minotaur of the same Greek legend.

I was just pondering the finer points of the heroic tale when I noticed a distinct change in the malodorous fumes we'd been inhaling. Gone was the atypical stench of feces and other human waste. Seriously, it was completely gone…replaced by something not quite so offensive, but foul in its own way. I took three quick whiffs then looked at my companions.

"You smell that?" I asked.

Nikki nodded. "Yeah, I do." She sniffed a few times, then added, "What do you think it is?"

I couldn't quite put my finger on it—or its significance. But forced to describe the strange odor, I'd have to say it was a slight mixture of sour milk and honey. The smell wasn't the biting, fierce stench that permeated the rest of the maze and I knew that somehow, whatever was causing it was neutral-izing the normal smells. Which begged the question: Why? What was it for?

But I knew the question would have to wait as we approached a portion of the tunnel curving sharply to the right and the sudden absence of any lights. As Arnold rounded the corner, he'd become almost completely enshrouded in darkness. Without the illumination of our own flashlights, we'd be unable to continue following the Jack Russell. Even more unnerv-ing to me was when Arnold suddenly stopped, took in a series of sniffs, and whined nervously. He ducked his head, huffed at the concrete slab near his feet once more, and turned to look at me.

"What's wrong?" I whispered to him.

In response, he just eyed me curiously, turned to look at the tunnel's bend, then back at me.

"I think he's found something," I whispered. "Only thing is, he seems a bit nervous. Doesn't want to move forward." I bent down and gave him a small dog biscuit. "Which worries me more than you can know." I had never told anyone this, but when I first met the little dog, he'd killed a creature that a full-grown sabre-tooth tiger had been unable to defeat. If Arnold was afraid, then there was more than a good chance that whatever lurked around the bend was not something any of us wanted to tangle with.

"Scott. Randy. What's your 10-20?"

Static.

"Dad? Any idea where Landers and Randy are?"

No answer from his end either.

I clicked the transmit button a few times, satisfied that the radio was working properly. Last year, when dealing with the tritons in the Cyclades Islands, the cryptids had developed a way of creating an electromagnetic pulse that effectively shorted out any electronic equipment within a certain radius. For a brief second, after not hearing back from the others on my team and finding the defective overhead lights, I was concerned that the same thing was happening here. But the crackle of static in the radio's tinny speakers told me we definitely had power.

"Guys?" I said again into the radio. "Can anyone read me?"

Still nothing.

I looked around at the curved walls of brick and mortar that surrounded us. It had been some time since we passed an exit ladder and I could only assume we'd moved steadily deeper into the sewers which might be causing interference.

Swell, I thought. *I've got no idea where our backup is, no clue what we're up against, an annoying newspaper reporter who might be working with one of my deadliest enemies, and a ticked-off ex-girlfriend with a tranq gun. What could possibly go wrong?*

The three of us stood silently, trying to peer through the murk and around the curve with the x-ray vision none of us had. No one spoke, nor offered any advice on how best to proceed. Apprehension coursed thick as Jell-O through each of our veins. None of us were anxious to move forward.

"Okay. There's nothing we can do about it," I said, absently mounting one more camera to the curved wall. "This is what we came here for. We've got to go forward." I nodded at Nikki's tranquilizer gun gripped tight in her hand. "But keep that thing up and ready just in case."

She nodded at this and idled up beside me, almost protectively. I smiled at the thought and took a single step forward.

The three of us rounded the corner with careful, deliberate steps. Our feet slid, rather than lifted, across the walkway as we pressed on. Arnold took up the rear, his hackles raised higher with each tenuous stride. Ten yards later, we suddenly found ourselves in an immense chamber—what appeared to be some sort of junction connecting four different sewer tunnels. In the darkness, there was no way to tell how expansive the room was, but I figured the ceiling was at least thirty feet high and the walls were fifty feet apart.

Our flashlight beams crisscrossed in sweeping arcs as we carefully explored the vast chamber. I signaled the team to stop their sweep the moment my light streaked across a splotch of crimson on the wall across the way. I held my index finger to my lips then pointed at the stains. As their eyes fixed on the tableau, I slowly moved the flashlight back and forth, illuminating more of the glistening red substance. The red stuff almost painted the algae-coated wall and walkway on the other side.

"Is...is that blood?" Davenport whispered; his voice cracking slightly.

In reply, I merely shrugged, lowered myself into the waste water, and sloshed over to the opposite side. With the flashlight held close to the nearest pool of red, I lowered my nose to it and inhaled. The scent of something sweet and aromatic wafted through my nasal passages, catching me off guard. Instinctively, I started coughing and covered my mouth with my shirt to muffle the sound.

Nikki hissed at the sudden noise and pulled the tranq gun into firing position as she swept the area for any movement my hacking might have elicited. When nothing stirred, she lowered the weapon and whispered over to me.

"Are you all right?"

I nodded and cleared my throat as best I could.

"It's not blood," I said after finally overcoming the coughing fit. I dipped a finger into the stuff and brought it to my tongue. It tasted just as sweet as it smelled. "It's some kind of berry juice. Lots and lots of berry juice."

"Dude!" Davenport croaked. "I can't believe you just tasted that."

I glared at him before turning my attention back to the stains.

"The same stuff as you found in the Central Park tree, you think?" Nikki asked. "The berries I mean."

Seeing nothing else of significance, I moved back over to where they was waiting, pulled myself over the rail and back onto the walkway.

"Yep. Seems to be their food source," I said, reaching into my pouch and pulling out a water bottle. I swished a capful of water around in my mouth and spat it into the sewer. "That stuff tastes nasty. Yuck!"

"Do you think those berries are what's causing the strange smell in here?" Nikki asked.

I shook my head. "I don't think so. The stains smell nothing like it. I don't think they're connected at all."

"Wait a minute," Davenport whispered. "So you think these creature things prefer these berries to human flesh?"

"What do you think?" I said with an edge of sarcasm. "We've already established that the JDs are more than likely herbivores. Our running theory is that they're some form of humanoid megabat. And if they keep to the dietary habits of most megabats—the flying fox or the fruit bat for instance—then their primary food would be either berries or nectar. I seriously doubt they have any interest in feeding on human flesh. Besides, none of the bodies we've examined looked gnawed upon." I shuddered at the memory of Aislynn's mutilated remains.

Nikki looked at me quizzically. "If this is no surprise to you, then why do I get the feeling that you're just a little freaked out right about now?"

I grimaced as I allowed my answer to ferment inside my head for a bit then decided the truth would be the best thing.

"It's the quantity that concerns me," I said. "We're talking enough berries to coat a highly porous brick wall. Enough to make it look like a blood bath occurred here as a matter of fact. I don't know exactly how much it would take to produce that much juice, but it's more than I would have ever dreamed necessary for two or three Jersey Devils."

"And that means?"

"It means that there might be more than *two or three* Jersey Devils down here. A heck of a lot more. As a matter of fact..."

Something warm and wet dropped from the ceiling onto my shoulder, stopping me in mid-sentence. I craned my head to see a droplet of crimson goo now splattered all over my Hawaiian-print shirt. At the sight of it, a shiver sent tremors down my spine and I immediately sent up a silent prayer that I would be wrong about the origin of the new stain. Slowly, I looked up into the high vaulted ceiling above. The FLIR imager followed my gaze and I gasped involuntarily at the ghastly sight it revealed.

Directly above me, hanging upside down by long taloned toes curled tightly around a series of water and drainage pipes, rested twelve bright red and orange shapes huddled tightly together. A grand total of twenty-four menacing red eyes reflected back at me as I looked from the small thermal imager screen to shadowy mass above me.

I'd been right. There were definitely a heck of lot more than two or three of these things and the confirmation sickened me. I'd seen firsthand what one of the creatures could do to a single human being. I had no interest in finding out what a dozen of them were capable of.

Still, the JDs simply stared back at us, completely disinterested. I figured we still had a chance to get out of this situation in one piece as long as no one did anything stupid.

"All right, here's what we're going to do," I whispered, hoping my voice didn't sound as terrified as I felt. From the looks on my team's faces, I had a feeling it wouldn't have mattered much if it did. They weren't exactly brimming over with loads of confidence themselves at that moment either. "Back up. Very slowly. Very carefully." I took a step backward to demonstrate my brilliant plan. "No sudden moves. No rash—"

Without warning, there were a series of flashes, clicks, and whirrs behind me. I spun around to see Davenport clicking away at an expensive looking Nikon with fevered enthusiasm. His eyes wide with wonder—if not dollar signs—his index finger clicked away furiously at the camera. The creatures began to stir at the brilliant cacophony of light and sound from the camera. Sharp piercing shrieks erupted from their equine-like mouths as they shuddered to life. Their leathery wings shook furiously as they unfurled in a display of aggressive defiance.

"—actions," I yelled. "No rash actions! Cripes, what the heck were you thinking?" I snatched the camera from the reporter's hand and tossed it into my pack. "Come on!"

Spinning around, we bolted from the junction chamber, running back the way we'd come as fast as our legs would move. The sound of two dozen bat-like wings and a choir of high-pitched screeches echoed menacingly behind us.

TWENTY-ONE

I MASHED THE TALK BUTTON ON MY RADIO AS WE RACED THROUGH THE labyrinth with twelve angry winged cryptids breathing down our necks. "Landers? Dad? Can you copy?" I shouted, rounding a corner and picking up speed. Davenport and Nikki were five feet ahead of me. I'd already lost track of where Arnold had gone, but figured he'd be fine. "Seriously guys, this ain't funny!"

A squeal of static erupted in my earpiece, nearly deafening me. Then Lander's garbled voice spoke up. "...can't hear...breaking...can you repeat?"

I risked a quick glance over my shoulder. Now that we'd made our way back into the portion of the sewer that had working overhead lights, the JDs had grown a bit more timid. They'd slowed down and I could only make out two or three of them as they scrambled hand over foot along the tunnel walls. One of them crawled upside down on the ceiling, crushing each light fixture as it passed to create a shadowy haven for its brethren to continue the pursuit.

"We really stirred up the hornets' nest down here!" I shouted into the headset. "We. Need. Help!"

I was breathing hard now, unable to continue the conversation as I negotiated another sharp turn and suddenly realized I'd completely lost sight of Nikki.

Swell. Why does everyone get lost in these situations but me?

"Jack?" Landers voice said into the ear bud. "Hang on...we're...to where...Just hang tight!" With another electronic squeal, the transmission ended.

I could only assume he was telling me they were on their way, but at the moment, I had no time to respond. The vanguard of my pursuers was now only a few feet away. If I didn't turn up the speed, I'd finally get an accurate demonstration of what it meant to be drawn and quartered.

"Nikki! Davenport!" I yelled while speeding down the tunnel. But there was no answer. Wherever they'd gotten themselves to, I could only assume they were a heck of a lot safer than me. Suddenly, a new well of panic bubbled up inside me. Nikki was now alone with Davenport...a man who may or may not be in the employ of Freakshow. If the madman wanted to take her from me, now would be the perfect opportunity to do it.

Crap. Crap. Crap. "Nikki," I mouthed as I rounded another turn. *Where are you, sweetie?*

But I couldn't worry about it now. Too much was at stake. If I got myself killed, I'd be no good to her if she was in trouble. And the screeches from the JDs behind me had become shorter, choppier; followed by the long string of clicks I'd heard in my last encounter with the creatures. They were signaling each other; using some form of primitive communication. I couldn't decipher what was being said. Of course, at that moment, I really didn't care.

I'd also noticed something else. The smell of soured milk and honey had given way once more to the horrific stench of waste and sewage. Whatever had expunged the normal odors earlier was apparently not being used in this section of the tunnels. I wasn't sure that was a good or a bad thing.

However, as I looked up ahead to see what looked like another junction, I realized it was all a moot point anyway. If this chamber was anything like the one in which we'd found the creatures nesting, I'd be able to slip down one of several tributaries and hopefully lose them in a maze. Besides, I hadn't been sprayed with Devil Juice any time lately. I had a feeling that once they cooled down from being roused from their slumber by Davenport's flashbulbs, their normally passive demeanors would kick in and they'd give up the chase. All I had to do was hold out for a bit longer and I'd be home free.

But my brief glimmer of optimism was quickly dashed as the overhead lights ahead were suddenly snuffed out. I made out the shadowy forms of four chimeric creatures scrambling in my direction. Suddenly, I knew what the clicking noises had been for. They'd been signaling their counterparts who were busy flanking me from the same tributaries I'd hoped to use for my own escape. Now, I was going to be trapped between the two groups like a bug between two fly-swatters.

"Swell," I said, wheeling around to look behind me. I could just discern the shapes of three Devils stalking closer. Their high speed pursuit had slowed the moment I came to a stop; to be replaced by a slow, steady gait. With their wings folded behind their backs, their long, muscular arms and short simian legs shuffled through the sewer water with ease. Their brethren, coming from the opposite direction met up with them and I quickly found myself surrounded on all sides. The only thing keeping them at bay was the rickety metal safety rail that ran along the walkway.

Not exactly Fort Knox, is it?

I just hoped it wouldn't be the Alamo either.

The water sloshed around their feet as they inched closer, while keeping a safe distance at the same time. I counted seven creatures in all. Where the other five had gone, I had no idea...but then, seven was more than enough to have to worry about. The biggest one presented himself in the center of the semi-circle they'd created to surround me. I couldn't see much more than inky silhouettes in the darkness, but the biggest—I assumed it was the alpha—shook its upper torso violently. Its long, course hair and leathery wing rose up to present an even larger, more threatening figure.

Compared to the others, the alpha was immense. While its brethren averaged about seven to eight feet in height, this one, at full stride, stood a whopping twelve feet tall if it stood an inch. Its girth easily equaled two of the smaller ones standing shoulder to shoulder. And though I couldn't make out the details of its fur, I could tell that it was much longer...fuller than the rest. But it was the creature's eyes that captivated me. The red pinprick of reflections seemed to burn right through me, chilling me in place. For the life of me, I couldn't tear my own wide eyes away.

Then, the alpha screeched. Loud and piercing, the shriek was like a hundred fingernails scraping the sides of as many blackboards. I jumped at the sound. My reaction seemed to embolden the creature and it took a single step forward. Then another. The water churned with each step, sending up waves of wastewater cresting over the catwalk. Finally, upon its third stride, it was leaning against the paint-chipped rail. Satisfied it was as close as it could get to me without crawling over the railing, the thing let out a series of clicks followed immediately by similar sounds by its companions. It dragged in a deep breath, exhaled, and clicked some more. But it also didn't move.

And neither did I.

The JDs hadn't completely blocked my path since they had remained down in the river of wastewater while I stood feebly on the walkway. But it would take very little effort for any one of them to clamber up to me if they chose and I quickly realized we were in a sort of standoff. No, that's not exactly right either. It was more like they were sizing me up. Assessing me. The strings of clicking seemed to corroborate my hypothesis.

Their behavior at that moment helped solidify my theory that they were normally docile unless provoked. Unfortunately, I honestly wasn't sure how that bit of information would help me at the moment. After all, they were still riled up and aggressively defending their territory. I was the uninvited guest who'd invaded it and threatened them with retinal-burning light from my flashlight. In short, though they were curious about me for the moment, I didn't know how much longer it would last. Eventually, they would have to decide what to do with me and I'd rather not be around when they did.

The big one took another series of sniffs in the air before continuing with their strange form of dialogue.

"Jack?" Landers voice crackled into my headset. "Are you there?"

I stiffened at the sudden intrusion into the very delicate standoff. On the one hand, every instinct in my body screamed at me to grab hold of the radio and shout for the ENIGMA agent to find me as soon as possible and blow these winged freaks to bloody bits. But the more rational, scientific side of me understood that A) it would be wrong from an ethical perspective. These were living creatures. Quite possibly nearly extinct. My time in Greece last year and the ecological homilies of Clarence Templeton had helped me realize that I'd callously killed far too many cryptids in my time. The pint-sized eco-terrorist might have been a radical, if not a little nuts, but his arguments had made a certain kind of sense. I'd sworn back then that I would change. I would strive to protect such creatures at any cost. But there was also the more practical Reason B. Quite frankly, it would probably prove to be a disaster if I gave into my panic and called for Landers to drop his own version of *Shock and Awe*. After all, any sudden movement…any escalation of noise…could set the monsters into another frenzy. With me at Ground Zero. No. I decided I'd see this through my own way. I'd figure a way out of this without harming any of them if at all possible.

That's when I noticed that all seven of the cryptids were now pressed up against the rail. Their clicking had stopped and the entire group was busy sniffing the air. One of the creatures gripped the railing and I heard it rattle in the gloom. My heart pounded as I sucked in a breath. Were they making their move or were they just trying to get a better look at me?

Look? I struggled with that word.

How exactly are *they seeing me?*

With the red glow of their eyes, I was convinced they had relatively poor night vision. Yet they insisted on clinging to the shadows. They'd destroyed each of the overhead lights as they'd chased me, as if illumination was repellant to them. Sure. The fact that their eyes glowed red in total darkness told me they had a layer of tissue in the back of the eye known as *tapetum lucidum*. The tissue, common in many animals, was known to reflect light back through the retina, increasing the amount of illumination available to be used in the dark. But the color reflected was the key. Amber and green generally meant excellent night vision. Red indicated poor night vision. Humans, who had no *tapetum lucidum*, hardly possessed any natural ability to see in the dark at all.

But though they most probably could see better within the darkened sewer than I could, I was confident the JDs' vision was nowhere near the ability of say, an owl or a cat. Or even other bats for that matter. So what could it be?

Infrared? Thermal?

My mind raced through the various animals that used such forms of sight, but something kept nagging at the back of my subconscious. Something obvious. Something I was missing.

Are you sure they don't use sonar like microbats? I asked myself.

No. From what I've seen of them, their ears are much too small. There's nothing to pick up the signals they send out.

Well, what about the horns? Could they not act as some sort of auditory receptors?

Don't be stupid. The only way the horns could act as receptors would be if...holy smoke! The horns. That's it! I'm a freakin' genius! Now all I have to do is—

"Jack? We're with Nikki and Alex," Landers' voice nearly made me jump; though I was elated to hear that Nikki was safe. The JDs, sensing my sudden start, tensed and their clicking began anew. "We're searching for you now. Reply if you copy."

My thumb moved down to the transmit button of the radio, but hovered there, unwilling to press it. If I did, this nerve-wracking, though oddly serene moment I was having with the colony of cryptids would be over. They might not tear me limb from limb, but this temporary reprieve would be finished and I'd once again be running for my life. My scientific curiosity was winning out over my instinct to survive.

The creature just to my left leaned past the railing, its snout brushing against my shirt and inhaling deeply as the others clicked feverishly at their companion.

My hand eased away from the radio.

I had to know. Sure, I had Davenport's camera tucked safely away in my pack. But a two-dimensional image on film was no substitute for an eye-witnessed observation. I had to know if my theory was right.

Realizing that I still clutched the flashlight in my right hand, I raised it up and pressed down on the power button. The beam shot out in a wide cone of brilliant light. In unison, the creatures reeled back, bringing their wings around the block the light from their eyes and let out another ear-piercing shriek. Instinctively, I shut off the flashlight once more. I'd seen what I needed in that brief two seconds of illumination.

Eyewitness descriptions had been uncannily accurate in their assess-ment of the creatures. Their torsos were long and broad with a thick, muscular frame covered in a pelt of course dark hair. I could see what Johnny meant when he said they resembled some mutated form of silver-backed gorilla with their short, stout legs and long, massive arms. Though they were capable of walking upright on two legs, they preferred to move on all four limbs. And their faces. I'd always assumed the equine features of legend had been mere hyperbole. But I'd been wrong. Their oval-shaped jaw line, broad snout, and large flat teeth gave the strangely chimeric impression that some insane god had haphazardly stuck the head of a mare on the body of an ape-shaped bat.

Then, of course, there were the objects I'd been determined to get a closer look at: the spiraled horns—ranging in length from six to about twelve inches—that adorned each of their heads. I still wasn't sure if they were what I suspected...but the strange grooves that spiraled around them were just another piece of evidence to support my theory.

But at the moment, I had bigger problems to deal with. The brief blast of light had only slightly stunned them. It wasn't enough to have been able to make my escape from their semi-circular prison. Now the seven large silhouettes were more agitated than before. Their clicking was reaching a fevered pitch and I watched as they shifted from their right to left feet as if getting ready to pounce. Against my better judgment, I'd wrecked the moment with my flashlight stunt and my irritated pursuers were slowly building into a frenzy.

Suddenly, the alpha shoved the creature to my left out of the way and leaned forward. Its simian-like arms whipped out, trying to grab me, but I dodged to the right with a duck.

Okay. Yeah, now you're screwed, Jackson.

Frustrated, the larger creature snarled, took hold of the oxidized railing, and shook it violently, trying to rip it from the platform. The six others, taking their cue from their leader, followed suit. The sound of metal twisting echoed throughout the vaulted tunnel. They could have easily just climbed over, but if they had any reasoning capability, it was being drowned out by their own bloodlust.

Okay, Jack, I thought. *Time to turn on the brilliance!*

I began mentally inventorying what I had at my disposal. A flashlight—but I'd already discovered that it wouldn't be enough. A walkie-talkie. Half a roll of duct tape. A cell phone. A pocket full of transmitter chips I often use to tag the cryptids I hunt. A pocket knife. And...

What's this in my cargo pocket?

I reached in, my fingers gripping a smooth glass container. I recognized it immediately as my dad's Aqua Velva bottle he'd given me just after my first trip down into the sewers. I'd completely forgotten to throw it away. I glanced skyward and mouthed a grateful "thank you." If my theory about how these creatures "see" was accurate, then this putrid stuff would be exactly what the doctor ordered...well, along with a few other odds and ends from my little MacGyver arsenal.

The sound of crumbling mortar and brick erupted to my right and I watched helplessly as the rail buckled under the sheer strength of seven pairs of muscular arms and was yanked from the walkway. Immediately, two of the creatures scrambled up on either side of me with the other five spreading their wings and pounding their chests with powerful fists.

"Yep," I said out loud. "Time's up."

I pulled my headset out from my ear, yanked the radio off my belt, and placed both items speaker to speaker. I then mashed the walkie-talkie's transmit button and quickly wrapped a ribbon of duct tape around the two objects. The radio erupted in a loud screech as the two speakers created a raucous wave of feedback that almost brought me to my knees. The creatures were as equally hindered by the sudden squelching, but they continued their slow advance while covering their ears with hairy hands.

Phase two, I thought, pulling the Aqua Velva bottle from my pocket and raising it above my head. I then hurled it at the walkway. The glass shattered, releasing an explosion of nine putrid ounces of men's aftershave all over the ground. Simultaneously, I powered up the flashlight once more and blasted their eyes with a beam of brilliant light. Instantly, the monsters froze. No screams. No shrieks or clicks. Just as I'd predicted, they'd become completely immobilized with sensory overload.

"Which leads me to phase three," I said as I turned and squeezed past the creature between me and the nearby junction I'd been running to earlier. I could still hear the horrible screech of the walkie-talkie feedback as I rounded the corner and dashed toward the nearest tunnel.

TWENTY-TWO

NAVIGATING THE TUNNEL AT A FULL SPRINT, I QUICKLY CAME TO A DEAD end to the catwalk and was forced to lower myself into the water. It wasn't the optimum situation, but I couldn't turn back and still had to put some distance between me and the creatures. I just couldn't be sure how long my makeshift flashbang would hold the JDs off, so a little dip in sewer water was the price I was going to have to pay.

Once down into the river of filth, I trudged more slowly; wary of finding a slick spot on the stone floor and slipping into the pool. It had taken at least three showers to get the smell out the last time and I wasn't looking forward to going through that again. I already had the feeling I'd need at least two just to get the Aqua Velva taint off me as it was.

Of course, if I could have found a stupid exit in the crazy sewer, all my troubles would be over and I would have gladly succumbed to as many showers as I needed. But I hadn't seen a single one since the chase had begun. The maze of tunnels reminded me of some sort of weird Escher woodcut with innumerable corridors that shifted and warped as I ventured further into them. The deeper into the sewers I delved, the more lost I seemed to become.

I moved as silently as possible, careful not to stir up a wake as my legs churned through the water. I'd already found a section of tunnel that had working overhead lights, so I stowed my flashlight, pulled out the FLIR, and scanned for signs of trouble as I walked. So far, so good. I'd stopped hearing the shriek of the walkie-talkie about five minutes ago—whether because of distance or equipment failure, I wasn't sure. But I had to assume my pursuers were on the prowl again.

Of course, the Jersey Devils weren't the only thing I was searching for. Thankfully, Landers had said he'd met up with Nikki and Davenport. They were even now scouring the labyrinth for me and I wanted to find them quick and get out while the getting was good. I had to assume we'd accomplished our mission and posted enough IR cameras down here to get enough footage to discover the secret behind their presence here in the city.

I was pondering that very question when a light from the far end of the tunnel blinked out, bringing me to a sudden halt. The FLIR's lens shot up, pointing in the direction of the burned out light.

Ah, crap.

In shades of red, orange, and yellow, I was able to make out a large winged outline skulking along the rounded ceiling ahead of me. I glanced over my shoulder, but could see nothing bringing up the rear. It had been several minutes since I'd seen my last tributary, but I knew if I started running toward it, there'd be no way of avoiding being spotted. I'd have an even poorer chance of outrunning the winged cryptid.

Think, Jackson. Think.

The next light popped, sparked, and went black; shrouding the entire far end of the corridor in darkness. My heart throbbed inside my chest as I nixed one option after another. I'd used up my best weapons in my earlier gambit. There wasn't much else I could do.

I heard a low growl just before the light nearest to me popped out of existence. I didn't need the thermal imager to make out the shape of a large black mass clinging to the ceiling. I stowed the camera in my pack and let out a breath. Fortunately, I didn't think my stalker had any backup.

Remembering my first encounter with them down here just the day before, I moved over the wall and pressed myself against it. My only hope was that its senses were still reeling from my rather ingenious move earlier, enough to make it blind to my presence.

That is, if it's one of the seven that surrounded you earlier, knucklehead. Remember, five were missing.

I rolled my eyes at my stupid pessimistic inner monologue.

Not now, I thought. *I'm in no mood.*

Don't worry. Stick around here too long and you'll never have another mood again. You need to run.

The shadowy silhouette scrambled closer, still clinging to the ceiling until it came to the light fixture almost directly overhead.

Yeah, Chuckles. That would be real smart, wouldn't it? Splashing through ankle high water, I wouldn't get five feet.

I heard the thing sniffing above me, just before it let out a series of eight staccato clicks. Then, it hissed and dropped down in front of me.

Déjà vu, I thought as my heart pounded even faster than the creature's incessant clicking. *If I get out of this, I swear...I swear...I swear...I will think long and hard about mucking around in dark tunnels ever again.*

Of course, God and I both knew I was lying through my teeth, but it sure felt good to pretend. That is, until the chimera turned to face me. Its luminescent eyes sliced through my courage like twin lasers burning through a child's balloon. Suddenly it hissed and lunged straight at me without warning. I tried to duck, but the creature's meaty hands grabbed me around the neck and lifted me off the ground. I tried to scream, but its grip strangled the air right out of me. My face reddened. I felt my ears burning and my cheeks flushing as I struggled for breath.

But I knew air was the least of my problems. If the creature's chokehold didn't ease soon, my circulation would be cut off; resulting in rapid multi-organ shutdown well before my oxygen ran out. Frantically, I tried prying its rough, leathery talons loose, but my strength was already failing.

Oddly, I sensed little hostility in the attack. The creature's actions bordered more on enthusiastic fascination more than rage—like a young boy who pulls of the wings off a butterfly to see what would happen.

Yeah. Either way, it ain't ever pleasant for the butterfly.

Red splotches danced in my field of vision. If there'd been any light, I knew things would be going dark. I was running out of time. Desperately, I swung my right foot forward, hoping to connect with its groin or any other tender area, but in my weakened condition, the kick did nothing but elicit a short huff of irritation. I felt its hands closing even tighter around my throat for the effort.

A splash of water from the opposite end of the tunnel caught both of our attention. The creature stiffened at the sound; the hair on its arms bristled against my probing fingers. Its grip loosened slightly as it bobbed its horse-like head around from left to right, tasting the air for a scent. The Devil let out another series of clicks, then a low, steady keening warbled from its throat. Whatever was lurking in the darkness at the other end of the tunnel answered back. Its voice, several octaves higher, matched the tone and pitch of the creature's whine.

The grip relaxed even further, as it slowly turned to face the newcomer. I could hear the newcomer moving toward us in slow, rhythmic splashes. But the cryptid didn't seem concerned. On the contrary, it almost seemed pleased with this new intrusion. Which, I figured, could only mean disaster for me.

"Dr. Jackson," spoke a low female voice in the darkness. "Listen to me very carefully."

Who the devil—er, I mean, who the heck is that?

As if reading my mind, the newcomer said in a calm, soothing voice, "It's me. Mia Leeds. I'm here to help you."

Though the creature's grip had eased, I still had very little air to hurl the string of curses that rushed through my mind at that very moment. No matter what she said, I figured the girl was here to kill me and was playing some kind of mind game with me. I struggled more violently against the beast, thrashing my arms against its torso in hope it would release me. But I only succeeded in forcing it to tighten its hold around my neck again.

"Don't struggle," she said. Her voice seemed to be right beside me now, though I knew it was merely a trick of the echoes within the tunnels. "The more threatening you behave, the more she'll react."

She?

"You're lucky it's Esther," Mia said with a soft chuckle. "If Goliath had wrapped his hands around you like that, your head would have already popped off your shoulder like a bad zit."

Is she talking about Bible stories now or am I going insane from oxygen deprivation?

Mia clucked her tongue a few more times, imitating the clicking noises so common among the JDs. Then she took another step and I was able to finally make out her slight figure in the gloom.

"I'd use my flashlight to let you see me better, but they hate any kind of light within their aeries," she said. "But I think you've already discovered that."

The silver-haired girl stopped within a foot of the winged monster. For its part, the creature seemed to relax a great deal in her presence and I felt its grip slacken even more. The simian beast turned to look at Mia, lowered its head as if curtsying, then let out a slight harrumph of acknowledgment. The scene reminded me of some wild re-imagining of Tarzan, with a great ape cowing before the Lord of the Jungle. Or considering I'm in the grip of an over-sized flying monkey, maybe a better analogy would be the Wicked Witch of the Oz.

"Now, Dr. Jackson, I'm about to do something," Mia cooed in her most soothing voice. "No matter what you think of me...no matter what you think I'm doing, do *not* react in any way. If you tense up, Esther will more than likely snap your neck. Do you understand?"

My eyes widened at her suggestion, but I knew she wouldn't be able to see me—I was merely a darker shade against the black.

"On second thought, maybe it's best you don't try to answer," she said. "But you might want to close your eyes for this."

Close my eyes? Is she crazy? It's already dark enough in here—

Before I finished the thought, she stepped up to Esther, reached out a hand, and with the hiss of a spray bottle pump, a shroud of mist drifted up toward my face, dousing my skin and hair with a cold liquid.

Holy crap! She's spraying me! She's spraying me!

Instinctively, I jerked my head away, trying to avoid any more exposure to the strange concoction the witch was squirting on me. Esther, sensing my apprehension, growled, then squeezed my throat even tighter. I struggled against her grip, swinging my fists wildly in a panicked fit. The knuckles of my right hand slammed against the Devil's snout, eliciting a shrill howl. But her grip remained firm. Once again, splotches of light flashed before my eyes. I was about to lose consciousness and there wasn't a darned thing I could do about it. The crazy silver-haired goth had actually succeeded in killing me.

"Shhhhhhh," I heard Mia say. "Easy girl. He didn't mean to hurt you."

He didn't mean to hurt you? I silently screamed. The only noise that managed to escape my strangling throat was little more than a whimpering growl. *What about me?*

She shushed the beast again, then followed it up with a another series of ticks from her tongue. I felt Esther relax slightly and once more, the sweet flood of air rushed into my lungs.

"It's all right Esther. Everything's going to be all right. Dr. Jackson here is going to help us find him for you. He's our friend," she said. "He's Phisto's friend too. But you have to release him. You have to let him go so he can find Phisto."

Pressure to my neck eased even more at Mia's calming words. The creature drew me closer, sniffing the air as she did.

Oh crap, I thought. *She's going to smell that stuff on me and that'll be it.*

But wait. That didn't make any sense. Why spray me with the homicidal cocktail only to try to talk the cryptid down? Why would she spend so much time trying to get her to relax...to let me go? And who on earth was *Phisto*? I wasn't sure whether it was due to some major oxygen deprivation or the adrenaline euphoria elicited by sheer terror—but I suddenly became aware that I honestly had no clue what was going on.

Luckily, it didn't seem to matter much to Esther whether I understood or not because she certainly seemed to. Slowly, after three more huffs of air, she lowered me to the ground and took a step back. Immediately, I drew in the largest breath I could muster, which sent me into a coughing fit as the cool air scraped against my irritated esophagus. At the commotion, Esther's hackles raised once more and she let out a slow, cautious growl.

"Shhhhhh...Esther, it's all right," Mia whispered. "It's fine. Go back to the others." I watched the girl's silhouette gesture with her hands, essentially shooing the winged beast away like a mangy mongrel. Esther instantly complied and I watched as her massive bulk leapt onto the ceiling again and melted away in the darkness beyond.

A very obedient mangy mongrel, apparently.

The thought no more entered my mind than I became acutely aware of another presence in the tunnel with us. The amber reflection of two round eyes beamed back at me at approximately where Mia's shins would be. The eyes blinked twice, followed by the panting whine of a dog.

"Arnold?" I asked with a gravelly voice. "Is that you?"

Another whine, then a slight whimper of acknowledgement. Then I remembered. I'd sent the mutt into the sewers to track Mia Leeds down. When we started getting chased by the chimeric cryptids, Arnold must have stayed on task and located her. But now the little traitor was actually *with* the crazy woman. The fact that he wasn't sucking on a toothpick right now over her cold, bloodless corpse told me that he didn't see her as any sort of threat. But that didn't make sense. The woman was trying to kill—wait a minute.

"What's going on here?" I said. "What just happened?"

She let out a soft giggle, which reminded me of the sound of rainfall on a thick canopy of trees. Almost elfin, if you really want to know the truth.

"I think I just saved your life," she said, flicking on a flashlight which nearly blinded me in the stark darkness. "But before I answer all your questions, maybe we should get back to your friends. They're probably very worried and quite honestly, I only want to tell my story once. So let's go. I'll take you to them."

She turned to leave, but I remained rooted in place.

"I ain't going anywhere until you tell me what you just sprayed on me," I growled. "Why did that stuff not send your friend *Esther* into a homicidal frenzy?"

She laughed again and shrugged. "My dear, Jack...why on earth would Esther attack someone with her own scent?"

"Excuse me?"

"Yeah, I keep forgetting he told me how dense you can be at times," she said before continuing. "The secretion that our killer is using was taken from the interaural gland of Phisto. That's why the colony tends to go a little nuts when they get a whiff of him. And it's also why they're own excretions doesn't create the same reaction."

"Huh?"

Yeah. Either I was still reeling from near asphyxia or nothing the girl said made any sense to me.

"I promise. I'll explain everything once we're with your team," she said. "Hey, if nothing else, you can say you caught me and look like a hero to your friends."

Trying my best to look uninterested in such petty ploys, I casually pretended to dust the Jersey Devil's course fur off my imaginary lapel. But then, it wasn't very often I got to outshine Landers, who'd give Robocop a run for his money. And, of course, showing up Davenport in front of Nikki wouldn't be a bad thing either.

"All right," I said. "I'll go along with this." Then I dug into my pack, pulled out my roll of duct tape, and threw her my most devilish smile while pulling a strip away from the roll and biting it off with my teeth. "But if we're going to do this, we're going to do it right."

TWENTY-THREE

"So how exactly did you figure your dad's aftershave would work to ward off the creatures?" Randy asked with a sly grin while walking over to the conference room table.

I rolled my eyes and nodded over at Mia Leeds, who was still bound with duct tape and secured to a chair. It had been a bear sneaking her into the hotel like that without raising any eyebrows, but we'd managed it thanks to the fact that one of the staff maids had taken a shine to my dad since he'd been staying there. "Um, *hello?* I think the important thing right now is to interview Mia here," I said as nonchalant as I could. Truth be told, I was dying to tell them about my awesome MacGyver moment. I just wanted to play it cool. "Not me."

"Actually, I'm kind of curious about that myself," our silver-haired prisoner said, with an infuriatingly self-assured smile.

I watched Landers double check the duct tape bonds while Arnold sauntered beside Mia, lay down next to her, and cautiously set up watch over her. Satisfied, I took my seat around the table. I was slightly surprised when Nikki strode over and plopped down in the chair next to me. She glanced my way and gave me a subtle wink.

Truth be told, when Mia and I finally caught up with the rest of the team, Nikki had been more excited to see me than I would have imagined. Surprisingly, she'd actually been worried about me. On the drive back to the hotel, I'd learned that the moment she'd realized we'd been separated, she'd demanded they turn around and find me, but Davenport—the jerk—would

have none of it. They'd become completely turned around in the maze and
Davenport didn't think they could find their way back to where we'd
originally split up. He'd claimed that it would be better to catch up with the
rest of the team and search the tunnels for me with them...for safety's sake.
If I was honest with myself, I'd have to admit, he'd made the right call. But
I'd never tell *him* that though.

Another thing I would never admit to anyone? When Nikki had so
gratefully wrapped her arms around me once we'd been re-united...well, it
almost made the entire Devil attack worth it.

"...think that any discoveries you have made regarding how best to deal
with the creatures would be beneficial for everyone, Jack," Landers was
saying when I finally pulled my eyes away from Nikki's. "We have time to
talk to Ms. Leeds. But for now, I think we should all hear about your
aftershave bomb."

"Yeah, I'd like to know too, Obadiah," Dad said with a scowl, clearly
annoyed that I hadn't used his gift the way he'd intended. He wadded up the
piece of paper with the maid's phone number scrawled on it and tossed it in
the trash before sitting down opposite me. "That stuff ain't cheap, ya know.
You owe me a bottle."

"Geeze, Dad...Sorry I used your aftershave to save my hide and all," I
said, briefly re-living the experience. I couldn't help but shudder at the
memory. Oh, don't get me wrong. It wasn't the close call with the vicious
cryptids that sent the uncontrollable chills down my spine. That happens
just all too often in my line of work. No, if you want to know the truth, it
was the filth. The smell. The sheer nastiness of those sewers that left me
with a queasy feeling. Even though, we'd taken a few minutes to get cleaned
up after we got back, I still felt the grime and stench clinging to me like
slime to a frog's back. "But the whole thing's really no big deal." I pointed
over to the white board, the red marker notes we'd taken during our last
meeting were still there. "It's been bugging me how these creatures see. My
first excursion into sewer seemed to indicate they didn't have the best night

vision in the world. But they didn't have the larger ears that are so common in animals that use echolocation."

I paused, taking a sip from the water bottle and glanced around the room. All eyes were fixed on me. Mia was not only staring, she was beaming from ear to ear, thoroughly enjoying my exposition. Of course, I had a feeling that none of this was news to her. She could easily fill us in on anything we wanted to know about the Jersey Devils and then some. Whether she would cooperate was another matter entirely.

"Anyway, as those things were circling me, I kept watching them—well, it was too dark to watch, but you know what I mean. I paid attention to their behavior patterns. And two things kept popping up over and over.

"The first thing I noticed was the clicking noises they were making. Sure sounded like echolocation to me. But it just didn't make any sense. Like I said before, their ears..."

"Could they use their horns to pick up sound waves?" Randy asked, stroking his soul patch in deep thought.

I just stared at his fingers as he played with it for several seconds. Couldn't take my eyes off it actually. After this investigation, I was going to have to have a serious talk with him about that ugly caterpillar-looking thing. Then, remembering his initial question, I shook my head. "No, I thought the same thing...until I figured out what the horns are actually used for. But I'll get to that in a second," I said, then took another drink. After the ordeal in the sewers, I could swear I could taste the putrid filth in my mouth. The water helped a little. "Back to the clicking. I noticed that they were doing it back and forth. It was a form of communication with each other. But what kind of communication? What could they be saying?"

"That you owe me a bottle of Aqua Velva," my dad growled, leaning back in his chair with a sideways grin.

Ignoring the old man's barb, I continued. "That's when I started concentrating on the second thing I noticed...the incessant sniffing. They constantly sniffed around, like a bloodhound after game. The only time they didn't sniff was when they exchanged clicks."

"Okay, Jack, stop milking this," Nikki said. "Unlike these guys, I agree with you, I'd rather be interviewing our captive. Just tell us without the drama, why the aftershave?"

I burst into a grin at the interruption and threw her a wink. That's my girl. She knew exactly what I did—the real information was going to come from Mia Leeds, not me. "Okay," I said. "No drama. Basically, Randy, you're right about the horns. They are integral to how they 'see,' but not through sound waves. They're actually a sort of sensory compiler."

"Come again?" Randy asked, genuinely amazed.

"Um, okay...let's put it this way. They do have eyes, but I believe their vision is rather poor. They have nostrils on their snout, which is where the sniffing comes from. And they can obviously hear, though they don't use echolocation. Just one of those senses aren't enough to create the visual picture they use to see by. I believe these horns act as a type of computer. It gathers all the sensory input, compiles and processes it to create an image in the creature's brain. It somehow sorts through all the different senses to provide a visual picture of their environment," I said. "It explains why the area near their nest had a distinctly different aroma than the rest of the sewers. It's my guess that they use some sort of secretion to neutralize foreign smells near their nests. That way, it will be easier to sense any danger that might enter their domain. It would sort of be the same thing as having spotlights with motion detectors installed around your bed. No one would be able to sneak up on you."

Landers shook his head. "So you're saying these things actually see by converting odors to visual images? That's a little far-fetched, don't you think?"

"Not necessarily," my dad said, leaning forward in his chair and propping his elbows on the table. "There are a number of reptiles—including many types of snakes—that use smells to see by. It's actually not as *far-fetched* as you might think."

"Plus, that's not the only way they see," I said. "As I said, the olfactory senses are just part of the big picture."

"And the clicking noises?" Nikki asked. "You're thinking it's some sort of cooperative effort. Maybe the sensory input is too much for a single creature to filter, so somehow they visualize in a communal system by the clicks? Like a hive mind?"

My smile broadened hearing this. "Exactly!" Not only was she gorgeous, she was a genius to boot. "That's what I figured out. So, I decided the only way to get away from them was too assault all their senses at the same time. Light, which they seemed to hate. The sound of my radio squelch to disrupt their auditory senses and hive communication. And the Aqua Velva—"

"To shut down their sense of smell," Randy said with a laugh. "That's awesome, dude! Brilliant!"

I swear I could feel my head swelling three times as big as when I'd entered the conference room at the accolades. They didn't come often or freely, so when they did, I enjoyed soaking them up. But a gentle buzz in the back of my mind kept nagging me. People were dying. Aislynn had been murdered. There was no time for pats on the back. Now was the time to put a stop to this once and for all.

I turned to glare at Mia. "Now, it's your turn," I said. "Start talking."

She cocked her head to one side and smiled. A swath of silver hair shifted, half obscuring her face, but from the shadows I could almost make out a mischievous gleam in them.

"What would you like to know?" she said. "I told you in the sewers it was time for you to know everything. All you have to do is ask."

I looked at the team and shrugged my incredulity. I could not believe just how ridiculous her statement sounded. Just like that? She's going to give it all up? No games? No tricks. Yeah, and I'm a Chinese rock star.

"Seriously?" I said. "All I have to do is *ask*? You'll tell me just like that?"

Her smile never wavered for a second. "Yep."

"Okay. Why don't we start with why you're doing this. Why have you been using those...those *things* to kill people?"

She suddenly turned serious and shook her head. "That, dear Jack, is the wrong question."

"What do you mean, it's the wrong question? You said you'd answer—"

"Did you do it?" Nikki broke in, leaning forward. "Are you saying we have it wrong?"

"Bingo!" Mia said, her smile returning. "Oh, he was right...you're definitely the smart one of the group, Nikki."

I glanced at Mia, then Nikki, and back to Mia. "Who? Who do you keep talking about? Who's *he?*"

"Sorry, that's the one question I can't answer. At least, not yet. But your girlfriend's right, Jack. I'm not responsible for what's going on. I came here to stop the killings actually."

"And your cohorts in the park?" Davenport chimed in. "The ones that attacked me? I suppose you're trying to tell me they're here to *help* too?"

"We attacked you because we couldn't let pictures of the *Houskaani*—at least, clear, professionally taken pictures anyway—ever see the light of day," she said, her eyes narrowing at the reporter. "We weren't really going to kill you, but we definitely wanted you to be afraid for your life, yes."

"Wait," I said. "A Houska-what now?"

"Houskaani. It's plural, by the way. Houskaan is singular. It's what we call the creatures the world knows as the Jersey Devil. It's what my family has called them since their discovery nearly eight hundred years ago."

"Eight hundred? I thought they were first witnessed during the colonial era. My research suggests the legend only dates back as far as 1735," I said.

"Well, that's true," she said. "As far as the modern *American* legend is concerned. But the creatures are far older than that. Much older. As far as we know, the first actual interaction with modern humans they've had was back around the thirteenth century, in the center of what's now the Czech Republic."

"Houska Castle," Landers said. When Mia gave him a quizzical look, he smiled and continued. "Jack had me do some research on something you had mentioned to him. The Gateway to Hell and the Czech Republic. Houska Castle was what kept popping up, but information about it is pretty scarce."

Mia nodded at this, returning his smile. "Hopefully, I'll be able to fill in those blanks then. The story that my family has told for generations is that in 1253, King Ottakar of Bohemia commissioned a very special castle to be built near Houska. He did so at the advice of three advisers who had hatched a pretty nasty plot to overthrow him. You see, believing the pit on which the castle was to be built was the gateway to Hell itself, the advisors wished to harness the dark powers of hell itself to wrest control of the kingdom. Only, their evil plans backfired.

"The story goes that construction released something that had been dormant for millennia...sleeping within the caverns below the earth. Large, winged creatures—believed to be demons from Hell itself—arose from the pit to tear asunder any who got in their way. Including the three advisors, by the way."

"Did she just use the word 'asunder'?" Randy asked, laughing.

"Shut up, Randy," I said, barely containing my own chuckle. To be fair, it was a game we played often, so I really couldn't blame him. Turning serious again, I looked at Mia and smirked. "Are you trying to tell me that these things really *are* demons?"

"Wait, Jack," Nikki said. "I've heard of this place. Back in Malaysia, a conversation came up with Marc about demons. He told me something about a place called Houska, which supposedly rested on top of a large pit that locals believed opened a doorway to hell. I can't remember the whole story, but he said something about sending prisoners down the pit on ropes—with the promise of exoneration if they would come back and tell people what they saw. Unfortunately, if I'm remembering correctly, the only person who ever came up from the pit alive had been driven insane. Soon after that, they decided to build a castle on top of it...but Marc never explained why."

The silver-haired teen rolled her eyes. "Well, if you all will let me finish, I'll continue with my tale."

With a smug nod, I urged her to continue with a promise that we wouldn't interrupt again.

"Okay," she said, "Where was I? Oh yeah. Anyway, with the people being ravaged by these creatures, Ottakar sent out an edict to anyone who was brave enough to answer. He promised a very handsome reward to anyone willing to vanquish the demons."

"Seriously...vanquish?" Randy asked. "Who talks like that anymore?"

I glared at him before nodding apologetically for Mia to continue.

"Anyway, priests and monks came from miles around to perform exorcisms, rites that were designed to seal the hellish Gates, and anything else they could think of. But the call for fortune and fame didn't just entice the clergy. It brought warriors, claiming to be dragon and monster slayers, to try their hand at killing the creatures. But they all failed. Every last one of them.

"Then, Ottakar gets a stroke of inspiration. Realizing how numerous his enemies are, he begins to wonder if perhaps taming such beasts might be a better use of his resources. So, the king seeks out the aid of a nearby alchemist, who, as a kid, had studied under St. Francis of Assisi himself."

"The same Francis that supposedly was able to communicate with animals?" my dad asked.

Mia nodded in reply and continued. "Yes. This alchemist supposedly had learned Francis' secrets, so Ottakar asked him to commune with the Houskaani and train them to become his own personal weapons of war.

"The alchemist, Ambrose of Leeds, reluctantly agreed and did manage to wrest a certain amount of control over the creatures, but no one knows exactly how. He started caring for them. Feeding them. Healing them when they were sick. In essence, he grew to become their shepherd of sorts...to love the creatures even. Actually, he loved them to the point where he eventually betrayed his king and fled with his pets to parts unknown. Eventually, the man's children carried on the tradition of shepherding them. Taking care of them. Protecting them...and, I should add, protecting humans from *them* as well.

"Then, in the early part of the eighteenth century, Ambrose's descendants decided to flee the persecution in England. He hired a ship, secreted the creatures on board, and brought them and his family to the New World. They landed in the colony of New Jersey and set up a settlement in what would one day be called the Pine Barrens."

"So this alchemist...his descendants...you're saying they are your family? The Leeds family?" I asked. I hated to admit it, but I was definitely hooked by her story.

Her smile widened at this and she nodded. "Exactly," she said, blowing a strand of silver hair out of her eyes. "And everything was going perfectly fine until, as you pointed out, 1735. Until one of the Houskaani developed a strange fever and slaughtered several of my ancestors. Because of how gruesome the killings were, my kin were unable to keep things quiet. Panic ensued and witch hunters from all over came to the region claiming we had practiced witchcraft and that 'Mother Leeds' had communed with the devil himself to birth this horrible abomination. Many were burned at the stake and the creature was hunted for days. Eventually, it was found and burned as well.

"Thankfully, its brothers and sisters, as well as a handful of my family, managed to survive in hiding for years until they once again re-emerged into society. But at that point, it was more and more difficult to keep the Houskaani away from the public eye. Every once in a while, there would be a spotting and then the hunt would begin anew."

Each of us sat silently, pondering the story we'd just heard. I couldn't help wondering how much of it was true and how much was just plain good ol' fashioned horse manure. None of what she was telling us was jiving with what Filmore had told me and Grigsby. And he'd apparently gotten his info straight from the horse's mouth—Senator Thomas Leeds himself. Why on earth would Leeds lie about his own family being devil worshippers? Witches? Why would he make up a story about how he had been running from his family for the last fifteen years, hoping they would never catch up to him. Why would he invent the threats? The danger that Mia represented? It just didn't make any sense.

Problem was, no matter how badly I wanted to disbelieve Mia's story, there was just something about it that rang true.

"All right," I said. "Supposing everything you said is true, you still haven't explained what's happening now. You haven't told us why we should actually believe you're not the one responsible for all this. Why the Houskaani, as you call them, are on this killing spree. And if it's not you manipulating them, then who is?"

Her face tightened as she nodded at me. "You're right," she said. "Of course. I haven't finished my story. But to cut right down to the heart of the manner, I honestly don't know who's responsible for the murders. Don't have a clue who's manipulating them or even how they figured out how to do it."

"Well, how about just start by telling us what you do know," Nikki said, her voice soothing and reasonable. She looked at our prisoner with a new sense of compassion on her face. Her eyes gleamed with understanding as she prodded Mia to continue. Although, I hadn't gotten the memo why, I could tell Nikki believed her story.

"Well, I know that my family has been looking over the Houskaani since the thirteenth century. During that time, we have become quite sophisticated in our ability to shepherd them from danger, prying eyes, and anything else that could cause complications in their adopted habitat. By the sixteenth century, we had forgotten the original techniques used by Ambrose. So, we were forced to develop other means.

"As you've already discovered, the creatures are capable of secreting a hormone from glands just inside their ears."

"The interaural glands you mentioned," I said.

She nodded. "These hormones are distinctive to the individual in much the same way a fingerprint is to a human. But unlike fingerprints, the secretions are capable of providing three separate sets of information. First, it identifies the Houskaani's colony—"

"Colony?" Randy said. "Wait. Are you telling me there is more than one colony out there?"

Mia shrugged in response. "Well, to my knowledge, not in America. There's only the one…unless the Mothman sightings are related in some way. However, my family has traveled the world through the centuries, trying to discover as much as they can about our charges. There have been rumors of similar creatures in other, more remote, parts of the world. Many of the stories you've heard about dragons—in particular the type known as the wyvern—seem to be linked to the Houskaani for instance. The Ahool of Indonesia is apparently another possible colony."

"Dude!" Randy said, glaring at me. "I told you! I told you the Ahool was real." He looked around the room and grinned. "Um, sorry. It's just that we investigated the Ahool a few years before joining ENIGMA. We didn't find squat and Jack pretty much decided the whole legend was bunk."

I returned my friend's glare for half a heartbeat before turning back to Mia. "All right. So it identifies its colony. What else do the secretions show?"

"Well, first, you need to understand that this colonial marker the secretion provides also is used to establish their territory. It creates that neutralizing effect on ambient odors you were just talking about. It works as a sign to any rival colonies that they're in occupied territory. That's very important for you to know. Remember that for later.

"The second thing it identifies is the creature's sex, as well as state of sexual maturity. It's used to attract potential mates. It's not really helpful for our current dilemma, but it's worth knowing nonetheless.

"But the big one—the thing that is most important is that it identifies the individual creature. No Houskaani discharges the exact same secretion. There is always a different scent attached to each one."

"Which is why Esther didn't attack me in the tunnels after your sprayed me with the stuff," I said.

"Exactly. It was her own blend. It would have confused the heck out of her," Mia said. "It's what made her docile once more. She couldn't reconcile her own scent on you."

"Okay, but how does any of this help us?" I asked. "How is this important to what's happening now?"

She looked down at her bound feet, shifting her gaze as if almost ashamed of what she was about to say next. "Um, well, you first need to understand that Houskaani colonies are, by default, always relatively small in number. There are never more than twenty-five or so of them in a single colony at any given time. Their lifespans are pretty long—living about one hundred to one hundred and fifty years. So, births are pretty rare. We were so excited when there was a new birth about eight years ago.

"Unfortunately, when the cub was only about three years old, it was stolen from the colony. We have no idea how or by who. All we know is that one day, the infant just disappeared without a trace. You need to know that the Houskaani are extremely social. Each adult is tasked with raising all of the offspring as if one big family. When the cub disappeared, the entire colony was devastated. They became dangerously despondent. They would hardly leave their dens to go out and hunt for food. It was torture to see them in such a state. It was all we could do to nurse the entire clan back to emotional well-being. It was so bad that we couldn't worry about who had taken the cub until after the colony snapped out of their malaise. It was only after we were confident that they were better that my cousin was tasked with investigating the theft and trying to bring her back.

"Though he hasn't made a great deal of progress in that regards, things had been looking up for the colony. They had finally returned to some degree of normality and once again seemed to be prospering. As a matter of fact, about a year ago, a new cub was born to the alpha male, Goliath, and his mate."

I shuddered at the name. The gigantic creature's sneering face flashed through my mind's eye, sending a sudden irrational bout of panic through my limbs.

Mia hadn't seemed to notice my discomfort and kept going. "It was a wonderful time. Everything seemed to be finally getting back to normal until—"

"Oh Lord in heaven," Nikki said, raising a hand up to her mouth in understanding.

I looked at her, then at Randy and Landers, who seemed equally as perplexed by her reaction as me. "What?" I said. "What happened?"

"Obadiah, you brick-for-brains," my dad said with a shake of his head. "The new cub was taken too. That's what all this is about."

I let that sink in for several seconds before uttering a single word, "Phisto."

�∻

Mia had gone on to explain the rest with quiet efficiency. Her devil-may-care attitude had all but disappeared as she'd finished the tale. A few tears streaking her porcelain cheeks as she stumbled over the words.

I'd been right. The cub in question was who she'd been referring to in the sewers as Phisto. Which, she'd explained, was short of Mephistopheles—not exactly a winning sales point in the "we're not devil worshippers" category, if you ask me.

Basically, somehow, the second cub in a decade had been abducted from the colony. This new disappearance had all but sent the Houskaani mad with grief. Instead of falling back to their previous behavior of despondent stoicism, the colony had quickly begun acting out. At first, it had been a few unsupervised excursions past their established territories—apparently, the Leeds clan had learned to corral the creatures by using the same hormone secretions as a type of invisible fence. Soon, even this barrier couldn't keep the cryptids at bay and they began venturing out in pairs as if in search of their missing offspring.

"We believe that when one of their kind is agitated or endangered, the hormonal compound is injected with a bit of adrenaline," Mia had explained. "It would act as a sort of warning mechanism to the others. A distress signal. I think our colony was picking up on Phisto's distressed secretions, which was making them even more riled up."

Then, one day, twelve of the twenty-two member colony just disappeared. Like the cub, they were just gone. The family had hoped that the missing Houskaani would return in a few days, but after a few weeks had gone by, it became abundantly clear that that wasn't going to happen. It wasn't until a little more than a month ago, when they'd heard of the first few sightings in Manhattan, that they pieced it all together. Somehow, the creatures had made their way north—to New York City. And to their horror, word quickly spread that they were responsible for the deaths of their first human killing in centuries.

A council of the Leeds' elders surmised what had happened. Whoever had kidnapped the cub had used the secretions to lure the others to the Big Apple in search of Phisto. The abductor had somehow discerned the method by which the Leeds clan had been corralling the Houskaani all these years and was employing the exact same methods to carry out cold-blooded murder. It was decided that Mia, along with a contingent of Shepherds, would be sent to track the creatures down and bring them back—unharmed if at all possible.

"But here's what I don't understand..." I paused. I was about to betray a huge confidence. Detective Grigsby and I had sworn to protect Chuck Filmore's testimony. But I could see no way of avoiding it if I was going to get to the truth. I was going to have to word this just right in order to keep the little weasel safe. "The police have a witness who swears up and down that *you're* the culprit. Says you've been hounding your brother for years, trying to get him to give up politics and come back to the fold. A witness who claims you are nothing more than a cult of devil worshippers who see the senator as a major threat to your way of life."

She rolled her eyes at this. "Oh please. You're not really going to listen to that sycophantic trouble-maker are you?" she asked. "Chuck Filmore has been spewing that garbage for years now."

I cringed as she said his name. My attempt at keeping Chuck's identity secret had apparently had failed miserably.

"He sees me as an obstacle to his own political aspirations," Mia continued. "The little cretin has been trying to drive a wedge between my brother and me since college."

"Wait, Thomas Leeds and Chuck Filmore went to college together?" I asked.

She nodded. "Sure. They were roommates. As a matter of fact, it was Chuck who convinced Tommy to go into politics. He'd always had his own political aspirations, but was smart enough to know he just wasn't charismatic enough to win elections. Tommy was. So, he started pushing my brother into the political arena." She paused, a strange looking coming over her. "I guess that's why he's never liked me much. He's always been afraid I'd pull the rug out from under his dreams."

I suddenly had a very different image of the little twerp. Maybe, just maybe, he wasn't as much a goofball as I'd original thought. Never in a million years had I considered the possibility that Chuck Filmore was the mastermind behind Thomas Leeds' political career. I mean, who would?

What power hungry political puppet master becomes the poorly dressed personal assistant with a bad comb-over to the man he's controlling?

A very smart one, I thought, letting my thoughts cycle through all the possibilities. *It's actually rather ingenious. He'd be present at most all the big events. He'd be right there during every important decision. And best of all, if things went bad, no one would hold him responsible.*

That's when another thought struck me like a Mack truck on a rainy night.

"Mia, what kind of relationship did Chuck have with Aislynn Sommers?" I asked.

She shrugged. "Not a good one, I can tell you that. I know that Ais despised him. She said he was nothing but a leech, riding along on my brother's coat tails and bleeding him dry of any substance. They always seemed to bicker. Sometimes, they had full blown shouting matches right inside the campaign headquarters."

"Could their fighting have anything to do with Chuck having feelings for her?"

She burst out laughing at the question. "Chuck have feelings for Aislynn?" she asked. "That's funny. She's not Chuck's type."

"Type?"

"Um, yeah," Mia said, her face twisting in disgust. "Rumor has it he kind of has a kinky side. Spends a lot of time down around the whips and chains district near Times Square. The way I hear it, he was into some pretty scary stuff. Ais was just too vanilla for him if you ask me."

My heart thumped hard against my chest as I exploded from my chair, pulled out my phone, and dialed Detective Grigsby. I paced anxiously as the line rang.

"What is it, Jack?" Nikki asked, moving to my side.

Before I could answer, the detective answered. "Grigsby," he said tersely.

"Hey, it's Jack," I said, turning on the speaker phone so everyone in the conference room could hear the conversation. "Listen. We've been duped. I know who our killer is—"

"Let me guess," he said. "Our good friend Mr. Filmore."

I paused, feeling my exhilaration deflate as his words sunk in. "Um, yeah. How'd you know?"

"Been doing some digging. Seems Victim Number Two, Theresa McUllen, had some major dirt on Filmore. Political-ending dirt. All this time, I'd figured the girl was killed to protect Leeds, but it seems that Filmore was the one who had had the most trouble with her."

"Now it's my turn to guess," I said. "He propositioned her. Thinking she was just an everyday prostitute, he'd try to solicit her services—"

"And she turned him down flat," Grigsby said. "Her roommate said she planned on filing a sexual harassment suit against him when the courthouse opened on the Monday before she died." I heard some rustling of papers on the other end of the phone, then Grigsby mumbled a few unintelligible words at someone and came back on the line. "But wait, it gets better. Once I found the connection with Filmore and McUllen, I started looking a little harder at Ted Enders."

"The first victim? The homeless guy?"

"Yep. And guess what."

"You found another connection?"

"You have no idea. You see, Enders got himself into some real trouble about six month ago. In New Jersey. Near the Pine Barrens."

"Okay, that's a little too coincidental," Randy interjected. "What happened in Jersey?"

Grigsby paused, barked an order to someone, then resumed talking. "Sorry about that," he said. "Things are a little chaotic right now. Anyway, looks like Enders was a suspect in a double homicide in Burlington County. Two other transients from New York were shot to death. Point blank in the head. Enders was found rifling through their pockets. When interrogated, he claims some guy—*some wealthy social-type*, as he put it—had hired the three of them to help him steal something. Enders swears up and down he never knew what was being stolen. His job had simply been to procure a moving van while his mysterious employer and the two other bums were the ones who did the actual theft. As soon as the three had loaded a big crate into the back of the truck, the guy who hired them started shooting. Enders ran and managed to get away. When he returned, he found his friends dead and the van gone."

"Why did the Burlington Sheriff's Office let Enders go?" I asked. "Sounds like they had a pretty good case against him."

"Not enough evidence," Grigsby explained. "No gunshot residue on his hand. No weapon. Plus there were a few locals who were able to confirm seeing the three homeless guys with a very well-dressed, well-spoken man. It was such a dichotomy, the quartet just stood out like a sore thumb. Made it easy for the locals to remember them."

"I wouldn't exactly describe Filmore as 'well-dressed' though," I said. "Looks like he gets his suits off the rack at Sears."

"Don't let that slob act full you," Mia chimed in. "He dresses that way to make Tommy look better when they stand side by side, but it's Chuck that is the fashion queen. He's the one who handles Tommy's wardrobe. When they're not campaigning, Chuck is dressed to the nines. Trust me."

"Um, who's that?" Grigsby asked.

"Oh, uh, no one," I said nervously. Last thing I needed was for the detective-sergeant to find out we'd caught Mia and hadn't advised him. "So was Enders or any of the witnesses able to give a description of this fourth man?"

"As a matter of fact, yeah," Grigsby said. "It matches our boy perfectly."

"So Enders was killed to tie up a loose end," Landers stepped into the conversation. He'd been so quiet, I'd almost forgotten he was even in the conference room with us. "McUllen was murdered just to keep her from filing her suit. Schildiner obviously was purely a killing of opportunity. One rival out of the way. But why Aislynn?"

A lump welled up in my throat at the question. It was obvious now that I actually knew what to look for. "She died because she'd been so free to talk with us," I answered. "He was afraid that she might inadvertently give us information that would eventually lead back to him."

"Sounds about right," the detective said. "And that's why we're gearing up to go after him. The warrant for his arrest has just been handed to me. We're about to head out and bring him downtown as soon as I get off the phone with you."

I glanced around the room, filtering through all the new information we'd just discovered. It was just so much to absorb in such a short amount of time. But something was nagging at me. Something about what the detective had just said. They were about to arrest him. That was a good thing, right? So why was the very thought of getting Chuck Filmore behind bars so disturbing to me?

"Hold on a second, Mike," I said into the receiver before pressing the mute button. I then turned and looked at Mia. "If you've known where the Houskaani have been nesting all this time, why haven't you corralled them back to New Jersey yet? Why are they still here?"

She shook her head at this. "Because without the cub, they'd just come back. In fact, they're currently so uncontrollable, there's just no way to corral them without Phisto's secretion. Even if we tranquilized them, they'd just return as soon as they got the chance. And with their flight speed, it doesn't take long for them to make the journey from the Pine Barrens to Manhattan. It just wouldn't do any good to even try. We have to find the cub first."

It's just what I was afraid of. As long as Phisto was hidden away somewhere on the island, there would be no controlling them. And even without Filmore manipulating them, the colony of Jersey Devils in New York City was a powder keg waiting to blow up. No one would be safe.

I mashed the mute button once more and spoke. "Detective, I hate to do this, but I'm going to have to pull Federal rank on you here," I said. "I can't let you arrest him. At least not yet."

TWENTY-FOUR

YEAH. THE REST OF MY CONVERSATION WITH GRIGSBY WENT ABOUT AS well as you might expect. I'd explained to him what we'd learned from Mia—by this point, keeping her capture a secret would have been counter-productive—and went on to tell him how the Houskaani would continue their rampage until we located their spawn. Since Chuck was the only one capable of leading us to it and since he would undoubtedly lawyer up once the Boys in Blue slapped on the cuffs, I told the detective that we needed to interrogate him first. I was even bold enough to tell him that we had unique methods for getting people to talk if necessary. The detective-sergeant hadn't liked that plan at all.

I was reflecting on Grigsby's rather warning while Landers, navigating through the strangled cluster of traffic along East 35th Street, drove us to our destination. Truth is, Grigsby had become downright unhinged at the very prospect of what I was asking and had threatened to arrest every single one of us if we so much as lifted a finger to interfere with Chuck's apprehension.

Swell, Jack, I thought as Landers negotiated a sharp left onto 9th Avenue. *Way to keep burning those bridges. At this rate, you'll be chilling in Sing Sing along with your buddy Chuck.*

"Turn right up here," Mia said from the back seat of our rented SUV. Her duct tape binding had been removed and she was nestled between two of her hooded henchmen, who we'd learned were her cousins. Six other Shepherds were following close behind in a dark-colored sedan with Nikki,

Randy, Davenport, and my dad bringing up the rear cramped in the cab of my dad's pickup. "Tommy's building is just up the next street on the left."

Our plan had been simple. Well, simple compared to my usual plans, that is. We had to keep the NYPD off Filmore long enough to find out where Phisto was being kept. But traipsing all over upper Manhattan just wasn't going to cut it. Our best bet would be to draw him to us and there was nobody the little weasel would respond to faster than his own bread-and-butter, Senator Thomas Leeds. After Mia had called him and explained what had been happening with the killings, the senator had agreed to call Chuck and ask him over to his penthouse suite to discuss the possibility of making the personal assistant into his new campaign manager now that Aislynn was dead. When Leeds had called back to tell us our target was on his way, we'd scrambled Mia's team and ours together and were now making our way there.

I glanced down at my watch. 8:18 PM. Filmore was scheduled to arrive at Leeds' penthouse around eight o'clock. While we *were* in a bit of hurry— you know, trying to prevent a cryptid-frenzied massacre in the city streets while avoiding the cops at all costs—we also didn't want to get there too soon. We wanted the little psychopath to get nice and relaxed in the comfort of his boss' study. Maybe even get a little cognac in him to make him feel warm and at ease.

"Here! That building right there," Mia shouted, pointing over to huge high-rise to our left.

Landers paused in the middle of the street. A few horns honked behind us as the ENIGMA agent hesitated with uncharacteristic indecision.

"What's wrong now?" I asked him with an anxious growl. I was getting antsy. I wasn't sure how good of an actor the senator was, but now that he knew the truth behind his old friend's schemes, I didn't know how well he could play his part. The last thing I wanted was for our quarry to get spooked before we had a chance to get to him.

Landers' head turned from side to side, scanning the street. "Um, where do I park?"

Mia shrugged. "I have no idea. I've never driven here. Just always took the subway or a cab."

The five us continued our search for a parking garage or an open space to pull the SUV into, but came up empty. The honking behind us grew more insistent.

"If that's my dad making all that racket, I'm going to kill him," I said, opening the car door and spilling out onto the street. "Mia..." I looked at her two cohorts. "Tweedle-Dee, Tweedle-Dum? Come with me. Landers, find a good place to park nearby and keep the engine running. If we have to do a snatch and grab, we'll need to make a fast getaway."

Mia and her two cousins clambered out of the SUV and pulled off their hoods in an attempt to blend in a little better. Despite the fact that the sun had gone down a few hours before, the yellow haze of the street lights washed over them, making their long black cloaks seem just as ridiculous even without the hoods. Ignoring them, I tapped the hood of the truck, sending Landers on his way, and waited for the sedan to pull up. Mia then ordered four of the car's occupants to get out and sent the other two to follow Landers and act as backup. Finally, my dad pulled forward and stopped.

The honking continued behind him and I turned to see a yellow cab behind him, its driver leaning furiously on the horn with enraged eyes and waving the most obscene hand gestures I'd ever seen.

"Keep your shirt on!" I yelled, feeling more and more like a New Yorker by the second. I then turned to my team and told them what was happening. My dad agreed to follow Landers while Randy and Nikki climbed out of the car. "Davenport, you stay with my dad."

"What? But I..."

"It's going to be hard enough to get the punk to talk to us," I said. "If he sees you there—a member of the press—he's going to clam up for sure."

It was a bald-faced lie. Fact is, I just didn't want the reporter tagging along. I still didn't trust him. Still didn't know what kind of relationship he had with Freakshow. And I didn't want him anywhere near us when we did our interrogation in case he resorted to some type of sabotage—or worse, he suddenly developed some journalistic integrity and decided to write about what he saw. Plus, a few minutes with my dad and the dapper Davenport would be willing to spill the beans on Freakshow just as a means of therapy. *It will be the worst of all possible punishments*, I thought, unable to contain the sly grin spreading across my face.

My dad drove off with the reporter still protesting in the passenger's seat of the truck and I heard Randy chuckle behind me. "Heh heh...I see what you did there," he said with a Cheshire grin.

"So do I, Dr. Jackson," Nikki said with a little bit of her old aloofness. Though, by the twinkle in her eye, I think she secretly was just as pleased with my trick as anyone. If I had to guess, I think the guy was starting to wear a little on her nerves too.

Putting a stop to the banter, I instructed two of Mia's goons to take positions across the street from the front entrance and another two at the rear exit, in case Filmore made a run for it. I then instructed the remaining two to take off their cloaks to avoid looking like rejects from a *Dungeons and Dragons* convention when we tried entering the building. With a nod of Mia's head, they complied. Without another word, the six of us crossed the street and came to an abrupt halt as a very stern and serious looking doorman walked up to us.

"Yes?" he said, a look of disapproval on his severe face as he gave us all a once-over. "May I help you?"

Mia stepped from behind me with a smile. "Hey, George," she said. "It's me. Here to see my brother."

If George liked the silver-haired teen, he certainly gave no indication. "I'm sorry, Miss, but I've been instructed that your brother is not to be disturbed at the moment. He's in a very important meeting."

"Yes, I know," she said, straining to keep her smile. "We're supposed to be there for the meeting. I'm sure he called down to let you know."

"Oh, he did," the haughty doorman said. "But Mr. Filmore asked me to give them at least an hour of privacy. Said the senator was still quite devastated over the loss of Ms. Sommers and that he wanted some time offer as much comfort to him as he could."

I felt my stomach tighten at the comment. The little weasel knew. Or at least, he suspected. And if he thought we were onto him, what might he have planned for Leeds?

"Look, Captain...um, Doorman," I said, stepping in front of Mia and putting on my best *don't-mess-with-me* persona. "I don't care what Mr. Filmore told you. I'm afraid the senator might be in danger. We need to get up there. Now."

George's lips twisted with irritation as he glared at me. Yeah, I know. I'd just chastised myself for burning those bridges, right?

"And I gave my word, sir," he said with a scowl. He looked me up and down. I could imagine what I must look like to him. My dark scraggly hair all askew and rough, unshaven face. The bruises around my eye still hadn't fully healed—now a mishmash of purple and yellow splotches above my cheekbone. A few cuts and scrapes to top everything off. Yeah, compared to Filmore—even in his disheveled guise—the doorman would obviously be wondering where the cat had gotten off to that had dragged me here. "And since I only just met Ms. Leeds a few weeks ago and have known Mr. Filmore for as long as the senator has taken up residence...forgive me if I give *him* the benefit of the doubt."

Somewhere between the pounding of my pulse inside my head, I thought I heard something amid the chaotic noise of the busy street behind us. Like a scream of some kind. High pitched. Abrupt. Intense.

Possibly a car horn in the distance? But my gut told me otherwise. *There it is again.*

That time, I heard it more clearly. It was louder. Closer. More familiar. More like a screech than a scream.

I glanced skyward, nearly blinded by the bright lights shining through the tower of glass above us. But once my eyes adjusted, I saw it. Briefly. A shadow and nothing more. But it was enough. I knew what it was, though I wasn't sure anyone else noticed it.

"And we don't have time for this crap," I said, reaching behind my back and pulling out my gun. I leveled it at his head.

"Jack!" Nikki shouted. "What are you doing?"

"I'm sorry, Nikki, but we're out of time," I said, nodding my chin up at the sky. My hand shook as I kept the barrel pointed at the doorman. Yeah, it was my first stickup. I have to admit—it looks much easier in the movies. "It's here. A Jersey Devil is circling the building while we waste our time with this bozo."

Everyone—including the doorman—glanced up at the midnight blue sky above, but saw nothing. The shadowy figure I'd seen just moments earlier was no longer circling the building. Panic welled up inside me.

Tick-tock.

"Are you sure?" Randy asked.

In response, I drew closer to George the Doorman, stuck the gun to his gut and hissed, "You need to let us in now. I promise you, we're not here to hurt anyone, but if you don't let us in, the senator is as good as dead."

George's eyes widened even more at my words. Then, the man nodded and pulled a card key up from an attached pulley wheel on his belt. Silently, he pointed at a rectangular pad mounted next to the door.

"Okay. Go ahead," I said. "But no funny business."

Really, Jack? No funny business? I rolled my eyes at the thought. *Why not just tell the man to stick 'em up while you're at it?*

Like I said, it was my first armed hold-up. My only excuse was that I panicked. Fortunately, if George was having similar criticisms of my clichéd performance, he didn't voice them. Instead, he slowly turned to the pad and laid the keycard against it. The red LED turned green and I heard the satisfying click of the door unlocking. Grabbing the man by the arm, we dashed inside only to be greeted by a very young, ruddy-faced security guard manning a station around the corner in the lobby. The kid couldn't have been much more than eighteen. Probably just out of high school. Completely inexperienced. Landers would have described him as *green*.

But no matter how inexperienced the kid might have been, he seemed pretty sharp. Alert. Seeing us, and the desperate terror on the doorman's face, the security officer glanced over at me. His eyes immediately dropped down at the Glock clutched tight in my hand.

"Ah, crap," I said out loud while bringing the gun up to point at him. "This just keeps getting better and better. Look, we need to get up to Senator Leeds' penthouse. He's in trouble. That's the only reason I—"

Before I could finish my sentence, the trembling security guard reached down to his side and pulled out his own sidearm.

"Freeze!" He shouted—a little too high pitched, not to mention delayed, to warrant much confidence in his determination. But I knew that a shaky gun-hand was just as dangerous—if not more so—than a coldblooded assassin's. "The s-silent alarm has...has already been triggered. The p-police are on their way."

Great. As if this night isn't bad enough.

"Jack, this is getting out of hand," Nikki said in her *everybody-stay-calm* voice.

"Yeah, dude," Randy agreed. "You're kind of racking up the felony points here, bud."

They were right, of course. But what could I do. I was already committed. Besides, Thomas Leeds didn't have much time left. Heck, for all I knew, we might already be too late. I had to do whatever I could to protect him, even if it meant breaking a few laws in the process. After all, it's not like I was really going to hurt anyone.

You big dope, that security guard doesn't know that, I thought. *If he so much as twitches, that revolver he's clutching is going to go off. Then what are you going to do?*

I glanced down at Mia, her face tense. She seemed to be just as conflicted as me. At the same time, no one knew the Houskaani better than she.

"What do you think?" I asked her. "How much time do we have?"

She shook her head. Her expression was grim, darkened by unvoiced doubts. "I don't know. Under normal circumstances, I'd say Tommy has nothing to worry about. He knows our secrets. He's quite skilled at corralling the Houskaani. But if Filmore has used the cub's secretions, I'm not sure anything he tries will do much good."

Sounded like none of us knew much of anything at that moment. But the one thing I definitely did know was that while we were in this standoff, nothing was being done. Leeds was in trouble and we were loitering in the lobby of his building. We might as well have been picking our noses for all the good we were doing him. Though at the moment, we couldn't do anything until I took care of Barney Fife.

"All right, easy buddy," I said, raising one hand in supplication while continuing to level my Glock at the doorman. "Why don't you put that pea shooter down before someone gets hurt. You said it yourself, the police are on their way. No need to play the hero any more. I promise. If you holster your weapon and I will *not* shoot you. But I don't have any more time to play with you. A man in your building is in a lot more danger than you at the moment. We're only here to help him."

Randy flashed an apologetic grin at the quivering security guard. "Yeah, man. Believe it or not, we're the good guys."

The security guard eyed us warily, then slowly eased his weapon onto the countertop of the security station and backed away. I nodded to Randy, who quickly retrieved the gun and tucked it into his jacket pocket.

"Great," he said, rolling his eyes. "Now I'm an accessory."

"Quit your whining. We have bigger problems to deal with," I said. Then I turned to look at the biggest of Mia's cousins. "What's your name?"

He looked at me, then at Mia. When she nodded a reply, he answered, "Timothy."

"All right Tim," I said. "First time we met, you guys were packing some pretty mean-looking knives. You have any weapons now?"

The big man nodded, reached around his back, and pulled out one of the biggest revolvers I'd ever seen from the waistband of his pants. With another swift motion he withdrew the deadly looking kukri knife Mia's people had used in Central Park.

"Good. Now Tim, I want you to stay here and keep an eye on these two." I turned my attention to the doorman. "First, though...George, I'm going to need you to secure the front door. We can't have any unwary residents traipsing in on us during the commission of our felonies, now can we?"

George shrugged nervously, then inched his way to another rectangular console beside the front entrance and punched a series of numbers into it.

"It's locked?" I asked. "No one can get in, right?"

The severe-looking man hesitated slightly.

"Georgie? Don't lie to me. Is it secure or not?" I tilted and twirled the barrel of the gun at him again in a lackadaisical fashion. I was hoping to show my indifference about pulling the trigger, or not. I wasn't sure how convincing I was, but he took the hint and once more punched in a series of numbers.

"All right," he said. "It's locked. Now please...let us go."

I grinned at him. "Don't worry George," I said. "It's almost over. If you'll be good enough to join your friend on the other side of the security station."

The doorman complied without another word and I turned back to Timothy. "Okay. Stay here and watch them." I grabbed a notepad off the security desk, scribbled my cell number, and handed it to him. "The moment you see the cops, call me and then get out of here. Don't worry about us. We'll find another way out, okay?"

The big man looked at Mia again, but when she merely shrugged in response, he said, "All right. But Dr. Jackson," he said as he pointed to the other goon. "Understand that if anything happens to Mia while you are up there, my brother Joseph here will kill you where you stand and ask questions later. She's *that* important to our clan. Am I clear?"

I gulped involuntarily at the threat, nodded, then motioned for the others to follow me to the elevator. Nervously, I pressed the button and after several excruciating seconds, the doors slid open and we climbed in. A sudden thought struck me as I studied the button panel.

"Hold the door," I said to no one in particular and I dashed back to the guard station. "Keys?" I asked the security guard, who was still visibly shaken.

"Um, why do you need the keys?" he asked.

With my patience wearing as thin the doorman's hairline, I shoved out my hand. "Because," I said. "Penthouse suites in these kinds of places are only accessible to authorized personnel. That means we need a key for the elevator to take us there, right?"

Reluctantly, the guard pulled a set of keys from a carabiner off his belt and handed them to me. Without another word, I ran back to the elevator.

"What floor is he on?" I asked Mia. When she told me, I inserted the elevator key and pressed the button for the forty-eighth floor penthouse. We rode the elevator up in silence, each of us staring nervously at the metallic doors and wondering just what we would find when they opened into the senator's apartment. I checked my clip nervously and looked over at Nikki, whose eyes were closed in silent prayer. *Good girl*, I thought while pulling the slide of my Glock back and chambering a round. *I have a feeling we'll need all the help we can get on this one.*

I closed my eyes for my own prayer, but was immediately interrupted by the chime that signified our arrival. As the doors slid open, I was aware of two things at the same time. The first was the unmistakable scent of the Houskaani hormone permeating the air. The second were the inhuman howls and terrified, all-too-human screams that exploded from the chaos of Thomas Leeds' penthouse.

We were too late.

TWENTY-FIVE

I STOOD TRANSFIXED. MY MIND NEEDED THE TIME TO PROCESS THE chaotic scene that played before my eyes. We stood in the foyer of the senator's penthouse suite. Polished black tile reflected the dim illumination of recessed light fixtures in the ceiling above us. Immaculate white furniture could be seen in the living room beyond the narrow hallway that led to the elevator. It was the quintessential bachelor's motif and it was now in shambles. I could make out a portion of a plate glass window that had been shattered, reminding me of the gruesome scene of Aislynn Sommers' murder.

An antique grandfather clock ticked away rhythmically to our immediate right. It's funny when I think about it now. How among the din of screams and shrieks and tossed furnishings and pounding feet I could still hear the pendulum of that old clock swinging back and forth. Maybe it had something to do with the blood-chilling tableau I was forced to watch the moment we entered the penthouse. Maybe it had something to do with the way our brains process scenes of pure terror. But whatever it was, the tick-tock of that ridiculous old clock seemed to me, at the moment, to be the drum beat prelude of some magnificent battle.

I'm not sure how long I stood there before my mind caught up to what I was seeing. It couldn't have been very long as the others hadn't moved either.

The expensive decor was being tossed around the room as if by a child having a tantrum, while an armed Chuck Filmore stood coolly to the side, watching his murder plot unfold before his eyes. Thomas Leeds, fighting for his life against a seven foot tall bipedal megabat with the raw power of a mountain gorilla, clung desperately to the creature's back as it stomped and thrashed through the apartment emitting high pitched shrieks.

Realizing our presence had not yet been discovered by either monster or murderer, I nodded to Randy and Joseph and pointed at Filmore, then to an open doorway that led into what looked like Leeds' kitchen. Understanding my silent command, the two padded into the kitchen where another door opened into the living room. It was my hope that, upon my next signal, the two would be able to snag the psychopathic weasel so I could deal with the JD without worrying about a bullet to the back of the head.

Of course, that left me with the daunting task of actually *dealing* with the frenzied Devil. I leaned toward Mia and whispered, "Any ideas?"

The silver-haired goth shook her head. "Not really, no," she said with an apologetic tone. "I can smell the cub's scent. It's driven Deborah mad with rage. There is no reasoning with her now."

"Deborah?" Nikki asked.

"Yes. If I'm not mistaken, that is who we call Deborah," Mia said. "We named her that after the female Judge of the Old Testament. Um, she's always been a bit more aggressive than the others, a warrior, so we thought it was an appropriate name."

The senator yelled again and we all looked up and saw the beast hurl him across the room and out of sight. Filmore grinned maniacally at this, his gun waving carelessly through the air with his frantic hand gestures.

"Kill him!" he shouted over the chaos. "Tear that pompous bag of bones to pieces!"

Time was up. With Leeds no longer on the creature's back, he was vulnerable to *Deborah*'s powerful arms. I was just about to signal Randy to make their move when a sudden thought struck me.

"Wait," I hissed. "The hormone. It's permeating the air. It's all over the place. Not just on your brother."

"So?" Mia said.

"So why isn't she going all Wookie on Chucky-boy now?"

"I'm not sure. He could be using the same trick I used in the sewers. Sprayed himself with her scent...or another one from the clan. It's a simple trick. We've used for centuries."

"Well, you and Nikki try to figure it out for sure," I said. "I've got to go rescue your big brother."

Without waiting for them to respond, I stuck my head into the kitchen doorway and nodded to Randy. Warily, the two immediately moved out of view and into the living room to carry out their portion of the mission. I could only trust they'd succeed as I dashed down the narrow hallway and leapt into the fray. From my peripheral vision, I could see Filmore struggling against the powerful grip of Mia's muscle-bound cousin while Randy clapped his hand over the personal assistant's mouth.

Without having to worry about the creep interfering now, I was able to turn my undivided attention to the beast, whose back was to me—its focus resting solely on its prey. Leeds was now backed up against the far wall, his eyes wide and supplicating. There was nowhere left for him to run and the Houskaan knew it. I watched helplessly as the creature's muscles tensed to lunge. I was out of time. There was nothing left for me to do but the unthinkable.

I raised my Glock and drew a bead on the back of its horned head. Even with my horrible aim, from this range, I couldn't miss. I hated myself for what I was about to do, but in this situation, I could see no alternative.

Exhaling slowly, my finger tensed on the trigger and I prepared to fire.

"No!" Mia shouted behind me. "Don't kill her!"

Hearing her screams, the creature whirled around; its red eyes glared malevolently at me, then drifted down to the firearm in my hand. As if recognizing it, the Houskaan howled with rage.

"Ah, crap," I said out loud, silently cursing the silver-haired minx for screwing up the element of surprise. "This is going to hurt."

Faster than anything with the creature's bulk should be able to move, it lunged at me and two things happened all at once. First, the creature extended its left wing, whipping it at my extended arm and sweeping the Glock from my hand. In the same swift motion, it stretched out its own hand, grabbed me by the lapel of my shirt, and threw me toward the shattered window directly behind me. Unable to stop myself, I flew through it and out into the open air of the city.

TWENTY-SIX

OKAY. A LITTLE KNOWN FACT ABOUT ME. I'M A HUGE BATMAN FAN. I can't help it. He's been my favorite superhero since I was a little kid. So, as I hovered out in open air, just outside the penthouse window, I couldn't help but reflect on just how easily the Dark Knight would have saved himself if he was in my shoes. In the split second before gravity took hold of me, I considered the various methods he might employ. Would he use his handy-dandy little gas-propelled grappling line maybe? Or perhaps, his highly trained acrobatic skills would allow him to somersault in mid-air, catch hold of an outstretched flag pole, and bounce back into the room from which he'd been thrown.

But no matter how badly I might have wished otherwise, I was no Batman. I didn't have his gadgets. Didn't have his skills. Heck, I didn't even have his snazzy fashion sense. All I had was my own body mass that now was racing toward the ground below. With the wind rushing past my head, I twisted my body around as best I could and reached out my arms; trying desperately to grab onto any handholds that protruded from the old 1930s Art Deco apartment building. A quick scan of my surroundings revealed that the nearest ledge—actually, it was more like a small veranda decorated with a row of potted plants—was about two floors down.

The good news was I was heading straight for it. The bad news—there was no way on earth I was going to be able to miss it. I was going to hit. Hard. And there wasn't time to twist around enough to land gracefully either. Earlier, just before being thrown from Leeds' window, I had underestimated my predicament. This was going to hurt a whole lot more than I originally thought.

Five. Four. Three. Two. I slammed hard against the jutting balcony ledge, shattering the ceramic pots of at least four gardenia plants. How the owners had kept the subtropical plant alive in New York City in early spring was beyond me...but then, it was now a moot point. The plants were as good as dead and the jury was, at that moment, still out on whether I'd suffer the same fate. I'd landed on my left shoulder and upper arm, followed immediately by a loud crack that had nothing whatsoever to do with the shattered ceramic. My momentum, only slightly delayed by the impact with the balcony, continued its course; forcing both my legs to flip over my head in a spiraling arc. I twirled, end over end, until I landed on my back on the small, seven by ten foot balcony. The air rushed out of my lungs and I heaved for breath while cradling my throbbing left arm. A shockwave of pain ripped through my shoulder as I writhed helplessly on the concrete floor.

I'd broken something. The pain was excruciating, but I guess that was good news. It could have been a whole lot worse. I could have been feeling nothing at all.

Slowly, I assessed possible injuries. I started with my toes. I felt them wiggle inside my sneakers. Then, had the same result with my fingers—though with considerable more effort given the agony I was in. Good. It meant that more than likely, my spine was still intact.

Okay. What's next?

Hesitantly, I glanced down at my shoulder and arm, but nothing looked broken. I took in a deep breath of relief and was rewarded immediately with a searing pain to my shoulder. I tried to move the arm, but even the slightest ambulation sent fire down my spine. As I screamed, my eyes rolled around in protest. That's when I saw the blood soaking through the upper portion of my black and white striped bowling shirt. With my right hand, I gently maneuvered the top four buttons of the shirt open and saw the horrid sight of my fractured clavicle tearing through the skin of my chest.

I had a compound fracture of my collarbone and I was bleeding out. The first dilemma, I could deal with. Twelve weeks of light duty would take care of that. The blood was another thing entirely. Since I wasn't spurting like a poor man's Old Faithful, I figured I hadn't lacerated an artery or anything, but I was bleeding enough to cause some major problems. I would need professional medical attention…which would take away time from the mission that we didn't have. It would also put me smack dab in the center of Detective Grigsby's radar. I'd get patched up and thrown in the pokey faster than you can say "Book 'em, Danno."

Then, of course, there was the unbearable pain I was going to have to endure even if I did manage to stop the bleeding. Here's something that might surprise you about me, considering how so unlike Chuck Norris I am: I have a very high tolerance for pain. It's true. I'm a lousy patient when I get the sniffles or flu, but physical injury has never really stopped me from doing what I want to do. Oh, I'll moan and complain about such injuries— for sympathy points mostly—but I've just always been too pig-headed to let it stop me when something really needed doing. However, in this particular predicament, I wondered if I'd met my match. The torment that shot through every nerve ending in my body kept me paralyzed on the veranda's floor. I struggled to move. Could barely lift my head.

It was moments like this when I missed my friend Vera more than ever. She had not only been one of the most wonderfully caring women I've ever known, she was also an amazing doctor to boot. But she was dead and couldn't help me now.

A light flicked on from the balcony's apartment interior. I glanced to my left as the blinds to the sliding glass doors shifted slightly and I saw a pair of wary, desperate eyes looking out at me.

"Who's out there?" came the shaky, garbled voice of an elderly female. "I've got a gun and I know how to use it."

Before I could reply, the door slid open slightly and the six-inch barrel of an ancient looking revolver poked out.

"I need help," I croaked, wheezing with each breath. "Please."

The gun tilted down to me as if its wielder could see through the barrel's opening. After a few seconds, it moved once left, then right, and back down to me.

"How'd you get out there?" the old woman, still hiding behind the blinds, asked. "Who are you?"

Okay. How the heck was I supposed to answer that?

Well, ma'am, I'm a member of a super-secret government agency that hunts down and studies monsters. I was in the middle of an assignment when a ticked-off gargoyle hurled me from the window two stories above yours.

That's when I remembered.

Nikki.

She was up there with that frenzied, murderous beast hell-bent on tearing everyone in Leeds' apartment to shreds. A creature that had thrown me out of a forty-eighth story window without a second thought. They were all in danger and I—

Blam! Blam! Blam!

The sound of three gunshots blasted into the night and I instinctively rolled into a fetal position with a panicked shout. But after a few heart-stopping seconds, I realized that the little crone hadn't been the one to pull the trigger. It had come from above. About two stories above.

I had to get up there. No matter how much pain I was in, or how much blood I had lost, I had to get up off my butt and move. Save Nikki. Stop the Houskaan before she killed everyone in the apartment.

I rolled over on my right side and used that arm to raise myself to my feet. It was then that I saw the shaking barrel of the gun pointing a mere twelve inches from my head. The little old lady, having heard the shots above, had stepped out onto the balcony and was looking me up and down suspiciously.

The woman, around eighty-something, was almost as big around as she was tall. She had dark wrinkled skin and white stringy hair that was pulled back in a loose bun. But if she seemed comical to look upon at first glance, any sense of humor was quickly eradicated by her fierce, bright brown eyes. The old lady was sharp.

"What's going on?" she asked. "And don't move. The police are on their way."

The sound of sirens from far below told me she wasn't joking—though I suspected their arrival had more to do with the silent alarm the security guard had tripped than any phone call to 911. Gingerly, I raised my right hand and pressed it against the open wound in my chest. I felt my blood oozing past my fingers as I struggled to remain upright.

"I-I can't go into detail now," I said, a brilliant cover story springing immediately to mind. "But I work for the government. I'm here to protect Senator Leeds, who lives two floors above you, from an assassination attempt. I have to get back up there."

She gave me an incredulous look, then tutted at my flimsy story. "When Mr. Sandusky was still alive—God rest his soul—he taught me a thing or two about hooligans like you," she said. "My husband was a wonderful man, you know, and he knew a few things about criminals and their ilk. I think you're some type of burglar, trying to break in."

I rolled my eyes. I didn't have time to deal with the woman's delusions. Nikki was in trouble.

"I promise you…I'm one of the good guys!" I said, irritation salting my words.

"Well, then, what are you doing trying to break into my home?" she shouted, her gun still aimed directly at my face. "'Good guys' don't exactly go around burgling helpless widows in the middle of the night, now do they?"

Another volley of shots exploded above us. The old woman's eyes shot up, following the sound of gunfire and leaving me with an opening. Ignoring the pain, I lunged forward and wrenched the revolver from her grip.

"Sorry, ma'am," I said, darting past her into her apartment and moving immediately to the door. "I don't have time to convince you."

I ran out into the hallway, stopped to search for the nearest bank of elevators and made my way to them. As I waited for the car to descend, Mrs. Sandusky shuffled from her apartment hurling a string of curses as well as two very worn, yet pointy, shoes in my direction. She followed immediately with a series of obscene hand gestures, then slipped back inside her apartment still muttering her obscenities as she went. When the elevator door opened, I mumbled a prayer of thanks and rushed inside. Inserting the security key, I hit the appropriate button and felt a lurch as the car moved upward. After two floors, the door opened once more into Thomas Leeds' apartment and I dashed back into the living room, still clutching the old lady's vintage revolver.

I came to a sudden halt when I saw the mutilated remains of Joseph splayed out on the living room floor. His right arm had been completely ripped from his torso and his throat was little more than shredded meat, making me feel a whole lot better about my own impairment. A few feet to the corpse's right, Mia knelt, cradling the winged creature's fallen body; her face buried in its course, stringy fur. Blood pooled around the creature's now disfigured head. My Glock rested on the tile next to her feet. The senator stood over his sister, his hand gently stroking her silver hair in easy, comforting motions.

"Jack!" Nikki shouted from somewhere behind me. "Thank God you're okay!" I turned around just in time to see her arms wrapping tight around me. I let out a cry of pain and she backed away with fearful eyes. "You're bleeding."

I nodded. "Broken clavicle. Just needs to be reset and bandaged up. I'll be okay." I paused, glancing erratically around the room. "Wait. Where's Randy? Filmore?"

Her eyes shifted to the floor as she bit her lower lip. After a few seconds of silence, she spoke. "They're gone."

TWENTY-SEVEN

"THERE WAS A PROBLEM," NIKKI CONTINUED ABOVE MIA'S HEARTBROKEN sobs. The creepy goth seemed more concerned about the death of the monster than that of her own cousin. At the moment, however, my only concern was Randy. "The Houskaan went after me when I rushed to the window to try to save you. Joseph let go of Chuck to help me. In the chaos, he managed to get hold of the gun Randy had taken from the security guard. Chuck took him hostage and they ran out of here. I didn't know what to do. I was so scared. I thought you were dead. I managed to call Scott—don't worry, I didn't tell him what had happened to you, so your dad won't be worried—and told him about Chuck's escape. Scott and Oliver are now searching for them on foot."

As Nikki recounted what happened, Freakshow's words hit me in the gut like a sledgehammer: "*Before your little investigation is over, one of your team-mates will be taken from you.*" How could he have known? Could Freakshow being orchestrating all this? Could Filmore and Freakshow somehow be working together? The very idea sounded ludicrous, but the homicidal voyeur had predicted this with almost prophetic precision.

I turned around, carefully scooped up my Glock on the floor while trying to keep the pain of the broken collarbone to a minimum, and started toward the elevator once again. "Come on," I said. "We've got to get after them."

"But Jack, we've got to get you some help," Nikki said, grabbing my good arm as I walked past and pointing at my shoulder. "You're bleeding. You're in no condition—"

"I've got to do something!" I shouted at her. "I can't let that maniac get Randy!"

"You don't even know if Chuck plans on hurting him," she said, misunderstanding which maniac I was talking about. "He'll probably let him go as soon as he feels he's home free. To our knowledge, he's never killed anyone with his own hands before. He's just used the Houskaani to do his dirty work. Randy will be fine."

"You're not getting it, Nik. It's not Filmore I'm worried about. It's Freakshow! I know he's behind all of this," I said. "He said one of my team would be taken from me and that's just what's happening."

Before she could respond, my cell phone buzzed inside my pocket. I couldn't believe the thing still worked after the fall I'd had, but its sudden ringing reminded me of an even more immediate problem. I'd told Mia's other cousin, Timothy, to call the moment the cops showed up. I suddenly remembered the sirens from Mrs. Sandusky's balcony. We were going to have to find an alternate path out of the building.

I reached into my pocket, pulled out the phone, and glanced down at the display. It was Randy's cell phone. My heart leapt as I accepted the call. "Randy?" I said. "Are you okay?"

"He's fine, Dr. Jackson," said the unnervingly cool voice on the other end that iced the blood in my veins. It was Chuck Filmore. "For now anyway. But you better call off your dogs. That spiky haired guy that looks like G.I. Joe almost nailed us. I see him or any of your other pals again, I swear I'll put a bullet in your friend's head."

I could hear police sirens through the other end of the speaker. Wherever Filmore and Randy were, it sounded as if they were outside, but still close to the apartment building. Which explained how he'd managed to spot Landers.

"You're not the only one who knows some nasty little cryptids who are easily manipulated, Filmore. If you hurt him, I'll be sure to do much, much worse to you," I growled into the phone. "But I'll call Scott off. Just let Randy go and you can be on your way."

He laughed scornfully through the phone's speaker. "Do you think I'm some kind of idiot? I have no idea how you're still alive after being thrown out of that window, but the fact that you are tells me you're resourceful. Your friend is my insurance policy that I'll be able to get out of town unscathed."

I shook my head, knowing full well he couldn't see the gesture. "Uh-uh. No way. There's no guarantee you'll let—"

"I don't care what you think," he said. His tone was suddenly rigid. "You know what to do if you want to see your buddy alive again. And if his safety isn't enough to keep you off my tail, you'll have another problem to deal with soon enough."

"What are you talking about?"

"Simple. I've been keeping those monsters controlled by systematically spraying the cub's scent at strategic locations around the sewers where they've made their nest," he said with an arrogant snort. "But the solution lasts approximately twelve hours. My last treatment of their nesting area was...oh, about ten hours ago. Once it dissolves, there will be nothing keeping them from entering the city and going on an all-out frenzy to find their child. When that happens, the only thing that will stop them is to either kill them or locate the object of their search." He paused, letting the gravity of what he said sink in. "So, I say that gives you just under two hours before all hell breaks loose. Oh, and by the way, I'll be leaving your friend with the cub. Find it and you'll find Randy."

And with that, the line went dead in my hand. Filmore hung up, leaving me to stew over this new turn of events. The situation was about as bad as I could possibly imagine. Soon, all of Manhattan would face the fierce onslaught of a colony of humanoid megabats who would stop at nothing to find their spawn. As Mia had demonstrated, they could be taken down with bullets easily enough, but that could effectively wipe out an entire uncatalogued species. If they weren't killed, then we'd doom hundreds of people to a gruesome death as well.

Rock? Meet hard place, I thought, absently staring at the now darkened screen of my phone. That's when I got an idea. I immediately scrolled down the contacts on my phone and called Wiley.

"Jack? Are you okay?" the computer nerd asked when he answered. "I've been monitoring the police band in the Manhattan area. Apparently, they've got a BOLO out on you right now."

"Yeah, Wiley, I'm okay. But we have more pressing matters at the moment," I said, not liking the fact that the police would "be on the lookout" for me. That didn't bode well for my future legal wellbeing. I knew Grigsby had been ticked at me for going after Filmore alone, but I hadn't thought he'd have the entire NYPD looking for me like a common street thug. I pushed the thought from my head and got back to the reason for the call. "We need to get a bead on Randy. He's been taken by the suspect and can lead us right to our target if we can find him."

"What?"

"I need you to trace his phone." I didn't have time to answer all the incessant questions I knew were coming, so I proceeded with my plan. "The bad guy just called me with it and—"

I heard the sound of computer keys clicking on the other end as I spoke, then was interrupted before I could finish. "I just checked," he said. "There's no signal. Guy probably turned it off and dumped it somewhere."

Crap. I knew that Filmore was devious, but I'd hoped that he wouldn't be street smart enough to consider we might use the phone to track them. Then again, these days, almost every TV show or movie made used the same gimmick. No, we were going to have to think outside the box a little with this one.

The phone to Senator Leeds' apartment rang, making me jump involuntarily. I knew who was calling and it wouldn't be good. I growled with an ever-escalating frustration. I was still in agonizing pain and had the weight of an entire species resting on my already injured shoulder…and things kept coming at me before I could even sort out the first dilemma. "Hold on a sec, Wiley. I'll be right back." I glanced over at Leeds, who was still comforting his sister and spoke. "You should get that. Pretty sure it's the cops. You need to buy us some time."

He nodded and started making his way to the cordless phone.

"Before you answer," Nikki said. "Do you have a first aid kit in here?"

"In the bathroom, down the hall. Third door on the left," he said. "Under the sink, I believe."

Nodding her thanks, she followed his directions while the senator answered the phone.

"Hello?" he said.

There was a pause while he listened to whoever had called.

"Yes, I'm fine, Detective Grigsby. I'm fine. Just a misunderstanding, really. I—"

Another pause.

"No, that won't be necessary," Leeds said. "No need for you to come up."

More talking on the other end of the phone.

"I have no idea what George or the security officer are talking about. There's no one here but some associates of mine…we're in the middle of a very important meeting. Now, I would really appreciate—"

There was one last pause before the senator said, "Fine. But only you, Detective. No one else. Is that clear?" After a second, he hung up the phone and looked at me. "Grigsby wouldn't take no for an answer. He knows you're up here. He promised he would come alone and that he would hear your side of the story." He shook his head in amazement. "I can't believe you pulled a gun on my doorman, Dr. Jackson. That was incredibly stupid."

"Seemed like a good idea when I was trying to save your life," I said, before resuming my conversation with Wiley. "You still there?"

"Yep. Just trying to think of a way to track Randy."

Track, I thought. *Track. Why is that such a buzz word for me?*

Nikki returned to the living room carrying an armful of supplies with her, just as the ping of the elevator sounded from the foyer.

"Wiley, I'll call you back," I said. "Keep brainstorming."

I hung up just as the elevator door slid open and a red-faced Grigsby stomped into Thomas Leeds' apartment and moved directly toward me. Nikki had already removed my shirt and was applying some stinging ointment to my injury.

"I'm going to have to set the bone in place," she said, ignoring the detective.

Some of the fire evaporated from Grigsby's eyes as he took in my shoulder. "Geeze, Jackson," he said. "What happened to you?" In response, I tilted my head to my right. His eyes drifted to where the dead Houskaan lay dormant in a pool of its own blood. "Holy Hannah! Is that what I think it is?"

He moved cautiously over to the creature and looked down at it inquisitively. Mia stood up to face the police officer, her face grim. While Nikki continued administering first aid to me, the Houskaani shepherdess filled Grigsby in on what had happened since we last spoke with him on the phone. Interestingly enough, she left out the part about the entire colony of Houskaani that would be rampaging through his city in a matter of hours. To his credit, he took it all in without a word until he was sure the tale was over, then turned to me.

"And this is why civilians don't take the law into their own hands, Jackson," he growled. "This could not be worse if you had tried."

Nikki's hand put a wet washcloth on my shoulder and I felt her palm press against the jutting bone. I tensed for what I knew was coming. She was not a trained medic, but her time as a missionary in some of the most volatile regions of the world had given her plenty of practice in mending injuries in one form or another. Still...this was going to hurt.

"Trust me," I said, gritting my teeth and closing my eyes as I waited for the inevitable. "It's even worse than you know."

Suddenly, white hot lightning shot through my body as Nikki pressed hard against my collarbone, pushing it back through my skin and adjusting it into place. Splotches of white and black, followed immediately by colors of the entire rainbow exploded in vivid clarity in front of my eyes. I screamed as agonal spasms coursed through every nerve in my body before everything went black and I slipped into a dark dream.

≈∽

I was in a thick, sweltering jungle. It was dark out. The sounds of insects and other less savory creatures echoed through the tree canopy. Sweat dripped from my brow as I sprinted through the foliage. Something was stalking me. Chasing me. I knew I had to get away from it, but there was a part of me that didn't want to. A part of me wanted to turn and face the thing that was now hot on my heels. Embrace it. Not let it go.

But that would be insane. I'd seen what the creature could do. I'd seen it drain the life out of its victims like a kid drinking from a box of fruit juice. To let it overtake me would be certain death. It would feed on me. Drain me dry like it had so many others.

Suddenly, I found myself at the edge of a steep gorge. I'd barely skidded to a halt in time and nearly plummeted to the abyss below. Letting out a sigh, I took a step back and peered across the ravine. Something about it seemed familiar to me, but I couldn't quite place where I'd seen it before. But didn't have time to ponder it. I could hear the thing in the jungle behind me. It was getting closer...moving more slowly now, but advancing none the less. I had to find a way to cross the gorge or I'd be monster food.

"Help!" I heard someone shout. I looked out at the ravine to see a pudgy little man hanging for dear life on a rope attached to unseen tree limbs above.

Nelson Daniels? Geeze, I hadn't seen him in over two years. The last time had been when he'd sponsored an excursion to the Amazon to search for an imp-like creature the locals called *El Pombero*. It had been when I'd first met Senator Stromwell and where I'd eventually learn about ENIGMA. Nelson and I had been stalked by a couple of hungry jaguars. We'd come to this very ravine and I'd convinced him to cross...well, calling it a rope bridge was being extremely generous. The rope had broken halfway across and he'd had to hold on with every ounce of his strength. *Just like now*, I thought.

"Nelson, what are you doing here?" I asked.

"Don't just stand there, Dr. Jackson!" he screamed back, rudely ignoring my question. "Help me!"

I glanced around, looking for a means to help him but couldn't find anything. Normally, I carried a spool of rope on jungle expeditions. As a matter of fact, I had carried one on this particular expedition as well...but for some reason, I had none with me at the moment.

"I'm sorry Nelson. I don't know what to do?"

My brain raced, trying to find a way to save the normally talkative little academic, but it felt sluggish. Too many ideas, thoughts, fears, and sorrow were clogging up the synapses. For the life of me—or rather for the life of Nelson—I couldn't come up with a single way of helping him.

"Jack! I'm slipping!"

This time, the voice coming from the gorge was not Nelson's. It was female. Soothing. Loving. But accusatorial as well. I watched as Nelson transformed in front of me into that of Vera Pietrova.

"Vera?"

"Jack. *Tovarisch*. I can't hold on much longer. I'm going to fall," she said. Her voice suddenly eerily calm, as if she was telling me about her day at work. "And you did nothing to prevent it. Nothing at all. You are going to let me die. You are going to let me—"

The radio on my belt squawked to life, drowning out Vera's deadpan accusations. "Jack? Buddy? Are you there?"

The voice over the radio was Randy's. A well of hope sprung up into my chest at the sound. I clutched the radio in my hands and pressed the call button.

"Randy! Get over here!" I shouted. "Vera's going to fall. We need you to—"

A growl from behind caused me to spin around and I found myself face to face with a macabre, chalk-white skull with no eyes and two needle-like fangs jutting from its lower jaw. A mane of golden straw-like hair sprouted from the creature's head, wriggling around in the stagnant air as if each strand had a life of its own.

A jenglot.

The thing—much larger than any I'd seen in life—hissed at me as it took a step closer. I couldn't tear my eyes away from the monstrosity as a strange, tube-like proboscis slithered out from its gaping maw toward my face. It wanted to feed on blood and I was the main course.

As it took another step forward, it hesitated. Its head cocked to the side curiously as it stared eyelessly at me. A single tear streaked down its bony cheek. That's when I realized who I was looking at. It was Vera. Or at least, how she appeared after the mad Russian geneticist known as Sashe Krenkin had had his way with her.

The radio crackled again, only this time, the voice was different. Tinged with a trace of a Latin accent. "She's beautiful, no?" Freakshow's voice warbled over the receiver. "The perfect killing machine. Powerful. Deadly." He paused, letting his words take root in my heart. "But she's flawed. She turned on her creator because of her love for you. In Vera, you failed twice..."

The Vera-Jenglot hissed again, regained its composure, and stepped forward. I glanced behind me to see Vera's human form still clutching tightly to the rope.

"Shut up!" I shouted into the radio. "Leave my friends alone!"

"You betrayed her twice, Jack," he said, oblivious to my demands. "First, when you allowed Dr. Krenkin to have her. And again, when you let her blow herself up, along with the madman's laboratory. She trusted you, Jack. She trusted you to come up with a way to keep her from falling and you failed."

"I said shut up!"

The Vera-Jenglot's tongue was close enough to feel its rough, spikey edges scraping against the skin of my cheek. I could smell the creature's hot, rancid breath as I closed my eyes and readied myself for what was to come.

"Jack?" Randy's voice was back in the radio again. "I asked where you are. I've got no way of finding you."

My eyes snapped open once more. The creature was gone, but I could still hear it in the shadows of the jungle. Stalking me with padded feet. I turned toward the gorge once more to see that Nelson Daniels had returned to his original precarious position. His short, thick legs kicked helplessly over the valley below.

Okay, Jackson, think, I thought. *How did you get out of this the first time?* My mind whirred, trying desperately to remember. Then, it hit me. *The tag!*

"Randy!" I shouted into my radio as I reached in my pocket and pulled out a small black plastic cube with a red LED mounted in its center. I pressed a button on the device's side and let out a breath of relief as I smiled broadly to myself. I knew what I had to do. "I've just activated Tag 23. Use it to track us."

"Jack?" I heard Nikki say from somewhere in the darkness of the jungle. "Are you okay?"

"Nikki? Is that you?"

"Come on, Jack, wake up," she said. I could hear the concern in her voice. "Please Lord, help him wake up."

The jungle landscape around me began to fade into nothingness once more and everything suddenly went black. But the darkness didn't last long. As Nikki continued to plead with me to awaken, I became acutely aware of a beam of comforting white light coming straight at me. Soon, it enveloped me…wrapping me in a gentle embrace. I felt something hot and wet touch my face and my eyelids fluttered open.

๛๛

I looked up to see Nikki's tear-stained face hovering over me. Another tear fell from her cheek to land on my own and I smiled up at her as best I could. I was still in immense physical pain, but the look of genuine concern on her face made my injuries almost worth it. She still cared about me. Still loved me, even. Still…

I suddenly sat up, wincing with pain at the exertion of it. I was resting on Thomas Leeds' white leather couch that had apparently been put back into proper place while I'd been out. I looked around the room to see my dad, Arnold, Grigsby, the senator, and Davenport hovering nearby; looks of concern on each of their faces. Well, the reporter didn't look as much concerned as he did apprehensive…but you get the point.

"How long was I out?" I asked.

"About an hour," Nikki said, putting a wet washcloth on my forehead. "Scott took Mia and her team out to look for Randy and the cub. We only have about another hour before the Houskaani take to the streets. We're out of time."

"I've got the department upping man power even as we speak," Detective Grigsby said. "We'll increase our patrols by fifty percent in case they start their rampage before we can find the cub." He paused for a second, then added. "Don't worry. They'll be carrying tranquilizer darts. Told the brass that we were hunting an endangered species of bear that I suspected was foraging in the city. They seemed to buy it."

I smiled at him, then shook my head. "Thanks, but I'm afraid once they see what they're really dealing with, they're not going to be too concerned with preserving an endangered species of anything," I said, taking the washcloth from Nikki's hand and dabbing at the sweat still pouring down my face. "Our only chance is to find Phisto and get it to the adults before they're even spotted."

"But that's exactly what we're trying to do," Nikki said. "That's why Scott and the others are out searching now."

I pulled my feet around and placed them unsteadily on the floor, then tried to stand. After a couple of attempts, and with my dad's help, I managed to get up and stand without tipping over. My shirt was still off and a swath of bandages were now wrapped tightly around my upper torso. My left arm hung uselessly in a makeshift sling. Seeing the work she'd done, I looked at Nikki and smiled. Then, I walked over to her, leaned in and kissed her softly on the lips.

"Thank you. For everything," I said, locking eyes with her for a few wordless seconds. Then, I turned to the rest of the group. "They're wasting their time. They'll never find the child or Randy," I said. "But I can."

I grinned at the entire group as I picked up my phone and called Wiley again.

"You still have the output frequencies for Specimen Tag 23," I asked him as soon as he answered the phone.

"Tag 23?"

"Yep."

"I think I might have them," he said. "But why?"

My grinned broadened.

"Because we're going to use it to find ourselves Randy and a baby Jersey Devil."

TWENTY-EIGHT

WE SPED ACROSS THE CITY AT BREAKNECK SPEEDS; GRIGSBY'S DASHBOARD
emergency lights sending out a swath of red and blue strobe lights ahead of
us. It was nearly midnight and traffic was still thick as a cup of Nikki's
coffee, but the police light managed to push us through some pretty tight
squeezes as the detective negotiated 11th Avenue into what appeared to be
the Meatpacking District.

Arnold and I sat in the front seat; I was favoring my wounded shoulder
while glancing down at the handheld GPS display in my lap. "Turn right,
three blocks ahead," I said before looking into the back seat at Nikki, who
was crammed next to my dad and Davenport. "How are the others doing?"

She shrugged. "Haven't heard anything in about five minutes, but you
know they'll let us know the moment the Houskaani start to move."

I turned back to watch the GPS in silence, my face drawn into a nervous
mask. I could only hope my *seat-of-the-pants* plan would hold together long
enough to do what needed to be done.

The dream I'd had after passing out had been the key to everything. I
supposed it was my subconscious trying to work through what my conscious mind couldn't. Though Filmore had tossed Randy's phone, there was
no way he could have known about Brazil...about how I was stalked in an
Amazonian jungle by a couple of big cats. He couldn't have possibly known
that I used a specimen tag—a tiny electronic device used to track animals
we capture in order to study their habits—as a means for Randy to find us
before the jaguars could eat Nelson and me. And he definitely had no way

of knowing that my oldest friend had decided the tag was a bit of "good luck" and had used it as a decorative piece on a leather strap he wore around his neck every day since we returned from Siberia on our first unofficial mission with ENIGMA.

Once Wiley managed to pinpoint the device's output frequency, all that remained was to track the signal back to its source and find both Randy and the cub. I'd brought Arnold along with us as a backup. I wasn't sure how precise the GPS could pinpoint Randy's location—even with the special modifications that gave the device the ability to beep as we drew closer to our target—so bringing the mutt would give us an additional method of tracking him once we were in the general area.

In the meantime, I had re-directed Landers, Mia, and her group back toward the sewers where the creatures nested. They were each positioned in the sewer's most strategic exit points in hopes of spotting them the moment they emerged into the city. Once they were seen, the plan was to have the team follow the cryptids and prevent any casualties. Each team member was accompanied by at least two police officers who had been briefed on what we were really up against. Telling them they were hunting a rare species of bear just wasn't going to cut it. I'd insisted they be told the truth before being allowed to partner with us. And thanks to Grigsby, everyone was carrying dart guns rather than high powered rifles or shotguns. If all went well, Landers' team could tranquilize all of the Houskaani before it even became an issue. But fortunately, I even had a contingency plan if all didn't go well.

Yeah, imagine that. Obadiah Jackson actually coming up with a backup plan. Stupid Landers was obviously having too much influence on me. I guess this operation wasn't so *by-the-seat-of-our-pants* now that I think about it.

"I believe we're almost there," I told Grigsby, turning my mind back to the task at hand. "Just a few more blocks. Up on the left."

It had taken us another hour, but we'd made it across town and into an industrial district near the Hudson River lined with docks, warehouses, and other places perfect for hiding a captured cryptid. I eyed the road as the detective turned into a do-it-yourself storage facility and pulled up to the gate. There was no guardhouse to the facility, only a keypad next to the gate that allowed entry onto the grounds for anyone who knew the code.

"Okay," Davenport said from the backseat. "What are you geniuses going to do now?" The reporter's words were tinged with spit and vinegar. He was still pretty sore at the way my team had been treating him once his connection with Freakshow had been made. But honestly, I think secretly he was more miffed that Nikki's affections had grown frigid the more she'd gotten to know him. Still, despite his sarcasm, the guy had a point.

"Guess I could climb over the fence," I said. "Then try to find a way to jimmy open the gate from inside."

Grigsby eyed me suspiciously then smiled. "Or we could avoid committing *another* felony all together, Dr. Jackson, and I can just use the passcode these places give us law enforcement types in case of emergencies." He pulled out his Blackberry and scrolled through a few apps until he let out a satisfied: "Got it."

He punched in the code and waited for the gate to pull back completely before gassing the vehicle through. The storage facility was comprised of a single, multi-story orange and white building made of corrugated metal. Except for a handful of tiny rectangular portholes that lined each corner of the structure, the only windows adorning it were built into large, automatic sliding doors at the entrance. Another keypad was mounted on the wall next to the doors.

Arnold let out a small whine as he scratched impatiently at the door.

"Looks like we're in the right spot," I said, handing the tracking unit to Nikki before pulling my Glock from the waistband of my pants.

"What are you doing with that?" asked Grigsby, punching the code into the keypad with a scowl. The doors slid open and he turned to glare at me with his arms folded across his broad chest. Arnold took two steps into the building, turned to look at us and let out soft bark. He obviously wanted to get moving and wasn't remotely interested in our current debate.

"You don't think I'm going in there unarmed, do you?"

He shook his head. "Uh-uh. No way," he said. "This is an NYPD operation, Jackson. You've already royally screwed this whole thing up. I'm not about to let you go in there guns blazing."

As the words were being spoken, my dad, who had stayed behind to get something out of the trunk of the car walked up to us; his Winchester rifle rested on his shoulder.

"Oh for the love of..." Grigsby threw up his hands in disgust. "You Jacksons are going to be the death of me."

"The way my boy shoots, Detective, chances of that are pretty good," Dad said with a chuckle.

Nikki joined in then, covering her mouth in an attempt to regain her composure as she eyed me apologetically.

"Fine," Grigsby finally said. "But you only discharge the firearms on my command. Understood?"

We both nodded our agreement.

We were about to step into the storage building when Nikki's phone buzzed. She glanced at it and said, "It's Scott." She answered it, mumbled a few unintelligible words and handed me the phone. "He wants to talk to you."

"What's happening, Scott?"

"The creatures have left the sewers," he said in an uncharacteristically nervous tone. "Four of them took flight and are heading northwest of Hell's Kitchen, moving toward Central Park. Mia, Timothy, and two NYPD officers are following them. Another four are heading southwest with the other Shepherds keeping tabs on them." He paused as if trying to figure out the best way to say what was coming. "But, Jack, two of them...well, they're on foot. Heading fast toward Times Square."

A lump formed in my throat. "Use your tranqs on them. You can't let them make it. I'm not sure what it's like at this time of night, but I'm betting it's still pretty crowded there."

"Tell me something I don't know," he said. "I've already tried. I personally sank three darts in one of them and it just barely slowed it down. It was enough Ketamine to drop a Yeti in heat and it only made the Houskaan dizzy. Jack, I'm afraid there might be only one way to deal with them."

Crap. This was not something I particularly wanted to hear at the moment. We were so close. So close to finding the cub and putting an end to this mess once and for all. I had wanted to do this without another person or creature losing its life in the process. But when it came down to it, protecting the human population took priority.

"Okay, Scott," I said. "I trust you to make the right call. In the meantime, I think we're in the facility where the Randy and the cub are being kept. Do what you can to give us as much time as possible."

"Will do," he said. "And Jack, good luck."

I ended the call and handed the phone back to Nikki. "Yeah, we're out of time," I told them, bringing the Glock up with my one good hand and stepping into the dimly lit corridor of the storage facility. "Screw subtlety. We have to get the cub and move."

"And you really think the rest of your plan is going to work?" Davenport asked, flipping on a flashlight and following us.

"Why wouldn't it?" I whispered, suddenly aware of how well our voices carried along the stark hallways.

"Because you stole it from *Jurassic Park 2*," he hissed. "Arguably, the weakest of the franchise, by the way—"

"First of all, I didn't *steal* the idea," I spat as we continued moving through the facility. "I was merely inspired by it. And second, anything with Jeff Goldblum in it is pure awesome and anyone who disagrees with that gets a punch in the face."

"Will you two stow it!" Dad growled under his breath. "Obadiah, we're on a hunt. And whether you think stealth is necessary right now or not, you two going at like a couple of fanboys fighting over who'd win in a fight between Superman and Batman is *not* going to help."

"Batman," I said.

"Superman, no doubt," said Davenport simultaneously.

I glared at him, but Dad was right. If Filmore was lurking somewhere around here, he would no doubt have heard our little bickerfest and might be lying in wait to ambush us.

From that point on, we strode silently through the corridors, following the four-inch display of the GPS unit, along with a series of soft staccato beeps to indicate proximity. As we came to a stairwell the tracking device indicated we should take, my dog continued moving further down the hallway.

"No Arnold," I said, holding the door open for him. "Randy's up here. We need to go upstairs."

The mutt just stared dumbly at me, huffed an exacerbated growl, then turned toward the direction he'd originally been heading.

"Cripes, Jackson," Davenport scoffed. "You can't even control one fleabag. How on earth do you plan on handling eleven Jersey Devils at the same time?"

My face reddened—as much from anger over the reporter calling Arnold a "fleabag" than from his insinuation that I might not know what I was doing. But I didn't give him the satisfaction of a retort. I simply stomped my foot and pointed to the stairs. The action caught Arnold's attention and with irritated reluctance, he complied. With I glance up into my eyes that seemed almost hurt, the dog trotted into the stairwell and started making his way up.

The rest of us followed close behind and as we ascended, my thoughts drifted back to Landers and the impending rampage of the winged cryptids. Something about the conversation had not sat right with me...something other than the possibility of having to put them down permanently. It had been something Landers had said.

Four of the creatures had taken flight and were heading east. Another four were flying south. And two were on the ground.

Four, four, and two, I thought as I rounded another corner for the third flight of stairs. *That's ten. But now that Deborah was dead, there's supposed to be eleven. Davenport just reiterated that there were eleven of them. Where's the eleventh one? Could Scott have miscounted?*

As we approached the door to the fourth floor landing, the tracking devices' beeps reached a crescendo, indicating we were on the right floor and all thoughts of my conversation with Landers instantly dissolved from mind. This was it. We were about to locate the cub, hopefully rescue Randy, and if we were lucky—I mean *really* lucky—we might just catch the culprit behind it all and stop a massacre at the same time.

Carefully, Grigsby pressed his palm against the pressure plate on the door and silently pushed it open. His gun trained in front of him, he crept into the hallway with my dad and I close on his heels. After clearing the hall, we nodded to Nikki and Davenport, who joined us. Arnold, however, was still reluctant to come, but a couple of quiet pats to my thighs egged him on. We then proceeded to search the floor as quietly as we could.

Just like all the levels of the storage facility, the layout was simple enough. We stood in what basically could have been viewed as a huge warehouse containing eight rows of ten air-conditioned storage units. Slowly, we moved from one row to the next, until coming to the sixth one away from the door we'd just entered.

My heart nearly froze inside my chest as I peered down at the far end to see a single unit, its garage-style door slid open. From our angle, nothing seemed to stir inside the confines of the unit. But in my gut, I knew we'd found it. No need to look at the GPS any more. We'd managed to find the place where Filmore had kept his stolen prize.

I took a single step forward before my dad's calloused hand reached out and snagged my uninjured shoulder. "Hold it, son," he said, glancing at Grigsby. "Anyone else think it strange the door is standing wide open like that?"

Arnold *harumphed* in answer, his wet, black nose turning toward the exit. But no one else stirred. No one else answered. All eyes were fixed on the storage unit.

"Maybe Filmore is still down there," Davenport whispered as he fiddled with the digital camera hanging around his neck. I heard the device hum as he powered it up. The sleazy reporter didn't want to miss a single moment of the action. "Maybe he's tying Randy up right now."

The detective nodded. "I doubt it," he said. "But we still need to take it slow and eas—"

"Screw that," I hissed. "We don't have time to play it safe." And before anyone could stop me, I ran toward the open door, aiming my gun as I spun to face the interior of the storage unit. Amid a string of curses from Detective Grigsby, the others caught up with me and shined their flashlights into the unit.

The warehouse aisle echoed with collective round of gasps as the contents of the unit's interior came into view. The interior was about eight feet by ten with only two objects inside. The first thing my eyes landed on was a large wire cage—the same kind one might use to crate a German Shepherd—resting unceremoniously against the back wall. A device was attached to the cage that would periodically release food and water at regular intervals to the cage's occupant. The occupant itself was no surprise. It was exactly what I expected to see—although, I have to admit, it was much cuter than I had ever pictured the little furball to be. More Ewok Wicket than demonic Phisto. Its orange-red eyes, bright and big, looked pleadingly as it keened pitifully at us.

But the baby cryptid wasn't what had caused the confused shock to our collective systems. It was the man, trussed up with layers and layers of duct tape, seated in a rickety wooden chair in the center of the room that was so out of place. We had expected to find Randy in a similar position, but the unconscious man before us now wasn't him. It was a badly beaten, bruised, and bleeding Chuck Filmore; Randy's leather necklace with the Tag 23 charm hung loosely from the man's neck.

We stood in silence, staring without comprehension. The sound of Davenport's camera clicking away was the only other sound in the room. Finally, someone spoke up but for the life of me, I can't remember who it was.

"Um, where's Randy?" they asked.

The words were enough to stir me into the present and I heard Detective Grigsby answer: "I don't know. The question I want to know is who did this."

From off in the distance, I heard a series of scratching noises, but I couldn't place it. I was just too taken aback by the discovery. On the one hand, we'd successfully located the cub...but I'd been so confident that my old friend would be here as well.

More scratches in the distance.

Where are you, buddy?

"I'm going to call Scott," I heard Nikki say as the blood pounded in my ears. "Let him know we've found Phisto and proceeding to phase two of the plan."

I nodded silently, still focused on the irritating scratching noises from somewhere in the warehouse. That's when I heard the whine.

"Arnold!" I said, turning on my heels and running toward the door that led to the stairwell. He'd been trying to tell me the whole time. He'd known Randy wasn't up here. He'd been trying to follow the scent from the moment we'd entered the building and I wouldn't let him.

"Obadiah?" my dad hollered behind me. "Where you going?"

"To get Randy!" I shouted, plowing through the door and down the steps with Arnold a few feet ahead. The nice thing about chasing monsters for a living is that one learns to run. Actually, you learn to run fast when there's plenty of room to maneuver and build up speed. Your life often depends on it. And though I wasn't as conditioned as Landers might have preferred—when it came to the life of my best friend, I really knew how to turn on the speed.

We made it to ground level in record time, bounding at least three or four steps at a time. I exploded through the stairwell door and turned left in the direction I'd seen Arnold moving when we'd first entered the storage facility. I could hear the sound of my dad's footsteps echoing down the stairs after me, but I didn't wait. I couldn't. We had already lost so much precious time. I couldn't bear the thought of being too late, though I knew that chances were more than good that I was.

We rounded a corner and I could see another set of automatic doors that must lead to the loading bay of the complex. Wherever Randy had gone, he must have gone through them. I slid to a stop just as I came up on them. A red LED flipped on inside the glass dome of the motion sensor above the door, which slowly hissed open and I dashed into the graveled back alley of the storage complex. Directly in front me sat a late model, luxury SUV—a black Mercedes with dark, tinted windows. A man in a very expensive-looking, tailored suit stood with his back to me outside the passenger-side backseat, busying himself with something—though from my position, I couldn't see what he was doing.

Suddenly, whether from hearing or sensing us, he spun around to face us; a look of surprise on his face. At first, I had suspected—no, it was more like hoped—that the man was Freakshow, but one look at his almost cotton-hued shade of blond hair and an immaculately trimmed goatee of the same color told me that he wasn't.

Instinctively, the man reached into his jacket and I could see the gleam of metal as he extracted a rather large caliber handgun. Faster than I could follow, Arnold lunged at my attacker and I watched in horrifying fascination as my loveable dog's jaws literally unhinged. His maw spread out to an impossible size as two viper-like fangs popped out and sank deep into the man's well-muscled arm. The gun clattered uselessly to the ground, followed immediately by the blond man and my dog. Screams exploded from the mystery man as the mutated mongrel began tearing meat away from his flesh.

While this happened, the SUV's backdoor slammed shut and I heard the engine roar to life. Instinctively, I ran toward it, my gun extended, and came to a gut-wrenching halt the moment the tinted windows slowly eased their way down. The sight inside the vehicle hit me like a baseball bat swung by Babe Ruth.

I saw Randy, tied up. His mouth gagged with a cloth bandana. Tears streaked his cheeks as he looked over at me. But why tears? That made no sense. Sure, Randy was in a bind...but he'd been through worse without so much as a whimper. Why was he crying now?

There was someone in the backseat next to him, but I wasn't paying attention. I couldn't take my eyes off my friend. I could just make out the barrel of a gun pressed tight against his temple.

Then a voice called out. "*Bozhe moi*, Jack. You look like crap," the voice said with a thick Russian accent. It was such a familiar voice. An unexpected voice. I noticed something hot and wet streaming down my own cheeks now, but I couldn't for the life of me figure out why I too was now crying. "You need to call Arnold off and let my friend get back into the car," the voice continued, as if my battered appearance had already been forgotten. "I don't want to hurt Randall, but I will if I have to."

The voice. Where had I heard it before? It seemed like eons since I'd last heard it, yet recent at the same time. But I just couldn't place it. My eyes still locked onto Randy's. I couldn't bring myself to look to the one who sat next to him, the one with the gun to his head. A few things had registered about the person with the gun, whose voice was so familiar to me...so comforting and so torturous at the same time. The flowing chestnut-colored hair. The blue-white eyes. The red, pouty and very feminine lips. Yes, those had registered as well, but still, I could not bring myself to look her in the face.

I realized suddenly that I didn't want to. By all I held holy, I couldn't look her in the face. And the tears began to pour even more.

Arnold must have recognized her as well, because he'd eased up on his attack and was now staring at her; a series of morose whimpers escaping his strangely deformed, unhinged jaws. Then, slowly, it reshaped back to normal and the dog stepped away from the man. He'd understood the woman's command—probably better than I did. I was still trying to process everything.

Who was she? Who was this woman and why couldn't I bring myself to look her in the face?

"Don't worry, Jack," she said. The accent was suggestive. Was it Ekaterina? No, Kat's accent was different. More well-traveled. Besides, I would never have such a visceral, tormented reaction to her like I was having at that moment. "Soon, Freakshow will contact you and all will be made clear. I'll take good care of Randy, I promise. After all, we have much to catch up on."

As I continued to stare at Randy, I was half aware that the blond man Arnold had mauled had scrambled to his feet, moved to the front passenger side door and slid in with a scream of pain. And still the tears fell from my eyes, soaking my shirt.

Jack, you need to look, I told myself.

But I don't want to.

And why do you think that is?

The SUV's front door slammed and I heard the driver put the vehicle in gear once more. It was about to drive off.

It's now or never, Jack. Look now!

No.

They're about to leave. This is your last chance to know for sure.

I heard movement behind me, then a sharp gasp. My dad had finally caught up to us. He was seeing what I refused to look at. I then heard the crunch of gravel as the vehicle started to pull forward.

Look! Look now!

"Nooooo!" I shouted aloud this time while simultaneously moving my gaze to the woman seated next to Randy. The woman with the gun. The woman I had met years before in a run-down hospital in a slum of St. Petersburg. The woman I'd grown to love as my very own sister. The woman who was supposed to be dead.

Without another word from its armed occupants, the SUV pulled away in a puff of gravel and dust. I could do nothing but stand there, my shoulders slouched as I absorbed what I'd just seen. Who I'd just seen. I felt my dad's comforting hand on my shoulder, but he didn't say a word. I was pretty sure he was crying too. After all, he'd loved her like a daughter himself.

After several minutes, I wiped the tears from my eyes, straightened myself up, and took a deep breath. Then I muttered a single name.

"Vera."

TWENTY-NINE

My Dad and I stood outside in the gloom of the alley for several minutes, not saying a word. Vera was alive. I didn't know how. Didn't know what had become of her these last two years. And had no idea how on earth she'd gotten mixed up with Freakshow. My mind reeled.

Then, of course, there was the question of what they wanted with Randy. Why had they taken him? Why had Vera been part of it? She'd loved him as much as any of us. What was going on?

Tears still running down my cheeks, I turned to face my dad. His eyes were red, but he was wiping away all evidence of his own tears. He smiled warmly at me before giving an understanding nod.

"I know you don't understand this, son," he said. "I don't either. But you've got to try to put this behind you for the moment. We have more immediate problems to deal with. Lives are at stake."

The Houskaani, I thought.

Every fiber of my being railed against the notion of not chasing after the Mercedes. Of not rescuing Randy and bringing Vera back into the family. I railed against the very idea of letting them get away. I'd lost my older brother, Zachariah, to leukemia when I was very young. It had been devastating. The emotional trauma of his death had nearly caused my own demise when I'd developed a severe fever after a bout with even more severe depression. Then, a few years afterwards, I'd met Randy. He'd quickly become an altogether different kind of brother to me. He'd helped me to deal with the turmoil, the emptiness, the hole that had been ripped from my soul when Zachariah had died. A few years after that, I'd met Vera and gained a sister I'd never had. And my dad was now asking me to turn my back on them? Just like that? Just give up and act like nothing happened? No way! There's no way on earth I could do that.

An image of Nikki suddenly flashed in my mind. Her warm, gentle eyes smiling at me in a way her lips never could. Her strength, that indomitable, unfathomable strength of hers, seemed to radiate from her. Stalwart. Strong. Faithful. All the things I had struggled my entire life to be.

I knew what my subconscious was doing. A scale had been erected in my mind. Weighing my options. Rationalizing and sorting through my fears and heart-felt desires. Would I do what was right? Or would I succumb to my baser needs—the need to never be alone? It's amazing what two years can do to a man. Before I'd met Nikki, the only person I ever concerned myself with was me. My friends came a very close second. Everyone else could go hang for all I cared. Now, however, I knew the answer before it ever officially formed in my thoughts. I could never allow innocents to be harmed—whether human or cryptid—at the expense of my own desires. It wouldn't be right. I'd never be able to live with myself and what was worse, neither could Randy or Vera. *No. I need to suck it up and finish this before anyone else gets hurt.*

I straightened myself up, wiped a few straggling tears away, and took a deep breath. "You're right," I said. "But I have a favor to ask you, Dad."

"Sure. What is it?" He bent down to pick Arnold up and began scratching the little guy behind the ears. He ignored the blood and gore caking the dog's whiskers and if he'd seen him go all monster on the gunman, he showed no sign of it.

"Don't tell anyone about this," I said. "Let's keep it between you and me."

If my dad was curious as to why I wanted to keep it secret, he didn't voice it. He merely nodded, then put his arm around my shoulder, and led me back to into the storage facility. He was right. We had a lot of work to do. Lives needed saving. But I swore to myself at that moment that once the job was done, I wouldn't rest until I rescued Randy and got to the bottom of Vera's apparent resurrection and her connection to Freakshow.

⁂

We were riding in the back of an NYPD SWAT van; the Houskaan cub brayed piteously at us from the cage that sat in the center aisle. I avoided looking at it as best I could. The fear in its eyes nearly broke my heart. The poor creature had been ripped from its family…kept locked away in some dark metal dungeon, so far away from the lush wooded forest it called home. From the numerous lacerations and dried blood-matted fur, I could tell that Filmore had been none too gentle with it, too.

I glared at the evil little bureaucrat who now sat handcuffed between Detective Grigsby and my dad. He sat silently, staring down at the chains that bound both wrists and ankles with a sour look on his face. Dried blood caked the bald spot on his head from a healing laceration. Both eyes were swollen shut from the pounding he'd sustained by…I shuddered at the thought of who might have given him such a beating. The man certainly deserved it for the misery and death he had caused, but I prayed to God above that Vera had had no part in the creep's torture. Her hands were designed for much gentler, nobler things.

Nikki and Davenport were sitting on the bench beside me. Arnold, whose muzzle still contained flecks of blood from Freakshow's blond henchman, rested casually against my leg. His steady gaze never faltering from Filmore.

"Okay, so what now?" Grigsby asked, breaking me away from my thoughts.

I wasn't sure what was worse—my mind focused on the suffering of the cute little winged version of an Ewok in front of me or the revelation that Vera was still alive and had possibly been turned into a heartless killer herself. I decided that neither was particularly healthy at the moment, so I struggled to come up with the best possible answer to the detective's question.

The news that the city was now in chaos made it a little easier to keep me focused. Reports from all across town were already coming in. At least six new attacks. Two disappearances. And Landers had indeed been forced to put down the two Houskaani that had attacked a handful of pedestrians in Times Square.

Even at such an early hour in the morning, the streets were in a near panic. The police and emergency management teams were struggling to keep up with an overflow of 911 calls describing strange demonic creatures flying overhead and howling into the night. A handful of the reports indicated that a few of the creatures had even tried to get inside people's homes. And things were only going to get worse. Mia's Shepherds had told us that they'd seen at least one posse armed with rifles taking to the streets, their mob-like minds gunning for the creatures. Even more worrying were reports that a handful of thrill-seekers were out and about, their camera phones at the ready to capture whatever images they could for the *fame and fortune* that can only be discovered on a YouTube feed. We had the makings of a major catastrophe waiting to happen and I still wasn't sure exactly how we were going to reunite the cub with its family.

"Right now, our priority is to get Wicket here as close to the colony as possible," I said. After seeing how adorable the fuzzy little critter was, I refused to call him something as sinister as Phisto. "The protein secretions apparently carry pretty far in the air, but without getting closer, there is no way of knowing for sure his family will latch onto the scent."

"And how, pray tell, do you intend to get close enough to them?" Davenport said. "I told you before, going all Jurassic Park and placing the cub in the backseat of a convertible and driving around town in hopes of drawing them out would be like throwing a worm in the ocean and hoping the Loch Ness Monster will bite."

"Um, for your information, Nessie...not a big fan of worms," I said. "Second, it lives in a lake. Not an ocean."

The reporter rolled his eyes. "You get my point," he said. New York is a big city and we have no idea where to even begin looking. Both teams hunting the airborne creatures have lost sight of them. Landers killed his targets and is now spinning his wheels trying to catch up. There's no way to know where they'll strike next. And remember, you now have *two* groups flying in different directions. Finding one group isn't good enough, you have to find both."

Nikki turned to look at the reporter and scowled. "Alex," she said. "Shut up or get out."

I smiled broadly at her. We'd long since decided that the reporter was more than free to leave our team whenever he chose. The damage Freakshow had planned was already done. There was little more that Davenport could do to us if he was, in fact, working with the madman. But the dapper tabloid reporter smelled too big a story to leave now. Whether we captured the creatures and saved New York City or we all died horribly gruesome deaths, he believed he was going to have one heck of a scoop. Then again, he'd never had to deal with a man named Anton Polk either. I doubted very seriously that the Director of ENIGMA would ever allow the press to print anything about today's events. It would be chalked up to a group of out of control weather balloons or something ridiculous like that. And he would do it with such finesse and eloquence and imagination that no one in their right mind would doubt the lame-brained story was true. Davenport could kick and scream all he wanted, but in the end, he would be horribly discredited. I almost felt sorry for the guy. Almost.

After Nikki returned my grin, I turned back to Grigsby. "Okay, last we heard, Mia's group was heading northwest. Their last known position—"

"Their last known position was near Central Park," Grigsby said.

"And Landers said the Times Square Houskaani had started moving toward Broadway just before they were killed," I said. "Which leaves Group Three—"

"Ooh, um, last report on the southwest-bound group put them just west of the Murray Hill area...around Park Avenue and East 34th Street," Nikki said as she glanced down at the Google Maps app on her iPad.

Suddenly, I sat up on the hard metal bench of the van. A pattern was beginning to emerge in my mind, but I wasn't sure if it was real or merely coincidence. I turned the facts over in my head for several seconds before I spoke.

"Hold on a second," I said. "Central Park. It was the place our first victim was attacked, right?"

Grigsby nodded, then shrugged. "So?"

"And the prostitute? Can't remember her name, but where was it that she was attacked exactly?"

"Theresa McUllen," Nikki said. "Um, she was killed on Park Avenue. Near the Union Square subway station at 4th Avenue."

Grigsby sat forward in his own seat as he began to see the pattern as well. "And the third victim, Schildiner, was at Broadway and 29th which, if Landers is correct, that's exactly where the two he was following had started moving before they were killed."

"Bingo," I said.

"Okay," Davenport said with a sneer. "Big freakin' deal. So they're returning to the scene of the crime. So what?"

Ignoring the comment, I dialed Landers' phone and waited for him to answer.

"Scott, I think I know where the Houskaani will head next," I said.

"Which group?" he asked.

"I'm hoping both of them will converge, actually," I said. "As far as I can figure out, they've got nowhere else to go. I'll text you an address as soon as we hang up. Just get everyone together and get over there. We'll meet you as soon as we can."

"And if they show up before you get there?"

I paused, considering the best answer. "Do whatever necessary to protect lives," I said. "But do your best not to kill any more."

"Roger that," he said before hanging up.

I texted the address then instructed the van's driver to get us to East 69th as soon as possible and sat back on my bench with a nervous sigh. Following my lead, Grigsby called HQ and told them to get the semi-tractor trailer we'd commandeered en route as soon as possible. The dispatcher advised that the truck was just leaving the Meatpacking District, but would get there as soon as it was able.

Filmore let out a derisive laugh at this. "You don't really think this will work, do you?" he asked. "Your reporter friend is correct, you know. The Houskaani are wickedly intelligent, but they're not human. They wouldn't possibly be returning to the scenes of their crimes. Human killers do such things as a matter of hubris. These creatures have no such ego. What on earth makes you think they'll be there?"

My dad, who'd been silently studying the young Houskaan in its crate during the entire conversation, guffawed. "You know, for someone as bright as you obviously are, able to pull this whole thing off, you really are about as dense as a blacksmith's anvil, aren't you, boy?" he said. "Of course they're returning to their murder scenes, but not for some human-like sense of pride."

"They're acting on instinct," I continued my dad's line of thought. "They're getting desperate. Without you providing them with regular doses of Wicket's hormone, they've completely lost his scent. They're backtracking now. Going to the last few places they had a hit on the scent you manipulated them with to try to pick up the trail."

"And their next stop will be the apartment where Aislynn Sommers lived," Nikki added. "On upper East 69th Street."

I grinned as I leaned forward to stare Filmore square in the eyes. "And that's where you're going to help us clean up your own mess, Bubba," I said, holding out a strange looking pump-action spray bottle we'd found in the man's jacket pocket. "You're gonna—"

Without warning, there was a fantastic crunch of metal and the SWAT van lurched to one side, nearly flipping over on its top-heavy side.

"—the heck was that?" I shouted, dropping the empty spray bottle to grab hold of a set of leather straps hanging from the van's ceiling.

Before anyone could answer, another impact slammed into the other side of the van. The reinforced steel of the armored vehicle bent inward, pushing against my dad's back and knocking him from his perch with a grunt.

"It's one of those...those things!" shouted the SWAT team officer seated in the front passenger seat. His eyes doubled in size as he craned his head to look out the window. "It's flying around, circling the van. What the heck *is* that thing?"

I staggered to my feet, still clutching the hand strap, and helped my dad back into his seat. "No, no, no!" I shouted. "Not yet. We're not ready yet."

"Sure," Grigsby said with a worried smile. "Why don't you go out there and tell it that?"

A third blow came, stronger than any we'd felt so far. The van lurched once more, this time with enough force to tip us completely over. The sound of screeching metal and car horns outside echoed through the closed confines of the cabin as we slid along the pavement, carried along by our momentum. The entire team was tossed throughout the back of the van like a set of dice in a Yahtzee cup. After a good six or seven seconds, we came to a stop and the sound of something large and heavy landed on the exterior of our overturned transport, followed immediately with a ghastly shriek and a hiss of air.

"Oh crap, oh crap, oh crap!" Filmore screamed as he attempted to un-tangle himself from a mess of riot gear that had fallen on top of him during the crash. "What are we going to do? What are we going to do? It'll kill us all!"

A series of bangs exploded against the side of the van as the maddened creature outside tried to claw its way to the infant keening wildly inside. I steadied myself, trying to gather my wits as I pulled my Glock from my waistband.

"Where are we now?" I shouted to the driver, who was struggling to unsnap his seatbelt. In his panic, his fingers couldn't quite find the latch. In his state of mind, he wasn't going to be able to answer my question. I looked over at his partner, whose head hung limply. Whether he was unconscious or dead, I wasn't sure. Then I searched for Nikki, who was just pushing herself to her feet. "Nikki, check our GPS coordinates. Are we close enough to attract the others?"

She eyed me with irritation as she checked a badly frazzled Arnold for injuries. "Oh, we're just fine Jack. No, I don't think we have a concussion or anything," she said wryly. "How are you?"

More bangs from the outside erupted in the tight confines of the cabin. "Nik!"

"Okay, okay," she said, opening her pack to pull out the GPS unit. "Looks like we're at 60th Street and 2nd Avenue. Just nine blocks south of our destination."

Cripes! Not sure that's close enough, I thought, pulling out my phone and tossing it to Nikki. "Call Landers. Tell him he's got to find some way to get the rest of the creatures to move this way." I then turned to Grigsby, who was assisting the driver with his seat belt. "Get on the horn. We need to redirect the semi our way."

After checking on the officer in the front passenger seat and verifying he was merely unconscious, Grigsby turned back to me. "I'll do what I can, but it only just left the Meatpacking District," he said. "It might take another thirty minutes for it to get here."

Suddenly, another bang sounded from outside, followed by the sound of metal splitting. A sliver of streetlamp light flooded through the crack in what was now the van's ceiling and I could just make out the glowing red eyes of the malicious creature on the other side. The Houskaan had managed to break through. Of course, the crack was still small enough that only its long, meaty fingers could fit through, but as the creature growled and huffed, I could see the metal giving way to its strength. It would have the van ripped open like a can of tuna in minutes.

Filmore screamed at the sight then started pulling uselessly at the steel chains attaching his feet to the interior of the vehicle. "Let me go!" he shrieked. "It's going to kill me! It's going to kill me!"

But our murder suspect wasn't the only one screaming, I could hear bystanders outside the van crying out in terror at the sight before them. And from my particular vantage point, I could understand why. As the creature now wedged both hands into the splitting seam, I was able to see more of the monstrosity than I ever had before. We'd met before and the creature's sheer immensity was enough to make Hercules quake in his sandals. It was Goliath and he looked plenty irked.

The mystery of the missing eleventh creature had suddenly become clear. While his colony had spread out to retrace their steps of the previous weeks, this one—the alpha male—had gone out on his own. For unfathomable reasons, he'd broken off from the others and had followed another trail—a trail that I couldn't for the life of me imagine. And he had succeeded where the others had failed.

For a brief second, I wondered what would happen if I simply opened the back door and allowed Wicket to go to his enraged sire. But as I stared into those cold, murderous eyes, I knew that action would be disastrous. From what I could see, the cub was the furthest thing from Goliath's mind. He'd never once given Wicket a second glance as he tore through the armored steel like cardboard. No, his goal was on something else...someone else. And as I followed his gaze through the crack in the ceiling, I knew exactly who his target was.

Chuck Filmore.

THIRTY

IT MADE NO SENSE. AN ENTIRE COLONY OF JERSEY DEVILS HAD TRAVELED hundreds of miles to New York City just to find their missing infant. So why, now that Goliath had finally found the object of their exhaustive search, was he more interested in the kidnapper than the cub? Why were those burning eyes…those hate-filled, murderous eyes…so intent on a mere human rather than its spawn?

As if trying to answer my unspoken question, the beast, its limbs trembling with each frustrated blow, belched out a ferocious howl as it spread the fissure even wider apart. Its equine head, now able to slide through the split, hissed in frustration when it could squeeze in no further. But it was slowly, systematically widening the gap with each powerful punch, twist, and pull of metal. Soon, it would be through and I shuddered to think what would happen after that.

Grigsby, resting beside me on the ground, pulled out his sidearm and took aim.

"No," I said. "Wait."

He looked at me quizzically, but complied without a word.

"*Wait?*" Davenport said as he sidled up to us. As a matter of fact, everyone in the van, except for Filmore, who was still chained in place, had crawled their way over to us by now. The one conscious SWAT officer had managed to extricate his teammate and had dragged him closer to the huddled group as well. We all kept ducking down, making sure to keep far out of the monster's grasping reach. During the rollover, the cage containing Wicket had slid toward the backdoor but the little furball inside only stared up at its sire with confident, knowing eyes. It didn't seem concerned in the slightest. "Why on earth would he wait?" the reporter continued. "He's got a clear shot. Why not take that thing out now?"

"Yeah!" Filmore cried, sweat pouring down his reddened face as he tugged at the chain that kept him tethered to the vehicle. "That thing wants to kill me."

That makes two of us, I thought, then directed my attention back to the cryptid above us. The thing had only once, that I could tell, even remotely acknowledged Wicket's presence. Its ire…its unmitigated wrath…had continuously been fixed on Filmore. *But why? And why is he not concerned about his little boy?*

The Houskaan barked out another howl, followed immediately by a distinct hiss of expelled air. But the sound didn't seem to come from the creature's mouth. It came from somewhere else…but where?

"Obadiah," my dad said with a concerned look on his face as he brought his Winchester to his shoulder and locked his sights on the creature. "They're right. If you're planning on doing something, sooner would be much better than later, I think."

"I know, I know…but something's wrong," I said, scratching absently behind Arnold's ears to calm him. "I can't quite put my finger on it, but—"

Another howl, then the now all-too-familiar hiss…and I saw it. I'd been looking for it. That's the only way I'd been able to catch it. Just below the beast's ear line—two slits that resembled some strange vestigial set of gills. The moment the Houskaan howled, the slits spread out, followed immediately by a puff of some vapor-like mist.

Goliath's hormonal secretion. It just sprayed it all over the SWAT van. It knows the child is here, but it also knows Filmore's a threat and has to—

"Cripes," I said, bringing myself up into a crouch and stretching my hand out at Grigsby. "I need the shackles' key."

"What? Why?"

"Don't have time to explain. Just give me the key. We've got to get Filmore out of here."

At this, the little creep's head poked up from where he had been cowering. "What? Uh-uh! No way I'm going out there with that...that thing on the loose!" he shouted. "I was never able to do anything with that one even when I was corralling the rest. It has a mind of its own."

"You'd rather stay here until the cavalry gets here then?" I asked.

"Cavalry?" Nikki asked. "Jack, what are you talking about?"

"We didn't need to worry about figuring a way to bring the colony here," I said, nodding up at the grinning horse-face as it squeezed further into the ever-widening crevice. "It's been signaling them the entire time. They know the cub's been found and will be on their way. That's why it's currently after Filmore. It knows he's the one that stole the cub...he's the biggest threat to their survival and Goliath wants to eliminate that threat before the others get here."

Grigsby handed me the keys. "And you really think taking him out in the open will protect him better than being in here?"

I rushed over to Filmore's side and reached down for the padlock bolted to the bulkhead. Slowly, I glanced up into his still swollen eyes and a flood of rage washed through me at the sight. For the first time in years, I knew what it was to thoroughly despise another human being. It was *his* fault. All of it was his fault. The current rampage of winged monsters through Manhattan; the deaths—including Aislynn's murder; Randy's abduction and the turmoil that Vera's apparent resurrection brought with it, in some completely irrational way, I blamed him for all of it. Whether it was fair or not, I held him responsible and I knew that part of me would not mourn if Goliath *did* get his hands on the man's scrawny little neck.

I glanced back at my friends and met Nikki's steady gaze. Silently, as if sensing my inner struggle, she smiled at me with a slight, sympathetic nod. And I knew. I knew that no matter how much I loathed the man known as Charles Filmore, I would do everything I could to protect him. I'd do whatever it took to keep him alive. To make sure that he lived long enough to see his trial and, God willing, justice.

Keep in mind, this knowledge had nothing to do with some untapped, hidden strength within me. Oh no. If I had my way, I'd probably have put a bullet in his head right there for all the misery I blamed him for— undeserved or not. No, the strength that kept me from pulling the trigger myself and ending our horrible ordeal right there was the compassion I saw in that one glimpse of Nikki's smile. That one look had assured me that all would be okay. That we'd get through this. That I would find Randy and be reunited with the same Vera I'd lost in a Siberian research facility. That I'd catch Freakshow and make him pay for his crimes against both humanity and nature. But most importantly, I knew that after everything, after all we'd been through and our own personal ups and downs, if she could still smile, I knew there was always hope for us.

"I think we have a much better chance out there…with lots of places to hide…than trapped in here by four walls and a gas tank," I said, popping the lock open and removing the shackles from around Filmore's ankles. I then removed the handcuffs around his wrists, grabbed him roughly by the shirt collar, and turned to face the others. "As soon as Goliath's attention has turned our way, get out. Leave Wicket here and when the other Hous- kaani arrives, let them take him." I grabbed Filmore by the wrist with my good hand and pulled him to the back of the van. As we passed underneath the creature, it screamed with rage and reached one muscular arm down to snag us. Keeping as low as we could, we slipped past him, though his clawed hand tore a four-digit gash in my already blood-soaked bowling shirt. Once at the back door, we stopped and I turned to look at Nikki one more time. "Call Landers. Fill him in on what's happening. Tell him that other than protecting lives, no one is to interfere with the Houskaani. We won't even need that semi any more to transport the creatures. I have a feeling they'll migrate back to the Pine Barrens on their own once he's safe. It's where the rest of their colony is. It's their home." I paused for a second, trying to find the real words I wanted to say to her. My possible *last* words.

But Grigsby spared me the embarrassment of saying something utterly foolish by scrambling over to me, his gun steadily trained between Goliath's red-glowing eyes. "Sorry, Jack," he said. "Filmore's my prisoner. You're not taking him anywhere without me."

I grinned at him, nodded, and tossed my shoulder sling to the floor. Although I knew I needed it to keep my reset collarbone in place, I figured it would encumber me too much when I ran. It was a toss-up—keep my clavicle secured or stumble and let a winged monster tear me apart at the seams. In the end, it wasn't much of a contest.

I put my good hand on the van's backdoor handle just as a huge shock-wave rippled through the entire van. The creature had once more slammed its powerful fists into the vehicle's hull, creating a large enough gap to squeeze its head and both arms through. There would be nothing stopping him from entering the tight confines of the transport now.

"That's our cue!" I shouted and threw open the door. In an instant, Arnold leapt out of the van and ran out of sight to the other side. Though I was worried the little guy might bite off more than he could chew, I forced myself to focus on the plan and pushed Filmore onto the street outside. Wincing from a sharp pain to my shoulder, I followed, scooping my prisoner up by his collar again and sprinting away from the wreckage.

Risking a glance back, I saw the creature jumping down from the van to follow, only to be confronted by the viper-fanged visage of my little Jack Russell Terrier lunging at him. To the average person, from a distance, the sight might have been ludicrous. Comical even. But I knew better. I knew what was happening to Arnold's physiology. Knew the changes that were occurring to his jaws…his musculature…his brain. I knew the feral ferocity that was about to be unleashed—a ferocity and bloodlust that had been glimpsed earlier that night with Freakshow's goon. And suddenly, I found myself wondering which monster I should be more concerned with.

With a preternatural growl, so deep and alien for such a small dog, Arnold circled around the Houskaan, leapt into the air, and brought his fangs down into the back of its right thigh. His unnaturally expanded jaws clamped down on the beast's hamstrings and tugged ferociously, whipping his head around in a frenzied motion until the tendons and muscles of Goliath's right leg were ripped away in a spray of blood.

Whoa! I thought, turning back in the direction in which we were running. No matter how many times I saw him in action, I would never get used to it and to be honest, he frightened me more than a little. I only hoped that none of my friends or teammates ever witnessed what he could do. They'd never accept him for what he was like I did. Polk would insist on locking him up. And they'd all have good reason for their concern. He'd just hamstrung a ten-foot tall, four-hundred pound winged monster and was hardly breaking a sweat—well, if dogs *could* sweat, that is.

The monstrous roar behind us, however, told me our problems were far from over. The Houskaan might not be able to run efficiently now, but I was pretty sure he could still fly, which meant the farther away we were when he figured that out, the better for all of us.

Of course, the crowded street was certainly not going to help us get the distance we needed. All around us, cars had come to a halt, creating a massive parking lot along East 60th. Even well after midnight, the streets were packed and the occupants of the idling vehicles hadn't had sense enough to run away while the beast's rampage was focused on us. Instead, like some perverse tailgating party, they'd gathered together, camera phones in quaking hands, and videoed the entire scene before them.

"Tell me you at least dialed 911!" I shouted at one of the amateur videographers as we ran past. *Geeze, Polk is going to have a stroke trying to suppress all this*, I thought.

"Jack," I heard Grigsby shout from behind. "I've got to clear the street. Gotta get these people away from here."

I waved back at him in agreement, trying to conserve my oxygen as I pushed Filmore forward. We weaved in and out of the haphazardly parked cars, attempting to create as hard a target as possible for the fast-moving flying *Wizard of Oz* monkey that I sensed was back on our trail. No matter how much damage Arnold had inflicted, I knew it would not be enough to stop the creature from having its revenge on the one who'd torn his family apart. A gut-wrenching realization came that I would either have to find a way to kill the beast or die trying to stop it. There would be no other alternative.

A shriek, followed immediately by a swooshing sound behind me, announced Goliath's airborne presence. Instinctively, I shoved Filmore to the ground and dove on top of him just as the flap of large leathery wings rushed past my head. I glanced around and saw a full-sized 4x4 pickup parked just three feet away; its large knobby tires spread wide and supporting the truck high off the ground with the help of a lift kit. Grabbing Filmore's arm, we dashed over to the truck and ducked underneath its carriage as we recouped our fleeting breath.

While we waited for the creature to double back, I had a sudden thought. Senator Leeds' apartment. Deborah. Filmore chortling like a madman as the scene unfolded before him.

"Why didn't she kill you?" I asked him without preamble.

"H-Huh?"

"Deborah. The female Houskaan at Leeds' penthouse," I explained. "She attacked me. Threw me out a window. She slaughtered Joseph. Yet, she didn't even give you a second glance." A dark shadow, highlighted by the sodium streetlights around us, zoomed over the blacktop and past the pickup we were now hiding under. "Why not?"

"I-I..." The little guy trembled violently, his mind and voice unable to connect with each other. He was scared out of his mind.

He jumped even more when a series of four gunshots rang out back down the street from where we'd just run. I figured Grigsby had had no choice but to open fire on Goliath. At this point, I couldn't say I blamed him much. I was sorely tempted to put the monster down myself. Still, despite the gunfire, I had a feeling our tormentor would soon be back and from the looks of things, so did my captive.

"This is important, Chuckles!" I shouted, grabbing him by the shirt and pulling him close to my face. I smacked him across his angular cheek, trying hard not to draw too much satisfaction from it. "Forget what's going on out there and tell me. Why didn't she attack you?"

His face flushed from my slap, he took a deep breath and attempted to steady his nerves. "I-I used an ultrasonic transmitter I bought from a hardware store...the kind used for invisible fences for dogs. It-it messes with their ability to hear. Has to do with the way...the way they see the world. With the device activated, she couldn't *see* me."

I shook my head. "That can't be it. They don't use echolocation. Their hearing makes up only a portion of how they see."

"But they need all of their senses to form a complete picture around them," he said, his eyes darting back and forth in search of the monster now stalking us. "Mess any one of those senses up and you create a major blind spot for them."

Geeze. The burgeoning ego I'd developed over my ingenious flashbang device I'd employed in the sewers yesterday was instantly deflated. Apparently, my dad's horrendous cologne alone would have been enough to do the trick.

"Okay. So where's the ultrasonic device now?" I asked.

He shook his head. "Gone. Whoever jumped me at the storage facility took it. Don't know why, but—"

The four wheel drive we hid under shuddered violently with a sudden impact as Goliath nose-dived into it. It bounced back onto all four tires once before being lifted again by two powerful fur-covered hands clutching the undercarriage.

"Gotta move!" I shouted, grabbing Filmore and scrambling out from under the truck's bed and back onto the street. I glanced around, searching for Grigsby. He was supposed to be my back up here, but was nowhere to be seen. Deciding we were on our own, I pointed toward a nearby subway entrance. "Let's try for that. Maybe we can lose him down there."

The shriek behind me told me we only had seconds to traverse the hundred and fifty yard dash to the stairs leading into the subway station. Even at my best, there was no way we'd both make it. There was just too much open space and the creature was too fast.

I turned my head, looking over my shoulder, and saw nearly twenty feet of leathery wing gliding in the air behind us. Goliath was only forty yards away and gaining fast. Making a conscious decision, I gave a gentle shove to Filmore's back.

"Go on! Head for the subway," I said, knowing full well that I might be handing a cold-blooded killer his walking papers. But I'd committed myself. I wasn't going to allow the Houskaan alpha to have him, no matter what. Besides, I made a living hunting things. If I survived what I was about to do, I would hunt him down too.

The little creep didn't hesitate. The moment I nudged him, he put on a burst of speed I wouldn't have thought possible for someone so ungainly and aimed for the subway. The moment he was far enough away, I spun around, just in time to see the creature swooping down in Filmore's direction. Instinctively, I leapt into Goliath's path, wrapped my arms around his shaggy torso and held on for dear life.

THIRTY-ONE

A FLASH OF PAIN RIPPED THROUGH MY SHOULDER AS I CLEAVED TO THE monster's waistline with every ounce of my strength. I was pretty sure my insane stunt had just re-injured my collarbone, but that wasn't the worse part. The cryptid bucked, then lurched skyward sending us up toward the jagged skyline above the city. The blurred shapes of Off-Broadway theaters flew past and underneath us as we barreled into the sky. My prey undoubtedly hoped to hurl me to my death once we reached our apex and with my throbbing shoulder, I doubted it would take much of an effort on his part.

My face pressed tight against the monster's belly as I struggled to pull myself up and onto its back. Wind howled past my ears, buffeting my shaggy hair as we sped above the streets. As if sensing my intentions, Goliath veered to his left then performed a perfect mid-air barrel roll that would have slung me free if my white-knuckled grip hadn't dug even tighter into its pelt. As the creature began to right himself, I pulled up with all my strength, allowing the momentum of the maneuver to swing me out and over from my ride. My hands slid precariously along Goliath's hide until they once more grabbed firmly onto the hair of its back and pulled myself in tight.

I'd made it. Perched on his back, my legs straddled the creature's waist while my arms wrapped tight around his neck. I tucked my head against its shoulder, keeping my torso bent low along its back in a strange aerial spooning position. Hey, if you were holding on for dear life and riding on a winged horse-headed demon from Hell nearly seventy stories above Manhattan, I'm pretty sure you wouldn't care how silly you looked either. The point was, I'd finally managed to gain a purchase where it would be easier for me to hang on.

"All right, Mr. Ed," I wheezed, clutching the beast around the neck in a tight bear hug while keeping my eyes clenched tight. The last thing I wanted to do was to see my own doom. "Be gentle. This is my first time."

The Houskaan, clearly unnerved by my new perch, ducked its head and folded its wings back. Without warning, my stomach lurched toward my feet as we dived straight down in a spiraling arc. My fingers bit deeper into the creature's neck as we plummeted from the sky.

Think Jackson. Think. Or you're gonna end up being the world's thinnest New York-style pizza.

But nothing came to me. Despite having grown up in the Bluegrass state, it might surprise you that I've never really cared much for horses. I spent some times in a few stables when my parents worked in Lexington. Learned to ride, sure. But I never enjoyed it very much. There are several perfectly good reasons for that. First of all, they bite. Second, they smell bad. And if that's not enough, they can be as mean as a rattlesnake, about as bipolar as half the women I've dated, and generally speaking, they attract a heck of a lot of flies. Riding on the back of a Jersey Devil was light years worse than riding a horse. Well, without the flies, that is. No sensible fly would be caught dead buzzing past a living gargoyle's head from nearly seven hundred feet above the New York City streets.

As far as I could figure, I was pretty much screwed…which only made my panic-addled brain even more sluggish than usual as we plummeted to our doom. The only hope I had was in Goliath's own instinct for survival. I was pretty sure he wouldn't go all Kamikaze on the street just to get rid of an unwanted hitchhiker and that brought me a certain amount of comfort. A small amount, to be sure, but enough to give me an extra ounce of courage. Courage enough to pop one eye open to see what was happening.

Oh, geeze. Wish I hadn't done that.

The sidewalk was racing up fast to greet us and so far, Goliath was showing no indication of having any of that *self-preservation instinct* I'd been counting on.

Stupid animal, I thought, wrapping my legs tighter around his waist as the Hot Wheels-sized cars below began to grow to full size. I could now make out the crowd of onlookers, a barrage of camera flashes blazing away the darkness. To my right, I could see the SWAT van, though there were no signs of my friends or the other Houskaani either.

Without any warning, I heard a loud clap from below, then another. Something struck Goliath hard in the shoulder eliciting a horrendous howl. I felt something warm and wet re-soaking my shirt as I pressed up against his back. I knew without looking that it was blood. Someone was shooting at us and from the blood, I'd say the bullet passed through the creature's shoulder and must have narrowly missed hitting me.

...the heck? Who's shooting at us down there?

Blam! Blam!

Two more shots rang out just as the beast let out another bellow and began spinning wildly, his downward trajectory speeding up in an uncontrolled drop. Inexplicably, as we fell, I felt the creature's left hand reach back and gently grab onto my leg. It wasn't an aggressive gesture. More like what you do when you have to stop real fast at a stop light and have to reach out to keep the passenger from flying through a windshield. It was as if Goliath was trying to keep me from falling off.

"Stop shooting! Stop shooting!" I shouted above the roar of wind in my ears. If Grigsby or my dad were responsible for this, and if I survived the next sixty seconds, they were going to get a major piece of my mind for this crazy cowboy stunt.

As we rotated another 360 degrees, I had my answer. Among the throng of on-lookers and amateur shutter-bugs all clustered together like some two-bit posse from a cheesy Spaghetti Western, stood about eight gun-toting men and women with their sights locked on us. That's when I remembered

Landers' report of a group of frightened New Yorkers taking to the streets to hunt the Houskaani. Part of me had thought he was joking about that. I should have known better. After all, the man had the sense of humor of an 18th century vicar. I had bets with Randy that the last time Landers told an actual joke was during the Clinton Administration. So I chided myself that the sight of the posse below me really shouldn't have surprised me as much as it had.

The group was a hodge-podge ensemble of adults and teens, men and women, blue-collar truck drivers and gang-banging punks. There was no demographic rhyme or reason to the makeup of the vigilantes—only fear. Or worse, a thirst for killing a monster.

But the throng of shooters wasn't the only thing I saw. A furtive figure, wearing a hood, darted from the same subway entrance that Filmore had fled. From the distance, I could just make out a patch of white from under the hood. Mia. And from the looks of things, she was heading straight toward the crowd.

Well, if I survive the drop, at least I'll have backup.

Three more shots went off. I felt another slug rip into Goliath's torso. The great beast screamed—I wasn't sure whether from pain or rage—then managed to regain a certain amount of control to our descent. I heard the leathery sound of wings unfurling and a sudden gust of air filling them. Our momentum slowed just as the creature veered to the left. We were still approaching the ground, but at a much slower, more controlled pace. When we were only twenty or twenty-five feet off the ground, the great wings began flapping at an even more fevered pitch and the creature righted himself for a landing.

"Stop shooting, you idiots!" I shouted again, now certain they'd be able to hear me.

Their eyes widened in collective shock as they caught their first sight of me clinging to the back of a living gargoyle. In unison, they each two a single step back, though they still kept their guns trained on us.

That's right. Nice and easy, I thought as we slowly approached the street. I wasn't exactly sure what I'd do once I landed. After all, I wasn't exactly an invited guest of *Air Houska*. Once we were on terra firma, he could just easily rip into me in front of the crazy nutjobs with all the guns. Then again, now that I thought about it, if he'd really wanted to, the Houskaan could have more than likely tossed me aside like an unwanted gnat. But he hadn't. As a matter of fact, unless I'd imagined it, not only had he seemed to try to keep me from falling off once the fireworks started, it almost felt as though he'd actually turned into the gunfire to shield me from any stray shots. *But that makes no sense. Why would he do that?*

But I had no more time to ponder the question as I felt the gentle thud of Goliath's massive feet touching down onto the pavement. My arms were still stretched tight around his neck as my legs dangled uselessly, nearly three and a half feet off the ground. The creature kept his wings unfurled and extended, presenting a nightmarish image to his attackers; then he turned his head, eyeing me over his shoulder, and let out a soft huff of air before giving me a slight nod.

Dude! Is this thing...is he sentient? Sure, I know all animals are to a point. But the Houskaan seemed...aware. Almost—I shuddered to believe—conscious. Aware. His eyes, crimson though they were, seemed to exude an otherworldly intelligence and understanding I'd not seen before in my previous glimpses of the creatures. He seemed almost...human.

He huffed again just before the coarse hair underneath me bristled and he turned his gaze toward his attackers. From the tension of muscle fibers beneath me, I guessed he was about to attack and was warning me to get away. *But that's crazy!*

"Buddy, you better get off of dat thing and get outta here!" shouted a large man with an overhanging belly bursting at the buttons of a plaid shirt. From his dress and the way he carried himself, I figured him to be a trucker of some kind. Or a lumberjack, though I doubted there was much call for a lumberjack in Manhattan. Whatever he was, he was holding what looked like a sawed-off shotgun in his meaty hands. "We're not gonna let that thing live to kill any more people."

I heard the tale-tale sound of a gun cocking and I glanced at a young Asian kid, dressed in colors and brandishing an old, rusted MAC-10 machine pistol. A smoldering joint hung loosely from his mouth as he glared at us with watery, red-rimmed eyes. To his left stood a middle-aged woman in office attire holding a .380 semi-automatic pistol. She looked nervous, but determined.

Taking all of this in, I refused to let go of my perch. They couldn't shoot at Goliath while I hung on without possibly committing murder and for some unfathomable reason, I had a hunch the Houskaan was reluctant to put me in harm's way as well.

"Who are you people?" I asked, trying to bide time for Grigsby or the others to come to my rescue. "Geeze, Lord knows I'm all for the Second Amendment, but put those stupid things away. You'll put someone's eye out."

"Mister, you better do what the man says," said the secretary-looking woman with the pistol. Her hands shook as she spoke. "Th-that...*thing*...has already killed a lot of people tonight. I saw it with my own eyes. We all did. And we're not going to let it...let it..." Her voice trailed off as she succumbed to a sobbing fit.

I glanced past the posse, looking for any signs of Mia. I was sure I'd just seen her running from the subway, so where was she? For that matter, I couldn't for the life of me figure out where my friends had gone. The SWAT van was nearly three hundred yards off and abandoned. I could just barely make out the wire cage that still contained the little furball, Wicket. But I couldn't spot Grigsby, my dad, or Nikki anywhere.

Come on, Grigs, where are you? Heck, at this point, I would have settled for Davenport. Anyone to talk these people out of doing something we'd *all* regret. I knew that with enough fire power, they'd be able to easily take Goliath down. Landers and his team of cops had proven that in Times

Square. But I wasn't sure they'd be able to kill him without a handful of the posse being slaughtered first.

I'd been in a number of standoffs in the years I'd been doing this kind of work. None of them had turned out well. Something told me that this one would be the worst I'd ever seen. And since the cavalry was nowhere in sight, I figured I'd been elected to be the negotiator for the moment. To save their lives. To save the life of Goliath.

Gently, soothingly, I stroked at the creature's pelt as I spoke calmly into his ears. "Okay, big guy, I'm getting down now," I said, continuing the petting. "No rash moves, okay?"

With a stomp of his foot, Goliath pulled back his wings and clicked three times. Remembering how Mia had interacted with Esther in the sewers, I mimicked the same string of clicks and eased myself off his back and onto the pavement. My hand still stroked at his fur as I moved in front, making myself a human shield against the gun-wielding mob.

"No one's going to kill anyone else tonight," I said, reaching into my pocket and pulling out a cigar. This situation called for slow, deliberate actions. One jerky, unsteady move could end it for all of us and I wanted the posse to know they were in no immediate danger. I stared at them without a word for several seconds before biting the tip of the stogey off and lighting it up. I pulled in a deep puff of smoke and exhaled slowly through my nostrils; savoring the sweet Cuban blend. Then, I held up one hand as a gesture of peace. "I'm with the government. We've got everything under control here. Now return to your homes and no charges will be brought against you for firing on a federal agent." It was a stretch, sure…but they had no idea this operation wasn't officially sanctioned.

"You must be nuts," the burly trucker growled. "That thing—and a few others just like it—ripped a man to shreds right in front of me. I ain't about to let it get away." In unison, the entire group hefted their weapons up as if to demonstrate their resolve.

I felt Goliath bristle behind me, a low growl rattled from his throat. Unconsciously, I reached behind me and patted it on the chest. Warm fluid seeped onto my hands, reminding me of the slugs he'd taken just before landing. "Easy, big guy," I whispered. "Just take it easy."

"Now, move away," the trucker continued, "or we won't be responsible for what happens to you."

"And I won't be responsible for what happens to any one of you," I said, clenching the cigar tight in my teeth as I pulled my Glock from my waistband and brought it up to aim directly at the big man's head. With only one good arm and a weary, battered body, it was almost a Herculean feat to keep the weapon steady. "Yeah. You might kill us both right where we stand, but I'll be sure to take as many of you knuckleheads with me as I can."

From a distance, I heard a piercing shriek, followed immediately by another one. The mob tensed, turning their heads skyward as they attempted to locate where the horrific noise was coming from.

This is not good, I thought. If the remaining Houskaani came and saw their patriarch in danger, there's no telling what they might do. *Where's my team?*

"Listen to me," I said, keeping a bead dead center on the trucker's forehead. "Those are the other creatures. They're heading this way. All they're interested in is getting back a cub that was taken from them. Let them do that and no one else gets hurt. If you don't drop your weapons and get out of here before they arrive, none of us will survive. You need to go." I paused as another shrill cry echoed against the canyon of buildings. The shriek was much closer than a few seconds before. "Now."

The crowd paused, uncertainty etched on each of their faces. A few actually lowered the guns, but no one dropped or holstered them. All eyes were fixed on the trucker—the impromptu leader of the pack.

Finally, the burly man spoke. "And what if we don't? We have more than enough fire power to stop the likes of dem."

"Then you will all die," purred a feline voice from behind the crowd. As one, they all turned to see the dark hooded robes of Mia and seven Shepherds who were only now materializing from the shadows cast by the overhead streetlights. All eight of them clutched their wicked-looking kukri knives tight in their hands. I glanced down at Mia's to see a dried brown stain on the blade. "At least one of you, already is."

Is that blood? And what did she mean by that last comment?

"Mia," I said, deciding to put the questions aside for the moment. "Am I glad to see you."

She smiled sadly at me, her silver hair partially covering dark eyes. "I'm afraid you won't be so glad soon enough, Jack," she said grimly. "One of these cretins murdered Esther tonight. The gentlest of them all, she'd never killed a single human and someone put a bullet in her head. Luke here saw it happen and we are now here for justice."

Goliath fidgeted behind me, a gentle harrumph belching from his lips.

"You said it, Chewie," I said to the Houskaan before directing my attention back to Mia. "I don't think so, toots. I'm going to tell you exactly what I told them: No one else *dies* tonight. I'm sick of it, Mia! Sick of the death. Sick of cryptids and humans alike dying, and I ain't going to stand here and let you raise the death toll." I took in a deep breath as I slowly eased the Glock's barrel in her direction. Goliath stiffened, but he made no move against me. "Do we understand each other?"

Mia's reaction surprised me. Where I'd pictured her becoming indignant or enraged, she merely laughed. That slight tinkling sound of some faery queen I'd noticed before. The sound was even more unnerving than the erratic screeching that now was coming from high above. The Houskaani were finally here. In my mind's eye, I imagined the winged creatures circling overhead like some breed of vicious Lovecraftian vultures.

"He said you were an idealist at heart," she said. "Oh, you might play the part of some apathetic scoundrel, a mercenary for the highest bidder, but when push comes to shove, you will always do whatever it takes to save lives. Even the lives of scum like these...or like Filmore."

My veins chilled at the way she said Filmore's name. There was something dark and cold-blooded about it. Something that cut to the quick. But something she said unnerved me even more. It wasn't the first time she'd mentioned someone telling her about me and I was determined to get to the bottom of it. My throat tightened as a dark and horrible thought seeped into my head. *Freakshow? Could she have been working with him the whole time?* "Who? Who do you keep talking about?"

She giggled again as she pulled one strand of her hair back behind her ear. "Why Dr. Jackson, I thought it would be obvious by now." She moved forward slowly; the bewildered posse spreading out nervously to open a path directly toward me like Moses and the Red Sea. She sheathed her blade as she walked and stopped mere inches from me. Her smile never faltered. It was a nice smile. A genuine one. Not an ounce of duplicity in it...which chilled me even more. "It's my cousin. Marc Leeds. Your former colleague."

THIRTY-TWO

THE BOTTOM DROPPED OUT OF MY STOMACH. MARC...THE MAN WHO betrayed us, betrayed me...the man who had allied himself with enemies unseen and had quite literally thrown me to a school of flesh-eating mermaids was Mia's cousin. The former folklorist and linguist of the team had disappeared after our excursion to Greece last year. The last time we'd had any contact with him at all was a break-in at my place shortly after we'd returned. Oh, I couldn't prove it mind you. Arnold had all but ripped two of his accomplices to pieces, but we'd never found a sign that the bookworm had even been involved. And we hadn't caught of a whiff of him since.

I suddenly remembered Nikki's comment about a possible connection to Marc when we'd learned about the Leeds' link to our current investigation, but I'd chalked it up to simple coincidence. Which was really stupid of me since time and again, I've discovered that there simply is no such thing.

"Marc Leeds?" I said, forcing a breath between each syllable. My pulse throbbed against my temples. This was almost as big as if she'd just given me Freakshow's real name, address, and social security number. "Is your cousin?"

She raised a gentle hand up to my cheek as she stared compassionately into my eyes. "Yes, Jack," she said, before cocking her head to one side as a tumultuous round of screeches and howls erupted above us. Distracted as I was with the news of Marc's connection to the Jersey Devil legend, I'd almost forgotten my precarious situation. "But we haven't time to discuss such things. Goliath is injured, the rest of his colony has now arrived, and it's time to meet vengeance to the one who murdered Esther." Suddenly, I felt something cold and rigid press against the seam of my pants, just below the crotch. Mia smiled devilishly at me when I recognized the feel of her curved blade against my inner thigh. "And you can do nothing to stop it, dear Jack. Our fight is not with you, but with him." With her other hand, she pointed to the Asian teenager with the MAC-10.

Before the boy could react, four Shepherds lunged, pulling his machine pistol from his grip and hurling him to the ground.

"Now wait just a minute!" the trucker said, lunging forward only to be grabbed from behind by another, equally burly Shepherd.

"Justice, Jack," Mia said. "That's all we're asking. It's already found our good friend Charles. Now, for the Asian murderer and we'll be on our way. Out of your hair. Out of your life. And all you have to do is do *nothing* at all. Just let it happen and you'll be free of all this."

Filmore? Is he dead? Then I remembered the ruddy-brown stains on her knife. The direction she'd come from when she'd materialized from the shadows…the same subway in which Filmore had fled. *Had she actually killed him?*

The blade pressed tighter against my leg as I let her words sink in. The Houskaani shrieks grew louder, closer. I was alone. Alone against a colony of living gargoyles. Alone against a murderous psychotic cult. Alone against a group of well-armed New York vigilantes. And against a kukri knife just six inches south of the family jewels. All I would have to do is sit back and let it all play out. Let Mia and her Shepherds kill a not-so-innocent gang-banging punk who was probably guilty of so many more heinous crimes. Just sit back and watch as an extremely rare animal species is wiped from the face of the earth by the New York equivalent of a pitchfork wielding mob. And then sit back and watch as Mia's forces and the lynch mob destroy each other out of some old world sense of retribution. It would be so easy. And I was so tired. Tired of the job. Tired of ENIGMA. Tired of being walked on by every ferret-faced bureaucrat or politician that came my way. Tired of my friends…my *true* friends…being in constant danger from every whackjob with delusions of grandeur.

I looked down at the Asian kid, a Shepherd's knife hovering mere inches from his throat. His almond-shaped eyes pled silently at me as he sobbed under the powerful restraints of four other Shepherds that now pinned him firmly to the ground. Just as they had done me in Central Park. A sacrificial lamb, awaiting his slaughter.

Yeah. It would be oh-so-easy to just give up at that point. Only, I wouldn't be easy to live with if I did.

"Your cousin seems to have told you an awful lot about me," I said casually.

She looked up at me curiously at my sudden change of subject. "He told me a great deal about you, yes."

"And did he ever tell you how I tended to react when I felt bullied? When I felt threatened?" I asked Mia, never taking my eyes off the terrified Asian kid.

"He said you didn't like it."

"Exactly." I raised my Glock and fired directly at the Shepherd who was holding the knife just inches from the kid's throat. The bullet whizzed through the air, striking the flat of the kukri blade and ripping it from the man's grasp with a shower of sparks and a sharp, metallic clang. My mouth flew open in utter astonishment for a moment before I whooped in delirious glee. "Dude! Did you see what I just did? That was freakin' awesome!" Of course, I would never tell a soul that I had been aiming for the man's head. I really am that lousy a shot, but I wasn't about to admit it.

But I would have to wait for the proper accolades to come later. For the moment, the miraculous shot had left my adversaries in a stunned stupor. Before Mia or her goons could react, I lunged forward, wrapping my injured arm around the Shepherdess' waist and dove to the ground, pulling her with me. We slammed hard into the asphalt, jarring the knife from her hand. I heard it clatter to the ground just as a guttural roar erupted from Goliath, obviously ticked off at my sudden act of violence against the woman he saw as his matron. A sudden gust of wind and the flapping of wings soon followed and I suddenly found myself surrounded by six angry cryptids.

I rolled off the stunned Mia and pointed at the crowd. "Get out of here!" I shouted. "Now!"

The posse stood there, mouths agape as they stared down at a now dented knife blade lying harmlessly on the ground. The hooded goon who'd been wielding it, rolled on his back, gripping an obviously injured hand in a fit of screams.

"Go!" I shouted once more as the other Shepherds, joining their monstrous charges, moved around to encircle me. I wasn't going to have to tell the mob a third time. Without another word, they turned tail and sped off toward 2nd Avenue, leaving the gang-banger still struggling against the massive arms of two of Mia's goons.

With my gun still raised, I watched as Mia climbed to her feet, dusted herself off, and laughed. "Okay," she said. "I have to admit, Marc didn't prepare me for *that* little stunt. Well played, good sir. Well played. But it changes nothing. We still have the boy and we will still have our justice."

"And then what, Mia? Who's next?" I asked. "Landers? He killed two of them in Times Square tonight. Are you and your goons going to kill him too? I gave him the order to do it. What about me? Am I on your nutty justice list too?"

The Houskaani, obviously not pleased with my raised voice and aggressive behavior toward their benefactor, hissed and growled. Their massive muscles tensed in unison as a series of clicks warbled from their throats.

"Of course not," she said, oblivious to the building tension of her pets. "Those kills were sanctioned. Human life was in danger."

"And human life isn't in danger now? You're talking about killing a man, Mia! You're planning on murdering a human being."

She belted out a scornful laugh. "Human being?" She pointed at the gang-banger with a scowl. "That's being awfully generous, wouldn't you say?

Besides, it's different. He killed Esther, who wasn't threatening anyone. He murdered her in cold blood and so, retribution will be ours."

"I can't let you—"

"Jack?" A familiar feminine voice spoke from behind the throng of Shepherds and Houskaani. I peered around them to see Nikki and a frazzled looking, Alex Davenport. Both were staring at the terrified kid on the street. "What's going on?"

"Nikki! Thank God you're here," I said. "Where's Grigsby? We need him here now."

"He-he and your dad went after Filmore. They found his trail in the subway system and are looking for him."

Mia let out a soft chuckle. I wheeled around on her and growled, "What?"

"Oh, it's just that providence has given us all a way out of this little standoff we're now finding ourselves in," she said.

"How so?"

"I've told you all along I've nothing against you or your friends. As a matter of fact, I see us as sort of kindred spirits. I've no wish to hurt you…which is exactly what would have happened if you continued to prevent us from our task." She turned, looking over at the SWAT van. I followed her gaze to find the cage that had housed Wicket empty. "Phisto has been rescued. The only thing keeping us here is the murderer and you're in our way."

My pulse quickened at her words. I wasn't sure where she was going with any of this. By my reckoning, we had her dead to rights. Between Nikki and myself, I was pretty sure we had enough fire power to take out the JDs and a few of the Shepherds along with them. Mia knew I was loathe to kill the creatures, but she had also been told of my previous exploits. She wouldn't have any illusions to the fact that when push came to shove, I would do it. Especially to save Nikki. And yet, the silver-haired strumpet was just as casually confident as the first day I'd encountered her. She knew something I didn't and that just didn't sit well with me.

"All I have to do is wait it out, sweetheart," I said. "Once Grigs finds Filmore's corpse, he'll be coming back this way. He'll arrest you and your band of Merry Men and all will be right with the world."

She laughed again. That tinkle of chimes laugh I'd come to know so well. "That, dear Jack, is where you're wrong. Chuck Filmore isn't dead. I didn't kill him. Just, um, incapacitated him slightly. He's hurt, yes. And bleeding a great deal. It will be a very easy trail to follow."

Nikki pushed her way through the Shepherds until she stood beside me, her chin turned up in steady defiance. A tail-wagging Arnold strode confidently beside her while Davenport nervously brought up the rear. There was a gleam of light in the reporter's hand, a reflection of a lens, hanging down at his side. The little weasel was snapping pictures of the entire thing.

"Then Detective Grigsby will charge you with assault," Nikki said. "It'll be the same basic outcome."

"But that's where you're wrong. The trail won't only be easy to follow by a homicide detective and your dad, Jack," Mia explained, her face suddenly looking genuinely concerned. "Look around you, Jack. Who's missing?"

I did as she asked. All around me was nothing but metal blades, burly hooded figures,   and fur-covered beasts. Four Shepherds encircled me. Two pinned the gangster to the ground. And one still lay on the ground, holding his injured hand where my bullet had slammed into his knife. Besides the human, there were five Houskaani intermingled in the mix.

But wait...Landers put down two of them and with Esther killed, there should be at least eight left. I figured that two had secured Wicket and taken him to safety. *But that leaves one missing. Who's missing?*

I spun around, my eyes slowly glancing down at the ground where a pool of blood was beginning to dry. Houskaani blood. I took a quick inventory of the creatures again before a wave of cold washed down my spine.

"Goliath. Where's Goliath?"

"And now you see how this is the end of our standoff," Mia said. "When you pulled your little stunt and attacked me, Goliath fled. He wasn't sure how to respond. You see, very few humans are ever allowed to mount the Houskaani. Those who do, and who survive, form an irreversible bond with each other. Much the same as a rider who breaks a wild steed."

The memory of how the beast had turned into the gunfire to shield me from the posse's barrage flooded through my mind. How he'd actually reached back to make sure I wouldn't fall off as we plummeted to the ground. How he bristled when the vigilantes had threatened me. Mia wasn't lying. Something had definitely happened during that weird flight...something I couldn't quite explain.

"You see, in Goliath's mind, you two are now brothers. His first instinct was to react to your attack. To defend me. But because of your newly formed bond, he couldn't. That's when he remembered his original objective..."

"Filmore," I whispered.

"Exactly. So now you have a choice. Stay here and save this little piece of riff-raff." She pointed to the kid. "Or go and protect your father and the detective from Goliath's wrath. After all, if they stand in his way, he won't have the same reservations about killing them as he did with you. They will be collateral damage to him. Nothing more."

For a moment, I could do nothing but glare at Mia. I couldn't figure her out. I truly believed that she wasn't the run-of-the-mill crazy weirdo I usually ran into on these investigations. She wasn't evil, per se. She didn't have the typical look-out-for-number-one mentality. I believed she honestly didn't mean me or my friends any harm. So I couldn't understand why she was doing this. Why she was allowing it to happen.

"Jack, go," Nikki said, pulling out a Smith and Wesson 9 mm and leveling it at Mia. "Arnold and I have this. And Scott's on his way. Just talked to him, he was only about ten minutes out. Go save your dad."

I stared at her dumbstruck, then looked over to Davenport who was now standing beside her in a protective posture. His camera had disappeared and his hands were now clinched into tight fists as if he was raring for a fight. With such uneven odds, it was a foolhardy gesture, yet one that caused my respect for the man to rise up a notch or too. Still when all was said and done, it would be crazy to abandon Nikki like that.

"There's no way I'm leaving you here with these nutjobs, Nik! No way!"

"And what did I tell you about trying to 'protect' me all the time?" she scowled. "We can handle this."

I paused. I'd lost so much recently that the weight of it all was really beginning to push me over the edge. My best friend had been kidnapped by the most insane man I'd ever encountered. Vera, who I'd believed to be long dead was now working for the same man who'd kidnapped Randy. And my relationship with Nikki had been on the rocks for the last few months. We'd only just now started mending some pretty damaged fences. I couldn't imagine what would happen if I lost her forever. I couldn't just leave her to fend for herself; even with the support of my dog and the squirrely journalist as backup.

"Tick tock, Jack," Mia said, a coy smile once more returning. "I promise not to hurt her or Arnold while you're gone. But at this moment, you're the only one who can talk Goliath down. You're the only one who can stop him from his hunt. He's injured, severely, which will make him even more dangerous. I doubt either your father or Detective Grigsby can do much against the savagery they will face if he catches up to them."

"Jack," Nikki said, her eyes silently pleading with me. "Please. Go."

I looked to her, then to Mia, and back to Nikki again. Then I pointed down at Arnold. "Watch her. You got that?"

The little mutt let out a short bark, before wagging his tail enthusiastical-
ly. I gave him a quick pat before stepping toward Nikki. Slowly, I leaned in
and pulled Nikki tight against me. My lips pressed against hers and I felt her
body melt into my hands. What the kiss lacked in longevity, it made up for
in sheer, unbridled intensity. After several seconds, I pulled away from her
and looked her square in the eyes. "I love you, Nikki Jenkins."

She nodded at me. "I love you too, Dr. Jackson," I heard her mumble as
I turned away and sped off toward the subway entrance, following a trail of
congealing blood left by the strange winged creature known as Goliath.

THIRTY-THREE

WITHOUT LOOKING BACK, I RAN STRAIGHT FOR THE STAIRS LEADING down into the New York City subway. Sure. I was concerned about Nikki, but ever since I first met her, she had never stopped surprising me by just how well she could fend for herself. Besides, Arnold would protect her if things got nasty. Granted, I wasn't sure how well she'd do in preventing the Asian kid's death, but push come to shove, I honestly didn't care. At that moment, the only people's safety I cared about were hers, my dad's, and to a lesser extent Grigsby's.

Priorities. When faced with life or death for those you love, priorities can certainly become crystal clear. My entire life, I'd never been much of a hero. Never concerned myself with anyone else's well-being but my own. After meeting Nikki, all that changed. I slowly discovered that day after day, I was putting other people ahead of myself. It was most definitely a strange sensation…though not entirely unpleasant. But at that moment, that old selfish side started boiling up from the depths in which I'd buried them. I would do whatever it took to protect the ones I loved…the rest of the world could go hang for all I cared.

Besides, the sound of sirens heading our way helped to ease a number of my fears. The cavalry were on their way and that meant Nikki and Arnold only had to hold on for a little while longer. Which was something that couldn't exactly be said for my stubborn, but well-intentioned father at the moment.

I pushed my tumultuous thoughts aside as I came to the railings of the staircase, grabbed hold, and allowed my momentum to swing me around. I took the stairs three at a time and halted only a second when I caught the gleam of crimson stains along the tiled steps—telltale signs of Goliath recently passing this way. At least I was on the right track.

I jumped the last four steps, stumbled briefly, then ran forward. I brushed past a cluster of pale-faced commuters who were huddled together, trembling with obvious fear, near the entrance.

"Dude!" cried a tall black man dressed to the nines as if he'd been out clubbing the night away. "Don't go that way. There's a freakin' monster down there!"

In response, I brandished my Glock, grinned, and said, "No kidding?" Then, I ran past, keeping my eyes glued to the trail of blood that led me to a set of turnstiles and a bewildered transit cop who was only just picking himself up off the ground. Not wanting to be delayed by having to explain the firearm, I tucked it into my waistband, made sure my bowling shirt was pulled over it, and approached the police officer.

"Which way did it go?" I asked without feeling the need to elaborate what "it" was.

The cop dusted himself off, wiped a stream of blood from a knick to his brow and shrugged. "No idea. It was the craziest thing. I was just doing my patrol when all of a sudden—"

I didn't wait around to listen to his tale. Without preamble, I vaulted the turnstile against the officer's protests and darted toward the escalators that led to the subway platform. Simultaneously, I pulled out my cell phone and dialed my dad. After the third ring, someone answered.

"Obadiah?" my dad growled. "We found Filmore. He's been stabbed, but seems to be—"

"Dad, shut up and listen!" I shouted. "The alpha is on its way to you guys. It's after Filmore. It's injured and royally ticked off. I'm coming to you now, but in the meantime, tell Grigsby not to engage. If it comes down to a choice between Filmore or the creature, let Goliath have him."

There was a brief pause, then dad cleared his throat. "You know we can't do that son. Filmore might be a piece of filth, but we can't let him be mauled to death either."

"Dad, listen to me—"

"No, son. We're not going to let this man die. It would be wrong and you know it."

Oh, for the love of... "Okay," I said, throwing up my hands in frustration. The sound of approaching footsteps and shouts from a couple of transit cops heading my way reminded me I had to get moving again. "Fine. Where are you now? I'm coming to help."

I heard a rustling sound as my dad put his hand over the phone and consulted with Grigsby in rushed, mumbled tones. After a moment, the rustling stopped and the detective's voice spoke into my ear. "Jack, we're halfway to the next station on Track 7B, heading east. Only about a quarter of a mile so you shouldn't—" An ear-piercing shriek exploded through the phone's speaker. "We're out of time. From the sound of it, it's still some distance off, but gaining on us fast. We gotta get Filmore out of here!"

"Grigsby, wait!" I shouted, but the other end had already gone dead. "Crap!"

I moved up the ledge of the platform and glanced down, scanning right to left until I found what I thought to be Track 7B. I was just about to scramble down onto the tracks when the cops caught up to me.

"Hold it right there!" One of them shouted. "Where do you think you're going?"

I craned my head around to see not two, but six transit officers standing in defensive positions with their hands hovering precariously over their gun belts. I noticed the officer I'd jumped the turnstile in front of was nowhere in sight. Probably getting bandaged up. Swell. That meant that unless they caught Goliath on security cameras and had had time to take a gander at it, I was about to sound like a stark, raving lunatic.

"Would you believe I'm down here hunting the legendary Jersey Devil?" I shot them a smile, but apparently it wasn't charming enough to be convincing. They merely rolled their eyes at the comment, unfastened their holsters, and casually rested their palms against the handle of their guns. "No? How about the Loch Ness Monster? Ogopogo? Mothman? Rabid Chihuahua?"

"Sir, I'm going to have to ask you to come with us," said one of the cops, obviously not amused. I watched silently while his five partners started flanking me…three on each side. "We don't want any trouble now, so just—"

Before he could finish, I leapt down onto the tracks, careful to avoid the rails. I was pretty sure only the so-called "third rail" was infused with more than six hundred volts of electricity to power the trains, but why take chances? Best to avoid them all, right? I ran over to the seventh set of tracks and turned left, moving toward the gaping tunnel. Vibrations from underfoot told me that a train was coming, but from my vantage point, I had no idea from which direction. How Filmore, Grigsby and dad, and now the Houskaan had made it through the tunnel without becoming subway pizza, I wasn't sure. But I hoped the trend would continue as I moved into the darkness of the tunnel.

Shouts from behind told me the cops were still in pursuit, but I couldn't worry about them for the moment. Even now, Goliath could be busy tearing my dad to shreds and no matter how infuriating the old man could be, I just couldn't let that happen.

Pulling my Glock and flashlight from my pocket, I ran through the shaft as fast as my legs would carry me. Even with the flashlight, the run was foolhardy. It was just too difficult to see anything within the tunnel to be sure-footed. Case in point: when I was only about two hundred yards in, my foot caught the top portion of a railroad tie and I stumbled, nearly striking the metal railing. Carefully, I picked myself up and renewed my trek through the subway, albeit at a slightly less frantic pace this time. I wouldn't do anyone any good if I got myself zapped before I rendezvoused with the others.

I'd walked about a quarter of a mile when the metallic screech of a train's brakes echoed around the concrete tunnel all around me. The close confines made the direction impossible to determine. The good news was that I couldn't hear a single footstep from my pursuers. I wasn't quite sure how, but it seemed as though I'd given the cops the slip.

Now, if I could just get a few more lucky breaks like that, I thought, carefully stepping between the iron rails of the tracks. My flashlight swayed back and forth in the gloom. *We'll be home free.*

Of course I should have known better. I hadn't so much as walked another fifty feet before coming to a fork in the tracks, fanning out into two distinct passages.

"You've got to be kidding me," I growled. Grigsby had said nothing about the tracks splitting up. As a matter of fact, he seemed to imply that 7B was a straight shot to where they were. Hadn't he? Or had I simply picked the wrong track to follow? "Swell. So, Jackson...time's running out. Which tunnel are you going to take?"

I swung my flashlight at the ground in sweeping arcs, looking for the blood trail I'd been following earlier. I found none, but whether because the creature was moving too fast through the tunnels or I'd taken the wrong one was anyone's guess. All I knew was that I was really starting to panic. I didn't have time to waste trying to figure out the best tunnel to take. Even this little mental roadblock was costing too many precious seconds. So, without giving it another thought, I opted for the multiple choice test approach. I took the path my instinct guided me to and veered left.

Though I'd stopped running through the dimly lit tunnel after my fall, I now picked up the pace in a near perfect mall-walker impersonation and hoped there were no security cameras down here to catch just how goofy I looked pumping my arms and legs like a geriatric Olympian. Five minutes later, the tunnel narrowed as it bent into a sharp right curve. The rumbling of trains was louder around here, but for the life of me, I still couldn't discern their direction. Or location. Because of this, I wasn't exactly comfortable moving forward. Up until now, the subway tunnels had been lined with walkways on either side of the tracks, clear spaces for transit employees to move safely without fear of being hit by an inbound train. Now, however, with the bottlenecking of the tunnel, the walkways disappeared. Only about a foot of graveled space separated an foolish pedestrian from a speeding train. And I still wasn't entirely sure this was the direction Goliath had come. For all I knew, I would have been better off taking the right-hand tunnel. Should I really take the chance by moving into the unknown of the curved shaft?

That's when a sweep of my flashlight caught sight of a few round stains coating the gravel. The stains were dried. Too old to have come from Goliath. But they had the dark, crimson hue of blood. Filmore. Mia had hurt the little weasel. Made him bleed. It was these drops that Goliath would be following to stalk his prey. It was also no doubt how Grigsby had tracked him as well; though what had prompted the detective to take Track 7B to begin with was a complete mystery. I'd seen no blood on the tracks below the platform at all. But I suppose that's why he was the homicide detective and why I hunted faery tale creatures for a living.

Of course, the blood could have just as easily come from some bum living in the bowels of the subway. For all I knew, I could follow the trail and end up on a wild goose chase. But honestly, what choice did I really have?

So I pressed on, moving into the tapering bend of the railway while carefully maneuvering around the third rail to keep from electrocuting myself. After several tense minutes, the curve straightened out and I could suddenly make out the sweep of a flashlight moving back and forth about two hundred yards up ahead, followed by a series of indecipherable shouts.

From this distance and in the gloom, I struggled to make out exactly what I was seeing. I stood transfixed, rooted in place, as my brain pieced together what was happening.

A man lay on the ground with his back leaning against the concrete wall of the subway, his hands clutched tight over his stomach. Another man, tall and sturdy, wearing a familiar flannel shirt knelt over him. His hands were pressed down on the other man's stomach—the gesture of someone trying desperately to stave off a flow of blood from a serious injury. A third man, obviously Detective Grigsby by his stature and demeanor, stood with his back to the other two. His legs were spread in a defensive posture as he steadied himself to fire his sidearm at something outside my field of vision. Suddenly, a mushroom of fire spat from his weapon's barrel, accompanied by the echoing percussion of a gunshot. A screech of fury and pain followed immediately after, just as a monstrous winged mass swooped down from the ceiling and lunged straight toward him.

The detective managed two more shots before the creature landed just in front of him and slapped the gun from his hand. Goliath's wings then spread out, presenting a menacing and formidable visage before lunging once more. The monster's Herculean hands grabbed hold of Grigsby's neck, lifted him off his feet, and hurled him across the tunnel where he slammed hard against the wall with a sickening whack.

"No!" I shouted, forcing myself from my paralysis. Somehow, I found my feet moving toward the horrifying tableau. My hand felt numb where I white-knuckled the handle of my Glock.

If Goliath had heard me, he gave no indication. With Grigsby down for the count, he moved toward my dad and Filmore with single-minded determination. His gait was by no means graceful as he stumbled over the gravel between railroad ties with a pronounced limp—evidence of the damage done by Arnold to his hamstrings. His left arm hung loosely at his side, as if the limb were merely a lifeless mass of flesh and bone. I imagined that the injury was from at least a few of the gunshot wounds he'd sustained from either the posse or Grigsby. One look into the Houskaan's crimson, but unnervingly intelligent eyes told me that the creature understood his own demise was unavoidable now. But I also knew that he wouldn't stop until his quarry—the man who'd brought such pain to his colony—was taken from this world as well. Unfortunately, that also meant that anyone who stood in his way would happily be considered nothing more than collateral damage.

A stream of blood pooled onto the gravel with each step Goliath made, but still he lurched forward. Dad, fully aware of his approach, stubbornly insisted on continuing his ministrations to Filmore's wounds. Now that I was closer, I could clearly see him tying off a makeshift bandage of strips of coarse fabric—from Grigsby's trench coat, if I wasn't mistaken—he'd wrapped around the man's torso. Securing the dressing with one more knot, he spun around to face the monster that now lumbered only a few feet away. He arose, chest out in defiance, and stood between the Houskaan and Filmore.

"I ain't gonna let you take him," Dad said as he squared off against the monster without a weapon in sight...which made no sense. The old man had had it with him while in the SWAT van, so where was it now? But I put the question in the back of my mind as I watched my dad in utter astonishment. And perhaps, a little bit of pride as well. Dr. Oliver Jackson, at that very moment, reminded me of some courageous Old Testament prophet that was staring down the enraged eyes of an ancient demigod ready to destroy an entire civilization. I couldn't help wondering who would blink first in the showdown, but wasn't about to let things play out on their own.

"Stop!" I shouted; now close enough for everyone to hear me. Dad and the creature both turned toward the sound of my voice. I pulled to a halt, nearly slipping on a pile of loose gravel, and brought my Glock up to aim directly at Goliath's head. "Don't make me shoot you. Please."

A grotesque, scornful sneer stretched slowly across his equine snout, followed immediately by an irritated snarl. From the contemptuous glare in the monster's eyes, I was beginning to think Mia had been full of crap about the bond we'd supposedly formed. But after staring the beast down for several nerve-wracking moments, he appeared to relax just a bit and took a single step back before letting out a sigh-like huff and a snort.

Slowly, steadily, I lowered the gun while letting out a series of soft clicks with my tongue and stepped forward. The Houskaan snuffled, ducked his head slightly, and took another step back. The winged-beast was calming down. Muscles loosening. His breathing deeper, slower…more steady. Granted, his eyes still burned as they glared down at Filmore's bleeding form, but it was looking as though the worst was behind us.

The next step would be to get Filmore to the hospital and Goliath and his clan back to the Pine Barrens. Then, I could begin my search for Randy and end Freakshow's madness once and for all.

But first things first.

"You okay, Dad?" I whispered without taking my eyes off the Houskaan. I kept my hands—even the one holding the gun—up in a calming gesture as I spoke. "Are you hurt?"

"Nah, son. I'm fine," he said. His voice was as calm and soothing as an Enya tune. "Though we really need to get going. Mr. Filmore seems to be stable, but Detective Grigsby took a nasty hit. I'm pretty sure he needs medical attention ASAP."

I glanced over to where Grigsby lay, twisted unnaturally in a heap against the tunnel wall. From where I stood, I could see his torso rising and falling in quick shallow breaths, which told me the gruff, annoying detective was still alive…well, at least for now. But I wasn't sure how much longer he'd last in his condition. Dad was right. We had to get him out of here and that meant turning my attention back to Goliath. "It's okay, big guy," I said, turning to the Houskaan and employing the soft, soothing tones I'd heard Mia use with Esther the day before. "We won't let him get away. But you need to go back. Back to your colony. They need you to—"

Click click.

The sudden sound of a hammer being cocked from behind made my blood run cold.

"Dad? Your rifle...where is it?"

There was a brief pause before he answered. "I...I set it down when I started bandaging Filmore up. It should be..."

We were both turning around just as the lever-action rifle gripped tight against the wounded creep's shoulder exploded in a blaze of light and sound. The shot went wide, missing Goliath by a mile, but before any of us could react, the murdering little weasel chambered another round and pulled the trigger. The slug jettisoned from the barrel and slammed straight into my dad, spinning him chaotically to the ground.

"No!" I shouted, bringing up my gun and taking aim. But before I could let off a single round, the Houskaan let out an ear-splitting howl and leapt forward. His ape-like arms knocked the rifle from Filmore's hands and scooped him up in a surprisingly graceful and fluid sweep, despite the creature's injuries. The wounded man was then thrown onto Goliath's good shoulder, who immediately turned and ran toward the southwest tunnel. Soon, they were both swallowed by the darkness and out of sight. Filmore's terror-filled screams were the only evidence the two had ever been there.

"Well boy, get after them," my dad said before bursting into a series of wet, hacking coughs. His hands clutched at his right thigh as blood oozed from between his fingers, soaking his jeans dark.

"I'm not going anywhere, Dad," I said. "You've been shot for crying out loud."

Dad pulled himself into a sitting position and winced. "Don't be an idiot, Obadiah. It's just a graze. I'll live. Which is something we can't say about the Filmore boy at the moment. Now go."

I glanced over at Grigsby, who hadn't so much as moved an inch since being hurled against the wall. "Well, you may be okay, but he's not. You said it yourself, we've got to get him to a doctor ASAP. I'm not about to put Filmore's life above his."

Dad croaked out a hoarse laugh. "That's funny, 'cause he certainly did so himself. That's why he stood up to the monster to begin with. It's the kind of man he is. He would gladly give up his own life to save another and you should respect that."

"Well, I'm not him. I'm not a cop. Fortunately, I didn't swear to *serve and protect*," I growled. "Dad, that man killed Aislynn Sommers. Just as surely as if he'd put a bullet in her head, he killed her. Without regret. Without remorse. He would just as easily kill Grigsby or you. Heck, he certainly tried hard enough! And you honestly want me to—"

"Do the right thing? Yes," he said with a weak, but compassionate smile. "Always. It's not for you to decide who deserves to live or die. Not for you to judge another man's actions. The only person on earth whose actions you're responsible for are your own." He ripped a strip of cloth from Grigsby's already tattered jacket that had been laying on the ground next to him and started working on dressing the bullet wound to his leg. "Now go. I'll take care of Mike. You go after Filmore before I get up and tan your stubborn hide."

Knowing better than to argue any further, I stood to my full height and took off in the direction Goliath had fled.

THIRTY-FOUR

TRACKING GOLIATH THROUGH THE SOUTHWEST TUNNEL WASN'T EXACTLY difficult. The big galloot was losing enough blood to keep a blood bank in hemoglobin for a year. Besides that, Filmore's girlish screams echoed for miles within the confined space. Since subway tunnels were, for the most part, a straight shot, it wasn't too tricky to keep pace with them.

I had traveled about a half a mile when the rumbling of trains picked up again, this time unnervingly close. I stopped for a few second, trying to discern from which direction the train was coming. It seemed to be coming from directly up ahead, but I'd long since realized that Track 7B had been a retired track and hadn't been used in some time. The corrosion and lack of maintenance in certain places were testament to this as well. But despite this, the presence of trains so nearby was a reminder that I'd have to be extra careful from this point forward.

I was just about to continue my pursuit of Goliath, when my phone buzzed silently inside my pocket. Reaching in, I pulled it out and glanced at the display. A spring of hope welled up inside me at the name.

"Landers!" I said after accepting the call. "Where are you?"

"Looking for you. I found Nikki, Arnold, and Davenport." He paused for a second as if someone nearby was talking to him. "Nikki wants me to tell you that they're all fine…although Alex seems to have sustained some broken bones after being attacked by one of the cryptids. Paramedics are looking at him now. The Asian kid is alive too, but Mia and her goons have disappeared. So have all the Houskaani, including Phisto."

"That's Wicket."

"Who?" he asked.

"Never mind," I said. "Right now, we've got bigger problems to deal with."

"Yeah, Nikki told me that you went down into the subway to look for your dad. Is that right?"

Filmore's cries for help were fading away quickly, which prompted me to start moving once more as I nestled the phone tighter in the crook of my neck.

"Yeah. Found them. Grigsby's hurt. Needs immediate medical attention," I said. "Goliath took Filmore and I'm currently tracking them deeper into the subway. Not exactly sure where I am at the moment, but you can find Dad by walking along Track 7B, at least a mile. When you come to a—" An ear-splitting scream erupted from just up ahead of me. Filmore's own cries were even more frantic now making me believe that the weasel was just about at the end of his rope. "Look, gotta go. Just find Dad. Get EMS down here to help Grigsby, then come find me. I have a feeling I'm going to need the help."

Without waiting for his response, I hung up, stuffed the phone back into my pocket, and ran toward the frantic screams. Only, I'd been wrong. When I caught up with the guy making all the racket, it wasn't Filmore at all. Instead, it was a horrified, and slightly battered, transit cop who I found cowering against the tunnel wall with his arms draped over his head in a classic "duck and cover" pose. The cop continued one prolonged scream; taking deep breaths every so often, only to go back to screaming again.

"Are you all right, buddy?" I asked.

The sound of my voice startled the cop. He spun around, frantic. Eyes wide and service sidearm pointed directly at my gut. His screams melted into a series of fevered keening. In his surprise, the gun discharged, narrowly missing my left ear.

"Holy—!" I jumped, immediately patting my entire body down to double check that I hadn't been hit. "Are you crazy?!" But between the strange look from those near catatonic eyes and the pathetic keening that bubbled up from the man's throat, I knew the answer to my own question. Yes. The police officer had grown completely unhinged. Nuts. Bonkers even. He'd be no help to me at all. "Look, officer," I continued in a soft, comforting tone. "I have friends on their way down here. They're bringing help. You're going to be okay."

But the pathetic whining continued without response. "Just try not to shoot anyone, okay?" I asked as I left him alone in the rumbling tunnel to fend for himself.

❧

Five minutes later, I heard a barrage of gunshots followed by a chorus of panicked shouts and screams—both human and Houskaan alike. I picked up my pace, running pell-mell toward the cacophony and completely forgetting about the dangers of high voltage running along the rails. A hundred and fifty yards farther, I came to a passage along the left hand wall that led into another subway tunnel. Pulling my Glock from my waistband, I turned into the passage and carefully strode out into the new tunnel, stopping short at a ghastly sight.

In the beam of my flashlight, I caught sight of four other police officers laying unmoving and bleeding on the other side of the tracks from me. Entrails and gore spattered the nearby wall. A fifth man clutched at a stump of his right arm as he rolled back and forth, screaming. The rest of the arm lay uselessly three feet away.

A few more yards away from the arm provided the most shocking display of all. Goliath lay immobile on the ground. The reflection of the dim overhead lights above glinted off the pool of blood spreading underneath his body. The amount of blood was shocking. I wouldn't have believed he'd be capable of having so much left after the amount he'd already lost.

The creature's massive arms covered his face and head as a man's much smaller form stood over him, a retractable police baton gripped tight in his hand. The man brought the baton down hard against the creature's skull as he laughed maniacally at his own violence.

"You idiot!" he shouted at Goliath, bringing another blow down against his shoulder. "I own you. I own all of you!" Another strike landed along the Houskaan's ribcage and the sickening snap of broken rips echoed through the chamber. "I know the secret. I know how to make every last one of you dance. And I'll make them *all* dance after you're long gone!"

As if understanding the words, Goliath growled and tried to sit up, but was struck once more against his brow. "Sit down!" the man shouted. The creature crumpled to the ground in a heap from the impact, eliciting even more cackling from the deranged man. "Good dog!"

In the few seconds of observation, I managed to piece together what had happened. While carrying the inert Filmore over his shoulder, Goliath had stumbled on the same transit cops who'd been chasing me. There'd been a struggle. The cops opened fire, inciting the creature into a rage and he'd mauled his attackers mercilessly. But their gunshots, coupled with the injuries he'd already sustained tonight had been too much for him. He collapsed, leaving a frantic—if not deranged—Chuck Filmore to beat out his own frustrations on the winged cryptid.

As the man raised the baton again, Goliath turned his head and found me staring. There was something in those sad, pathetic red eyes…something in the creature's whine of agony that tore deep into my heart and something inside me snapped.

"Filmore!" I shouted, rushing furiously toward him. He spun around, a crazed look in his eyes, but before I could cross the tracks to stop him from another blow, the tumultuous rumble of a train brought me to a dead stop.

Seconds later, the train zoomed past, completely obliterating my view of the other side.

My fury still burned in my chest as the train screamed by me. When it had passed, Filmore was nowhere to be seen. Though I wanted to rush to Goliath's side and check on him, I knew my primary obligation was to the fallen law enforcement officers who lay sprawled along the narrow concrete walkway. One by one, I crouched down and felt for a pulse, but the only one still alive was the same man who had clutched feverishly to his severed arm. Mercifully, he'd eventually passed out, but was still breathing. He wouldn't be for much longer, I knew, unless I figured a way to stop the bleeding.

Laying my gun on the ground beside me, I yanked my belt from the loops of my pants and wrapped it around the bicep of the injured arm. Cinching it tight, I locked it in place with the buckle. The cop stirred as I brought the belt around his arm for another pass and tucked it underneath the strap, but he didn't speak. His eyes fluttered open. Wild. Pain-filled. Terrified even.

"Shhhhh," I said. "Everything's going to be okay. Help's on the way and—"

The man's eyes looked past me, growing wider. He tried to scream, but it was too late. Something heavy and metallic crashed against the side of my head. My ears rang from the impact and I bit back the cry of pain that threatened to unravel any semblance of machismo in me. Fortunately, I had no time to nurture the pain. As I crashed the ground, I immediately rolled to see a crazed Chuck Filmore bearing down on me with the same metal baton he'd been using on Goliath. As the steel balled tip swept down at my head, I rolled out of the way again, grabbing hold of the Glock on the ground as I did. I brought the gun up as I rolled onto my back, but the baton knocked it from my grip and it clattered to the floor a few feet away. Before I could scramble to retrieve it, Filmore kicked me in the jaw. When the black spots in front of my eyes had finally cleared, he stood over me with my own gun gripped tight in his hand.

"*You!*" he growled with spittle streaking his chin. "This is all your fault. Everything was going fine before you came along. I was finally gaining the respect I deserved. All the hard work I'd put into Tommy's political career was finally paying off. Then you showed up and..." He paused; his face twitching with rage. "You ruined everything! You and that smart mouth of yours."

"Sure," I mumbled, still reeling from multiple blows to my head. "Like nobody was going to look into a series of murders committed by a group of winged monsters. Something like that's bound to draw attention. Not the subtlest of ways to kill someone, Chuckles."

The man's face contorted with rage. "Even now you want to disrespect me? Make fun of me?" He inched closer, the gun barrel continued to point directly at me. "But you *will* respect me, Jackson! Everyone will come to respect me."

"You know," I said, still flat on my back. Casually, as if I had all the time in the world, I reached into my shirt pocket and pulled out a cigar. After biting the tip off and gripping it in my teeth, I continued. "That has got to be the worst Dangerfield impression I ever heard." I flashed him an unconcerned grin. "You're supposed to say, 'I don't get no respect.'" For emphasis, I pantomimed straightening an invisible tie while bulging out my eyes in an even worse impersonation.

"Shut up! Shut up! Shut up!" he screamed, stomping a foot against the concrete like a ticked off two-year-old. "I have had it with you. Had it!" His breath wheezed as he spoke. "I'm twice the man you are! I have an Ivey League post-graduate education. A man of sophistication. Refinement. Class. You're nothing but a brutish goon. A slack-jawed yokel who's probably gotten by his entire life based solely on his over-inflated charm and good looks. I've been second place to guys like you my entire life and I'm sick of it! Sick of it!"

I'd apparently punched all the right buttons. He was about ready to fill me with enough lead to keep Superman going to the ophthalmologist for weeks. And though I wanted to keep him talking to buy more time, I didn't want to press my luck either. Landers and a SWAT team were on their way. I just needed to stall long enough to give the cavalry enough time to get here without becoming a bullet magnet while I was at it.

"So I'm starting to see a theme here," I said, trying to sit up on my elbows. Filmore made no move to stop me. He simply kept the gun barrel trained at my head. "Everything. All of this. The murders. The Houskaani. Every last bit of it has to do with you trying to gain a little bit of respectability."

"It's what I deserve!" he shouted. "I have stuck with that buffoon of a senator since college. Through thick and thin. Through amazing victories to heart-breaking losses. I never left his side and that pompous blowhard didn't even know I existed. He couldn't even so much as look in my direction once his lecherous eyes landed on Aislynn Sommers. Of course, I don't know why *that* surprised me. Everybody always fawned over her. Even you, Jackson...even you couldn't take your eyes off her. But she was a *nobody*! A *nothing* before I introduced her to Tommy. Soon, she was running his entire campaign. She was in charge of the entire empire and I was discarded like scraps to a pack of strays. I became completely invisible. Immaterial. Resigned to the status of menial gopher duty."

"So you concocted this scheme to set things right...to regain the respect Aislynn stole from you?" I asked, shifting the cigar to the other side of my mouth while wishing I could light it. Oh, what I would have given at that moment to be able to take in the warm embrace of the Cuban's smoke, but I dared not break the spell I was trying to weave. "So tell me...how did you do it? How did you discover the Houskaani? How did you figure out how to manipulate them to do your dirty work for you?"

His eyes sunken within his ashen, sweat covered face narrowed at me. His lips curled in a rictus of pain, rage, and possibly confusion. Something dark and red, just above his belt caught my eye. A stain of blood oozed from the makeshift bandage Dad had made for him. A trail of it streaked down his grime-soaked trousers.

"Oh, I know what you're doing!" he spat. "You're trying to trick me. Trying to get me to tell you everything. But it's not going to work. You're going to die never knowing the truth. Never knowing how I did it." Laughter started hissing from between his trembling lips as he focused once more on the gun in his hand. "This is for every creep who ever made fun of me. Every square-jawed jock who ever humiliated me. Every bully who ever..."

Without finishing his train of thought, he pulled the trigger.

❧

White hot pain flared through every nerve in my body just before my vision began to dim. The only awareness I had came from the unwavering memory of the roar of the gunshot just before a .40 caliber slug ripped through my gut. Or was the roar a product of a deluge of blood rushing through my body and into my head. I remember the *thump thump thump* of my heartbeat slowly diminishing. Slowly fading. But not the roar. It went on without mercy, bombarding my ears, my skull, my mind with its incessant rumble; all while I clutched numbly at my abdomen, oblivious to the blood coursing so freely between my fingers.

I struggled to open my heavy lidded eyes. Struggled to focus. To take in my surroundings. Everything was blurry. Hazy. Dark. As if someone had slipped a pair of ultra-dark Ray-Bans over my eyes when I wasn't looking. The only constant...the only solid thing I was assured of in that lifetime of seconds was the infernal roar raging all around me.

I suppose it could have been coming from the speeding subway train that I saw zipping past in my haze-addled mind. Or maybe it was simply the ridiculous diatribe Filmore was still spewing.

"...no one will ever push me around again! No one!" he was saying when I willed myself to focus on him once more.

"Oh, just put another bullet in me and shut up already!" I screamed. Or at least, I thought I did. Can't really be too sure. I couldn't hear anything past the roar in my head. But by the wild eyed rage plastered across his worn, ashen face, I thought maybe he had, indeed, heard me.

That is, until he cocked his head to the left as if listening to something. Suddenly he spun around and I realized right then that he'd hear the roaring too. Which meant, it couldn't have been from the rush of blood to my head or the pounding of my heart. Since he turned around in the opposite direction of the tracks, I knew it couldn't have come from the subway train either.

And there it was again. That roar, mixed with something else. It wasn't a deep rumble as I'd originally envisioned. There was something else in that sound. A whining sort of noise. No, a high-pitched shrieking, followed immediately by a series of sharp, staccato clicks.

Filmore was screaming now as he pointed the Glock away from me and fired into the gloom. Fired again. And again. And again.

After that, the roaring seem to stop and the only sound that could be heard was coming from my own labored breathing and the whimpering fear-induced cries of Filmore as he glanced all around as if he'd lost sight of his prey.

"Where are you? Why aren't you dead already?" he shouted into the darkness. His own frail voice bounced chaotically off the concrete walls. "I won't let you take me. I won't let you best me! I am your master! I own you! I will not—"

The sudden rumble of another train moving in fast swallowed the rest of Filmore's threats, but I didn't need to hear the rest to know I was already bored with his insane tirade. I was just about to start begging him to end my misery when two things happened simultaneously.

First, the tunnel we were in filled with blinding white light as the new train rounded the corner and rushed past us with blinding speed. I felt the cool, dust-filled air whirling around my shoulders, soothing my feverish body. The second thing, which was barely visible to me as darkness continued to engulf the corners of my vision, was the quickening of a living shadow molded to the ceiling above. It was almost imperceptible at first. Just a slight shift of light and darkness against the gloom. Then, like a liquid snake coiling itself in preparation of a strike, Goliath slithered along the ceiling until he was almost directly overhead, spread his wings to their full span, and pushed off with an ear-splitting screech.

Before Filmore could react and bring the gun up to fire, the Houskaan swooped down, wrapped his thick, fur-covered arms around the little man and shot directly for the speeding train. The two crashed headlong into the steel behemoth's side, shattering windows and crunching metal. A wet, crunching sound followed soon after and then all was silent.

I wanted to scream. Wanted to rail against the cruelty of it all. Goliath, a strong, noble being sacrificed his own life. Had given all he had to protect his colony. Maybe even to protect me. A creature—a rare and beautiful animal—had once again been tainted by the greed and indifference of humanity. I'd seen so much of it in my time. No matter whether the humans were insane, sociopathic murderers such as Chuck Filmore or Freakshow or they were wrapped in the spirit of patriotism and commissioned by the federal government, these creatures would always be victims of evil men. And I knew that I could be counted among them and it sickened me as I lay bleeding in that subway tunnel.

Though I could barely move, I struggled to turn my head to see what I knew all too well what I would find. When my eyes rested on the bloody mess just a few feet away, I knew my assumptions had been correct. There wasn't much left of either Goliath or Filmore. Arms, legs, and necks were all twisted in a grizzly tangle that only the seriously dead can master.

I clenched my eyes tight again after only a short second or two. I didn't want to see it anymore. Didn't want to have that image permanently locked in my mind's eye the way so many similar scenes already were. Fortunately, when the coughing fit seized me and a fountain of blood started gurgling up from my lungs, I knew the image would soon fade. So would all the others. Death was fast approaching for me and strangely, I was fine with that. I knew exactly where I would wind up at the end of all things. The thought of it was strangely comforting.

But I had one regret though, as consciousness began to drift out of reach. One nagging, angry thought echoed loudly at the back of my mind. I would never find Randy now. I could never rescue him. Never put an end to Freakshow's insanity. And as unconsciousness enshrouded me, I remember having another thought that overpowered the first: *No. That is not gonna happen.*

Then, all went dark.

THIRTY-FIVE

Pine Barrens, New Jersey
Six months later

"WHAT'S THE GAME PLAN, BOOMER?" JOHNNY STEPHENS ASKED, handing me the binoculars.

I took them and looked through the eye piece, absorbing every green-glowing detail of the Day-For-Night goggles. There were at least eighteen Houskaani milling around the thickly wooded landscape, picking insects off each other's backs like mountain gorillas. A compliment of nine Shepherds—fully armed, I might add—lounged lazily against the trees, watching their charges with casual disinterest. And though she'd not come out of the cavern set into the side of hill underneath us for the last two days I knew without question that the Clan's current matriarch, Ms. Mia Leeds, and her brother Thomas were down there as well.

Oddly, despite the chaotic activity below, we'd seen no sign of Wicket at all since setting up our surveillance, which troubled me a little bit.

Johnny and I had spent the better part of a week camping out on the highest point overlooking a secluded valley nestled deep within the Pine Barrens. We'd been getting a feel for the land, and most importantly gathering intelligence on the Leeds' clan. Despite their efforts to cover their tracks and hide from the federal authorities now currently hunting Mia and a few other members of her family—including the good senator, who'd been linked to the New York City murders by the press—we'd found them with hardly any effort at all. But then, the Feds weren't best pals with one of the top five professional hunters in the world either.

Now, after hours of surveillance and planning, I finally felt comfortable enough to make our move. Finally felt that we had enough of an advantage to pull off my crazy scheme.

From my crouched position, I pivoted around and uncovered a small wire cage. A good sized raccoon rested comfortably inside, though I wasn't sure for how much longer. The sedative I'd given it earlier that afternoon would be wearing off pretty soon.

"Well, Phase One of the plan is to let Bandit here stretch his legs some," I said, smiling at the name I'd given the little guy. Arnold would have probably been more dependable for what I had in mind, but I just couldn't risk what would happen if one of the Houskaani managed to catch him. For this particular operation, Bandit the Raccoon would just have to be good enough. "After he wakes up and takes off, we'll need to move to another position along the ridge. We'll wait things out until it's safe enough to enter the valley and make our next move then."

"I've already marked out the path for our next blind," my friend said, wiping a stream of sweat from his brow. Considering it was early October in southern New Jersey, the weather was unseasonably warm. "But what I don't get is how that little critter is gonna to get everyone down there— including th-those monster things—scrambling up here." My friend's wide eyes spoke volumes about his courage. It had only been a few months ago that he had been savagely mauled by one of those creatures. Though his physical injuries had healed, he was still suffering from post-traumatic stress. Still having intense nightmares about his ordeal. The fact that he had agreed to help me, to be so close to the monsters of his nightmares, meant more to me than he could possibly know.

"Don't you worry about that," I said, forcing a confident smile as I reached into my jacket pocket and pulled out a small, non-descript vial. I shuddered as I gazed at the clear liquid from within. Truth be told, the bottle represented everything I'd come to loathe about my current career choice. It represented mankind's own revolting hubris and his constant desire to usurp the very throne of God.

A slight scratching sound emanated from the cage. I turned to see Bandit's eyes flickering open. He wasn't quite fully awake, but it truly wouldn't be much longer. With time running out, I opened the small door to the cage before I pulled the stopper out of the vial and inserted a small dropper into its contents. "Keep your eyes on the Houskaani," I whispered. "If they so much as glance our way, we'll have to run. Got it?"

He nodded back at me from behind the night vision goggles, his dark skin making his movements extremely difficult to see in the woodland darkness.

Confident that my friend had my back, I pulled out the dropper and sent five even drops of clear liquid onto the raccoon's bristly hairs. The sudden jolt of cold liquid seemed to excite the animal, eliciting a hiss as it raised its head up to take in its surroundings.

"Okay, it's done and Bandit's almost ready. We should move. Now."

In unison, we crouch-ran along the pre-established path Johnny had created to our new hunter's blind, almost directly opposite our original position across the valley. As we marched, I sent up a silent prayer in hopes that all this would not be in vain…that many of the answers I sought were only a few minutes away.

Fortunately, it didn't take nearly as long as I'd anticipated for the Houskaani in the valley below to work themselves into a frenzy. I watched with fascination as one by one, each creature would stop what it was doing, sniff furiously at the air, and bristle with agitated rage. The Houskaan secretion I'd discovered deep in the vaults of ENIGMA just a few weeks before was definitely doing the trick. But the thought of the discovery ate at my soul. The complete betrayal I'd felt when I'd found out about it was more than I ever imagined possible. Involuntarily, my mind drifted to the series of events that led to my current rogue operation.

෫෧

After being shot in the subway six months earlier, I'd slipped into a coma. Hadn't even been aware of my own rescue. Didn't see the remains of Goliath or Filmore carried off to God only knew where. There was nothing but darkness for me for more than three weeks. The slug had apparently torn through the lining of my stomach and I'd quickly developed sepsis. This inevitably led to pneumonia, which resulted in me lying comatose in a hospital bed for weeks.

Detective Grigsby hadn't fared much better than me. Goliath's brutal attack had left him in traction for weeks. Numerous bones shattered. Internal bleeding. Even a cracked vertebra. The prognosis for both of us had been rather grim. Fortunately, we had both pulled through—in a manner of speaking—though Grigsby was now on an indefinite leave of absence as he underwent extensive physical therapy. His bones were healed nicely, but that didn't mean his mobility hadn't been drastically hampered, possibly forever.

My own injuries had mended much more cleanly. After two and a half months in the hospital, I had finally been released and assigned to desk duty at ENIGMA. Of course, I was having none of that. Despite the fact that Senator Stromwell assured me how lucky I was to A) be alive and B) to still have my job after completely disregarding Polk's orders, my primary focus was on finding Freakshow, rescuing Randy, and discovering the truth behind Vera's apparent resurrection from the dead. Once again, Stromwell had assured me that they were doing everything within their power to do just that, and I had been ordered to stand down. In fact, Polk had threatened me with criminal charges if I proceeded with my own investigation. To ensure my cooperation, he'd gone so far as to have Wiley transferred to an undisclosed location, severing all communication between us. Polk had known that my best link to Freakshow was in tracking his Internet presence and that the little nerd was essential to doing that.

To get my mind off everything, Polk had tried to get me focused on the Leeds' Clan—to help in the apprehension and capturing the Houskaani for preservation. But I'd refused. I'd simply lost all interest in them. Besides, after being released from the hospital, there was no mystery left as far as I was concerned. Although Filmore had refused to spill the beans to me about how he'd known of the Houskaani to begin with, let alone known how to manipulate them, a journal discovered in his apartment had pretty much filled in all the blanks. Years before, while in college, a very intoxicated Thomas Leeds had freaked out about going home during a semester break. There had apparently been a family emergency which required his immediate attention and Filmore had described Leeds' moods as "strange and distrustful". Then, on the night before he was supposed to head back home, the two had gotten drunk and Thomas had told him everything. At first, Filmore hadn't believed him. Thought the entire tale was a figment of Leeds' alcohol addled imagination or a possibly some sort of nervous breakdown. But the more he pondered what his friend had told him, the more obsessed he became with anything to do with the Jersey Devil. About a year later, when Leeds made a similar trip home, Filmore had followed him in secret and discovered all he needed to pull off the recent murders.

So without anything to occupy my mind, I became more and more frustrated over the red tape that was being thrown at me in regards to finding Randy and Vera. After a few weeks of trying to search for them on my own, I found myself completely stymied. Even worse, my trust in my own organization was rapidly eroding. I began to believe that there was a concerted effort between the top brass to keep me from digging too deep into Freakshow and I didn't know why.

My obsession, of course, led to more issues with Nikki and me. Although our relationship had improved drastically since the New York investigation (not to mention the shooting), my various mood swings, and ny growing frustration with her father's pet organization began to put a strain on us all over again. She'd said I was being unreasonable. Even called me paranoid. Claimed that I was seeing conspiracies everywhere. Personally, I think she just didn't like anyone questioning her father's motives. The last time I'd seen her, she was boarding a flight to the Ukraine to help out a missionary pal over there. In truth, she didn't leave angry. If anything, she'd truly seemed sympathetic. Even concerned. She'd told me that she wasn't "pulling the plug" on us, but thought she needed to give me some space to deal with everything that was going on. Her sudden departure felt like the biggest betrayal of all. When I'd needed her most, she'd basically called me crazy and left town. I'd thought she was better than that. Apparently, I'd been wrong.

Landers, of course, hadn't been much help either. Though I know without question that he sympathized with my situation—was worried about Randy himself, though skeptical over what I'd told him about Vera—he was a soldier at heart. If he was told not to assist me in my own search, he would follow those orders to the letter, without question. Not so much a betrayal to me, because I expected no more from him.

The answer to my dilemma, and maybe the key to truly opening my eyes about the agency I'd been working for came in the most unusual of sources. Two days after Nikki flew to the Ukraine, I received an email from the tabloid reporter, Alex Davenport. The experience in New York had indelibly changed the man since the day I first met him. First of all, after I'd left Nikki and Arnold to go after my dad, there had apparently been some kind of skirmish when Mia and her clan attempted to leave. In the melee, a Houskaan female had lunged at Nikki. Davenport had tried to intervene and the encounter had left him with three broken ribs and a fractured hip for his troubles. Even now he has to use a cane to walk around. I'm not sure if it was that one stupid, but heroic move or something else, but he was different now. Better. More courageous. Less sure of himself. Humble. He even visited me in the hospital during my convalescence a number of times and quite frankly, I'd grown to like the guy quite a bit in spite of myself. After countless hours of debating the nature of the "message" Freakshow said he would leave with him, Alex had insisted he'd never been contacted by the madman again. We had both pretty much chalked the whole thing up to the mind games of a lunatic. But the day I received that email, everything changed. And I do mean *everything*.

Alex had received a new email from Freakshow. The message was simple. It had merely been a string of names put together in relational order, followed immediately by a smiley face:

```
Marc Leeds :: Ekaterina Stolnakanova :: Me ☺
```

In short, "Marc is to Kat as Kat is to me."

It had only taken a few minutes to understand its meaning. Last time I'd seen Marc Leeds, he'd been with Kat on a boat in the Aegean Sea. Freakshow himself had told me that he and Kat had some sort of strange working relationship. Therefore, if I find her, I'll find Freakshow. The quickest way to get to her was by finding Marc and there was no better way to find him than through his very own family.

I started digging into any information ENIGMA had on the Leeds' Clan. At first, there was very little to go on...just a few references here and there over the years. Whispers and obscure allusions to them in various investigative reports over the last few decades. But nothing substantial. So, I'd decided to try a different tact. As oppose to looking for a paper trail that might easily be glossed over by anyone trying to keep a lid on something, I decided to look for physical evidence instead. Evidence was key to the day to day operations of ENIGMA. It was too hard to come by to simply discard it the way one might shred a paper trail. I knew that if there was any sort of cover up within the agency concerning the Houskaani, they more than likely wouldn't have touched any of the physical stuff. It was just too valuable.

So, I began exploring the evidence vault buried within the lower levels of ENIGMA HQ. This was no small feat, let me tell you. The vault is huge, lined with shelves containing jars of pickled biological samples, a few hundred taxidermical specimens, and even a few well-designed artificial habitats that housed several highly-endangered live cryptid species.

It took me some time, but eventually I found what I didn't know I was looking for. It had been a clear vial of liquid. The markings on the label were in code, but easily decipherable by anyone who'd been around the agency for a while. It had simply read: Sample of Interaural Secretion from Infant Jersey Devil. It was dated five years ago...roughly around the same time as the first Houskaan cub kidnapping. The same kidnapping that had prompted Marc to set out on his own to discover who was responsible and later to betray my team and me.

With the discovery of the vial, my own mistrust of ENIGMA was cemented. Now, it was more important than ever to find Marc. Not only to use him to find Randy, but to discover just how far the corruption within the agency went. And in order to do that, I was going to have to do something really crazy. Crazy even for me!

Which brings us to where I found myself now. On the bluff overlooking the small valley in the Pine Barrens patiently waiting for the opportunity to make my next move.

⚜

"Looks like the camp is nearly cleared out," Johnny whispered, bringing the night vision binoculars from his face. "I think it's now or never."

I watched as the very last Shepherd scrambled up the northeastern embankment, chasing after three Houskaani now hunting the secretion-soaked raccoon on what I hoped would be a very long goose chase.

Nodding, I turned to my old friend. "I think you're right," I said while standing to my feet.

Leaving Johnny perched opposite the cave entrance, a rifle barrel pulled tight against his shoulder as he covered my back, I made my way down the embankment as nimbly and quietly as I could. Once reaching the bottom, I crouched behind a large birch tree and looked around.

The Houskaani and their Shepherds were still on the hunt, leaving the entire valley bereft of life. I glanced over at the cavern, a warm glow of a burning fire danced off the walls from inside. Other than that, I could see nothing. For all I knew, the cavern could be as empty as Anton Polk's soul. Perhaps Mia and her brother had taken some unseen back passageway and exited some time ago. What if all this was for nothing? I mean, it was just plain strange for anyone to remain hidden within a cave for days on end. Sure, a few of the Shepherds had been seen coming and going. Food was brought in. Empty baskets and plates were brought out. But I'd never quite figured out what the silver-haired minx and the former senator could be doing in there or why they'd not taken a single step outside for at least two days.

Okay, Jack. Quit your belly-achin', I thought, pulling my Glock from its shoulder holster and making sure a round was chambered. *There's only one way to find out what's going on and you're quickly running out of time to do it. So get moving.*

Taking three deep breaths, I darted out from behind the tree and bee-lined it toward the cave. Once there, I pressed up against the rock wall to the left of the entrance, which was low to the ground. From my current vantage point, I could tell that it opened up into a vast chamber immediately upon entering. Now that I was closer, I could hear sounds coming from inside as well. A radio echoed off the walls, the clipped staccato cadence of a news anchor was reading the script of current events with practiced precision. I also heard the soft murmurs of people talking, though I couldn't make out what was being said.

After several minutes of trying to decipher the dialogue, I glanced up at the bluff where I knew Johnny to be and nodded at him to let him know to be ready for anything. And with that, I spun around, ducked my head, and stalked into Mia Leeds' cave.

The place was not what I'd expected. It reminded me more of a hobbit hole than some dank, monster's den. A fully operational wood burning stove sat in one corner of the chamber, a kettle steamed on top of it. In the center of the room, a fire crackled; it's smoke drifting up toward the ceiling and gliding through hundreds of naturally formed crevices that acted as chimneys. Around the fire sat two plush reading chairs. A small end table with a stack of books rested next to each chair.

And then, there were the occupants of the cave itself. They didn't see me at first. Their backs were to me and they were obviously far too consumed with what they were doing to pay any notice to anyone slipping into their hideout.

Of course, I'd been right. Both Mia and Thomas were there, bending over something in what looked like an old, battered baby crib. I watched silently, taking in as much detail as I could and soon pieced together exactly what had kept them so engrossed within the cave for the last few days.

Inside the crib, I could make out the soft contours of a fur-covered body...a series of short, soft clicks, coos, and gurgles coming from it. The creature was slightly too big for the crib, but it lay on its back allowing the two human caretakers to run damp washcloths over its pony-like face. From the hair color—and the similarities it had with Goliath—I was pretty sure I was looking at a very ill, very weak Wicket. Or Phisto. Whatever you wanted to call him. The poor thing looked emaciated, the ribs protruding from its distended belly.

"He's not eaten well since his ordeal in New York," Mia said, not turning around to face me. "We think he keeps expecting Goliath to return home soon. We're doing everything we can just to keep him alive, but it's not looking good."

So I reckon I wasn't as much a ninja as I'd hoped. She'd known I was there all along.

"How'd you know it was me?" I asked, clutching my gun tight in my hand.

She gave me a quick glance over her shoulder and smiled. "We knew you were here spying on us after the first couple of days."

"Which is actually rather impressive," Thomas Leeds explained while inserting a syringe into a vial of medicine and injecting it into Wicket's arm. "I know Mia has already told you how the Houskaani mark their territory and their uncanny ability to detect intruders. It's no easy feat to fool them for as long as you did."

I shrugged. "Trust me, that has more to do with my friend out there than anything I did," I said, taking a step forward into the cavern. "But now that reunion is over, it's time to get to business. I need to talk with Marc."

At this, Mia turned around completely, her eyes bright and wide under a radiant smile. "Do you, now?" she asked with that same annoying faerie laugh I'd come to know so well.

"I'm serious," I said, holstering my gun to show her I meant no harm. "I need to see him. I don't care about the past. Don't care what he's done. As a matter of fact, I kind of understand his betrayal a little bit better now."

"So why is it you need to see him then?"

"Because..." My face grew even more somber and my eyes narrowed as I tried to come up with the best answer to the question. In the end, I realized that the truth was the only one I could give her. "...Because I need him to help me find a homicidal maniac."

At this, Mia's expression began to mirror my own. Then, she gestured toward a reading chair resting cozily next to the fire in the center of the chamber and took the seat opposite. Once I sat down, she spoke. "Well, then...it sounds as though you and I have a great deal to discuss, Dr. Jackson. A great deal to discuss indeed."

EPILOGUE

THE SLENDER WOMAN LEANED BACK IN THE METAL CHAIR OF THE outdoor café nestled among the exquisite shops and clothiers along the *Rue de Rivoli* in Paris. It was such a beautiful day for this time of year and she had promised herself that she would savor every second of her trip. It had been far too long since her last visit. Of course, she'd been entirely too busy to do much traveling except where her own research called for it. So now, she basked in the bright glow of the nighttime landscape of the aptly named City of Light and slowly sipped at the near perfect cup of coffee steaming in her one good hand.

My hand. Ekaterina Stolnakanova nearly smoldered at the thought of what had happened to it a little over a year earlier, in the Cyclades. What Obadiah Jackson had done to her. He'd thought himself so clever, attaching the device that summoned what he'd so ridiculously dubbed the *tritons* to her boat. She and Marc Leeds had barely escaped with their lives. As it happened, one of the mermaid-like creatures had clamped down it's thick, shark-like jaw on her right hand, severing it completely. And now, the hideous prosthetic monstrosity was the only thing that marred her near flawless appearance.

"Is this seat taken, my dear?" asked an older gentleman with a full head of silvery-white hair and a hint of a New England accent.

She looked up at him, then nodded silently to the chair across from her. She was certainly in no mood for pleasantries. Once he'd taken the chair, she leaned forward, snubbed out her cigarette, and glared at him.

"So what is going on?" she asked in a hushed but venomous tone. "What on earth happened?"

The old man held up a hand, waved over a waiter, and placed his own order in almost perfect French. He then casually lit his own cigarette and leaned back in the chair to study her.

"Be careful how you speak to me, Katherine," he finally said. He'd always refused to call her by her Russian name, preferring the more barbaric, in her opinion, American equivalent. It was just one of the many subtle ways Gregory Sanderson maintained tight control of his most recent employee. "Remember your place in this relationship."

She bit her lip in irritation. She had no time for this. The buffoon calling himself Freakshow, a man Sanderson himself had insisted she become partners with, had apparently gone rogue and threatened to ruin everything the Nephilim Project had worked for. Oh, she knew better than anyone what it was to revile the insufferable Jackson. Not only had he taken her hand, he'd also murdered her grandfather in a Siberian laboratory two and a half years before. So, she could completely sympathize with Freakshow's obsession with revenge. Still, there was a time and place for everything. Truth be told, if he'd come to her, told her his plan, she might have ditched Sanderson's cause and joined him. As it stood, he'd left her out in the cold which infuriated her beyond belief. And Ekaterina was not a woman to have on your bad side. She had vowed since first hearing of the snafu that the lunatic would pay dearly for this transgression.

"My apologies," she said. "I meant no disrespect."

Sanderson eyed her up and down, as if trying to assess her sincerity. Whether he believed her or not, she'd never know. Though she knew the man was smart enough to see through servile platitudes with ease. After several long moments, he finally spoke.

"Dr. Jackson has gone off the grid," he said as casually as if he'd just mentioned the weather.

"What? How do you mean?"

"Just like it sounds," he said after taking a quick sip of his chai tea. "He's resigned from ENIGMA and disappeared without a trace. No one within the agency has any clue where he's gone or what he's up to."

"And what about us? Has our own intelligence network fared any better?"

He chuckled at this, though there was no mirth to it. "Last we heard, he made contact with Clarence Templeton. We believe he's approaching him about joining his network."

It was Kat's turn to laugh at this. "There's no way. Jack is too much of an idealist. He would never throw his hat in the ring with someone like Templeton." She paused for a second before continuing. "Unless..."

"Yes?"

"Unless the little twerp has promised Jack answers."

"He doesn't have any answers," Sanderson scoffed. "He's not been part of our organization in a very long while."

"But he does have resources. Resources Jack will need if he hopes to discover where his mouthy friend has been taken."

"It gets worse." Sanderson leaned back in his chair and lit a cigarette while the waiter refilled his china cup.

"How can it get any worse?"

"That's never a wise question to ask, my dear. Never wise at all." The old man dropped a manila folder on the table and shoved it over to her. "Surveillance footage from the warehouse where Cunningham was taken."

She opened the envelope and pulled out the five glossy black and white photos inside, nearly gasping when she saw who was captured on them.

"So he saw her? Jackson knows about her now?" she asked, her heart racing. If she'd thought Freakshow had screwed things up before, he'd made a complete cluster of things now. "Why on earth would he have used her for...I mean, he had to know what kind of a risk..."

"Precisely," Sanderson said. Though his face was a mask of indifference, she could tell that the old man was upset. Possibly the most she'd ever seen him. "I wonder if that's why he used her to begin with...because of how it would affect our own project."

"So you're saying he's intentionally sabotaging us? That he's broken away from the program?"

The old man shook his head as he slid fingers through his thinning hair. "No, I don't think so. But you and I both know that he plays by his own rules. In order to utilize his numerous assets, I've been forced to give him certain leeway for his own operations. Though even this was a bit too much even for me. We've had words. He's assured me that she's been returned to her cell and won't be employed for any future games."

Kat allowed this to sink in for a while. When the waiter came to refill her own cup, she placed a hand over it and waved him away.

"So what do we do now?" she asked. "Jack will undoubtedly be hell bent on finding Mr. Cunningham, not to mention trying to uncover the mystery behind Ms. Pietrova's sudden re-appearance from the dead."

"It's worse than you know. Before quitting ENIGMA, Dr. Jackson paid a visit to the Pine Barrens."

"So what? I'm sure it was just follow-up on his most recent case," she said.

Sanderson shook his head. "I don't think so. According to one of my contacts within the agency, Jackson was completely indifferent toward the Houskaani investigation after being released from the hospital. He refused to help the Director and other federal agencies in their own investigation of the Leeds' family."

"So what changed his mind?"

In answer, Sanderson pushed himself away from the table, buttoned his suit jacket, and leaned forward on the table. His hot, rancid breath washed over Ekaterina as he spoke. "Let me put it this way, Katherine," he said. "Dr. Jackson isn't the only person who has gone off the grid in recent days."

A lump swelled up in her throat. "Marc?"

The old man hesitated, then nodded. "We've lost all contact with him. It's as though he's completely fallen off the face of the world."

"You don't think that he and Jack have..."

"I daresay that they better not," he growled as he straightened himself up. Three non-descript men in suits materialized from nowhere to surround him protectively. "Dr. Jackson and Leeds can never form an alliance, Ms. Stolnakanova. Never. I don't care what you have to do, but find Mr. Leeds. Take care of him once and for all. Don't let him make contact with Jackson, do you hear me?"

She tried to swallow, but couldn't. The fierceness in his eyes was more intimidating than even her own grandfather's.

"Wouldn't it be easier just to eliminate Jackson?" she asked.

"No! Dr. Jackson is not to be harmed. Not yet. Do you understand?"

Kat nodded. "I understand. I will make sure that Marc Leeds and Jack never meet again. On my grandfather's memory, I swear it."

AUTHOR'S NOTE

If you have only read the previous *ENIGMA Directive* novels in the print and didn't manage to pick up the anthology entitled *THE GAME*, then many of you may be scratching your heads at this moment concerning the character known only as Freakshow. "Where did *he* come from you?" you may be asking. "I don't remember him mentioned before." Some might say. And still others are completely perplexed about Arnold and his, um, unusual characteristics.

For you, I humbly apologize. I didn't mean to slap you with so many surprises in a single volume…but it was rather unavoidable. You see, in 2011, Seven Realms Publishing produced *THE GAME*…an anthology of short stories inspired by the classic Richard Connell tale *The Most Dangerous Game*. My entry in the anthology was called FREAKSHOW and, taking place approximately three years prior to *PRIMAL THIRST*, was a prequel of sorts.

In it, I introduced the world to a madman who hosted his own unique Internet reality show where men would be kidnapped, placed in some remote place, and then forced to survive an onslaught of nasty cryptids. The show, which could only be viewed by invitation and only by the richest of the rich, would then place wagers on a variety of factors such as how long one might survive or how one might get away from a particular monster.

In the short story, Jack finds himself kidnapped and dumped in a decrepit old amusement park on a desert island and the adventure begins. It was also the beginning of a deep-seeded obsession for Freakshow, who felt cheated over the entire ordeal.

It was on this island, also, that Jack meets his loveable dog…Arnold. Right from the beginning, Jack discovers that the furry little friend isn't exactly what he appears to be. As a matter of fact, all of the creatures Jack faces on this island seem to be the product of strange genetic manipulation and Arnold appears to be no different. Still, for the most part, Arnold is just a dog…who licks people's faces, wags his tail, and occasionally barks at the mailman. Jack prefers to keep it this way, of course, and therefore has never told a single soul about his dog's unusual pedigree.

Point is, I ask that you not feel cheated by me throwing this strange new character into the mix without a word of warning. I honestly didn't plop a character out of thin air and hurl him at our hero. There most definitely is both rhyme and reason for it all. I just ask you to trust me a bit longer and all will be made clear soon. In the meantime, if you're curious about Freakshow, then I encourage you to read it! It's not only available in The Game anthology, but can now be purchased as a standalone e-book short story for only $0.99 wherever ebooks are sold.

Thanks for everything!
J. Kent Holloway

ABOUT THE AUTHOR

J. Kent Holloway is an adventure author with a passion for edge-of-your-seat thrillers. A real-life paranormal investigator, his work explores the realms of the unknown. When not writing or scouring the southeastern United States for ghosts and cryptids, he works as a forensic death investigator.

You can learn more about him at his website: www.kenthollowayonline.com

CPSIA information can be obtained at www.ICGtesting.com
Printed in the USA
BVOW03s1048240314

348580BV00003B/210/P